Praise for *The Narrator*

"Michael Cisco is of a different kind and league from almost anyone writing today, and *The Narrator* is Cisco at his startling best."

—CHINA MIEVILLE, author of *Perdido Street Station*

"An extraordinary story of war and the supernatural that combines the creepiness of *Alien* with the clear-eyed gaze of *Full Metal Jacket*. Like *The Other Side* if it included soldiers who could glide over the water, a mysterious tower right out of early David Lynch, and infused with Kafka's sense of the bizarre. Destined to be a classic."

—JEFF VANDERMEER, author of the *Southern Reach* trilogy

"*The Narrator* is not a subversive fantasy novel. It eliminates all other fantasy novels and starts the genre anew. You must begin your journey here."

—NICK MAMATAS, author of *Move Under Ground* and *Love is the Law*

THE NARRATOR
Michael Cisco

LAZY FASCIST PRESS

Lazy Fascist Press
PO Box 10065
Portland, OR 97296

www.lazyfascistpress.com

ISBN: 978-1-62105-185-5

THE NARRATOR

The American Kafka: An Introduction

by Jeff VanderMeer

Few writers within the realm of nonrealist or "weird" fiction have created more original work than **Michael Cisco**, who over the course of two decades and several novels, including his critically acclaimed debut, *The Divinity Student*, has forged a singular path in creating visionary, phantasmagorical settings, uniquely alienated anti-heroes, and genuinely creepy happenings—while also exhibiting a healthy absurdism and dark sense of humor. The work he has created sits comfortably between that of Thomas

Ligotti and Caitlin R. Kiernan, compares favorably to that of Thomas Bernhard and, yes, Kafka. In short, he is one of the most interesting writers I've encountered in the past 30 years.

In Michael Cisco's *The Narrator*, the narrator Low is conscripted into an army to fight against the "blackbirds," who possess lighter-than-air armor. But first, our hero must play a waiting game in a city of cannibal queens and uncanny dead things, with priests for both the living and the dead. The Edak, strange remnants of a mighty imperial power, must be avoided at all costs. Once his unit is mobilized, Low sets off on a journey that is by turns absurd, surreal, deadly, and one of the great feats of the imagination thus far in this century.

These feats depend on a layering that's extraordinary for weird fiction and is given rare power by the attention to detail in the brilliant set pieces that Cisco strings together to tell his tale. I've rarely come across so many instances where I was simultaneously in the moment of the novel but also recognizing that I was encountering images and situations unlike any I'd ever read before. Sleepwalkers that bruise the skin of reality, assailants who skim the surface of the water in armor that's lighter than air, guns that are not guns, conjurings with unexpected consequences, a huge ship "like a black egg," refugees from an insane asylum who assemble as soldiers. "*As if a giant were pushing us along the road, blithering to itself.*"

Yet the true wonder of *The Narrator* is that in addition to the hauntings and unique marvels of the supernatural on offer, the novel is also an extended treatise on the negation of meaning that is war. There are many battle sequences in *The Narrator*, and they all translate as action without meaning, sometimes so chaotic that even individual action is hard to discern within the movements. As near as is possible in text, Cisco conveys the jerky, roving, incomprehensible experience of men on foot shooting at each other across broken, often hilly ground. The individual meaninglessness of it and the group rationalization of it. The result is to come close to conveying the derangement required to wage war. *"An army is a horror. It's a horrible thing."*

But the uncanny and the hook of a powerful theme are rarely enough to sustain any novel. The next element at which Cisco excels is in creating characters like Saskia, a woman "all in armor" who "has a short sword with a basket hilt on her right side and a flapped holster on her left hip." If there's a hero of *The Narrator* besides Low, it is this battle-tested woman who never falters in her bravery under fire. She's a deliberate counterpoint to the senselessness of war—an entity with a tactical purpose who brings order by simple focus. Saskia is also perhaps the only character who remains consistent from beginning to end, and in a sense she gains her own agency as narrator because of it. (But she's not alone: Makemin, Nardac, Punkinflake, Thrushchurl. You'll remember all of them. By the end, the book will be buried in your skull.

What does Cisco layer on top of searing scenes of the uncanny and of war, in the context of unforgettable characters? A series of experiments in narration, eel-slippery. The narrator of *The Narrator* may not be the narrator of the entire novel. Where does his narration really begin and end? What to make of the asides between chapters? Of meeting another narrator, who in a sense begins to narrate the tale in a different way? What of the accounts of others, which the narrator narrates by adding notes like "an unhurried, slow inhalation" and "Her voice dropped there." And "She caressed the air by her knees with stiff old hands, seeming to coax the guillotine blade out of the sparkling air so that I for a moment saw it."

Should we be worried? I think instead we should relax into reading a work of true originality, verve, and intellectual rigor.

First Chapter

An army is a horror. It's a horrible thing. They say you might change your mind about that when the country is invaded and your people are suffering wrong, but for me this is all just more horror, more army-horror.

It's through rags of fast-moving smoke that I first catch sight of Tref. I'm standing in the pass, to one side of the pumice road, looking down from my perch on the massed roots of some dusty old cork oaks. The city below me is like a shining, smoking lake, thrusting its troubled glints into my eyes and making them smart. Overhead, the sun is lost in a white sky without circumference, above the flashing waters of the city.

One flash of the sun and I am down in its streets. Why is the station so far out of the city limits anyway? Most likely a collusion between the builders of stations and the builders of long roads. I walk into Tref unremarked as a ghost, and now this is me, here, in its bare broad avenues. The sky showers the street in volleys of sharp light. I take step after step, feeling the street and the city existing all around me, like figuring out all the parts of an unfamiliar flavor. My mind is too tired and weak from travel to do much of it. The city washes by me and its outlines dance and glitter as they will, playing their fairy games with me. I stumble along in a boulevard so wide the opposite side seems to sit on the horizon and the whole world bulging in between me and there. Out from my pocket I pull again to look at the implacable pink lot that tells me that I am *drafted* ...

drafted ...

I put in for an *exemption*

and I got *drafted* ...

I look up just as the sun quits the sky. I am sprawling in a white wrought-iron chair in the paved court of cafes, the iron finery is biting into my back a little, the table is streaked with sunset bands on the glass top. Heavy and tippy at once. Bands of gold and rust light cut across my coffee ring. The ticket is still there in my right hand on my right thigh. A little wind toys with it there, the battered paper is soft and tough as a piece of linen. Why can't I awake from this dream? This is an ugly dream. These words seem to come from an old song. I came from the village ... the village named for the sheep fold that was the first thing probably built there, where the high way broadens on the mountain of the heavens/constellations of the spring. When I was in my third year at the College of Narrators, Twisse, who was our ward resident, passed word of the draft around and told us to get in our exemption forms early. Next thing I know I pull a pink lot from an envelope in the mail room and stand staring at it, welded to the spot.

"How did *that* happen?" Twisse asked, peering over my shoulder. He took the paper gingerly in his hands. "No," his head shaking, "you should go to see the Uz about this."

Twisse walked away with his sharp, upturned nose in the air. My friend Spiena was with me and rested a hand on my shoulder.

"Run away," he said.

I looked at him.

"Stay with Blue Loom Pigsty, or—your other uncle, whatever his name was."

"Lard Loom Blossom."

"If you can keep out of sight for a few months, you'll probably be forgotten."

"I'd be killed."

"You might," he says sadly. "But you take the same chance in the war."

"What about my degree?"

"You can forget your degree. Everyone here would certainly sympathize with you."

"I should try at least to clear this up with the Uz," I say. My mind is like a motionless reflection in a piece of glass. My thoughts are frozen in place, too frightened to move.

"Oh he won't do anything!" Spiena said with a look of disgust. "You might as well tell your troubles to these chairs."

"I have my copies of the documents. I have my dated registration. I kept everything just in case."

"Eh. I suppose he might listen, but, that's only because

anything is possible with these administrators. He's white."

Spiena shrugged his meaty shoulders.

"I honestly don't believe they really think at all."

"—Where would I go, if I had to run?"

"Back into the mountains ...?" Spiena said unhelpfully.

Winter comes so swiftly in the mountains that the leaves are frozen green on the trees, the grass in the meadows. The foliage never turns color or falls, but hibernates in clear ice casings until the spring thaw restores their interrupted life again. So the winter landscape is tinkling green, dazzling with flakes of light, crisp through the snow. The many rock-lipped streams freeze clear as well, and the fish are suspended in place like spangles of precious metal until spring. I walked to the small cluster of administrative buildings, a clutch of cottages and shops connected by a tangle of gravel paths and baffled from sight like an embarrassment by several echelons of yew hedges. I passed through these under boughs of cherry trees, the scarlet cherries still on the branches, glowing like embers through the ice that outlined every leaf and twig in shining white thread, and I saw myself endlessly multiplied in all that pure ice, even on the yew branches, their deep green almost black, and webs of gossamer ice in the recesses of the hedges. A dark, bulbous, top-heavy figure loomed in and out of them as I passed, arms anxiously swinging.

I never have been able to find out how the administrators get their posts, or why they all seem so unqualified and unhelpful. I walked in among the dozen or so buildings with smoke in my face, blown down toward the ground from the chimneys of the cottages to my left. One of the administrators, a white old woman in a shawl, was spinning in a doorway, muttering around a short clay pipe to a sharply-dressed aide who avidly took down her dictation. The woman eyed me as I passed, without slowing her spinning or her smoky speaking. I glanced at her, then at once dropped my eyes to the thick ankles slotted into shoes so tight they seemed painted on. While her look was cryptic, her aide, who was red, shot me a glance of unmistakable disapproval. I was tempted to fling a handful of snow at them, but after all I might need to persuade them of my good will later, so I belatedly turned, as I had already passed nearly altogether out of sight of them, and made a sort of half wave half salute, along with what I felt was a strained and unappealing smile. Some smiles break a face and some smiles tear across.

Stark white and clean as a surgery, Uz Leimme's office was like an ice cave all year. A small white box of a building, with two nearly wall-sized windows in the front, square door in the middle that swings back silently on big hinges. His secretary, absent when I came, would sit behind a high marble-topped counter. Bright sunlight from the windows was reflected and re-reflected all throughout the open office, and I could see Leimme back there in the rearmost recesses. His desk was steel with a marble top, and there were chrome and marble counters and frigid glass-fronted cabinets on the walls. Some had files in them and some had bright steel implements, most of which looked medical but some were clerical—staplers and hole punchers.

When he saw me, Leimme crossed to the sink and, humming, began soaping his hands wildly, flipping gobs of foam in all directions. He then undulated forward up to his desk, his gait deformed by a wooden right leg. He was a large, round-headed man, with white hair parted on the left. Like most administrators, and this was always attributed to chance, he was a white person from the valleys on the other side of the mountains. His shirt and satin cravat, his long waistcoat and longer jacket were white, his trousers were black and white checked, his leg was white wood. He dropped with one loud crack into his seat and waved me forward with a rather inane grin.

I sat stupidly before his desk and concisely explained my problem, laying out my paperwork with ostentatious care in the desolation in front of him.

"I have just received this draft notice." I placed my finger straight up and down on it, on the desk. "Even though I submitted a valid application for exemption as a student at the College of Narrators, well in advance of the application deadline."

Uz Leimme's expression hadn't changed. "So?" he grinned at me.

"So there's been a mistake."

"And?"

"And I'd like you to fix it."

"Don't be an ass!" he said unctuously.

"Who's an ass?" I cried. "I *applied* for an *exemption* and I *got* a *draft notice*. Now is this application in order and on time or isn't it?"

He looked at me, and the light was very bright all around. He didn't answer. I might not even be there anymore, from his point of view.

"This is idiotic," I said helplessly. "I have to matriculate!"

His fingertips rebounded cheerily off each other like rubber bladders. I could hear his cheeks creaking as his smile winched itself up his face. His smile would handle me; now that it had put in its appearance, he could abscond from behind it. The smile shook at me, as though this were an excellently thorough explanation. And then it was the train, smiling at me through clouds of steam and grunts of smoke. No family there, not much family to speak of, and Spiena had already said goodbye to me the night before. I hear a voice call my name, turn to see a reed-thin old man in a sort of cassock advancing on me with an envelope in his hand. The letter:

My Dear Loulle!

How foolish of you, you know it was foolish, not to register with the Documents Registrar! They have, at this moment, three excellent positions open for persons fluid in Lashlache, and you, with the sole exception of professor Tmendo himself, would have been the only candidate locally available. There naturally is nothing now to be done, poor thing, about it, because your draught notice establishes prior government service in the military which obviously invalidates a Documents Registry exemption.

Don't imagine, however, that the question of your military service is in any way settled, however. I have composed a letter to the regional advocate etc., explaining your case in detail, and we believe a response is pending. I have also informed a friend of mine in the military administration of your predicament, and he has seen to it you will be given an interpreter's assignment, which official recognition of yourself as an interpreter will represent a distinct advantage in putting forward your case for transfer to the Documentary Board, which case I am taking *personally in hand.*

Uz Leimme

My name is Low, not "Loulle," he wrote "fluid" for "fluent" "draught" for "draft" and repeated "however" inappropriately at the end of the first sentence of the second paragraph. Furthermore, I *had* registered with Documents Registry *through* professor Tmendo, who was my Lashlache instructor, two years ago. Had he forgotten to file it?

The messenger stood waiting with his hand out. I dropped a coin in it, and he angrily dashed it to the ground and reopened his palm. I looked at him interrogatively.

"What did you do that for?"

"I need your original draft notice," he snapped, and pointed violently to the new pink lot that remained in the envelope. I pulled from my pocket my original, yellow, lot and gave it to him, whereupon he whipped around on his heel and stormed off the platform. I picked up my coin and then looked at the new lot. I looked a long time without understanding.

My original lot had me joining the local battalion, the so-called "Fifteen Milers," whose rallying point was in Qul Elboe, about three miles down into the river valley on this side of the mountains. The lot I was then holding assigned me to an entirely other army, "Red Expedition Chapter," rallying three hundred miles away in Tref. I was dealing with agents of an offended spirit or capricious god.

I eat, and step out onto the streets, nearly colliding with a pale man. He is lean and tall with a small head and blazing round blue pinpoint eyes, staring up at the sun in amazed ecstasy, and oblivious to me. His thin red hair hangs lifelessly down in ragged locks, his arms hang down at his sides, and his smocked outline seems to wobble in the intense, chilled light. Behind the man, an Edek emerges from her underground den. The Edek is taller than this tall man who is her helper, and like all Edeks she wears a close hood of dun cloth with two holes for her eyes, fitted into a bandage of thin gauze tape wound many times around the long neck. This one is dressed in a uniform of velvety brown corduroy, with the straps of her binoculars criss-crossing the narrow chest, and knee-high boots of soft laced pigskin. The rooty, gloved hands glow a little, one reaches to pinch a bit of material at the back of her helper's smock, and her helper, whose eyes are the Edek's to use, leads her past me. The Edek's head swivels in my direction as she goes by, and the fierce thrust of her gaze nearly knocks me against the wall. I rub the sparks from my eyes, and when I look again, the two are gone. Too late—she *saw* me!

Train to Qulo, shrugs, bored looks from the officers I spoke to there—you will have to go on. With regret I went back and forth in broad daylight lanes, brightly-colored cottages outlined in gleaming silver ice, and then the sky was swept with glowing indigo clouds. I wrote to my uncles, to Dull Hill Bramble, and to Found Horse Whistle. Two days of black soda bread and stewed fruit soup, then I sat on the train pulling out again in dusk snow flurries; dark blue light closed over the landscape as the station slid by, snow bearding the rough mortared edges of its bricks.

I watched the land flatten out into a piebald mat of inky blue rock and phosphorescent snow, lone naked trees studded with black birds. Fewer and fewer red faces. I had a book called *Syntax for Personal Narrative* in my lap; I can't recall reading it. "The responsibility of those who preserve events in language must be to ..."—to something something. Something about narrative grid of the weft of the archive to creative intuitive form, a slot-rhythm ingrained into writers, reciters, and listeners until even those events observed firsthand are experienced as if they were already written and being read back. Flatter and flatter the land, mountains always in the distance growing lower smoother and more rolling, taking me away from the land of Mnemosems maybe once and for all. We dropped out of the snow and the ground turned brown, then grey and pale gold as we dropped into the desert.

Festive music warbles in the cafe behind me, but I am the only customer here. The wind is moving trash in the empty street. I imagine releasing the lot I hold in my hand and permitting it to escape along this street. The trembling stars shout down to me, and the life that is in me shouts back. That I know I'm living goes up levels in me like surf rising against the tide marks. I've never been to the ocean, never seen it. How can I use such metaphors?

"... I'm sure it's all very amusing," says a woman's voice going past in the dark.

You aren't on your way to death, and I am; this is my moment—you get out of it.

I put the money on the table and go inside. The counterman's doughy face makes him seem older than he is.

"Is there anywhere I can stay around here?" I ask in Cvaivrenew.

"Spare room upstairs I could let you have." He holds up

three fingers. I put three coins down on the counter and he waves me along behind him, points me up the stairs to the door. The room is tiny, without windows but not close, because the roof is nearly half gone; an irregular, round hole shows bare timbers. Warm air eddies around the room softly, there are stacks of boxes, ladder against the plaster wall, a hammock strung beneath the gap in the roof. I spin in place a little, back and forth—not much chance, I decide, of rising sun shining on me here. Huddle under a thin felt blanket in the hammock, head down on my chest. Sound of the wind lightly dragging its fingers over the city. Tears spill from my eyes in silence. Over me is pulled a cap of vigilantly staring night.

*

Among the constellations I can see the flitting shapes of the Imperial deputies, the Predicanten, to whose persistent attentiveness I owe my entanglement here. Although they can be any size, take any shape, now they are like little winged men, naked, hairless, and rubbery, flapping convulsively high overhead, or clinging like bats under the eaves of the buildings. Do I dream it, or does one perch above me, peering down a long moment as I sleep? Running away? Would you be ... running away?

The next morning I find I am long looking at the changing blue sky, and rising all around me is soft foam of treading feet. I am lying on my side now, looking at this mummy-ape hand of mine, a preserved leathery paw or fleshy antler, with a dot of reflected light glowing at each fingertip, the light going down into the tissue makes a pinkish ember of each finger; the palm is a webbing of fine creases and deep. I work my muscles and balance myself, rising onto my feet. I can just peer out the hole in the roof. I watch in fascination this white girl walking down the street, the precision bipedal movement, setting the weight down first on this foot then on that.

Downstairs I sway out guardedly into the cafe, where people tap crockery and talk. It's hard not to rub my eyes or my head, but my college haircut is hard to muss and I believe I look presentable enough. Up to the counter, I point to a heap of rolls. The proprietor deftly sweeps one of them onto the plate just bussed and set before him, still covered with the crumbs which technically are still the property of the previous customer, and hands it to me, so that's how it is.

Sitting at the table are obvious old hands, taking their time. They will eat, and stroll at their leisure to their places of business, jingling their keys and gradually opening up shop. Most regular business is confined to a commercial district straddling the river at the butt end of the town.

Now I'm alone. The street launches me without warning into the great sluice of another of these vast boulevards where the air is never still, flooded with sparkling bicycles that shoot dart and veer in shoals. The city is ribbed with vaulting aqueducts, which step high on tall stone pylons with arched stone groins in several leaping lines over the streets and rooftops. These aqueducts vent their water into elevated cisterns and, more spectacularly, into public fountains, descending many stories through the air in clear, discrete streams bearded with refreshing mist. The sun strikes them making transparent membranes around the jets like a flame calyx.

I wander ... wander over to a newspaper and tobacco kiosk, ask the woman if she knows where the mustering point is, or Captain Makemin. She just smiles and shakes her head. I try Chiprena, Hiuv, and Bouzenush and get just the head shake.

"Got yourself drafted?"

Big friendly-looking fellow with a thinning black beard. He thinks the mustering point is in a place I've already checked but I don't correct him, sound him out instead. He turns out to be a know-it-all, attached to the surveyor's fund. I take him up on his invitation to accompany him to his office.

"The natives have always called this place Tref, at the base of the mountain, and so the city acquired that name because it was built here. Its real name is Dusktemper—bit strange, right? Religious separatists from Sjilte were the founders, and, in addition to the *Manual of Techniques*, they had their own holy book, a kind of allegorical short story. I can't recall its name, but most of the local place names here they drew from it. Anyway, that's why the Subashi of Dusktemper is called a Precentor instead."

"What was Dusktemper named in the story?"

He thinks, and puffs out his mouth a little.

"It was an inner property of man, like spirit, or maybe it was a particular spirit. I think it might have meant holiness, but they had their own ideas about that." He gives me a frank look that admits he's told all he knows.

"And they divided the city into the two precincts?"

"I'm not sure. It seems right, and the city I know has had no other plan, but these priests, and people," he waves vaguely around, "aren't separatists. And I think this division involves a separate association of places that had been determined by the natives. They buried people over there—" he gestures over the river, "and had birth huts over on this side. The huts were raised up on high stilts and the women would hunker down in a frame over a hatch in the floor, and the midwife or whoever would reach up and lower down the child."

I ask about the separatists. He tells me there probably aren't any left anymore, or very few.

A carefully ramified division of labor regulates the operation of the life and death priests. Life priests, urbane, serene, dressed in satiny white and cream gowns, preside at weddings, naming ceremonies, tend the sick and perform healings when they can; death priests, subdolous and mordant, dressed in shabby subfusc, officiate at funerals, conduct autopsies and embalm bodies, attend to the dying and insane, and cast out or even imbibe possessing demons. Life priests are permitted and encouraged to marry; death priests, while not enjoined to celibacy, are forbidden to marry or to bear children. The life priests exhibit dazzling vitality; they eat only the freshest and most pure food, drink only water and fruit juice, abstain from smoking, and are alone permitted to chew bennoch resin, which gives them balsamic breath, shining teeth and sparkling eyes. They smell sweet, even the old ones. The death priests, on the other hand, are sallow or even greenish in complexion—whatever their original color—with grey whites of eyes and yellow hyena teeth. They smell stale, or wear olfactorily-garish perfume, and shed whiffs of carrion where they go. They are forbidden more than a minimum of nourishing food, and eat almost nothing that has not been dead preserved or fermenting a long time. They all drink ardent spirits, smoke copiously, and most are inveterate sweet eaters. There is no enmity between these two groups of priests, although they are compelled to avoid each other as a rule in order to maintain a pure distinction. When they do meet, a complicated protocol governs the exchange of formalities. In fact, since no one is ever born in the death precincts, all death priests are delivered into this life by life priests of the previous generation. Naturally, all life priests are ushered into whatever dream comes after by the generation of death priests who will bury them in the death district.

The separatists' city charter forbids the construction of churches and bans all but a handful of religious writings, and even these cannot be bought and sold in the city. They may however be given away. Printing religious matter is banned, although copying books by hand is not. The life and death priests conduct their ritual observations in cemeteries, hospitals, offices, libraries, basements, attics. The lifers tend to change venue often, the death priests change far less often.

I was told, or read, that everyone visits Veciofeni's cave sooner or later. He stood in there and wept himself to death, evidently, and this manner of dying, so gently incremental, brought about the perfect preservation of his body as a consequence of his mummy-like dehydration and the saturation of his person with his own lachrymal salt. His remains stand there still, unsupported, hands folded over his heart; the flesh of his face is pliable, his hands, his nose, even his ears are unshrivelled. The air in the cave is redolent of the odor of his tears, a salty air like sea breath, but without the underlying, living mustiness. Two deacons, with feathers in their hair, sit on the floor by his side. They live in the cave, keep watch over the saint, and further his medicine with their singing. Each takes his turn echoing the other, and the song is long deep sinus notes that hum in the stone, consonants as light as rustling leaves.

Visitors come daily, bearing offerings of flowers and votive body parts. Organs lie embedded in enormous bouquets of flowers, and the walls, which in places have been terraced, glow with vivid ruby hearts, piles of severed arms and hands, muscles like bundles of carmine wire, platinum braids of nerves, topaz pancreases, lungs pale rose as dusk's first shadings, plaited rivers of hair, majestic livers of royal purple, slabs of snowy fat, fragrant pink brains smelling of soluble minerals, elaborately knotted ivory intestines ... by the entrance, air sluices through grates of stretched human vocal cords, the sound joining the deacons' song. All these treasures are fresh and glowing with dismembered life. They glitter in the vaults of my imagination as Beardo describes them, and seeing them so vividly in there I feel as though a voyage to the cave itself would be redundant now.

Shade of trees with long-bladed leaves, a dusty corner courtyard with cool sunlight on the stone walls. Flat, leathery pods, like bumpy little belts, litter the pavement. He waves me into his small office, all leather this and rosewood that. I am shown ranks and ranks of uniform volumes with gold edgings; these are the encyclopedic writings of Alak specialists about the natives here—their history, language, religion. Of course, no Alak has ever actually visited Tref; or if any have, they didn't draw attention to themselves, and that would have been out of character. The books were written in the capital, on the other side of the world, and brought here—unless they are copies made somewhere in between, in which case nothing of the capital adheres to them. Like most of the citizens of the Empire, I have never laid eyes on an Alak.

*

Air fresh and cool round my shoulders, still early in the year.

Everything seems to spin away from me as though I were near the center of a vast level wheel, which collects and disperses and collects again out of the substance and people of the city. I can feel the dizziness whirling up to me, and I have to stop and hold my head in my hands. How can I leave this place in uniform, march and get shot at? It's a bad dream. The worst dream.

I duck into the post office and line up in the clammy gloom under a low arched ceiling. Like being inside a clam, I imagine, deep under the sea I've never seen. The counter is marble topped with greasy steel and the clerk behind it is no less impassive, explaining to me that the money I was told my parents would wire to me here has not come, pointing numbly again and again to the spot in his thumby ledger where my name would be if there were any legitimate reason for me to expect such a money order which there isn't. I feel something cold and disgusting splash behind my face, trying to ooze out of my eyes, but satisfied with warping my voice so that I can hardly make myself understood. This, on the assumption that there were any human beings present to understand me. I am sickly trying to explain myself to a glazed crust filled with grey clam mush. The other patrons are understandably curious about this adventure of mine, and I can feel their runty eyes peer after me as I leave in a hurry.

It all seems less gay and diverting in the stark blare of sunlight outside. I have only the few lonely amber coins of Shoanly clacking in my pocket, already too little to send a message of explanation back home. What do you do with a good explanation no one can hear? I feel conspicuous and cursed. I take those ways which seem likely to lead me away from all these people who have places in the world. Of course, so do I, but it's not one I want. I reject it. I would reject it. The Edek …

Wherever I turn my head, small panes of glass shoot light spears at me, hunting my eyes. Now I wend along bookstall streets, funnelled in light as air on the wind. Bits of paper hurry around me, in and out of shop doorways and alleys, cross and recross the street in front of me. As paper goes, it's a busy street. The books stand in neat rows sandwiched in together, and among them sit figures perched atop tall stools within the obscurity of a deep doorway, barely visible in the gloom. My finger etches a groove in the dust that clings to spines patched with gilt titles. Look at this *The Seven* [dull old] *Syntagmas*. I had to read that. Here's a bright new copy I'd buy if I had the money of *Séance Paralogia* by Hathebeth Huthebie, who used to be my teacher. Perhaps I could trade my *Syntax* for it.

I may never be anything better than a journeyman narrator now. If I ever were to write an account of these events, which are in any case written, my narrative would be incoherent and inconclusive; I never know enough to say. Neither buying nor selling, I keep on my walking feet that take me out from this lane of cool dust to brighter streets with shop windows, a blonde square with indistinct people strolling in the shade of a few half-sized trees in the distance. The light recoiling from the bright ground distempers the shadows and makes these people resemble figures in an old and faded picture. I beguile myself enjoying the grimaces of ranks of iron gargoyles, which rise from the gutter all the way to the dizzy steeple above. Crouch and pull faces all day—that's a good job. They're well fed and healthy, with bulbous muscles thickly rippling. I wouldn't half fit in as a woman sails by, the uplit light reflecting from her white blouse barely tints her wan face with its glow. She's not for you, nor any of them, as you know. That wasn't a very kind thought. Icy wind blows into the deepest of my spirit's stiff fractures. Still hypnotized, thinking you can when you know these are impossibilities we're talking about; known only to me as my vision is clearest—clear, clear as a bell. From the steeple, the bell can see everything in the town. Meet a woman, you will meet another. They always enter in twos.

Now, how would a callow youth like myself know that?

Once you see an Edek, or once one sees you, you will see others. Two of them, hooded like hostages, now stalk out of the church with their wan-faced helpers leading them. Edeks are blind to this world, mostly, and see vicariously through their assistants. I don't know whether or not these helpers all wear the same mindless look because they've been put through some sort of procedure, or if an Edek's presence or influence brings on this condition, but it seems like a mercy to me.

The foremost Edek wears a long belted black coat, badly

faded; she has the air of a wasted invalid just emerging from her sick chamber with an uncanny, almost supernatural new vigor. Her companion is in an officer's tunic, a long scarf wound round her neck many times. They angle away in the direction I came, taking long powerful strides in near unison, and in near unison they both abruptly turn their puncturing gaze on me, four frigid pools of congealed ink .... They do not pause, their heads reswivel, and they go.

I search for the mustering point, and the day passes. Now I am in the outer skirts, where the streets swell and contract as they please. Fewer people, and older. A hat in one of the windows catches my eye and I stop to look at it; my eye drifts over wooden heads on stands, past the sill and down to where an anxious cloud of dust is tumbling against the base of the building, in the dry alley. Indirect sunlight sifting down from everywhere illuminates the dust faintly, and I watch the motes rise and fall in vertical orbits, on a current, I guess, of air crushed against the bricks and forced aloft. The dust looks like a woman, with a long dress and a wide hat; and now she seems closer, as though she had traversed a wide space between us and were peering through a window at me. I see her eyes, not the luster of her eyes although there was light in the face—like a face of gold ash on a wax head—and her gaze "glowed" into me, without light. Water splutters from a drainpipe opposite me, and spills down a shallow channel in the dirt along the middle of the alley, thickening with dust until its front end is a bulbous brown lip. I can't see the woman any more, nor can I remember her face.

The ground is elevated here, the view is unobstructed and full of wind. The sheer black trench of the Idle runs away from me, black wrinkles in a grey ribbon, and on its far side is the spiracle mound of the death precinct, from which on some nights it is recounted one can see the titan form of a grinning mortuary student rearing up to set a green death taper in the sky. There's the Embalmer's College, crouched like a toad dropsically bloated with venom and warted over with cupolas; its presence exceeds its size, and draws attention to it among these other buildings as the eyes draw attention in the face.

I walk toward the river, and in less than a quarter of a mile I find a bridge to cross into the death district. Shreds of black crepe, and the dried husks of flowers that might have come from funeral wreaths rasp along the ground, are toyed with by the air. The bridge is encrusted with what look like brass teacups broken in half, like scales growing out of any order, embedded in yellow solder. I cross the empty bridge as the sun begins to slide down toward the backs of the mountains, and night's elaborate mechanism whirs to life all around me. It's just tuning up.

So this is the death precinct. I find willows sighing over strewn empty streets, dust and attentive calm on the other side of the bridge. Sunset takes hours, and there are no lights lit anywhere yet. No sound but rustling skirts of air, the half-hearted whine of a shutter's hinges, crickets who chirp two or three times and stop. I wander without thinking, and as the darkness falls I am picking my way through unlit streets with bushes growing from the pavements; in the gathering night, everything is felty and dim, the stone buildings luminous pink and silver with bare lividity, patched with lichen and veiled in ivy. I am thirsty, but the stone trough I find is too scummed over to drink from. I haven't eaten since the morning, and so imagine the state I am in. I have wandered too long to go back, and my mind is unclear. I start pushing in at doors and even windows, and here one door opens. For a moment my thoughts are sharp again. Charred beams and broken plaster on the floor, smashed furniture, walls glow white-blue like cheeses. Here on the window sill a chipped tin cup with a little sand at the bottom is nearly full of rainwater. I drink it down carefully so as not to drink the sand. I can feel it pouring down cold into my empty stomach. There's even a thin, narrow mattress or pad here folded on the floor. I pull my jacket around myself and lie down on my side. My body groans with fatigue but it takes me a while, or so it seems, to get to sleep, listening to the wind, and the faint sound of settling dust.

*

Ravenous morning. I am already in the streets before I wake up all the way. I hear the voices long before I begin to see people, and then only a face here a face there. Mostly white people. I am blinking all the time, but it's hard to see. There are mortuary students everywhere, the males in vested suits with cutaways and cravats, silk hats with black crepe around the band, and the females in black dresses and flowered hats. Only those who have matriculated may wear veils. I wash my face in a fountain and take another drink—a belly filled with water doesn't hurt so much. I decide I have to spend something; two rolls vanish without a trace. I sit for a while and wait for them to percolate through me. Then I spend the rest of my money on a proper meal.

The cemetery gardens of Dusktemper truly are the finest imaginable. Every few blocks the land opens up in stately rolling green and dark cypress yew and willow, lawns spangled with lank stones, peopled with sculptures and mausolea. Some are in immaculate condition and some falling into picturesquely complete disrepair. The eerie serenity of these places hums with an undercurrent of menace that I find appeals to me. What is the nature of this oddly soothing feeling? I have seen the gardens of the life priests and they are tranquil and beautiful, but these fantastically still, entranced graveyards fascinate me.

So now I am moving among these monuments, trembling phosphorescence in the pale stones beneath lost grey sky. The path descends across the cemetery, and now the few distant visitors and groundskeepers drop out of sight. The path cuts into the ground, and becomes something like a stone-lined trench as I follow it around the base of a low hill. I am thinking of dead men, and the stories that they leave behind for us to repeat. It was to this task that I had proposed to dedicate my life, and now the fiat of someone I'll never know or see has quashed that purpose.

I catch sight of a woman laying flowers on a grave. The lane I walk is baffled by a stone retaining wall on my right, and as I pass I keep gazing at this woman. The grave is marked with an upright stone, and she, the stone, and the colossal beech that overhangs it, are stark against a cream sky. No I didn't actually see any flowers; she had been bent over the grave and straightened her back gracefully as I came. Only now does she notice me, turns her entire body toward me. An impenetrable veil is draped across her hat's extremely wide brim, and gathers into the grey lace of her chin-high collar, and hat and veil together look like two saucers stacked mouth to mouth. A voluminous sooty cone from the waist down, her dress is cinched tight around her, blooming out from waist to taper back into her long neck, a grey fabric with a darker shell of transparent gauze web, dotted with tiny black flowers like evenly-spaced flies. She stands with her arms at her sides, staring at me with her invisible face. I think of charred wood burning black in the grate, creaking and whispering with cryptic fire deep beneath the scorch, when I look at her black and grey shape against the lividity overhead. I must be at or below the level of the occupant of that grave.

As though a string tugged it, my head keeps swivelling back to the woman, who seems to turn in place to follow me with a gaze emanating from the entire front of her body. Further on down the lane as I look back a little light shines across the veil and I glimpse the contour of a tapering face—there it is the green flash I've heard about that happens just at sunset in this part of the world, trickling around this tapering face through the veil. I seem to see or imagine two intense round grave stares like a pair of black pits or pools fixed and sucking at my image greedy as quicksand. I hurry to get out of her sight—I don't enjoy this feeling, being watched, and this looking and hurrying, all too affected by someone else, and here I am mangy with poverty uncertainty and lostness.

The cemetery peters out into long-weeded lots and listing stone buildings shaggy with vines, all under the sprawling dry shade of ancient black-leaved beeches. Everywhere the cool air is settling gradually toward the earth like dust, tugging almost imperceptibly at me. In the wan light of this drugged day I pick my way through grave wrack tumbled up in lots, broken stone basins filled with clear rain water and brown scum at the bottom like a mat of tea leaves, watched over by stone angels their faces half-lathered with moss.

A sickening recollection of my reason for being in this city washes over me, nearly buckling my knees. These sharp sensations of coolness, quietness, beauty, all to be stolen from me for no reason, for nothing—I don't even know what this draft is for. Epitaph collage of broken slate and granite tombstones knitted together by the weeds, "Rest In Autumn Loving Wife," "Where We Shall Be Killed In Fire," and protracted lines of numbers. The iron-piked wall is interrupted by a partially collapsed house and as this is the only exit that presents itself I part the curtain of vines and enter the house through the wall, setting my feet down with care on the slippery floorboards.

I hear voices near me. In the next room, three mortuary students are throwing dice against the far corner; a fourth lies with his head on a split cushion along another vine-draped hole in the wall, the day's beaded light gleaming on his long legs and checked vest. He is watching the dice players and smiling. They turn to nod and grin at me, bent cigarettes at their lips, then return their attention to the dice. A fifth student lies nearby in the room's darkest corner, his outstretched legs crossed at the ankles and his shoulders propped against a door in a deep doorway.

I can see the whites of his eyes, and the dim motions of his face as he speaks.

"As you honor death, buy me a drink!" he calls, smiling. It sounds like a quotation. If I were a wit, I'd know from where and give the countersign.

"I have no money," I say, pinching at my empty pockets.

"Then you are my brother," he replies at once, and lithely rolls himself into a crouch with his arms between his knees like a frog, but still sitting on the stone jam of the doorway. His face is round with a slightly tapering chin, skin white as custard and a sharky grin on red baby lips, faded grey irises in eyes like yellowed ivory. Straight pale brown hair bells from his top hat in a bowl cut.

"I'm Jil Punkinflake." He says this as though he expects me to have heard of him, smiles up at me and offers his hand. "Go ahead and laugh if you like, but it's my name."

I don't laugh, but we smile at each other.

"What's yours?" he asks.

"Low," I say.

"Just Low?"

"Low Loom Column is my complete name outside the country."

"What country?"

"My country."

"Mm," he says. "What is it inside?"

"I can't say it here. I'm not inside."

Jil Punkinflake gets up and tugs the ladder from his vest. A large death's-head moth, clinging to his lapel like a boutanier, opens and closes its wings meditatively. We sit down together on a piano bench by the wall. I explain my problem, how I come to be here.

"An exemption?" he asks.

"A narrator's exemption; they'll give it to you if you've already done your obligatory service, or trained for something."

"So you get out of it if you're a veteran?"

"No, I mean you go into the army when you come of age and serve a year, war or peace. It's a standing army."

"That's what you did, Low?"

"No, I took medical training. The Sodality in town made me an award of the fees, because my marks were good in school."

"But what possible good is it to the army training you if you can use that to get an exemption?"

"I imagine they reckon on being able to entice you to stay, having you right there. And there's always the chance war will break out during your training period—there's always one going on somewhere—*then* they can enlist you for a full tour without discounting your training time."

"And just to whom are you assigned, Low?"

I have to check the ticket to be certain.

Jil Punkinflake's head tilts back as though he'd just been lightly buffeted on the chin. "Makemin's unit is understaffed. Half his troops have deserted already. Why don't you run? Your chances are good."

"I was seen by an Edek," I say with a sheepish smile and toss of the hands.

"An Edek saw you?" he asks sharply.

"Yes."

He shakes his head.

Twilight shows violet fire in the sky as we make our way to the dormitories. Skulls hang in net bags from the street lights, which are not lit.

One of the students grabs my arm and points, and the other students are watching in rapt attention as a hearse rattles by in the square terraced below this one. The horses are large and burly, with glistening curried hides and quivering tails painstakingly bundled atop their buttocks. Their plumed heads bend in the same direction at the same time, their dishevilled manes seem especially wildly to contrast with their otherwise impeccable grooming. A hatless man in a plain black suit is driving them. I crane my neck to see inside, but the windows are curtained. A veiled black wreath adorns the back. My comrades sigh and coo to themselves over it, and sagaciously evaluate the style of the brass fittings, the magnificent lacquering of the wood.

"It's built low," the one who took my arm says, "because the coffin rides in a compartment *above* the passengers. *Isn't that dreamy?*"

We go on. Now, here and there, I see a few faltering lanterns. Most of the people of the district seem either to be old or ill, but not for that reason lacking in street vigor. There are no doctors in the death precinct, only morticians; if you get sick they'll be happy to embalm you. We stop on the way before one of the many haunted houses that line this route. I am told of strangled voices from mouths clotted with earth, bellowing curses and prophesies from the basements and stairways; a stirring of the embroidered hem of the arras, and a certain object no one has ever seen because it is shrouded in darkness even in the noonday sun. The students hang on the gate, looking eagerly from one black window to the next. Finally, having evidently seen nothing, they straggle back into the street, ragged yellow smiles kneading faces that glow blue as though dusted with lead powder.

"You've seen ghosts in there?" I ask.

"Naturally. There are ghosts all over the district." Jil Punkinflake turns one of these hyena grins on me, his eyes like luminous toadstools in the fluorescent dusk. He waves his hand at his three dice-playing companions. "There were five of us, you know."

We spin through brilliant salons of butter-colored candle light and twinkling crystal, straight-backed lady plays remote music on the spinet as the room darkens with burgundy shadow, and a breath stirs webs in the empty hallway. As we pass the mouth of a sunken arcade lined with heavy wooden doors, a crazed pounding breaks on the air, resounding down the long arcade from somewhere out of sight. One of Jil Punkinflake's friends, a plummy-voiced boy named Nectar, explains adipocere to me. "It's an entirely distinct variety of decay, and quite ubiquitous, but you seldom see it expressed because the other, more common variety seems to drive it out. In those rare circumstances in which it does gain the ascendancy, it transforms the flesh into a kind of wax. We have a little girl at the school who's all adipocere; eighty years ago, or more now, she died—and hasn't changed a hair since."

"She's gone the color of weak tea," Jil Punkinflake adds.

Nectar points to a sunken burying ground about the area of a modest house. The grave markers are tumbled in disarray and half buried in firm mud, marbled throughout with a thick pale substance that in places has oozed onto the surface in smooth, flat wads.

"There's a real welter of the stuff down there," says Jil Punkinflake. "Water main broke a few years back, when all of those—" he flips his hand at the stones, and now I see fragments of coffin, a dull bronze handle "—were just in." And we pass by. "Wouldn't you love to have a cake of *that*?" They grin at each other. "Fine *laaadyyyy soooaaap*." "Or make candles, for a slow steady cremation." "Remember Cinto's—with the flower candles?" "We haven't had one as good as that this year. Did you go to Tehute's? Wasn't very good. Just two mutes at Tehute's." Drain pipes, slimy soot-blackened brick, clouds hurtling past far overhead. I feel as though I'm all muffled up, stifling warm but not sweating, not hot. Why am I so warm? Jil Punkinflake and the others all seem warm too, in fact they give off a palpable, febrile heat. They lead me back through streets and derelict houses, over a broken mausoleum, its marble dimly radiant in the starlight, to the Embalmer's College. A bearded man in a black skull cap or is it a toque is waving in a cart laden with bodies, puffing a blunt black cigar. Students dash excitedly from cellar doors and collect the bodies, carrying them inside. My companions saunter toward one of the wings, full under the gaze of one of the gaunter deans, who sits on horseback veiled from the crown of his silk hat down past his knees in nearly opaque black gauze.

I follow through dingy halls lined with matted dust, grimy wallpaper whose pattern is nearly browned out by years of smoke. The whole place is impregnated with an oppressive odor of stale smoke, rotting meat, embalmer's preparations, clashing with my hunger so that my head spins and I don't know whether or not to be disgusted. Banging lockers—the halls are thronged with students. Jil Punkinflake takes my hand in his hot dry fingers and leads me to the refectory, yellowed tiles over every surface in the room, over the elaborate groined vaults and niches, even the cenotaphs are tiled. I am shown to a bench at one of many long steel tables whiskered with tiny scratches, and presently Jil Punkinflake brings me a steel tray of food.

Black bread, a bowl of brine to season it with, hard dry cheese that thankfully is not too ripe and the mold is all on the outside and easily cut away, leathery preserved meat dished with stewed prunes, a beaker of thick porter so bitter my eyes tear up drinking it. Jil Punkinflake bangs his beaker against mine and toasts, "To the Cannibal Queen!" A few of the masters enter veiled, glide past us, receive their trays of food and set them in niches hewn like dictionary tabs into the sides of the cenotaphs. They pull up their chairs and raise their veils, eat soberly with their heads thrust into those niches. Now my head really is spinning, and Jil Punkinflake leads me by the hand to the dormitory room he shares with Nectar and a few others. I am guided into a nearly invisible bed and I can barely see Jil Punkinflake's broadcloth back lying down beside me.

There was a remote time when long darkness fell, when I fell—I saw snow, and the snow glare dimmed ... some first darkness came over me in something like a fit—it lifted, and soon I was enrolled in the College of Narrators—I don't trust these words ... A vibrating metal grate in falling asleep behind my eyes behind my face, a vibrating or a shuddering, in and out through fixed stations, blurring or accordioning back into sleep in the dark. Still the weird feeling of being just slightly too warm, not enough to perspire, and my throat is parched.

The next morning I rise and somehow get out of bed without waking my companions. I climb onto a chair and peer out the high window, watch a speckled black and white pigeon fly along the ground with a twig in its beak. A puff of air as I open the window; I try to smell some fresh air but the breeze misses my nose and taps my bare shoulder to say time to go.

*

The rally point, according to my ticket, is supposed to be on the fringe of the commercial area, on the death district side of the river. I've looked there repeatedly and found nothing, now I widen my search area. If I don't report, the Edek will know. They don't need to find out. They simply know. Once I've reported, though—perhaps then.

The day is blinding. I walk through one chimney of light after another. No sign of any rallying. The small oblong square is nearly deserted and the buildings dwindle in number like scattered wooden blocks here, as though they were marching down into the wheat-colored dust and white weeds. A portable office stands at one end of the square, hauled here by aurochs—I can still see their dried-out droppings there underneath. The office is a long narrow box on heavy wooden wheels, the axles at least three feet from the ground. A flimsy wooden stairway leads up to a two-piece door, and there's a glassless window beside it as well. Under the window, a limp, haphazardly hung army banner slouches from two nails. I collect my breath, walk up to the window and call to the sergeant.

Hollow footsteps sound unhurriedly in the box. A man with a face like crumpled suede and stiff backswept boar bristle black and grey hair appears at the window, then opens the upper half of the door and holds out a hand like a faded old garden glove, looking at something inside the door jam in a manner highly expressive of utter boredom. I put my ticket in his hand and he clumps back into the office. I see the back of his head lower just as he drops out of sight, only then actually looking at my ticket. The time that follows is so empty I can hear the sunlight sprinkling down on me and this square, time ground down to a halt like a clock worn out its spring.

Feet scrape on dry boards. He leans out with a flat packet wrapped in red paper and tied up with string level on his left palm right hand on the upright jamb, my ticket slid in under the string, looks me in the face and says—

"Douche."

I stare at him.

"Douche," he says again in the same tone a little louder and pumps the packet once in the air.

I point at my chest.

"*Low.*"

"Hanh?" He looks at me now.

"*Low* is my name."

The tip of his tongue flicks in and out once.

"That's not my name," I say measuredly.

He is visibly thinking, but not the right way. He half-thrusts the pack at my hand with a look that as much as says all this were a bit much coming from me. "Look, I don't—... It's not—" he says.

"I want *my* pack."

"There's no *Loo.*"

He shakes his head at there's no and then pushes it a little forward at what he takes for my name, all very expressive.

"Well I'm here aren't I? Here's my name, here's my regiment, same as your flag."

I take and flap the ticket at him and he fans his fingers at it like a man declining to give to a tramp. He stands upright and turns a little away from me, resting his eyes on the familiar entrails of his store. His mouth is open and he has a nonplussed look, like why don't I just melt into the rest of this dream.

"Loo—Douche ..." he says bobbing his head to the left and to the right and follows the words with an uncouth sound like "egkhhh," flipping his free hand. He looks back at me and tosses me the pack.

"Here."

I catch it to my chest.

"I don't want this."

The sergeant just mashes his mouth tighter closed and shakes his head, strides into the back of the store lifting his feet over bundles.

Should I toss it back? It's not really an idea. I'm already walking away, turning this pack over—no name, Douche or otherwise, no number, no marking. It must have had its own labelled cubbyhole.

I sit on a white rock by the road, set the packet across my knees, and open it. The first thing I see as the stiff wine-colored paper opens its folds are the arm bands marked with antique scarlet plusses—so this is a medic's kit, anyway. I open the oilskin wallet underneath them, and rock back a bit on my rock. A passing man in a white canvas uniform sees me, first soldier I've set eyes on here, nods his head back as he comes up without at all going over to me.

"It's good?" he asks, tilting his upper lip. He's leaning forward, holds the base of his rucksack with both his hands.

"I'm in authority, it says here."

As a member of the medical corps with incomplete commission I am to be assigned the rank of *second lieutenant*, and, in what is called "concurrent conferral," I am designated on the NCO index as a *warrant officer third class*, followed by the word <u>interpreter</u> capitalized and in parentheses.

The soldier nods and his gaze wanders. He goes by me, saying to the air in front of him, "Should be good. Interpreters are paid a little more."

Here's a dull bit of bronze with a quill heavily embossed on it, and rays. Attached are a pair of cerulean blue ribbons to put on my shoulder straps, which will make my double role clear to anyone who cares to know. There's even a small blue star embroidered under the red Xs on my arm bands, in fresh thread. Another scrap of print informs me my medical kit, helmet, sidearm, and other gear will be presented to me when I report to Captain-Adjutant A. Makemin.

I put the packet in my satchel and wander over to the river. The light and the dryness give me a disembodied feeling like being high in the mountains where the air is thin, and your vision distorts as though the world were a convex mirror. I sit under a tree and look at the sparkling until I feel better, then paw open my pack again. After some travail I locate in its folds a simple envelope of brown parchment, and saints be praised there's a chaw of soldier's scrip in it. The cellulite paper is shiny and a little transparent, so that the brown yellow and charcoal dyes are like tiny grains floating in it; there's a finely engraved portrait of some general or other, the relevant numbers in their swirling ornamental foliage, and unwholesomely frenetic webbing underlying it all. Glancing up, I see the rally point.

Resignedly I make my way back past the office and into the camp, which spills out of the city limits onto the fringes of the foothills and scabland. There are rows of packing crates here, like a warehouse. A droop-faced man in a floppy turban and dingy tweed leans his elbows on one of the crates at the end of a row tracing circles with his knuckle on the wood. I ask him about Makemin. He rubs his nose on the side of his finger.

"MAH-keh-min, you mean?"

(I'd said "MAKE-min.")

"Is that how you say it?"

He looks bored.

"... Yes, unless there's another," I say.

"Not in, bub."

"Do you know where he is? I'm supposed to report."

The man is turning, hobbling off, the level of his shoulders seesaws as he goes back between the freight.

"He's off griping up a storm with the dispatcher. Come back again later—nobody's going anywhere."

The camp is mostly deserted; I see dun tents, bales of mosquito netting, churns of benzoin, all manner of things I can't readily identify, but that I somehow know have been sitting here a long time, dust duning up against the crates.

"You're looking for Makemin?" That voice is thickly accented and ragged, coming from a strongly-built man in a long dark sweater, sitting on a canvas seat surrounded by nothing in particular. I go over to him. He smokes, and seeps the smoke out horizontally into the wind from his mouth.

"Wait 'til you see what mood he's in before you try to talk to him. If he dislikes you when he meets you, he'll always dislike you."

I introduce myself and he tells me his name is Silichieh. He's part of Makemin's unit—a veteran, although he hasn't served with Makemin before. He shows me his green engineer's armband. When I exhibit my red X's, he pouts and says, "We're both professionals," smiling.

He has a broad square face covered in bristles and a rabbit mouth. I sit down on a low heap of bricks, and now his head is above me, against the oceanic sky. I tell him about my exemption problem and he nods philosophically.

"It's an old story. Just don't tell it to him—" whenever Makemin comes up, Silichieh points vaguely in the direction of one of the tents, "—no matter how good your case is he won't listen, and things will be worse for you then. He'll think you're shirking."

"Do you know where we are going?" Surprising I haven't thought to ask this earlier.

"Meqhasset," he says, and his eyes light up strangely. "You know Meqhasset?"

I shake my head no.

"It's an island. We're going to Port Conget; there's a boat there we will take to Meqhasset."

"Is it very far?"

"Not visible from mainland, but not far."

"There are Yeseg on the islands?"

"Not yet, but Meqhasset—you don't know?"

Again I shake my head.

"Well, it's complicated. Meqhasset is federated with other islands. They're all independent internally but they are all supposed to cooperate for each other's defense, and they mount strong defenses, particularly their navy. Meqhasset is very strategically placed because it's so close to land; from Meqhasset you can really have coastal control here, or pile up troops there to bring anywhere here. Now, lately business there is bad, money's gone and so, when either we or Wacagan men cross into their waters, other islands' navy don't come around. With no money, there's no help from anyone else, so now Meqhasset is vulnerable, and we race to see who gets there first. That's why Makemin is so frantic to move."

"I thought we were fighting to put down a Yeseg rebellion or something."

Silichieh smiles. "No, no. It's Wacagan versus Alaks again, as always. Wacagan are backing Tewsetonta, who's King of Yesegs, and encourage him to break with Alak Emperor, so now Emperor is behind Tewsetonta's brother Tewsetonka to take his place. Alaks and Wacagan fight through them. Taking Meqhasset is Tewsetonta's idea, and now we are supposed to head them off before they can get it."

He looks past me.

"There he is."

The camp is bordered on the town side by a few long low buildings, and from between them a group is emerging not far from us. I see a man talking agitatedly with a few others, starting and stopping, and they are nodding and making brief comments. Makemin is beside himself. He talks, gesticulating vehemently, his face drawn. Suddenly his whole body snaps and his fist staves in the side of a crate. He storms across the camp, his knuckles dripping blood into the dust. I take him in as he passes. His cropped hair and his skin are the same color and that makes his scalp look splintered. Drab tan uniform with something like a split skirt hanging from under the tunic, over his trousers, short boots and gaiters, cross-chest strap to his belt and a large buttoned holster. Medium sized and solid man, boiling with fury, and nearly all one color, clothes and person. He looks like a lot of light brown dust just congealed itself around his eyes. I've never seen more rage in one face.

Makemin storms by and disappears into his tent, the one Silichieh kept pointing to, with a furious dashing aside of the flap door. I glance at Silichieh and he makes an expressive face, what's the use?

"He's no jolly good fellow."

He tells me to try again in a few days. If anything comes up, there will surely be an announcement.

"Well, he's been getting divorced for months now, and she's not just divorcing him, but there's this lawsuit about some property or some land. That case is separate but related. So he spends every free minute he gets in there, writing letters and filling out forms or something. He can't possibly have wanted this assignment, and I don't know what he did to get stuck with it but it must have been pretty bad or pretty stupid. And now he has to deal with half his soldiers deserting, and no more can be spared, and so on, and they won't let him leave. It's all pretty bad shape."

"Did an Edek see you, too?"

"An Edek? No! Did one see you?"

I nod ruefully.

He runs his hand over the top of his head, then drops it into his lap and sniffs thoughtfully at the air.

"Why do you stay?" I ask.

He looks up at and a little into me. "Meqhasset is enchanted, everyone says. I want to see it."

"Enchanted how?"

He drops his eyes sideways.

"I don't know exactly. Whatever it is, is interior. No inhabitants have anything to do with it, and they don't talk about it. I heard about it from my cousin. He had to go there, on a boat, and he heard stories. And he saw something too, I think, but he would never talk about it."

"What does he think of you going?"

"Oh, he's dead. My whole family is dead. No wife, nobody waiting, so," he shrugs, "I can throw my life around if I want to. And I've been on campaigns before. I learned always to avoid glorious campaigns—everyone is more likely to die in glorious campaigns. You get yourself assigned to something small-time deal like Meqhasset, where you spend half your tour getting there, and you'll come back alive. Probably alive."

*

I follow the river into the commercial area. There are kiosks selling mineral water and witch hazel, porters rushing everywhere with heavy bales of cinnamon, camphor, cotton and kegs of sea salt. Here's an overwhelmingly fragrant row of tobacco women with barrels and great swatches of the leaves, cured and fresh, camphorated or spiced. In the meat market, they have whole ambuloceti for sale, hunted by the unusually brave and well-armed in the marshier land down river where the camphor grows.

Representatives of the Embalmer's College wander among aisles of corpses, heaped in pyramidal piles. They're soft and spotty like overripe fruit, the students and masters pinch, sniff, and squeeze with judiciously long faces and expertly-seeking eyes. The merchants sit wooden-faced on stools impassively fanning away the flies. Barrels of hands, feet, and genitals quiver as heavily-laden carts rumble by, and here a beefy woman dressed in a black leotard and brown leather apron sells skin and hair. On her foot-long wooden spools, ranged upright in a sort of abacus along the back of her stall, are glowing, convex cylinders of lustrous blonde, umbrous red, slick black hair glistening like onyx, feathery curls and hair straight and thick as wire, and sheets of skin in various widths from tapes to broad sheets, from sheerest transparency to skin like granulated oil over a barely-perceptible, delicate pink. Gland dealers are set well to one side, with the intestine men, who wear their wares in discrete coils around their arms and legs. The smell among the gland dealers is a cool sour haze of pungent ammonia, deep biting musks, rancid cheese reek, and woven in with the rest is a weird platinum note that glides through the sinuses like a love spell, casually drawing all attention and will together into a long elastic cone pulling me along until I blunder transfixed into the nearest counter. Steel trays and salvers, jars, metal urns, strings of dried gonads like bundles of garlic hanging in the drafty air.

An embalming professor from the school is tying up a tall stack of severed hands with twine, her veil held in place by a black petalled chaplet. She snaps the fingers on her own hand, the tips exposed by the fingerless lace gloves, and Jil Punkinflake appears from one of the aisles adjacent, pulling the ladder from his vest and smiling unctuously. The death's-head moth holds its wings out at full length.

He helps her carry her parcels to her phaeton standing by and winks at me. She clips away, and he ambles over, hands in pockets.

"Well? Are you an army man?"

I explain.

"It stinks," he shrugs. "Let's go drink some of your scrip, Low."

*

I find unaccountable difficulties always arise in searching out the narrative sections of any marketplace, but of course how could I know that? Anyhow there always seems to be some distraction, or the sort of wrong turn that, having drawn you into the trammels of its mischief, dodges behind the innocent turns and loses itself among them like an absconding pickpocket. No shortage of the real ones either—at the wine store, Jil Punkinflake took my wallet slowly from my hand as I was about to restore it to my pocket, and deftly slipped it into my shirt, where my vest holds it now against my skin. I ask him about the narrative market and he gives me a swift, canny look. With a nearly invisible toss of his head I realize he is one of those go-betweens who are involved with the narrative merchants, the storiers and letterers and calligraphers and abecedarians. We flit out into trough-like stone lanes.

"I'm one of many at the college," he avers. "Our work and their work can be compared. Properly compared. A feel for one is a feel for the other, often."

Past the indigo dyers and a suave aproned ink maker, and here is the narrative section, a long row of small, elegant shops with teak fronts adorned with gleaming brass and magnificent tumbling window displays. Here all the world's alphabets, abjads, and syllabaries are sold. Jil Punkinflake's face grows tight and sharp, he seems etched in the air. His eyes shimmer. There's a casino atmosphere

here; I can see great whirlwinds of invisible loss and gain churning in the sky down into the earth. But these stores sell only the general sort of alphabet, the vast majority of which were created long ago by a handful of ancient masters and gods. The current alphabet makers are skilled copyists, and talented embellishers—at least, this is true of those who sell their wares in these stores.

Another class of symbolists exists, who conduct their trade in secret, against both city and royal law, meeting clients in clandestine assignations, fashioning unique, customized writing ways for them. Hidden as they are, their presence is palpable everywhere, and accounts for this heady atmosphere. These underground artificers, trained by anonymous teachers, read copy and circulate books long lost to memory in the perfectly ordered, perfectly maintained, perfectly complete, never-read archives of the Alaks. The creation of a new symbola is not simply a matter of drawing a series of substitute markings; it is a magical undertaking, in which an ordination must be created that will allow for the improvisation of signs that will become permanent, and which must be commensurate with the client's requirements and expressive, at every point, of a rigorous internal coherence. Some clients will get phonetic alphabets, others syllabaries; some symbols, others pictures, depending upon their needs, wants, personalities, whatever exigency is expressed in their need for a writing way of their own. Furthermore, the characters must *seem appropriate* to their sounds, or concepts, and this is where no amount of unassisted technical ability avails. The association of symbols is conducted in often gruelling, if simple, rituals that can last for weeks; some accomplished artisans have died in pursuit of them. There is no telling at the outset what will cause the most difficulty; in some cases, extreme refinement of nuance may bring the symbolist to the point of complete collapse, while in other cases it may be an intolerable simplicity and directness that suffocates her.

Jil Punkinflake hops up on a sawhorse, and leaning forward looking into my eyes he tells me the story of a prodigy who sat in the grass by the wayside of the capital road in a shapeless black garment of many different materials and dashed off in the dust of the road immaculate alphabets on the spot, even sometimes for every single passer by. People looked down at the rows of letters and saw so much of themselves they broke down then and there, or instantly decorporated. One is better advised to be alone when one first looks on one's *own* alphabet, even those specifically designed to conceal the nature of the buyer from himself always show too much in showing too frankly this desire to hide in the letters.

Suddenly a look of detestation, such as I'd never imagined he could be capable of, let alone see myself, creases his face; his eyes darken and he hops down from the sawhorse. It's as if his expression were being corrupted by the effect of a corrosive poison.

He is looking past me—I follow his eyes, I see the crowd, the stalls, the buildings, but I don't know what, among these things, he is glaring at so fixedly. He touches my arm, and pulls me a little way aside, into the mouth of a narrow alley, still looking beyond me.

"What is it?" I ask. I must have been asking that for a while already.

Jil Punkinflake is actually panting with emotion, and

his grip on my arm is uncomfortably firm. I begin to get alarmed, and try again to align my gaze with his. Now I'm sure—a young woman, or a girl, maybe twelve years old, oblivious, composed, her head flowing with dense, long dark hair, is walking past us. She looks neither right nor left, but down toward the street, and people seem unconsciously to recoil from her. Some glower, but most simply move out of her way without apparently being aware of her at all. She is dressed in a white nightgown, and, though it hangs still and straight from her shoulders, it seems to undulate, and now she seems older than she had at first.

"A sleepwalker?" I ask, but I get no answer.

As she passes nearest to us, I feel something hit me, like the blow of a loud sound, that seems to fracture something in my chest. I feel the fracture's sick edges, and I want to gasp. The feeling dims as she passes, dwindling away down the street. I feel as though my life somehow adheres to her, and that it dwindles with her as she goes, and that I am helpless ...

Now I improve.

Jil Punkinflake watches her pass with an ugly and uncharacteristic look of loathing.

"Who was that? You seemed to know her ..."

"That," he says as though it cost him pain, "was a *dreamer.*"

"A sleepwalker?"

His eyes close like lowering blinds; his face is rigid. His teeth are almost chattering.

"We all hate them here, and soon you'll learn to as well."

"Why should I hate someone for dreaming?"

"*This* is their dream," he says pointing vehemently at the earth, and then adds in a bitter, wounded tone, "and we are *their* creatures. They disguise themselves and trick us, toy with us, draw us into their empty themes, leave us stuck in their follies ... trifling with us and then, when we need them—where are they? They're *gone!*"

And then he turns away from me and plunges his face into his hands.

Later, he looks up again, to the sky, the street, and murmurs, "Now we forget, now is the time."

*

I want to browse the stores. Jil Punkinflake, same again as ever, shrugs at them.

"Be around tonight and I'll show you something better."

... and he's gone in a twinkling like a fairy man.

I look at fine calfskin notebooks, bales of foolscap, ranks of somber iron type, casks of ink. This purplish-skinned man sells pencils so soft you can sharpen them with your breath. A stunning woman in a low-cut blouse sells fountain pens, and I stand there for I don't know how long transfixedly turning back and forth in my fingers a pen all made of an intermittently translucent, hard yet elastic substance. There is powdery smoke in it forming a minutely-worked interlocking pattern of silky tongues and smart hooks, the nib is gold, laced in a sinuous engraved line narrower than a hair. The pattern is engulfing, and I wander through it like a garden maze.

For all my looking, I haven't been able to find much of anything in the way of stories. I found only one storier, and it seemed to be closed, or perhaps sealed for a private party, behind its boxy wooden gates. I cross the commercial area, heading back toward the Embalmer's College. Hoofbeats bang in the street and I hang back to let the carriage pass. It's the hearse I'd seen earlier, which had wrung words of rapturous praise from the mortuary students. The horses are massive up close, and pass me with weightless power. I watch the carriage sail along the road and note the coffin hatch up above the wreath on the back. The hearse slows as it passes away; the window opens, and a well-shaped, woman's arm, in a tiny-flowered grey sleeve, unfolds from the passenger compartment. The laced hand drops a handkerchief in the street, and vanishes; the carriage turns the corner with weird sharpness and is gone.

I am alone in the street. The handkerchief retains the pinched point where her fingers held it a moment, and is faithfully embroidered with a beautiful character I don't recognize. The smell is like grape lees, wind chimes, rotting roses. When I raise my eyes from it, I notice a maybe four-year-old girl walking along the pavement opposite me, one hand in her mother's hand and the other pointing at me; and she does a funny thing. Grinning, her chubby face lit up with an expression of incandescent surprise, she peels her lips back from her little white teeth and red gums, and bites the air three or four times, looking me in the eye and pointing.

*

My route back to the College strays through an administrations corridor. There are few businesses here, all down at heel, customers and proprietors alike in ragged clothes. Deputies in short, belted leather jackets creak superciliously through the often thickly packed warrens with menacing ease.

The Succentor's subalterns are selected for their uncommon knack with emotion weapons, although most of these are never used and may not even be taught any more. It is not usual for persons who have had any dealings with the deputies, in their official capacity—and most of these deputies are fantastically devoted to their work and seldom allow themselves any respite in its pursuit even when invited, even when ordered to, by their superiors—to bear away with them any clear impression or recollection of them. A surprisingly dense mass of unshiftable complacency or satisfaction seems to set in, and it takes unpleasant, determined effort to claw through it to the real memories. The deputies move through the city at will, for the most part safe behind an indifference repulsion, and no one is the wiser who does not recognize the equivocal signs of the procedure. The deputy is brisk, smiling quietly to himself and going about his business. Citizens are pushed back and aside without taking offense; they are unwittingly darted with a infusion of obliging helpfulness, and it would seem to them a shame or even an outrage that anyone should mar this picture of happy efficiency, represented by the deputy in the flesh. Nothing is more important than that things should operate smoothly, with cheery smiles; anyone who disrupts this smooth operation in any one place threatens to send out friction ripples that will ...?

Emotion weapons are precisely aimed with focussing ways, like artillery; heavy guns are aimed by calculating the arc of trajectory required to hit the target and then carving away all remaining space in excess of that arc so that it, the ball, may only go along that arc: just so, the emotion weapon will have no effect unless certain questions are, and even the occasion of questioning is, carved away, so no one asks what it really is that the disruptive individual disrupts, or why friction is so wholly to be avoided, and smoothness elevated to holiness. Of all considerations in the use of emotion weapons the principal is to cause inversion, or the transferral of hostility to the victim, so that he or she is rebuffed for causing trouble. Uniformed in their repulsion, the deputies glide through the city without the slightest effort, leaving behind them smooth wakes of assiduously busy citizens.

I need to find my unit, to get some sort of documentation renewed or acknowledged, not that I can recall now ... I gather my courage and duck into one of the many small offices on the lane. The officer is brisk, smartly filing and typing, with a funny little smile on her face. The need I fling out to her like an open hand slides back and falls to my hip, as though she were on the other side of a pane of glass, too thick to shatter. She is humming away to herself inside her glass barrier, asleep even as she politely answers my questions. The barrier answers me: give up, give up. "Happiness is the intensest sort of prosperity and all Prosperity, I find, hardens the Heart—and happy people become so very prudent and far-sighted ..." She sees far past me.

The light seems to change (where did that voice come from?) its place of origin, shining now from down low, as if the world had flipped, and the deputy's face has become a mask, not a lineament changed. It is the face of a corpse exhumed from permafrost ground I saw when I was a boy. The eyes stare at me, and a voice inside them says, directly to me, "It won't be hard to break you, either."

I leave the office without a word, and without taking

my eyes from the sidewalk I feel a burden in the air, like a boulder rolling down the street behind me. I turn into a narrow alley, take two or three steps and a cold fist lodges in my stomach and dissolves there. This is the wrong way. I turn slowly, without wanting to, and face four deputies who are striding toward me down the alley like a human wall. I know they are supposed to seem solicitous and concerned but I can see black crumbling leers rending their dead soap faces, and I smell their breath of decaying bogs thick with frigid scum. Chuckling thickly in putrid scum they are coming for me. I try to turn with a body of lead, pushing out my heavy hand for a door standing ajar in the opposite wall, and I know I will grind to a stop and be caught and lost there forever in that hopeless moment turning to run from these deputies. It's royal power, flowing from the capital through them. What do they want? Unbuckling their belts. Dry finger tips brush the wrinkles standing across the back of my shirt.

The handle of the door is rebounding from my hand, the hallway flies around me as though I were falling headlong. Out of control I burst through a flimsy door and nearly tangle myself in low washing lines. But I manage to bend and avoid them, the shapeless woman hanging these clothes stares at me too shocked to curse, stares after me, I can feel it, as I run away.

*

They were talking about fortune telling, and I said I wanted to know my fortune—

"Come on, narrator, you can write down what we do."

I fall in with Jil Punkinflake, Nectar, a pair of women named Dusty and Lilly, and a puppyalonging freshman named Keen. It's an hour after sunset, and the country road is a livid silver scar in dark blue earth. Our hands and faces all seem to glow in the blue dark, swinging and streaking through the air. Giddy, sick-looking stars are tumbling around above us, through the empty branches. The road is gauntly lined with trees, and fallow fields striped blue silver and black behind them.

They are taking me to see one of their teachers, an immigrant or refugee who teaches at the college under an assumed name, Dr. Mellaart. They speak of him with a combination of reverent enthusiasm and a more childish excitement, as though he were only an entertainer. His group meets in a suburb outside the city, abandoned now the tributary dried. Many grand old houses there are gradually blowing away. The water never came back.

I like Lilly. She has a long jaunty stride and a face lit inside like a paper lantern. She shows me her side by side ten gauge with a garland of lacy bowels carved into the butt; entelodonts are still seen here occasionally, and respond with interest to the carrion smell of the mortuary students. Lilly looks very sporting with her gun and her little hat. Jil Punkinflake feeds his death's-head from a glass dropper as we walk.

The house comes into view on the right, through a break in the trees. A residual violet light stands in smears of thick water on pale clay soil, trees feebly claw the air in a copse off one wing, and the bare, scattered land beyond the house is creased with a shallow, oozing stream, little more than an inky scrape in the ground. An eerie, resonant stillness pours down in an avalanche from the sky, settling about the house like an invisible plume of dust. Lilly glances up at me with iodine whited eyes.

"It used to belong to a big camphor man," she says. "Once, his detectives caught up with a man who'd hijacked one of his cargos. They brought him here, and camphor man cut both his legs off him in one of the upstairs rooms."

She sidles up to me and takes my arm with her free hand.

"The man broke loose somehow and got as far as the front door before they shot him dead. From that time, now and then, people have heard him thumping down the stairs without his legs."

She gives my arm a playful squeeze. As we approach, I can see a shadow emerge from the high grass to one side of the house and pull itself instantly up through one of the windows. It's a brick house, with acute gables at either end like a cat's head. The windows are large panes of glass in scalloped stone frames, and as we bunch up to follow the stingy path through high weeds dried to wheezing husks I glance up in time to see a candlelit face recede from one of the sills upstairs. Are they coming in through the roof?

The veranda is deep but not broad; the steps and planks groan at our every move. Dusty opens the door, which chitters as it swings back. The house closes around me, and I am aware of a vibrant stillness, produced by tensions in something below or behind me. We are pushing back the invisible, ponderous fabric of presence inside the walls; the moulding on the walls shivers, and the doorknobs seem to cringe back into the shadows. A hand takes mine, and I am led a few steps down the hall, with the stairway barely discernible to my left, and through a wide single door of darkly reflective polished wood, into a parlour. I can make out many figures in the gloom, and Jil Punkinflake is already making the rounds with his cheroot in his hand, lighting the gas mantles.

A single round table in the center of the room, oilskin cloth and a big doily in the middle, tables all round. Dim light from the hollowly breathing mantles, tiled fireplace, mirror above it, fronded wallpaper and ponderous carved ornaments everywhere. The ceiling is bunched and wrinkled in a funereally heavy floral pattern, and a ghoulish rosette in the center. I am directed to a seat at the table with the door not far behind me; Nectar sits on my left and Dusty on my right, Jil Punkinflake beside her and Keen sits opposite me with his back to the window, the curtains nearly brushing his shoulders. I hear the boxed-in ticking of the clock for the first time as Jil Punkinflake says, "Lilly, it's time to bring him in."

Lilly clomps into the obscurity at the far end of the room, where darkness has collected like smoke. I can see her seat herself on a low stool and roll up alongside an enormous object nearly filling the space in that half of the room. Lilly is looking down at something on one side of this object and I can make out her pale hands manipulating what look like organ stops. A granulated light gathers around the base of the object which I now see is a four-poster bed with a beyond-elaborate sculpted frame. Lilly has a pair of earphones clapped to her head, connected to the bed with a length of heavy coiled wire in an embroidered sleeve. She is turning cherub's-head knobs the size of tomatoes, and sliding gilded wooden flowers, cherries, leaves, and grapes expertly back and forth, peering with bunched eyebrows at the results. Every few moments she flicks her eyes up at a deep curving groove, notched like a ruler, cut into the headboard, where a burnished copper needle sails back and forth along the notches as she turns a heavy cherub bulb with her left hand. Through the window, I can see high black clouds rolling up from the horizon and passing over the house; some of them slip in through the window and slither up the wall and along the ceiling. The big doily begins to flip end over end in place, apparently passing through the substance of the table, faster and faster with a sound like a thick rope being spun in the air. Jil Punkinflake's death's-head moth is sprouting long licorice-like tendrils with a liquid crackling sound; they loop and twine along his lapels and up his shoulder.

I can see a figure on the bed now, a large pale man all shining, wearing what seems to be a rough white linen suit. His hands and feet are wrapped in gauze, as is his fleshy throat up to the heavy chin densely stubbled with white. The high-browed head is pasty and his heavy lids sag over glittering dark eyes.

The door adjacent the base of the stairs stands blackly open directly before me and a round white head is bowed there, rising and coalescing like a ball of smoke. A leg swings out at the knee and a foot of solid darkness comes down across the threshold—the flesh of half my body is tugged aside in gooseflesh withering in my chest and Jil Punkinflake slams the door shut in my face. "Don't look in the hall," he tells me sternly, and then scans the others with vehemence in his eyes, leaving me weakly to drag my seat to the circle again. My back to the door feels alive with creeping cold fire.

Dr. Mellart is coming into view, propped up on the bed, and Lilly rises and open a shutter above the backboard, revealing a bough-raked sunset sky, although the window opposite me remains bottomless night. The sunken face speaks. His voice is thin and weak, projected from some other narrative, as he is not at home in this one. His speech seems to emit sense directly into my imagination. Linguistic elementals. The séance contacts disembodied narratives and raw images, imperfect memories, and dreams; the medium gives up voice to that idiom-phantom. I see why I was brought here—I am to record what will come through the others, who are all mediums.

In my mind's eye, a vividly colored green and blue map of the world running off into infinity on all sides—I see myself as I must appear sitting in this chair, from a point of view high in a corner of the room—rows of tattered, torn-open books dribbling leaves to the floor, tables and a stone floor strewn with paragraphs, verses, illustrations, choruses, familiar endings. Ripples in the air like heat waves, that gather in flowing ribbons, ascending and then gradually sinking again.

The figure on the bed grows dim, and Lilly seems to climb up onto the bed as its unluminous light ebbs out of the air. There in the glow I faintly see the fabric of her dress indented by fingers of gauze. I glance up, as though my attention were a thing hanging in the wind and liable to be tossed this way and that by the least breeze. Without a sound, the silhouette of a leaping naked man interrupts the light of the window opposite me as Keen bolts to his feet screaming with raucous laughter. Keen flies forward springing bounding chalk-faced his arms and legs jerk and snap—the laughter lacerating his throat, the table isn't there between us—he bites his hands inhumanly his blazing eyes draw streaks in the air. The two students who disappeared earlier lunge from their hiding place within the chimney and in a flash the rope is about him. Keen resists wildly, his laughter is a bellow that will blast the walls down. Now all the students are grappling with him; he veers again and again into the air like a puppet yanked up by a string, a skirt of black-sleeved arms clinging to his waist. His spine whips back and forth flinging his legs this way and that, twisting against their hands as they pin him flat to the floor. Every second, Keen wrenches his entire body a foot into the air against all their arms and slams flat to the floor, roaring with laughter hideous black implacable and bitter as death. The students hold him down with all their weight and strength—Keen's crackling eyes are smeared with blood and he bleeds from his torn lips. A dark figure flashes around the room near the ceiling gambolling and writhing like a man in an oven. Keen is pinned. He throws his head back eyes staring mouth gaping, laughing without smiling, it is only a fractured howl. As each howl reaches its loudest I become aware there's another sound inside it, an inhuman drone like a resonating box. He writhes on the ground pale as paper, throws back his head and voids a throat-wracking belch of corpse gas, the retching noise hums through him as it would a plucked harp string.

The laughter suddenly erupts from him again.

"The war!" he raves.

"The warrr! We won!"

His head snaps up on his neck and he stares into my eyes, hissing—"*We* won!"

Keen subsides into idiotic chuckling, his face folded down against his throat. He's laughed himself out. His laughter trickles around the room, his voice comes from the walls, the furniture, the fireplace. It jumps from the window, runs cackling into the distance. We can hear it go, we can hear it for a long time.

Jil Punkinflake, catching his breath, holds one of Keen's arms. He looks into the depraved face, eyes like jellied blood twitch in their sockets with a faint slick sound.

"Where's Keen?" Jil Punkinflake asks.

"In paradise." The voice chuckles in vomit. It gurgles in his throat and he tosses his head aside spattering the floor with a little.

"You are there now?" I ask.

"Now I am there there I now am now I am there."

He takes a deep shuddering breath, and grows even more shockingly pale, as though he were suffused with longing for something near. As he speaks, the room fades, and I am there, living the words he says, which have become colorless, toneless, have merged entirely with events and sensations.

"Who are you?"

"I am the one that balances the flood and the it's what I can say to you is only that there is a dead one in the choice way, I speak faster than it is in your power to follow. Right now you are speaking not I. Now is the time for I to speak through I."

"What is your name?" I ask, not knowing why. "Tell me who you are."

"I am trailing along balancing bodies with time. The way you choose is all spattered with peculiar lights and your selection is waiting. You have already waited. By water from his face, by the street stretching past me, by taking time away from me, taking him away from me, taking them away from me. Time without I, without it, is me."

"Where is Keen?"

"Pouring rain spilled down his face. He blows rain in spurts away from his lips. I speak faster. In the rain his young face seems to melt. I have to speak faster. I struggle to record on what I say on a water sheet but the music must allow time enough for whatever it is to come through these streets to me right now. He speak in doorways, am looking at me."

"What does he say?" I ask.

Blobs of rain tremble cold on his face. He shivers. Congealed vomit webs his lips in thick yarns.

"What are you saying, Keen?" I ask, raising my voice and speaking distinctly. "Keen?"

His white lips tremble open, letting rain run down onto his teeth.

"If his own train were wrecked, and this were yet no spur, then it would be she and he. Intimate in the half-light. She was the one who started, who hid, like her kind will. There is always more second wind, hidden or trapped in pockets below the earth, or in the trees, or in each other. You spread more whenever you shall sit down to write. That's the difference between lives; try it, and there shall be some wind to move the *death* out of your path. Boneless mummified words sifted through your writing fingers will receive and hold the death there, present before you and even trapped. You turn over death and life, passing them back and forth through something like a window, and drive the death sentences through what you did not know ..."

*

I visit the camp again. It's nearly deserted, and I'm thankful, but presently I come across a soldier who tells me our new orders will be delayed by about a week, according to the latest dispatch. That means there are orders, after all.

I spend several more days at the college. In vaulted cellars filled with a dense, clammy haze I watch from the visitor's pew in a corner as ranks of students whisk through timed autopsies. The crews are ranked by speed and neatness on a chalk-smirched board; a grandly-whiskered instructor holds up a stopwatch the size of an apple. His round cheeks are red and shiny in an otherwise waxy, greenish face, and a variety of dissecting tools hang jingling from the front of his apron. Bodies are slung up onto the tables one after another, eviscerated and binned; Jil Punkinflake and his team are highly rated. Red hands pull open the body cavities and a meaty, excremental, liverish perfume is emitted; then he and Keen, their hands flitting here and there like birds hopping in the lane, isolate and remove each organ, handing them to Nectar. He plops them one by one into a produce scale hanging from the ceiling and notes their weights on his smeary clipboard.

Slack human bodies are bustled and tossed everywhere I look, sliding across the floor in low heaps, pushed along by oilskin-aproned dieners with slick rubber spades. As each fresh cadaver is positioned on the dissecting table, Jil Punkinflake takes the temples gently in his grisly hands and gazes down into the dead face with a look like mother love. That look trembles on every face in the room, their caressing knives part skin, muscle and fat, and the bodies seem to offer up their contents to these hands with blissful abandon like dreamers unhasping their grip on the brink and allowing themselves to drop away into deep, balmy waters.

Last glimmers of sun blaze in the narrow arch linking two terraced buildings. The sunset is turning the sky to red and orange sherbet, and a few lamps are already lit, swinging under the eaves of the buildings. Amber cones of light fall from the lamps and splash along the walls, wind scuttles in dry weeds, brings me a gust of smoke, dust, oil frying.

I hear a rattle of wheels and hooves; a hearse—*the* hearse—pulls up before me and stops. The driver, dim against the half-blue sky, gestures me inside.

My hand trembles on the latch—I pull the door open and the compartment is empty. I climb in and not quite knowing why nor why not sit; falling in place not really under control, not used to climbing in and out of carriages. We go a short distance and then stop. Suddenly a hatch opens in the roof opposite me and the driver clambers down, with know-how if not with grace, into the carriage. He shuts the compartment and sits across from me with a piping sigh.

"Well," he smiles, enjoying the softness. "Comfortable? How d'ye do?"

He puts out his hand.

"Orvar," he says, "just Orvar, no mister." As if he wanted to spare me any unnecessary trouble. He repeated my name as I pronounced it, nodding once and sweeping his face down and back, reaching into his jacket for something. His eyes seem alternately drawn and repelled by my face. He pulls out a small metal bottle wrapped in a leather sleeve, undoes the cap and offers it to me—"Tea?"

It's brackish and slightly viscous, going down my throat in one cool lump. As he takes a neat swig, without touching his lips to the bottle, as I had done, I feel a sort of inner dislocation, and it's as though a dirt robe were slid under and around me.

He gives me a friendly smile. "It's a bit too strong, but it's no poison." Puts the bottle away and thrusts his fingers between each other.

"Well," he says, talking down toward my shoes. "Well."

I can hear the rasp and unrasp of his fingers against each other as he jams their webs together. I wait. His smile refreshes itself as a thought visibly occurs to him.

"She *normally* sits there," he says, indicating the spot to my right as though she were there now. The seat is draped with a rich silver fur lined in peach satin. With a surprisingly strong pang I recognize its perfume, and it now seems more intimate a smell, as if it were rising still warm from her body. It seems somehow very dear to me. I tenderly imagine a woman's body, with skin like peach satin, like dunes glowing orange in the sun.

"That's *her* scent."

"Oh," I blink. I feel as though I'd been caught pulling off my clothes in a trance.

"Yes, she's something of a fixture here in town. You may have heard of her?"—A guarded note entered in there.

"No," I say. It's true. I suspect he is probing for signs of guile in me.

"Well, then." He sits back, pushing his shoulders into the cushions. He seems to have relaxed his suspicion, but his face has taken on a hardness I wouldn't have expected of it. Cold twinges in my intestines from the tea, but it isn't an entirely unwholesome sensation. I feel massive and solid, settled heavily in place like an anvil.

"You seem to have attracted her interest," he says. There's no mistaking his meaning, or that he is her go-between in these matters.

"'Madame' means she's married, isn't she?" My voice sounds more confused than it should. I think of the grave she visited. Orvar's head lifts back, and some leavening shadow flits across his serious face.

"A widow now ... You really haven't heard anything? No, I wouldn't suppose you had ... You're from up north, aren't you?"

"I'm from the mountains."

"She was very attached to her husband and family." He waves at all the black, the funereal trappings. "I don't know how many years it's been, but she's still in mourning."

I blink and say nothing. This approach seems to work best.

"It's no secret. A story most people know something about, if not enough. Not their business, but—" he shrugs and purses his lips, then suddenly fixes me, points. "Now she's taken an interest in you, it's liable to become your business. That's why I have to tell you. You understand—it's something you should hear first from *me,* and not from some gossip or other."

I can still beg off, just barely—but her perfume wafts over me, holding me there like a giant, gently firm hand.

"Her husband held an administrative position; I wasn't associated with the family then, so I can't say what it was exactly. Evidently he overdid it, worked himself too hard. A trip to Cadassis and back in the snow gave him brain fever and he died in her arms, up at the house."

He pauses and glances out the window. Someone seems to be strolling by.

When the stroller is gone, Orvar says, tonelessly, "Her daughter was away at the time. She was alone in the house with her husband. She was very attached to him. She deeply loved him."

The sun goes below the horizon, and darkness closes around the carriage like the wings of a cape. Orvar is looking very dim there across from me.

"I don't think she could bear to lose him."

I measure with my eyes the distance between my hand and the door latch.

"Mr. Collumn—her husband's physician had passed word of his death to the embalmers, as a matter of course."

He inhales through his mouth.

"And they went to the house within three days' time of his death. They only found his bones, mostly, in the bed ... and her there with them ... and nothing else."

After long silence, Orvar coughs quietly and I hear the jostle of fluid in the bottle.

"Well, there was a scandal, as you can imagine. You see, everyone knew she had lost a baby boy a few years before. Crib death. Happened when she was away. Evidently too much. Too much for her. Her husband was supposed to be looking after the boy when it happened; he fell asleep, it seems, and when he next checked on the child, it was already over. Boy was fine before. The child was buried privately, on the grounds. Grounds of their estate. She refused the embalmers. Very unusual. Everyone remembered that *then*, you understand? She was very attached to the boy. Couldn't stand to lose him."

I nod, unsure he can see me in the gloom. My mind is not in motion.

"She blamed her husband. Apparently was cold with him after that. I was not yet in her employ then, but this is what I gather. She still loved him, you understand. When she knew he was dying, she repented it—her coldness—but he was so low by then that she really couldn't tell if he could know that or not. Forgive her. She's so sensitive ... and the uncertainty ..."

He makes a face I can't quite make out. Now, finally, my mind takes a step or two, and I remember.

"They called her the Cannibal Queen."

He starts at that.

"Please, sir!" he says sharply. "*Honestly!*"

He sits back, disapproval radiating from his invisible face. "She deserves better than that. It made her so ill, she suffered so—and for a woman like that, to be *ostracized* ... made a *pariah* ... Or worse, to be slandered. Made a figure of infamy. Of ribaldry—it's cruel, sir."

"No," he says a moment later, as if I had asked him. "You see there was an inquiry, and certain arrangements were made. The judgement, you understand, was sealed, out of respect for the family—not that there's anyone but her left, now her daughter's gone away. After that ... it's all nothing but vulgar speculation.

"... She's free. She could leave the city, if she pleased. But she won't abandon her graves. There's no question of punishment, at least ... not exactly, as she was, it was felt, *ill* at the time."

"No one thought to ... if she's ill ..." I say without really knowing what I mean.

He looks at me gravely.

"I mean that, if she's so ill, as you say ..." Now he is looking forbidding, face thrust forward in the shadows, and I falter, "—well, how is it she's free to—you're her keeper," I realize.

"I'm her keeper," he says, and his face goes up and down once, lips moued out.

"Her daughter disappeared, you know, and she couldn't help but think it was as a consequence of the rumors, although the girl absolutely refused to countenance them."

He leans forward again and looks me in the eye. His voice has become insinuating and confidential, a strange contrast with the man.

"So, you see, she's a *very lonely woman*. It's been *years* since anyone came to the house."

The fur slides down the seat, volubly sighing out its scent, and that delectable smell just landslides over me. I see again her cheek outlined in a green flash through the veil, and his voice is an echo the wind carries to me from below the horizon as I stand in the cemetery lane below her, in the past.

"She saw you in the cemetery, and she has seen you in the street. She asked me about you. She asked me very particularly. She instructed me that, if I were to see you again, I should invite you, in her name, to call at the house."

I am on the street beneath windy sky, and Orvar is speaking to me from the roof of the carriage.

"She receives in the late afternoon, past three."

There is a crisp card in my hand, pale lavender with metallic print, an address in the death district not far from here.

"Come soon, won't you?" he says almost merrily.

I hold the card up to my face and that scent unfolds its petals for me again. A rattle of hooves, and then no sound but the rustle of wind against the eaves. A tin can clambers down the street behind me.

*

What at a distance I took for rags of hanging moss prove instead to be enormous veils festooning every bough of every tree on the grounds. I have wasted my time wondering how I will get inside the high stone walls, if there will be a bell or if I will have to stand in the street and shout like a fool, because Orvar emerges from the small door in the elephantine wooden gates pimpled over with bronze busses as I approach. He is thumbing his keys in his palm. As I approach, he looks up without surprise and stands away from the door.

"Go on through. The Girl will show you in."

He seems brisk and cheerful as he pulls loose from the house.

"Good of you to come," he says even jauntily now, and waving. "So long."

I have to raise my feet high to get through the door, and the greasy black lock snaps noisily as I draw it to behind me. There is no gap in the wall here, I see as we go through, rather the walls fold inward to form a causeway leading to the front of the house, where they fold again to form a high, narrow gravel court. The fluttering trees appear to be imprisoned, like zoo animals, behind these unbroken walls. The branches are robust and beneath the floating veils the soil sports a rich pelt of luxurious black grass soft as sable. The house presents a flat and undemonstrative front of windows shuttered in discolored ivory and a bronze door and footplate level with the ground. Above this, a bronze canopy, its outer ring studded with round baubles, and topped with two life-sized bronze foxes, mirrored, creeping along the edges of the canopy with the far forepaw raised and matching sidelong looks. A human expressiveness has been inharmoniously grafted onto their faces, and the resulting look mingles derision, rapacity, idiocy and yawning in equal parts.

In the gloom under the canopy I am injected with nervous excitement. How do you knock on a bronze slab like this? Now I see the metal rod to one side; I have to hold it in the fingers of my left hand, while my right turns a crank at the end. I'm not sure I hear any responding action from inside; I wait.

A few wisecracking birds, a slurred gush of wind over the ground.

The door opens silently, all the way back, and the Girl, smiling shyly at me and a little shielded by the door, waves me in with an easy sweep of her left hand. The Girl closes the door as I come in to the dim house. Everything is shining and dark, polished wood and metal. The entryway is round and not very wide, with a flight of many low steps rising three or four feet to the level of the hall. The house is perfectly still, as if it and everything in it were one completely solid block. The Girl's skirts rustle, and the trailing white ribbons of her apron, which stream from both the small of her back and the top of her spine, leave trails of fragrance behind them.

The door closed, she steps in front of me and repeats her

gesture, still smiling shyly, and I follow her up the steps. She is indiscriminatably young, with dark hair. Her dress seems unusually sumptuous to me, and I note the large, dark stones dangling from her ears. While cinched very tightly into this dress, and most likely into a corset, her waist moves with athletic elasticity. She flows ahead of me, guiding me to the staircase. The hall is neither deep nor wide, but it is evidently tall—just above the staircase all is pitch dark. The ceiling could be hundreds of feet overhead.

The Girl leads me across the second floor landing and into the wings. Though the house is large, I get the feeling it has no spacious rooms; it's all narrow halls, closets and chambers. Everything gleams beautifully, not a speck of dust, not a trace of the earwax smell of old mildewed houses, rather an odor like generations of incense smoke molded into wood and brass. The Girl turns and stops me with an outstretched palm and a smile, knocks softly on a door, her shoulder nearly against it and her head leaning in. If there is a reply, I don't hear it, but the Girl opens the door and gestures me through it.

I step into a small room filled with pale, even light. The ceiling is less than a foot from my head, the walls papered above the wainscotting with faintly violet fronds on an ash background ... potted ferns, a screen, a virginal ... The windows are all on the left, a continuous bank of glass like the wall of a greenhouse. As I turn that way, I see that *she* sits there at a round table by the windows, a book open in front of her. She only that moment lifts and her eyes.

The dress is the same, or nearly.

I am wafting forward into the room, confusedly aware that the door has been closed quietly behind me, and that

I am in the hold of a undertow of light from the windows, which streams past her face toward me.

*

"Have you ever seen a ghost?"

The words come out from under her parasol, which she holds low enough to conceal her face from view. Not from my view, however. We are crossing an enclosed area, a walled space around a monument tower which is now open to curiosity seekers. Coming here was her idea.

"No," I say.

"How do you know you've never seen one?"

"I suppose I'd know that!"

"Why do you suppose? I think they are there to be seen all the time. I roll through the streets here, and the people flash by my carriage. How can I know that every one I see is solid flesh and blood?"

"Wouldn't there be something otherworldly about them? I thought ghosts were always obviously ghosts."

"Sometimes I lie awake and hear noises in the house, and despite myself I'm frightened. Then I hear some familiar sound—a clock strikes, or a train whistles somewhere—and my fear abates. But why should those sounds comfort me, and others frighten me? Why couldn't a ghost make the sound of a train?"

The wind rises along her length where she parts its current, and there stream from her head two or three calligraphic locks. Her hair is a deep black with grey spun in almost imperceptibly.

She squeezes the money into my palm, and I pay our

way into the tower. We ascend slowly, past suits of armor and tapestries woven specially to exploit the curvature of the tower wall. There is only one floor, a bare round room at the summit with a stone bench to the right of the entrance. An archway leads out onto a windswept promenade where we take in the view together.

I feel her distraction.

I place my palm lightly on the center of her back, expecting her to step forward toward the battlement, and moving forward a little myself. She doesn't move forward, but allows me to come up near to her, my hand sliding a little forward toward her right shoulder. I am within her warmth now, and the climate of her breath, her hair, and she seems to bend slightly into me, so now she is leaning with her shoulder and part of her bosom on my chest. I feel her hand gently alight on one of my shoulder blades. I drop my gaze to her face, but meet only the sight of her lowered eyelids; her features taper away from me, her lips are parted. She is strangely well-preserved, her face is unlined. A ghost lifts my left hand from my side, and I watch it settle uncertainly at her waist. She turns a little more in my direction, still not looking at me. Sparkling fingers touch my left hand, and she guides it smoothly up her body; I feel the sweep of her ribs flow beneath my palm, and flex out with her breathing. She tosses back her head, I am looking down into her shadowed mouth, and the lips I kiss are plated with cold over warm. The tip of her nose is cold, and draws a line like a stylus on my cheek.

Now she looks into my eyes. Hers are nearly black, with a deep light in them.

"Let's get inside, you might be seen with me."

Hand in hand we go back into the tower. I walk right over to the stone seat, pulling her. I sit, and draw her to me. She seems to feel this daring but drapes herself sidesaddle on my lap and twines her arms around my neck; her eyes are warm, luminous black. A fleeting look that tugs one sharp corner of her mouth up in a smile expresses pleasure and surprise at me. A few moments later there is a step on the stair below and instantly she bounds away from me. Straightening herself, she steps out again into the air.

"Closing soon, ma'am."

Then, as I yank casually at my shoelaces (which are tied), "Closing."

What do I feel inside me? A succession of warmly glowing haloes rise in layers in my heart and burst like bubbles without vanishing.

*

"Come on loverboy," Jil Punkinflake swings a shovel up onto his shoulder. "Tonight we're for some good old-fashioned grave robbing."

An anticipatory gurgle of laughter draws a ring around me.

The embalming students make their pocket money by distilling a tincture from the spiracles of young female cadavers and use it to make grigrio, a depilatory agent favored by courtesans and discreet wives.

They drop the latest batch of grigrio off in the market and we slide in line through the alleys, passing again along the row of alphabet stores. It's deepest night, and I see clandestine runners slip in and out of the backs of the stores like daring lovers keeping forbidden trysts, all dressed in tight velvet liveries, capes and masks. We run beyond the city limits and into a no man's land of crumbling walls and listing wrought iron, riven graves and heaps of unburied remains, animal and man bones and meat tangled all in red and black, striped with fat, lined with sinew and fine skeins of grease, tingling with flies. Here slumps in the mud a collapsed set of shelves spilling bottled animal specimens onto the ground, and from shells of broken glass have emerged frail, custard-fleshed creatures quivering like mute newborns.

Still in a madcap row we make our way faster and faster, hurdling over huge fallen trees and burping sloughs, cut through a derelict crematorium whose brick stacks tower into the sky. The moon rolls between them. Bodies here were burned to papery ash flakes and bone shards, and some of the ovens stand open, gagged with the stuff, spilling down the fronts and onto the ground in a petrified vomit. On the other side of the crematorium we bound over a low wall, and now we are making our way much more slowly and with greater care across a cemetery where the ground is upholstered with moss, and big standing stones interrupt the regular disposition of the graves. I think Lilly takes my hand in the dark. The fingers that hold mine are cool and wet and cling, like slugs. The stimulant wind that blows down the sluice of the Idle, past the tombs, wants to spatter us with cold, jingling silver spray, and make weightless ghosts out of us.

Nectar drops to one knee periodically and thrusts a bronze probe into the ground. Eventually the little propeller at the top spins and he nods showing his teeth. Shovels and picks chough into the ground. I have one myself and am digging. Thunk of wood sends a shock up my arm, and we withdraw to let Jil Punkinflake do his work; he snaps the nails up and out with his fingers as though they were so many pinecone spines and then lunges from the grave with the lid in his hands. A feeble stink, the meagre welcome this old grave is able to afford, clambers out to us. Nectar and the others are pointing—one side of the empty coffin is bored out in a circular hole leading sideways into the earth, and I can just make out a pallid trunk glistening there in the foggy shadow.

More digging reveals many other graves are in the same condition, their tenants having burrowed or perhaps digested their way through the ground, drawn to each other by an overpowering desire out of mind. Where they conflow, we uncover—with an eruption of stench that scatters us retching and snickering—a massive starfish hump, leprous and trickling with spermy ooze. The thick surface shivers at intervals, and, when exposed to the air, a dancing plume of cold white ethereal fire jets from the low cone at the center, or just above it. The bodies have melted together here, sighing and cooing ... That pungent smell is less and less like decay, and more and more like the must of a living thing, like a stable or a pig wallow.

The odor claws at me, and somehow I am pulling at Lilly, or was it Dusty?, and remembering. We all are falling into remembering ... I see darting windows and halls, these endless halls of mine, dark except for the blazing windows ... parallel lines of the floorboards to the walled horizon, and the mortal webs of the spiders matted with dust ... A huge crescent-shaped building seen from a window, ruins all around. A resonation in the air—I'm in a terrible place I never should have come ...

Someone jostles me and I watch Jil Punkinflake, hanging from a metal pole protruding from the ground and bent over the excavation, a thick canvas glove up to the elbow on his right hand, collecting that ether fire in bottles relayed to him by Keen. Jil Punkinflake avoids touching the thing as he works; when the last bottle is filled, he inches back along the pole and we all help pull him onto sound land.

"Let's get it covered again," he says.

Dirt flies, and in no time it is reburied. Nectar is carefully setting the bottles in his grigrio box. Jil Punkinflake plucks up a smaller one, blue and square, and swaggers over to me smiling. He puts it in my hand. Though the icy glass seems empty, I can feel an abrasive swirling through the glass, and without thinking I tamp down on the cork firmly with my thumb.

"Give it to your lady friend," Jil Punkinflake says, the moon white in his pupils.

*

The Girl beams at me as she opens the door. I am led into the house, and she turns to look at me several times. Once, on the staircase, she stops outright, and turns to smile at me.

She stands and smiles at me, for a long time.

Then she turns and we continue to the landing, her opulent hips swaying with a rustle of silk to the right, and to the left, before my eyes. She does not accompany me to the door, but waves me on, her smile unchanged. I go down the hall, to the door I passed through before. When I turn to look back, to ask the Girl with my eyes if this is the right thing I'm doing, she is not looking at me. The Girl shivers, her hand comes up to her breast, where her other hand seizes and folds it around its thumb. She lifts her face slowly, still holding one hand in another hand, and gazes into the air in front of her.

I open the door, and enter the small room, the tepid air close with her fragrance. Light from a grey day sifts from the windows, and she sits soft and remote as a figure in a painting.

We are going downstairs this time, to sit together in the rare gloom beneath the veiled trees. She has gone for her hat. I wait at the window, looking down at the dark grass, the stingy flowered border, the strict line of the upright house. There is a protruding what-do-you-call-it, a cupola? Some sort of fistula. A light is there now, where there hadn't been before. It is moving around the room, now bright, now faint. That's the Girl there, at the window, moving about the room in that light, which is now still. She is voluptuously in her slip, and now she sees me. I am smiled at again, across these windows. I can see even the strip of pink ribbon that cinches the slip around her narrow waist. Looking straight at me, she looses the slip and lets it fall about her feet, and I fly through stair and hallways and doorways, ways and spaces, lights and darks unmoor and spin smoothly and rapidly around me until through what I seem to know is the right door I am flung headlong into darkness, into bare, enfolding arms.

Later, I join the veiled woman who waits for me beneath the veiled branches, in a small paved spot by an airy pavilion. The thick crepe folded down from her great hat is impermeable to my sight, and the waxy light lances in between us, making her even harder to see. There is little said, and less meant maybe, before it is suggested to me that I might go. But, I am also tersely instructed to come again tomorrow. She sounds different. I agree to go, but for the moment I am a little faint, and wait a little to collect myself. I rub my brow, and my face is tickled by three long grey hairs, tangled round the fingers of the hand that rubs my brow, fluttering in the wind.

I peer at her, who sits there under the trees, and then up at the cupola window. In a spell, I wander out through the house. Of all the doors I see, I pass only one that stands open. The room beyond is black, but fragrance, and the sound of breathing, comes from it. I pause to look. Teeth glint in the dark. I go on toward the front door. Bare feet pat the floor behind me. I feel two firm hands on my shoulders.

On my way back to the college, the swift-coming rain catches me, and I have to hurry along the sloughing path with my lapels turned up. The trees here are bare, it takes me a while to find one with enough leaves to offer me any shelter. I stand there shaking the rain from my hair. Already the trunks around me are soaked, glistening and brown like hard turds planted upright in the ground. I put my hand in my pocket and with a shock I feel it close on the whirring bottle. I forgot to give it to her.

*

I am drinking with Jil Punkinflake when the word comes, just within the one vast hour. Separating the glass from my lip to which it had lightly adhered makes it ring, and I pick up the envelope from the rough boards of the table.

From a nest of shredded newspaper comes a small card with Makemin's name embossed in what I know at once to be real gold near the top: my orders. We move out tomorrow. I look up at Jil Punkinflake, and in my mind I see her, walking high above me against the horizon, her arms at her sides, her veiled head lowered, rolling a little wearily with each step and her long skirts undulating lazily against red and orange sky, like waves on the sea. Orders brought me to these people that I learned to love the moment I saw them, now orders from the same source will take me from them.

We take his lantern and make our way through the wreckage to the river. I make a magic knot from cadaver hair, make a hole in the soil with my finger, put the knot in, cover it, sprinkle it with water from a rain barrel there. I bend down and speak into the ground, saying whatever comes into my head. A transparent shoot shaped like a budding oak leaf slips from the ground and brushes my lip like a mineral noodle, before it bends at a sharp angle and points in a particular direction. I take a bearing from it.

We follow the line to a building with steps going down to the river. An adjacent tree is growing down through the roof and the long naked branches white as bones bore into the shelves. The pungent odor of decaying paper blends with the usual musty neglect smell, and I hear mice flit along the walls. With Jil Punkinflake's scalpel I cut along a thickly embossed leather membrane covered with golden curlicues and letters stretched all out of shape, which has grown over the shelves here. Most of the shelves are wrapped up like sleeping bats in folds of thick binding leather. I make a number of lateral cuts, and immediately the pages begin to dribble out onto the floor.

"Catch them! Don't let them touch the ground!"

Jil Punkinflake darts back and forth snatching pages out of the air, starting to laugh a little, and I am, with mounting silliness, slashing at this groaning leather membrane. The leaves sail out, and Jil Punkinflake's deft hands catch them.

"All right now," I say, "Give me those pages."

I carry them outside and hold them out, let the wind rattle them in my hand. Then I shove them into my satchel.

"This will take a little time."

I write up the now single screed on a roll of fine creamy paper, with a pen that audibly cuts the ink into the fibres, and bind that paper up with black crepe. That shows a bit of flair. I give this to Jil Punkinflake by the starlight of early that morning, and he takes it in his outstretched hand, then inbrings his hand holding the roll, gazing down at it as though it were an infant.

The mist lifts and lowers; it does this languid dance dreamily over the dank earth and lifts long shoots, limp and elastic, above its level, and I watch a slender probe trailing off and losing itself in the air in front of me. The body of the mist forgets and expends this pinch of its stuff without noticing it; before it vanishes, it acquires a sort of demeanor, like something not far short of a tranquil personality.

The kinked wand of mist is turning invisible and is reflected in the steelly bus of a tiny concave mirror in a bronze frame, and what I had taken for small green leaves nearly swallowed up in black I now see is a dark and green patterned sheet of wallpaper ... on the wall ... on which hangs the mirror ... in front of which I stand ... but in which I don't appear.

I see through it, that this is the landing of the staircase of her house, and here I have stood for who knows how long, where nothing has come nor gone, nothing has happened, and no light has been. There is a little light of the kind that makes mist glow, and now I see a panel of moonlight at my feet. Am I narrating now? It creeps snailishly along the bare boards and the wafer of wan rug, leaving behind it an oyster track of nacreous sperm. All a dream, that's certain. I find I can see the motion of this patch of moonlight; the leading edge is cloudy but firm, but for some reason my vision imparts a trickling to it. It shines now on the hem of a skirt, so that the color of the skirt and the color of the moonlight can't be differentiated.

I look to my left, and see a face in the dim, inches away. I see the scattered light of her face and her hands, interrupted by leopard spots of dark as though she were spattered with paint, or piebald with sores. Perhaps her fragrant, rich dress is only paint? Is she only painted on the door? There's a spot of paint on her right cheek, or isn't there? One of those ghostly hands rises and presses itself to my chest, sliding luxuriously inside my jacket and up past my heart.

Hollowly she says, "I want to love you" and it seems to be a variety of similar phrasings all said at once.

Her living skirts rise up closing around me and her hand, glued on my chest, pulls me forward. She draws me into her shade as weightless as a spirit, and I watch from some distance as we drift backwards together and dwindle out of sight like a starved candle ebbing out.

*

I go to her door that morning, but it is dusty, and no one

comes when I knock. There is no motion, nothing but the sopping hiss of the trees. So I take the bottle, which I have adorned with a silly pink satin bow I found in the street, and leave it, with a card, in the lee of the stone doorway.

Hands in pockets I trudge through the streets and there at my back I have the weight of my uniform, my medic's pack, waiting to take me over and make a soldier out of me. What will I do with my school uniform? Perhaps I ought to bury it with a brief service. I don't want to change.

The gates of the college are barred, the windows are broken and empty. The district is empty. I turn and see only the distempered movements of trash, leaves. Not even a rat stirs in the gutters, nothing.

I sit by the wayside and watch the high, emaciated clouds drift. The days are shorter and shorter, and the sky is already becoming funereally ornate with another sunset. No lights come out, anywhere. The city and the landscape sing to themselves, and from the cave of the saint far above something reflective turns and flashes occasionally. If I wait long enough, I will calmly disappear too. Death is what I feel.

Has the camp disappeared? Somehow it's more difficult to find my way there in the empty streets. Numbed branches tap with vacant insistence on the glass of a caved-in store. Hooves beat sharply behind me coming fast and I am seized up bodily by the shoulders—she lifts me with her fingertips as though I were a paper doll and flips me into the carriage, into her arms. She kisses me through the veil, her ardent mouth now soft now hard through the crepe. Her fingers sharp as daggers rake me up and down; I will sigh with bliss when they cut me open and plunge deep into me, greedily seizing and fondling my organs, won't I?

—Now she crumples against the cushions. I see the soft open outline of her lips, where the veil clings to them. They speak.

"Don't go _____ ..." she says quietly, calling me by her husband's name. "Let me hide you."

I look at her, whose first name I don't even know, and I love her. I want to worship her. But when she speaks with her lips glued to her veil, calling me by the name of the husband whose body she devoured, I shrink. I think of soldiers on the road, and I think of hiding in her house, watching helplessly from the windows as the Edeks pass again and again in the street, closing in, loitering longer and more intently each time they return.

"I was seen by an Edek."

"I can hide you ... from them ..." she's falling asleep, cooing and smiling.

A light flickers by me and I seem to see the Girl climbing hastily into the carriage, but it may be I am confused again.

Orvar coughs up on the box. Are we alone again? Have we been? She sits bolt upright and she turns this way and that from the waist, her hands in the air.

"There's a festival tonight! We should stay out of the streets."

She lunges forward to rap on the hatch, but I take her in my arms. I feel the delectable firmness of her flesh under my grip, and her fragrance, and it's as though I'd only just learned to love her.

"What are you worried about? They won't hurt you— and I want to see if I can find Jil Punkinflake."

"No—they want *me*." Her eyes are alarmed, I can see them grow wide. "They want to put me up in a sedan chair and parade me up and down like a pagan idol. They want me to stand there in the midst of them high on a dais, head to foot wearing only my veil and the garlands of flowers they grow for me."

She thrusts her head hard against my chest and drives her fists against me, shuddering and almost sobbing.

"They want me to *bless them*," she says bitterly. "You have no idea how they talk about me, what it's like to be talked about and written about and to be the object of speculation."

I catch sight of Jil Punkinflake slipping into an alley, accompanied by Nectar. I cry out to them, and lunge without thinking from the carriage. Her hands brush my back as she tries to draw me in, but now another group of mortuary students cries, "The Cannibal Queen! The Cannibal!" and immediately converges on the carriage. With a whipsnap Orvar drives the carriage away—and now I am trying to get back to it, waving frenziedly to her, but I am only one of many doing that now.

I watch in horror as a brazen hand snatches the veil from her face—she covers her face with her hands, crying out in anguish, and recoils into the carriage. She escapes as one of the mortuary students, a woman, brandishes the veil overhead howling in triumph. Furious, I shove my way through the crowd to her, as many others are trying to get hold of the veil or tear a piece of it off for themselves. The student is as yet keeping it from them, laughing and bounding up onto any elevating thing, the base of a lamp post, a stone block, a post box. I get around behind her while she crows from atop the post box and give her a shove. She reels into the air and throws out her arms to break her fall loses her grip on the veil and before it can strike the earth I have it, and I run like a madman up the street as they pursue me.

*

They emerge slowly from cellars, sewer grates, tunnels and culverts, panting and grinning, like dead men drawn from their graves by the pull of a magic song. I can hear a sound coming up all around me, like chuckling, muffled and reverberating in burrows and caves. Catching sight of each other they begin to draw together at crossroads, walking with swift little steps, like a trot-walk, with their heads down, smiling bizarrely to themselves, passing and repassing each other in back-and-forth walking, and when they pass they touch each other lightly on the chest or shoulder, or on the back. That muttering chuckle rolls around them like smoke; I feel my throat tighten as if these chuckles were being forced down into it.

I can see some of them tremble. They fidget as they walk back and forth, they are becoming weightless, they are overflowing with energy. Now at no signal their walking becomes dancing, they link arms and spin in a crouch counterbalanced, they break ranks and radiate outward clapping their hands and stomping in unison. Two white shapeless flapping things batter against the chest of the one nearest to me, like moths ramming a lamp. I can feel the bow wave of their force roll me back from the inside and then I see those two white things are severed human hands hanging from a lanyard around his neck. Many of them are so adorned, with hands, feet, and dried hearts.

91

They all crack a riotous human whip in the streets. They brandish riding crops and woolly flails of human hair, thongs of pale curious leather—they charge through the streets shrieking like banshees lashing out at each other and everyone they see with their crops thongs and flails. The lifers recoil and dodge away laughing as they are struck. I see a streaked stark-eyed face whiz by flapping its arms, a soft blow flutters down my face and breast and power crackles down my body, I catch my breath and my legs and arms shiver with a mindless desire to leap and flail.

I'm in a group of lifers following the students now, panting and shivering. The students are clashing in the crossroads; some have picked up heavy steel garbage cans and bang them one-handed on the ground in a swift driving rhythm while others whirl with locked arms and stamp their feet. Rushing together in pairs, they take each other by the waist, and butt heads with a sound like wood mallets striking wood. They bash their skulls against each other, and their top hats seem riveted in place never budging, seize each other and hurl each other up ten feet in the air— now they have pulled searing-white knives from their coats and slash each other across the face, knife arms swinging regularly backhand and forehand. I can hear the thud of the knives as they hit, but there is no blood, their faces are unmarred, even when the knives hack at their eyes.

They stop and dance, then run again through the streets, belaboring crowds that shout with glee and alarm, wildly trampling the flowers that are strewn down for them from the windows. Now they have come to a dilapidated square on the river, the faces of the buildings here are tall and blank, with blasted windows and rent masonry. Beside a listing stone fountain a few students are waiting for the others, with a rough wooden wagon piled high with human heads. The sight stops me in my tracks and that moment I am set to one side by a pair of decisive hands under my armpits. Some invisible companion, perhaps every follower of the students has one, has put me out of the stream, but that current of blazing excitement is crazing me again and I fling myself back in, rush along with the others and take my place among them by the maimed, outflung arm of a collapsed bridge.

The boulevards belch students into the square. They form a jostling rampart around the fountain and heads are distributed rapidly from the cart. Two men stand atop the pile and fling heads down to upraised arms. A bad smell trickles in my nose and screws itself in behind my face—then it softens, dissolves in other odors like a buttery perfume, and cold autumn wood smoke. Some heads are mounted on wooden poles draped with black shrouds and strapped to the student's backs. The other two corners are attached to rods with human hands at the ends, making the dancers into crude carnival giants with real human heads and hands flapping as they gambol around the square. Even through the shouts and howls, the pounding of impossibly coordinated stamping feet, the clapping hands and ecstatic shouts, I can hear that chuckle scattered everywhere, and perhaps even from the heads.

I am watching them take up heads and at first I think they kiss them—but they sink their teeth into the dead lips, and a helper ties a black band around the crowns of both dead and living heads so that they are clamped eye-to-eye together, noses side by side. The students dance with heads bound to their faces—I see one with a woman's head shaking his whole torso so that her long black hair is a cloud around his shoulders. They brandish their rods and flails, one in each hand, and begin striking these together in frightening precise patterns like a vast duel with interchanging partners. These dancers form a ring within the ranks of the shroud dancers, and another group comes forward—they take a head in each hand, by the hair, by the nose, by the lips or ears, by the shreds of skin hanging from the neck. Two rush forward with a slopping, heavy basin, and I smell something like creosote. The heads are dipped in a two-part fluid unmixed clear and brackish like oil and water, and touched to the green flames of long corpse candles in the hands of giggling little boys and girls. Then the dancers spin around the fountain tracing green and blue comet streaks with faces that are only shadow blots in gobs of fire, whirl until they are only underlit smudges in hoops of fire. I can hear the hollow rustle of the flames as they whip grunting through the air. The dancers spin faster and faster and some of them smash their heads against the stone of the fountain or on the ground, and the crowd seems to want to be spattered with the sparks and dead matter that splash out from among the students. The lifers, with nervous smiles, edge closer and then scamper back into the crowd like someone playing tag with the surf. They seem to want to feel the sparks hit them.

The dancers slam the ground, they pound the stones with their feet and flail heads and hands, fire and cries in the air—cobblestones and severed heads fly crashing into the windows and crazed celebrants fling themselves on the buildings, the street, the fountain, ripping the stone with bare hands, snapping off teeth biting the stones, everywhere a sound of flesh beating stone. Now they take their burning heads and running off down all the boulevards of the city, where all other lights, I see, have been extinguished. The only light until dawn will be the streaking fire of burning heads in runners' hands, racing up and down the streets of the life precinct at random. Even when dawn begins to well up in the sky, I will catch sight of a few last funereal rioters, bounding along the streets with long, graceful ten-foot strides, bundles of orange fire spilling from their upraised hands.

You first drew breath as you were then in a den of ruined shelves, where the bindings had grown to drown the structures of the shelves like skin grown over a skeleton, the skeleton being the shelves, the wood, and as well over the flesh, of wood pulp, that is the paper pages. You were, prior to that first breath, slashed and rifled, as gravity had been permitted by some agency to draw your pages to earth. You were always remote from earth but all the same still as connected to it as breath, for example, is to earth.

That was you then, that emerged the night of the death's heads ritual games. Those cuts in the skin widened themselves somehow, with a steady crackling like a fire smouldering, the fibers popping apart one by one, and then you sluiced out with a motion that would require many pages to describe; you were quiring up papers as they tumbled down, all to your white body runnelled with creases. A ragged, ribbony body dripping with thick water, you abided there under the hood of ruptured leather like a saint in a wall sconce. Your angular head was slipcovered with thin and drooping white locks, and you were all over just as white and wrinkled as the head of a molar, except for the black ribbons beneath your fingernails.

Your eyes were running pits of ink, black and sparkling, and glue trickled from your nostrils and filled the pleats to either side of your lipless mouth, fringed with hairline wrinkles. You drew breath at once, not to breathe, but to began to speak, and since speaking and vomiting always go together with you, so that to speak for you is also to vomit if to vomit is not always to speak, as you always vomit whenever you speak, the fragrant black ink ran in curds down your chin and spattered down your front, where your body folds like lapels and like clothes. You spoke clotted words in a ripely decayed tone, like a voice out of a hive. Your lips flinging out a froth of black spray, your lips writhed around long white needles in black gums between which your succulent vomit slid and behind which your tongue, like a larva, slopped and coiled.

What did you say? The letters dripped onto your white paper body from your drawn back bowed black mouth.

You were talking hands, and so you had two good long hands; you talked legs and there they were, not so good. You talked feet and they came out worse still. Then your hands waved feebly at you from the floor, and you talked arms and shoulders to connect them to your lean serpent's trunk, since that seemed appropriate. There they were. Hands were content.

As the last of your particular pages accumulated into you, you were free to separate yourself from the motherly wreckage that gave birth to you, but you didn't do it just then. You perched and sat there on the floor beneath the ruptured hood of leather, and spoke words that meant themselves for the brotherly thief that had made those cuts and taken those pages.

You waited, and whatever you called to didn't respond, didn't come. Outside the moon shone down white on a whole world, white over black, and in the streets there was a dance of burning heads. It was in the midst of this chaos that you dragged yourself finally from the shelves, tearing loose, and you had to crouch and scuttle on your bad legs, bent double and brailling along with your fingers on the ground. Eyes of ink you turned this way and that weirdly to see your way through the door, and you lifted them to catch the moon's reflection in them and in the black rheum that dangled from them. You are drawn, the moon told you, to the letters Low, Loom, Column, the black sky explained to you in a whisper, who will leave Dusktemper tomorrow. Don't be surprised—you knew all the names that were ever said from the start, and even said them all already. That time, you were born after there were names, you saw. See. Lapsed again there. Go on, you went on, drawn to him. So you, the narrative, gradually draw nearer. Coming for us.

Second Chapter

We are mustering to go, what's left of the unit scrabbles to and fro gathering its materials and raising the swarming dust.

"Oh shut up, shut *up*. Quit *talking* like that—you're always *talking* like that." With whinging irritation in his voice, Nectar shoves me in the shoulder, and waspishly takes his leave.

I am watching the operation. Makemin stands in the middle of all the activity, pivoting in place, calling out orders, and pointing, knuckles of his left hand rest on the back of his hip. From time to time his assistant, a small, unflappable, owl-faced blue man named Nikhinoch, will walk up to him, moving with dispatch but never with haste, receive some order or other, and walk away in the same manner to relay his master's words or carry out some not unimportant task. The men are shouting and murmuring; I hear bellicose talk without getting more than a vague sense of its meaning, and my spirit sickens. Up to now I'd been grateful Tref is not what could be called a boisterous city; the lifers are too clean and the embalming students, for all their wildness, are too ghastly. I'd always looked on bellowing, back-thumping men and their drinking ways and braying heartiness with a combination of fear and disdain. In the mountains, you don't raise your voice idly. You don't want to whoop it up.

It's time for me to change. I pull up the flap and enclose myself in the narrow tent. My uniform exhibits a strong disinclination to abandon its square packeted shape. All a nameless straw color, like pale mud puddle. After a moment's reflection, I divest myself of my school clothes and begin putting on my uniform; I'm going through with it. The shirt is surprisingly comfortable. Pulling the collar to around my neck I find I haven't the slightest inclination to scratch there. Good. Bit loose, better than a bit tight. The stockings are thick. I suppose that's good, although they are a little too warm. The corduroy trousers are ungainly in my hands, flapping and dangling around like a dead albatross. Good inch of extra room between my waist and the band—I'll need that belt. Buttons tightly to the leg from the knee to the ankle. Silly looking. Next there's this vest I don't know why I have, double breasted with peg-and-loop buttons. Over that, the jacket, with thick cookie-like buttons and pockets everywhere, and a belt built in. The boots are a disgrace. They're flimsy and crumbling, with hardly any soles to speak of. I flip them into the corner.

The shoes I came with are excellent, and despite my failure even to shine them once and a while, they gleam like new, without so much as a scuff. I'll keep them and hope nobody notices.

I swap everything into my new pockets. It's tricky trying to get the shoulder ribbons and armbands to look convincing. Finally the unfortunate hat. I carefully pack away my former clothes, put the parcel under my arm, step out through the flap. Feeling strange and self-conscious I cross the camp looking for Silichieh. Passing the darkened window of one of the warehouses I glimpse myself and the sight jars me—my uniform is so complete that I am vanishing into it. If I'm going to appear at all, then I'll have to insert something discordant. I take off my hat and at once the figure in the glass, performing the same action, becomes me again.

"You want replacement? Talk to Tabliq Quibli." Silichieh points to the man in the floppy turban.

Turban looks at my hat, pushing his cheek out with his tongue.

"Something more, just a little maybe."

I run back to the tent and return with my appalling boots. He takes them.

"Yeah," he says, and staggers off with them. After a long time he comes back with a different one. It looks better, and doesn't at all match my uniform. I put it on. It fits. Good. Swap is done.

Silichieh grabs the back of his seat behind him and gets up; with a bearlike wave he invites me to follow. He speaks familiarly in Chiprena to a drawn-faced man with fierce black stubble all over his jaw, and in a moment or two I am handed a sidearm and holster.

I pull out the heavy revolver. It has a fin running under the barrel, and a heavy hinge where the gun breaks open. The barrel is octagonal, and the grip is very curved and polished with long handling. Silichieh explains the gun to me, and gives me a hand-dragging leather case of shells. He watches as I load the gun. The shells go in my pack, although he tells me to keep another seven loose in my left outer lower jacket pocket. Good. I duck out of sight take off my belt holding my pants up by bowing my legs and string the holster onto it.

Silichieh shows me how to loop the barrel end to my thigh. I walk, and the holster does not impede my movement or slap against my leg. Good.

An Edek, maybe the Edek, is crossing the camp now behind her helper. Again I am clamped a moment by that gaze, and then the Edek moves on. A bolt of rage flashes through me—that Edek is here *checking up on me*. She stops at the edge of the camp, by a ruined arch delicate against the sky, bends her bound head to the ear of her helper, who in turn speaks morosely to Nikhinoch, who proceeds at once to speak to Makemin.

A few moments later we are ordered to fall in for inspection. Silichieh has transferred his engineer's band and stripes to his sweater. I scan the ranks.

No women.

I say as much to Silichieh.

"It's that divorce. He doesn't want to know women exist."

A few moments later, Makemin is staring me in the eye.

"What's become of your hat?"

"I wasn't issued a hat, sir. The dispatcher—"

"Acchhh," he says, disgusted.

We've both been put upon by the incompetence of the dispatcher.

"*Those* idiots," he goes on. "You did well to provide for yourself."

Under clenched brows, his eyes have dropped from my face and wander, clawing their way through black storm clouds. He moves on to the next man.

Silichieh's sweater doesn't seem to register, but further down the line Makemin is beet red, barking with no small dispensation of froth into the face of a wincing pockmarked man. Evidently his cartridge belt is not regulation.

We break ranks, and as we mill aimlessly around the air is split again by Makemin's voice.

"*You!*"

He is pointing at Jil Punkinflake, and the Edek is at his side. My friend is marched away by a corporal. When Jil Punkinflake turns his eyes to me, there's something fragile in his look, and my heart goes out to him. I've had time to get used to the idea, but it's more than the shock I'm seeing.

Why in the world would he have come here? Here is all the fresh enlivening haste of setting forth.

A tug at my elbow, and Jil Punkinflake smiles ruefully at me. They've left him most of his clothes, but swapped his tail coat for a jacket like mine, and given him a skimpy kepi. He's criss-crossed with straps and a harness, and a light lever action rifle sticks up like a chimney from his back.

"They got me," he says.

Makemin, now wearing his goggles and a stovepipe helmet plated in brass and draped in a white canvas havelock, mounts his horse and gives the order for us to assemble in march formation. Nikhinoch comes scrambling up with the company standard, a triangular pennant on a flimsy bamboo pole—the design is extremely complicated with a great many interlocking figures and much badly-rendered writing. It is presented with outstretched fist to Makemin, who takes it as his horse shifts its feet.

"Drums!"

Nothing.

"Well?"

Tabliq Quibli slouches past saying "The drummer boy is—" and he flips his hand in a gesture that plainly means away, run off. The familiar expression of disgust on Makemin's face screws a notch tighter.

"Piglets, move up!"

We obligingly begin tramping by him in ragged lines. Nikhinoch, still in his smart civilian small clothes, his dark wavy hair parted like mine in the middle and swinging down like cottage's eaves past his ears, clips up on a chubby pony and takes his position beside Makemin. As I come by he suddenly flings the standard at Jil Punkinflake, who catches it startled.

"You carry the standard," Makemin says, the creases hard on his mouth's two sides. "Try not to smudge it."

Jil Punkinflake looks at me miserably. And now we are going.

*

Through the partial arch and out of the city, turning immediately onto a dirt road that runs more or less directly into the foothills. The soil bleaches as we walk, leaving

Tref behind us, the sun is bright but the air is cool and in motion. There's a gradual slope up into the hills. Our feet raise small plumes of colorless dust, air rustles with sage and rosemary, the pungent smells of miserly, resinous desert plants. Some have spring-action seeds that bore themselves into your stockings and trousers, poke and irritate your skin. Not too many horses—only Makemin and Nikhinoch are riding. The lieutenants evidently deserted as well, so their horses are pulling an extra cart. We have three. The entire company, by my estimate, is not more than seventy. This includes the Clappers, who walk in a compact mass toward the rear of the column; they wear jingling apparatus, all manner of bones, wooden and metal things hanging on thongs around their necks, dangling from their brims like bead curtains in front of their faces. When soldiers fight with their bodies the Clappers fight with their spirits by means of complicated interlocking clapping and chants to Eihoi the Wild Horse.

"The mountains received us in stony silence yuk yuk," I say inanely. I'm possessed by an imp who slaps such stupidities out of me all the time.

Nikhinoch informs me—as I am one of the officers, I keep forgetting—that our route will take us through the foothills, skirting the mountains, round to the sea and Port Conget. Silichieh estimates the journey will take us less than a week. There's a brief slow down where the road was washed out by a slide some months ago, forcing us to climb for a bit. Jil Punkinflake stretches out his leg spinning his foot in the air feeling gingerly for a foothold; Silichieh powering up the slope, his body bunching, unbunching, rebunching; and Makemin's indefatigable ascent, one steady planted step after another. We camp that night well into the mountains, in a series of clearings strung along the way, ledging out into the valleys and commanding enormous views. Jil Punkinflake is gazing abroad wondering at the landscape. He's never been in the mountains before. The slopes are bare white rock, dark vegetation spatters them like ink spots, and in the light of the full moon that white stone phosphoresces a wan blue both pale and warm. The path is a bright streak in a luminous field dappled with dimly waving, fragrant shrubs.

The next day, at dawn, I want to be a naked and tender-fleshed young gargoyle, perched up on high, the bottomless wind sliding deliciously over me and I am blank, hurtling from on high coming to rest again in all this rustling quiet. I want to linger over the fantasy, but the story won't let me. The column is moving.

The second day passes much as the first. Did. Luckily the path, high in the mountains, is more or less level.

The third day, we come to a broad place with many roads. The signpost lists nearly to the ground, peeled battered and useless, but there are characters carved into the adjacent rocks.

"Interpreter!"

I come forward.

"Lulom, isn't it?"

"Low."

Makemin points to the stone—"Anything?"

"Is it in Lashlache?" Nikhinoch asks.

"I think not," I say, stepping up.

I examine the inscription.

"It's Wiczu!" I say this in astonishment only because I

hadn't expected to recognize the language at all. "It says Ciawixde is ten miles down that road"—I point the way—"through the hills and over a bridge. Then that way goes to the sea."

Makemin has pulled out his waterproof map and is scanning it intently. Evidently his ordained route is marked there—I can see red lines.

"They'd have us go through Ciawixde," he says in a moment. "But an old bridge is liable to turn up wrecked after so much time. And there are Wacagan in the area."

I hadn't known that. I look around me, trying to see menace in this unchanged scenery.

He goes on peering. Now he dashes the map into his lap.

"I'm sure those imbeciles have the wrong idea. The lay of the land over there," he points with his tightly brown-gloved hand, "is far better. I say we go round to the sea. Check for more."

I look.

"Blank."

"Fine.—Where did you learn your languages?"

"The Narrator's College, sir. In the mountains, near Qulo."

He visibly registers this information.

"You're a narrator?" he raps out sharply.

"Yes, sir." Am I getting myself into trouble or out of it?

"Nikhinoch."

Up comes Nikhinoch on his pony.

"Mm?"

"This one's a narrator. Can you get him a horse, a pony?"

Nikhinoch shakes his head.

Makemin looks back at me.

"You'll walk near to me in the ranks from now on. Right?"

"Can my friends walk with me?"

"Go on, go on, what do I care?" He waves us on and we begin again to march, on the heading he has chosen.

The path descends shallowly for a time, and the land opens out to our left in a high, flat-bottomed valley with pale new green and mild breezes. The men keep striking up loud atonal songs behind me. Now, not only do we have a faster, more even road before us, but we will have the solace of shade, too. The column is moving; we mark the earth with our perishable steps and make the heel song of our foot beats, an exhalation chorus layered on top.

Around sunset we make camp, and Makemin indicates he wants me near. He draws a long satchel from among his paraphenalia and brings out his rifle. He exposes it proudly; a Galvanophre Thunderbolt, a heavy double-barreled over-and-under bolt action rifle with two six round magazines, one per, that slot into a box on the receiver's left side, two bolts which can be snapped together to throw both chambers at once, two barrels for the quick follow-up shot so crucial in sniping, or so he says. Trigger has four settings—only top barrel, only bottom barrel, half and half which means the trigger fires the top barrel on the first half of the pull and the bottom barrel on the second half, and alternating full pull. Makemin draws and chambers two long but not especially heavy rounds from a pouch inside his kidney belt. He lifts the rifle to his shoulder sights and fires instantly, and again. Two plumes of dust spurt from a stone clear across the valley. With a grim smile he lowers the weapon and pulls the bolts one at a time. The action seems extremely stiff, and Makemin impresses me with his strength pulling them back so smartly, expelling two spinning, spent shells. Each flashes once in the sun on its way to the ground.

"I was second in a thousand ranked in sharping," he says mixedly, something souring his pride. "And was one of seventeen commenced directly to adjutant."

"They must be faring well at the front to spare you here,"— ugh. Just because I'm good at it doesn't make buttering him up feel any better. I want his story, for my own sake.

He practically spits.

"They're miserable at the front! They're pitiful! Men who graduated at half my standing are giving orders at the front while I'm pissing away my life on this assignment!"

His gaze takes hold of me and I realize I'm in for the story.

"When I was twenty. I was arrested. For stealing dirt."

He says this levelly.

"My cousin needed fill earth to build a new post office in a town it doesn't matter the name. For years there had been an enormous mound of displaced earth standing in a lot by the river; they had built a footbridge there to connect some islands in the river. When I was a boy we would visit my cousin and together we used to play in it. Only because people constantly were walking through the lot was it clear of vines, and that's the only reason the mound wasn't overgrown. No one touched it—it was like a feature of nature. So when my cousin needed the fill earth I said to him, 'let's go take some.'

"We went at night and started to load the cart. I looked up and saw the footbridge sway, and the handcar rolling towards us in the rust lights, so we tried to hide in the shadow of the bridge—then there were bullseyes shining. A fine and a reprimand—that's all."

He shrugs, sets his lower lip angrily.

"But it went on the record."

Now we are sitting around in the evening, digesting and resting. I can see Makemin through the transparent front of his tent, sitting at his desk with a bale of papers, writing frenetically. From time to time, Nikhinoch will come to attend him. Once I see Makemin take up a small container, slide the lid aside, pull out a pinch of some peach-colored snuff, and sniff it vigorously first in one and then the other nostril. I refer my querying eyebrows to Silichieh, who smiles, his voice muffled by a mouthful of smoke.

"Oh, that stuff. Keeps him alert, I think. I don't know exactly what it is but it fits him. I wouldn't touch it myself."

I sit and listen as the breeze blows through my ears, and the sunset lights go colors down over my scalp.

I pass on the dirt story, and Silichieh snorts a little, lying back against a stump with his hands in the pockets of his sweater.

"That's typical."

After a moment he says, thoughtfully, "But that's good for us, I think, because it means he's not going to stick to nice little points of decorum too much. That's best kind of commander."

A worrying thought—"What if he tries to heroically—heroically to recoup his name?"

"Oh, you mean with a something big? He's tried that too. He has a decoration though he doesn't wear it."

Tell, tell ...

Makemin had belonged to a sharp shooter unit that fought at some place on the far side of the mountains called Galleh. The Alaks there had been talking to the Laughing Gas and went over to the blackbirds—that's Wacagan, the

Enemy, you students—and it was a matter of putting the insurrection down.

Soldiers marching on the road through fields and copses. They run right into the rebels set up in a village. Shock, scrambling, shots. Neither side is prepared to pull back, and no reinforcements are coming to the soldiers; head of the local garrison died of the Influence and had not yet been replaced—without him, no good organization.

The fighting breaks up, drags on in skirmishes and both sides find themselves killing their own in the confusion, and through a tormented night of aching watchfulness and impossibly sudden explosions of violence, dying. A flashing steel wing flickers over you and in the next instant half your unit is gone, breaking twigs and random shots all around you, and in the next second it's just as quiet as before, and you reel bewildered from cover to cover not knowing what you are.

Here's young Makemin pinned down in a burned-out farm house, the last of his unit. No knowing where the rest of the soldiers are, where the line, if any, is, if there has been a retreat or advance, if there are any soldiers but him left. A distant shot startles the rooks and he shrinks. Hoofbeats, he glances through the window. In watery light just before the dawn he sees one of the rebels ride past at an angle heading for broken ground at the horizon. Makemin can see, in the turmoil of the man's wildly flailing cloak and loose clothing, that he wears a sword—that makes him one of the leaders. Not having a clear shot Makemin crazily breaks from cover and begins sprinting after the horse. He raises his rifle and sights it on the veering horseman, holding the gun level as he runs all out, his legs slithering and swivelling beneath him to keep his upper body plumb on the perpendicular.

Shots on his left—one or two guns, a shot cracks against the charred trunk of a tree to his right and behind barely missing but still he runs sighting grinding his teeth in frustration as the figure before him slips in and out of his line and now as the rider sinks below the ridge furrowed into the ground and wheels to the right, the horse tosses back its head a bit and in so doing lifts it above the level of the furrow into Makemin's sight—the gun barks and shears off the top of the horse's head sending ears flying two different directions and a shank of skull whirling onto the top of the ridge. Makemin lowers his gun and keeps running up the ridge vaults over the fallen horse where the fallen rider scrambles for his thrown rifle. Makemin rams the leaded stock of his gun into the man's head and up and down he swings it like a butter churn, moils the butt in his brains and the spatter of ejected blood joins red flecks to the motes of foam clinging to Makemin's lips.

Some time later a small group of soldiers, led by Makemin's commanding officer, will appear, having driven off the shooters in the distance, and having witnessed Makemin's kill. They find him still panting not far from his man, sitting on the dirt bank, distractedly dragging his rifle's grisly butt in a clump of reddened grass.

*

The next day is all soft light and wind; pale green new leaves stand out brilliantly against trunks and branches blackened by night rain. Welcome relief for smarting feet that afternoon when Makemin, who heads the column, stopped short to accost a pair of anxious-looking locals. These are the first people we've encountered, and I worry what we are going to do to them. I am brought forward to translate—the moment Makemin refers them to me, their eyes follow his hand and slip onto my face from his, and at once they begin again their halting speech in Cvaivrenew.

When it peters out, I turn to Makemin.

"Someone stole two of their chickens."

Makemin makes an unusual, wry face.

"Tell them we'll keep our eyes open."

They stand by the road, arms at sides, evidently intent on watching the entire group pass and shouting encouragement as we go by, as though they were dispatching us personally.

As the afternoon dreams on, the road begins to climb slightly and the trees become more dense.

One of the forward pickets comes back stepping high and reports seeing a figure darting in among the trees at our approach. We continue, now everyone is looking this way and that.

There in the bracken I see a white flash in a little handful of scattered sun. Nothing to be heard over all our clanking and thudding. Another flash—the figure veers in mid leap, magically dropping out of sight again.

"Is it a talku?" Someone asks in a low voice.

(Talkus are mountain spirits one is especially liable to encounter when lost, and in confusing winter weather. They often take on the appearance of persons familiar to their victims, by a kind of imagination mirror effect.

"What are *you* doing up here?"

"Oh, just poking around. You know how it is."

"But—you're barefoot?!"

"We don't feel the cold," he says equably.

"Don't feel the—why it must be 40 below!"

"Is that very cold?"

"... Stay away from me ... You stay away!"

"Why is that any way to pa-la-la-la-la-laver *oooooollld fffrrrriieennnddd?*")

Makemin, without stopping the column, turns his head this way and that. He dons his goggles and looks some more.

"He'll have to cross the path up ahead, unless he has already crossed the path."

He wavingly indicates the slope, which is on our right, where this white errancy has been up until now.

"The slope ahead is too sheer on that side."

At his order a few sergeants trot up, and he sends them fanned out ahead. There's commotion in almost no time. One of the sergeants has collared someone.

"Who are you?"

"Spih-ch duwa!"

The sergeant gives him a shake. His defiance collapses.

I am to translate.

"Your name?"

"Megrodowite," he says sullenly (Me-GRAW-do-weet-eh; the r is soft, last syllable very short). He's a young man with dark curly hair, wearing a long white shirt and nothing else. His feet and lower legs are well shaped and mucky, and in his right fist he holds two limp chickens by their snapped necks.

"Where are you from?"

"I live here."

"In the woods? Not with nice soft legs like those."

"I live here I tell you."

Another shake.

"You're a thief, that's one thing."

"So what are you?"

"Don't bother," he holds up his hand to the sergeant who's priming another shake. "I don't care what you take— where are you from? Is there a village here?"

"All right, but I'm not from there."

"Where are you from then?"

"It's empty now anyway."

"The village?"

"Yeah the village. They've all gone and left everything."

"Was there an attack?"

"No, but they thought there would be or something."

"But you're not from there. Where are you from?"

Megrodowite is brooding.

"Let him go."

The sergeant releases him but does not move away. Megrodowite stands there shuffling his feet and swaying a little, making up his mind. Makemin gives him time to do it in. In which to do it. He rubs the back of his neck and adjusts his thready collar.

"'M from the asylum," he says uncertainly.

"What asylum? ... Show me."

Megrodowite just looks at him, his head half ducked as if he expects to be cuffed.

"Is there anyone else there?"

"Yes, many of us," his spirit revives in him. "At first word of the blackbirds, the doctors ran off, all the staff, left the patients on their own, half still locked in their cells and can't get out."

He holds up the chickens.

"We've got to feed them. We can't just leave them to starve!"

"Well then, let's see what we can do about that. Show me the way."

Megrodowite rises at once to the occasion and draws us along the path into an overgrown tree tube, leading into the folded elbows of the mountains. There is a gradual ascent on matted leaves and spongy flakes of cork bark. We make our way along the writhing back of this snaking path, and a shrill, far-away cry stops us all in our tracks. Megrodowite goes on unfazed, and the column begins undulatingly to move again. Now the path is close in a dry rock flume, and we are switching back and forth nervously as we climb. The column has grown silent and hearkening. A moment later, the flume opens out like a funnel of rock and we emerge into opener land again, much less bouldery and glowing with new grass, particolor canopies of leaves.

The asylum nearly spans a woody hollow with steep green slopes rising all around it. A clammy fog clings to the ground here and seeps around the foundations and through the open windows like vast ghostly tongues licking the building. The walls are all deep rich and surly red brick, but, while the walls and windows are weirdly crisp in outline, the pile still seems to be slouching and half-dissolved because its high-peaked roof of thick grey thatch has a roving outline along the top. It's like the shoulders of the building, as though the asylum were a body lying headlong towards us and wrapped in a woolly hide, the face flung forward resting its chin on the ground.

We begin to see inmates in among the foliage, or in the clear space in front of the building, and a few apparently stranded on the slopes, although we've met none in the road but Megrodowite. Now we are in the clear space, and they emerge and come out to us like a band of gentle spirits, all different, all uncanny, quiet, and wary. Some are naked or nearly so, some still wear their formless garments of stained and stiff linen, their bare legs under; and some are dressed all outlandish, in crude follies of their own making.

Here they come out to meet us in our uniforms and helmets and clanking equipment, with our indecipherable banner and our rummaged, half-scavenged gear. Some of the nearer ones instantly respond to our martial appearance with snappy salutes, some serious, some silly. Dull thuds of bare heels thumping together. I pass close to a young man with yellow curls, in white shift and thin cotton breeches, with the fly wide open, sitting on his bottom by the path, legs out before him, soles of feet stained green by the grass, drawing spirals and tic-tac-toes in the dirt with his fingers. He glances up at me and smiles and I smile back.

Hullo, loonies.

Makemin halts the column before the asylum, and, with his finger, jabbingly appoints a detail to venture inside. He will lead personally.

"Intepreter, come with me. Always with me."

Silichieh and I fall in. There are eight of us entering the asylum now.

One of the heavy, double front doors is still shut and locked with bolts at top and bottom, the other is dangling inward on one hinge, with obvious marks of violence all over it. The lock looks as though it had been bitten away by a huge animal, and the wood all round that is savagely scored. Step onto an uneven tile floor, white with black diamonds, dotted with puddles that reflect the meager light. The fog roams here and there like a living thing, coiling under the stairs or slithering down into the basement. The inmates have put tinted paper around some lamps and set them down at random, creating whorls of colored mist.

I hear muffled cries, words and howls intermingled, knocks and bangs, like fists or feet against metal doors. The noise swarms up all around us as though the building groaned and racked itself in troubled sleep. To our left, a long hallway lined with doors, paint and plaster hang in flakes from the walls and clutter everywhere, like room-vomit. The ceiling is low, there is a sort of reception bar here, a blackened painting hung over it, a panel lined with cubbys, now mostly torn out. Behind heavy grilles facing us are two stairways that bend right and left up into black. The building shivers. To the right, double doors with smashed panes.

Megrodowite looks hangdog and points lifelessly to the hall on the right. At once Makemin leads us there, Megrodowite hanging back. The double doors squeal as we thrust them apart, and above and behind us, and far away, a high-pitched voice howls a long descending note.

This hall is abbreviated, a heap of rubble—charred remains of wooden chairs, it looks like—blocks the far door too deep in shadow to see. Megrodowite indicates another pair of doors, these solid. Makemin pushes open one side, takes a step over the threshold and immediately turns back letting the door fall to. In the puff of air the closing door forces out into the hall I smell the mortuary smell of decomposing bodies.

"Nobody knew what to do," Megrodowite says lamely.

"Shall I go see if any ... still live?" I ask.

Makemin nods at once.

"Be as quick as you can. See if there are any medical supplies or stretchers. What ailing we find in the cells we'll triage out in front." He tells Silichieh to fetch my "embalmer friend," and a moment later Jil Punkinflake and I are through the doors and searching.

"Hmmm," he says, sniffing philosophically. "Mighty ripe!"

He gently brushes the temple locks of what once was a man, withered and streaked like a candle with dark putrescence, lying in a bed by the door. The room is long, tall, and white, with squat windows high by the ceiling. Half the beds are filled, all their contents alive with decay. The fog plays under the springs, and seeps between the fingers of drooping hands that hang from the edges of thin mattresses. I am less acclimated to the smell than I had hoped to be. They're all so badly rotted not a one could be alive, but I have the intolerable idea that perhaps some neglected patient lies here, maggotty and gangrenous, but living and in agony. I check each body. Each is dead. Jil Punkinflake solemnly draws the sheets over them, one by one, as I rifle the cabinets for supplies, dumping what little I find into a pillow case. I grab a stretcher, set the sack in the middle, then stack that on top of the two other stretchers—these, like the beds, I notice, have straps ... and then we carry them all out at once. As the doors swing open, Makemin and the others roll back away from us. The doors are flapping back and forth, fanning infirmary air into the hall.

I set up the triage area, and we ready ourselves to go inside again. The ayslum is looking down at us, banging and shouting, and I hear again the same shrill, plunging howl, fringed with a shallow echo as it rolls down the halls. The asylum has the fixed expression of someone whose mind collapses, and not fast enough. The occupants are gradually becoming agitated, as each, I suppose, becomes aware of our arrival—in his or her own way. We go back in.

Makemin notices a small metal door between the stairs, set down a truncated shaft angling into the floor.

"The closet! Oh, I forgot it!"

Megrodowite staggers back with his face in his hands— his voice trembles.

After an exchange of looks, Makemin bids Silichieh break the lock. Light falls in the dim confine of the cell beyond, its contracted floor huddled with figures pale as flour sacks ... trembling, naked, frail as a clutch of baby birds. They slump against each other, knees up, and from this huddle rises a shaking face with sightless eyes, responding perhaps to the sound of the door. The mouth opens, and a cracked voice cries

"Sir is a genius!"

Other voices feebly join in, the heads stay lowered.

"Sir is a genius!"

Makemin turns to me.

"Get them out."

Their flimsy bodies, as we convey them out of doors and into light for them unseen and unseeable, shiver and cringe even from our gentlest touch. Disgendered by neglect, they chant their slogan and raise their bent wrists toward their faces. The other inmates fall silent as we carry them out, nearly a dozen, and, with indescribable looks in their eyes, they gather around the cots to stare at them. There's no treatment for these, except perhaps water.

Makemin asks me if I think it likely any will recover, and I tell him no.

"Screen them," he says. "Use the tarps and tent poles for now. They are upsetting these others. ... And I don't want to look at them."

*

In no time the yard in front of the asylum is filled with milling persons. With Silichieh, I retrieve the handful who are either too stupefied or weakened by neglect to move on their own. The whole place is swarming with shadows, with sounds, but as we release the trapped patients, a trembling calm leaks down.

Makemin is consulting with Nikhinoch and the rest of us are grouped together under the trees. I've done what I can with the ailing ones, and rejoin my friends wondering what's going on. Megrodowite comes over and stands next to me.

"You're taking good care of them," he says.

Here comes, from somewhere behind the asylum, a woman all in armor. She has a short sword with a basket hilt on her right side and a flapped holster on her left hip. She approaches Makemin boldly, homing in on his authority. A pleasing, and weirdly familiar face. I could say she looks like da Vinci's "Lady with Ermine" if there had ever been such a thing. Strange thing to think. Jil Punkinflake flaps Megrodowite on the shoulder and points.

"Who's *that?*" he asks, eyes riveted.

"Saskia," Megrodowite says simply. "She was one of the locked-ins. I brung her food a few times."

Jil Punkinflake draws closer to Makemin and watches her come. Silichieh, Megrodowite and I are drawn along.

"Must have retrieved her things from the attic."

"You've come for me, haven't you?" she calls in Yesge.

Everyone pauses, including Makemin, because her satiny voice is as deep as a man's. Our unconcealed astonishment obviously irritates her, as though she presumed we might have the grace to overlook this peculiarity.

"Yes yes my throat was injured during the arrest," she draws nearer. It's unnerving; a very sensuous bass and she's not much over five feet.

"Have you any message for me from Tewsetonka?"

"She wears Yeseg colors," I comment to Silichieh, who nods.

Makemin answers.

"I wasn't looking for anyone in particular, and I have no message for you."

She seems to calculate, with what I reckon to be her poker face—it's a good one. Just a slight slackness around the mouth shows she's putting together and reframing within herself.

"Why did you come, then? You are Tewsetonka's men, aren't you?"

"We are from the Alak army, and we are going to Port Conget and from there to Meqhasset."

Makemin seems to want to break off his conversation with her and resume consultation with Nikhinoch.

Saskia reacts at mention of the Alak army, and her next words are in Alakan, with high-class enunciation.

"You're off the road, you know. I can show you the way, should you need a guide."

"I need no guide," Makemin actually smiles a little. "I am here to recruit."

Some of the officers standing nearby are visibly taken aback by this and trundle forward, preparing their protests. He is distracted by them and does not hear her insistance that she was wrongfully imprisoned here.

"Surely you don't propose giving these people arms?" the sergeant asks incredulously.

But Makemin is decided. "I'm damned if I'll go off short-handed."

"I volunteer!" Saskia says loudly.

"I wouldn't trust this bunch with a pile of spoons, let alone with our stocks—we can recruit in town!"

Saskia is striding nearer.

One of the inmates, a small man bald on top, turns excitedly to his neighbor, who has wiry ginger hair.

"They want us to fight! Bring Thrushchurl!"

Ginger nods with a concerned look ploughing his face above the eyebrows and dashes off, back toward the asylum.

"The towns have all been picked dry. What do you think I do with my time?" Makemin asks bitterly. "I've written every dispatcher and hamlet within a hundred miles and nobody has anyone to spare. Should we find anyone in town, I'll bring them on, too, but as I can assure you we won't, we take *them—now.*"

He sends Nikhinoch and sergeant Yarn to bring up the carts. Word is already filtering around and a number of inmates are tentatively approaching, listening.

"Sir!"

Saskia thrusts herself forward through the arguing officers at Makemin, her face brilliant with an eager smile.

"Sir, I was formerly retainer to Prince Qiprit in Ziwr', who fought and bled as I have done for Tewsetonka. You must permit me to join you!"

Ginger trots up to rejoin Bald Spot and they are whispering together. Past them perhaps only I, of our company, see him come from beneath the asylum, loping, glowering and grinning. He is dressed like a mortuary student, complete with his top hat, climbs seemingly on all fours out of total darkness, up the basement steps, through the slanting storm cellar doors. Pausing, he squints in the afternoon light, his eyes pinched into two crescents, his long yellow teeth exposed. Somehow I anticipate learning that this is his habitual expression in almost all circumstances.

Saskia: "The usurper's men put me here for the trouble I caused them, though they dared not take my life.—I promise you I am not mad! If I were, would they have sent me caparisoned like this? With my sword and my guns?"

"I will take any able fighter," Makemin says in answer to both her and his clamoring officers, his hands in the air.

At the fretful promptings of Ginger and Bald Spot, who wave with both arms, the man from the cellar ambles in this direction, throwing out one leg after another like a crane and cocking his head. When this man has drawn within about a dozen feet of us, Bald Spot turns to Makemin and holds out his hand sideways.

"Thrushchurl is head of our party," he says helpfully.

Thrushchurl doffs his hat from his rat tails a moment, then resettles it, his grin fluctuating through a number of expressions without ever disappearing.

"They're trying to induct us!" Bald Spot tells him.

"Oh, yes?" Thrushchurl says. His voice is unctuous and he pants a little as he speaks.

Saskia: "I was trained as an officer at the Academy in

Ziwr'. I do expect to ranked accordingly."

Makemin's arm snaps straight up into the air pistol in his grip and fires once; it's a high-caliber hold-out gun and the shock of its percussion slaps against my ears and makes them ring. The officers crowding Makemin recoil, and the inmates squawk and dodge around, hands to ears.

"All able-bodied inmates will arrange themselves before me in three—equal—ranks!"

Nikhinoch stalks aside rattling his finger in his ear.

"You!"

Makemin points to Megrodowite, who walks forward diffidently. Taking a sabre ferrule and sash in his fist, Makemin drops them into Megrodowite's arms.

"I'm making you corporal. You will stay here and look after the ones who can't take care of themselves, *hein?* Go to the nearest town and show them these things, tell them I gave them to you, and get them to help. Detail porters and bring the weak ones down to the village. See that they are taken care of there. Can you do that?"

"I don't think they—"

"You'll do it. Write to me in Port Conget and let me know how things go with you. You can write, can't you?"

"Kind of."

"Keep it simple. Let me know if you are not receiving cooperation. You will find I am able to enforce my authority through my deputies." Makemin begins turning away. "Tell them that from the start and you'll have a better time of it."

He faces the milling patients.

"Ranks! Ranks! What is this nonsense?! Sergeant!"

The line officers presently put the ranks in order. Thrushchurl and a few others stand off to one side. Saskia stands by herself in front of the leftmost rank, eyes sternly fixed forward. Makemin gives her charge of the group, then calls on Thrushchurl, who lopes forward at once, as servile as a dog.

"You captain that lot," Makemin says, pointing to the middle rank.

Thrushchurl's reply is a sort of nasal gasp accompanied by an expansion of his grin. He silkily takes his place there at the head of the column, to the evident satisfaction of the few there who had identified themselves as being of his party. Sergeant Yarn, who, after the full toll of desertions was reckoned, had lost nearly all his men, is assigned the third group.

Tabliq Quibli burps softly and climbs down from his cart, unhurriedly unfolds the canvas coverings from his stores of supplies. There are enough guns but everything else is scarce. The asylum soldiers are randomly accoutered in bits and pieces, a helmet here and a gauntlet there, boots here and hats there. I watch Thrushchurl seize up a carbine in his huge hands, beaming at it.

"I'm an excellent shot," he croons, rocking the gun this way and that.

Megrodowite puts out his hand with a rueful mouth, something not strong enough to call a smile, and we shake.

"I'm glad you got out of this," I tell him.

"No, I-I don't want to fight," he says sorrowfully.

"Neither do I."

"Why don't you run?"

"I was seen by an Edek."

"What's that?"

"They're embodiments of imperial power."

"And that means you can't run?"

"It means that," I say with a sigh, "if you run, there's no escape."

"And then jail?"

I shake my head.

"Death."

His eyes fall, and suddenly fill with tears. He puts his arms around me. Now I'm comforting him.

*

The asylum soldiers are not all that unruly and seem for the most part delighted with the excursion. They make a shapeless larking mass in our rear, with sound corresponding, a jangling of spur-like voices, fragments of songs often belted out in shameless ugliness, laughter and hoots. It's as though a delirious giant were pushing us along the road, blithering to itself. Makemin doesn't seem to care, as long as the columns stay together and keep moving. The madmen keep up the pace admirably, and we skirt the mountains in a few days, scavenge a few supplies at an abandoned farm, where Jil Punkinflake befriends a hungry-looking dog, blonde, with two different-colored eyes.

At the heads of our columns, we march in close proximity to Thrushchurl.

"How'd they get you?" Jil Punkinflake asks him.

Thrushchurl just goes on grinning and draws a partial circle in the air with the tip of his nose. His parents bestowed size on him; proportioned like other men but he is a size or two bigger, with elongated arms and fascinatingly large powerful and beautiful snowy hands. Below the brim of his silk hat, his ears are so white they seem daubed with silver paint. He doesn't talk about himself. Rifle strap across his chest, his hands are free to rove from pocket to pocket, or to finger an invisible piano. I've noticed he has his own anthem, a dismal snatch of song he tirelessly repeats under his breath,

"Little mice, little mice,
Even cats have got their lice,
Run-run-run, get far away—"

When we set camp, we sleep in no particular order, under our makeshift shelters. Thrushchurl matter-of-factly sets his cot down near Jil Punkinflake's, and seems to enjoy our raillery without much partaking of it. I've noticed he keeps turning his head suddenly, and peering at the ground, his vapid smile taking on a weird, predatory look. I've seen him start out of his dozing to do it—what does he see? There's never anything there.

One night, I am trammled along in dreams of love. I draw her back onto my lap and press my lips to her throat. In the shadowy obscurity of my dream sight I see her face both as it is and stylized at once: the exquisitely molded nose whose curve is asymptotic to that of her nearly circular cheeks, and the sail-shaped eye above and the thrilling scalloped lips below. The skin of her back slides along my lips trailing grated nerves, and more intense than life I feel the warmth and smell the fragrance of her hair, which only becomes more intense as I sit up awake, wondering how the mountain, the wind, the camp can bear her fragrance or press her warmth to my face. And there I see Thrushchurl sitting furtively hunched on his cot, doing something sloppy with his hands in his lap. I am yet too dazed to think to look away, but now I realize he's fondling and playing with something that shimmers like mirage through his fingers. It's mercury. He has a pool of it in the hollow of his blanket and he's running it through his fingers, and chasing beads of it across the cloth. I lie back and watch. His face is stark in the moonlight, the eyes are hollow, his grin unvaryingly fixed. I may or may not nod, but I see him collect the mercury and transfer it swiftly to various of his pockets, trousers jacket and vest. Like a cadaver he now reclines flat on his back, and his hands droop over each other on his chest like swan's wings.

Jil Punkinflake is doing everything he can to get next to Saskia, but she is repellently brisk and busy, not unlike the deputies of Tref. So naturally he turns to me for help—few people can resist the temptation to tell their stories. Most people *are* their stories. How wise that makes me feel, but I doubt that feeling. I am obliged to her or to fate for this story, in that she presented me with occasion to hear it.

"Medic, what's that star?" she asks me sharply, pointing to my armband. I explain, and an interest shimmers in her lovely eyes.

"Ah," she says, preludally.

Then: "No, I didn't belong there."

Jil Punkinflake, marching uncoordinatedly next to me, pipes up before I can ask anything.

"How did you come to be there?"

"I was abducted by my cowardly enemies, who thought to put me out of their way without daring to face me. The administrator was related to one or the other of them. I will find *that* one out, I assure you."

The way she says it, I believe it.

"How did it happen?"

"In Ziwr'," she says, as though a different question had been asked. "Prince Qiprit was my foster father, and Tewsetonta's Sattvi had him killed when he took Tewsetonka's side. He was stifled in bed, with a pillow," she adds bitterly.

"I knew who to blame, and I and my retainers went to the Sattvi's house. His courtiers came out to protect him, and we slew them. But then more arrived from other parts of the city, and at once they were like wind all around us. They killed my men on their knees, in the street, in front of me. But the Sattvi directed them to spare me, because he had moved too quickly to kill Prince Qiprit, and so had made more enemies than he could handle, faster than he had expected. As usual, he was afraid, and thought that killing me would set more faces against him. They jailed me instead."

It's almost too compressed to follow. Plainly, she has been working and reworking this account—in her cell, probably.

A sinister and understated smile appears on her lips, beneath her eyes hard and clear as crystal.

"I strangled my guard and got away. The Sattvi had already left Ziwr', but he had left his son behind. My knife parted his throat like it was water. I put ribbons in his hair, and put his head into a pillow case. I spread the rest of him around the garden," she gestures as though she were arranging small objects on a mantlepiece.

"One by one, Prince Qiprit's old friends turned me down when I asked them for help in putting down this mutiny. I wanted to take the town for Tewsetonka, but only a handful had spirit enough to stand with me. Now of course I realize the sattvi's friends wanted to get me out of there before his return, because they knew I would kill him. So they set a pack of skulking quakers on me."

Muscles work in her face.

"I let myself be distracted—next thing, I'm off my feet and flung into a closed cart, like a bale of hay. They brought me to the asylum."

"That's when your voice changed," Thrushchurl says. I hadn't noticed him creep up.

"I have Prince Qiprit's voice now," she says lividly, without turning to look at Thrushchurl. "And I'll keep it until His Travesty is dead and the true King of the Yesegs is restored."

So, there's her mission, in black and white. Jil Punkinflake is beside himself with admiration.

*

Now we are on the far skirts of the mountains, and Makemin is tightening up discipline, setting pickets and look outs.

"Wacagan are moving through this area in quick bands," he says, always broadcasting his eyes, goggles tight against his sockets.

"—They come up fast. No straggling. Keep together. Don't thin the line."

We camp in the hollow of three hills, gather in tents to watch night come on. I am in my tent, resting after mess with the others. Thrushchurl gives me his piece of jelly. I chew it gingerly, having bitten my tongue rather badly the night before.

I chew slower and slower ... the flavor is numbing out of my mouth, the cake is turning to sawdust in my mouth. Out of the stillness a feeling sinks long feelers into me, into my bladder, my intestines, creeping up into my heart and lungs, shortening my breath, tingling sick feeling in the scalp ...

"There's something ..." I look around meaninglessly at the others, who blink at me in innocent incomprehension as I stand up.

"I think ..."

I can't finish the sentence. My mouth is bone dry; it's a struggle to swallow.

Then Thrushchurl looks up at me, and says, "Yes ..." with a sort of listening hoist of his upper lip.

Silichieh's brows contract, looking from one of us to the other.

Rapid footfalls—we all turn our heads at once and there's Nikhinoch dashing for Makemin's tent.

Silichieh bolts to his feet saying, "It's trouble."

He lunges through the tent flap and hurries off somewhere, shouting—"It's trouble! Get up! Get up!"

We look at each other. Thrushchurl snatches up his carbine and clutches it. His whole body vibrates with nervous energy like a frightened animal and that song trembles in and out the brink of his lips. Nikhinoch emerges from Makemin's tent, puts the alarm to his lips and blows an endless fixed ringing note like a baby wailing in a cistern, and Makemin erupts helmeted from the flaps, holding his rifle.

"Soldiers!" he roars. "Soldiers! Get to the edges of camp! Under cover!"

Sergeant Kaladze races by clapping on his helmet stops when he sees us.

"Come on!" he screams. He looks at Thrushchurl—"Get to your column!"

Thrushchurl immediately lopes out into the night. Kaladze runs to a cart near our tent and overturns it, waving us to join him behind it. Other men are now doing the same all around us, stumbling out of tents pulling up trousers and fumbling with their guns, their eyes stark white in the dark as lamps all over are extinguished.

I hear cries.

Screams, from the forward margin of the camp. Without thinking I pop up, trying to drill my vision into the dark.

"Drop down!" Kaladze barks at me as something that whirs like a giant bumblebee passes me on the right. I cower behind the cart, Jil Punkinflake's grip convulsively tight on my arm, and bullets whack into the wood by our faces. His face seeks mine and he has become a petrified creature, starts to shake, shakes so hard it's turning into a fit.

A strangled cry from close by us. Kaladze points and I automatically follow his arm. One of the asylum inmates is curled up on the ground there, covered in blood, pain locked up in knots all over his face.

"Get him! Be quick! I'll keep them off you!"

With empty mind I dart out to the wounded man, feeling myself tear loose from Jil Punkinflake's grip. Resounding crashes from where I came, and another flash whir bare inches from my nose. I awkwardly drag the man, who cries out as I pull him, back under cover, and begin to tend him. He relaxes as I do my work, and dies.

A shout from somewhere cut off in the middle, and

more voices raised in pain. The dark crawls with screams.

"This is a bad spot," Kaladze says. "Come on!"

"He won't go," I point to Jil Punkinflake, who has shrunk into a ball.

Kaladze takes me roughly by the shoulder and drags me to a heap of stones, so that my legs whip up into the air as I am yanked along. He rushes back and overturns the cart on top of Jil Punkinflake, covering him like a turtle in a shell, and somehow gets back to me in one piece. The rock I hide behind snaps hard against my hand and stone chips flicker everywhere.

I follow Kaladze through the stones and trunks in toward the front where the cover is best. What I pass on the way I barely see and can't describe.

Now I am flung into an enclosure of carts and barrels and I don't know what, making a hasty barricade. Makemin has hacked a thin slit in the enclosure and snipes through it.

"Where are the grenadiers?!" he rants. "Where are my sharp shooters?!"

Nikhinoch, calm but blanched, his blue skin turned grey as ash, flits back and forth like a helper spirit. Bullets pelt and crack against the wood, ping off metal. The Clappers have congregated in a tight knot and their bleating chant drones in the gaps between blasts.

Bald Spot streaks across the open space and folds sideways not three steps from cover, his face crushed in shock his mouth a tight O and a despairing grunt forced out of his abdomen, his hands swing instantly to his right side where his body bends. His momentum takes him one swerving step more and he drops backward onto his left side. I rush to him and turn him over. He is rigid his eyes blank. His right side is smashed in, soft moonlight on jagged ends of his broken ribs. Blood from his wound has swept up onto his grey face, and spattered even his eyes.

"There's nothing—there's nothing! Get back!" Yarn calls, and I dart back to cover.

I peer about me desperately looking for Kaladze, but he's not there. Yarn slips away into the shadows. Who was my sergeant anyway? Am I supposed to be giving orders? I am down now in the shelter of one of the carts, and I peer out through a chink in the wood. In the gloom, I can dimly make out the groove of the road between the slopes. As I watch, three or four blackbirds, all in a row as though linked at the shoulder, fly sideways across the road. I am trying to spot them—the slopes around the road I now see are seething with motion, small groups of soldiers sailing in long bounding arcs, black against the dark, and here and there the muzzle flashes as they fire on us, still moving. They swing back and forth in the air just above the ground like ghosts, silent except for the shooting, effortless, weightless. Makemin's rifle cracks near me just as another group wafts out nearly too swift to see into the road, and the last one in the group is hit—he flips over his center again and again, arms and legs flailing. He floats in the air toward us, down the slope, limp, turning now shoulder over shoulder as if he tumbled along in the current of a sluggish stream, arms and legs flop and flop. I watch fascinated as the dark body drifts to a halt by the side of the road, backs of its hands dragging in the dust.

Thumping feet behind me—the grenadiers have gathered now. They work in teams, one kneeling primes the grenades and puts them in slings, hands them to the other who stands, twirls the sling and launches the grenade, then crouches again. Loud bangs from the road and slope.

"They are trying to get above us," Makemin says sharply, pointing to the slope on my right. He orders the grenadiers to concentrate on the road, to cover us as we move to defend the slope. I am ordered to help carry one of the lighter carts. A bullet bonks into the wood near my ear, and shaves splinters onto my cheek.

We clamber up on to the slope randomly dropping our cover, and I stop panting there. Shots rain in from all over and I throw myself down in total confusion. I turn my head this way and that, see at least a dozen men fall before us, and the long-springing arcs of enemy soldiers zig-zagging above us on the slope. I drag the man nearest me behind a boulder and bandage him. He is doing nothing whatever but breathing for all he's worth, eyes starting from his head. When I look up, I see Yarn come holding the front end of a heavy box, and Silichieh behind holding the rear end. Silichieh shouts something and they drop the box—he begins fiddling with it.

Yarn sprints over to us and his shoulder explodes just above the bicep—he falls on his side his head towards me and, after one numb moment, a howl is forced out of him as though he were being run through a mangle.

His groin ruptures, then his belly and chest at nearly the same moment, and immediately he is lifeless as a stone. A few more bullets pat noisily into his leg, and one dings his ear, causing his head to rock back and forth two times.

A boulder topples and falls away on my left, and two dark figures silently bound through the gap. I am frozen. One of them is in the light now; I see his short beard is white. Something crashes down on me, only sound, and the one I am looking at jerks, his left arm parts from his body, and I can see through the shredded uniform the white of his collarbone in a spray of blood. He glides weightlessly backward into the second one, who is lit too briefly to see by a muzzle flash. I think the bullet strikes his comrade. Another crash above me and now there is only a dim concatenation of whirling shapes there in the vague gap. I look up at Makemin, who has already rechambered his gun. He glances down.

"Get back to the cart!"

I follow him there. Silichieh is crouched down behind the box, which has unfolded to expose something like a metal cask that narrows to a blunt bottle neck. He is reaching and adjusting. I am hidden. Thrushchurl comes stalking up and begins firing around the cart that hides me, and Makemin is aiming and shooting, deliberate and steady. I peer out and see shapes massing high on the slope, all black streaks popping with gunfire.

"Shoot damn you!" someone yells at me.

I pull my pistol, but I can't clearly see anything to shoot at. My hands rest on the rock in front of me, pistol in my right hand. Explosions all around. My right hand hurts—I glance at it and smoke is puffing from my gun. I suppose I must have been firing it. It was pointing up the slope. It was full, now it's empty.

Something white, far up on the slope, and almost wholly concealed behind a stone—it's there only for an instant— an indistinct shape that pulls itself in and is gone.

A sound like popping stitches thunders up behind me. I drop down looking. Silichieh is pumping these two handcranks on either side of his metal barrel, which is mounted on hinges attached to a shield. I see the shield blacken in one spot and the whole thing vibrates, a bullet deflected there. Discrete packets of brown smoke snap from the front of the barrel, and Silichieh, pumping frantically, is peering through a wire circle on top of the barrel, swinging it deliberately from side to side, and Makemin is ordering everyone to shoot. The bottom of the slope, where we are, is exploding with flashes and blasts, and above us I can see the enemy soldiers going down, tumbling in air without hitting the ground. Brown gobs of smoke are growing here and there on the slope, like ghost rocks, and around them the enemy begin to writhe and paw their faces. I hear retching and belching howls. I see an arm spin against the stars, and I hear screams, orders, a weird bleating horn is blowing.

The arcing lines of Wacagan soldiers glide away from us now, back and forth, and turning from side to side in the air. They vanish over the brow of the hills and up the road.

*

It's dawn as we finally regroup. A quarter of our number is lost or injured. I attend the wounded I find, and presently a triage is organized. Jil Punkinflake I discover asleep, clutching the scroll I'd made him, still under the cart. His dog managed to crawl in beside him, raises his head and looks sorrily at me, one eye pale blue, the other crimson brown. I shake Jil Punkinflake's shoulder, and he stirs, smiling woozily.

"Was it a dream?"

The cart is riddled with holes. The scroll I take from him

is bare—seems he made use of it.

I am taken by the arm and guided into a tent, where Saskia sits angry and weary on her cot. She pays me no mind as I salve and cover an abrasion on her right shoulder, where a bullet had hammered her armor. Her skin is creamy, and there is a thin, soft layer of flesh over strenuous muscle like a flat sheaf of wire. She is scowling at the ground, living the injury time and again.

"Pig! ... Pig!" she curses softly.

I find Sergeant Kaladze among the wounded. They hit him in the gut, and he is unconscious when I get to him. The wound is bad, and I do not think he will survive it. I do what I can for him, but as I lift him up onto the cart he gives a long sigh and his brown face goes instantly grey. No pulse. I leave him in the cart—let them bury him in a proper cemetery.

Thrushchurl is moving in and out among the dead, peering eagerly this way and that. Now and then he will pick up and drop a flaccid arm, or turn a cheek.

During the fighting, I felt alarm, but no real fear. Now that the fighting is over, I tremble. I tremble with fear. It comes and goes in icy waves. It breaks open an icy cave inside me. When I think about what happened I sss-ss-s-stutt-tu-tut-tut-tut-tt-tt-t-t

*

Eventually we break camp and move out. Makemin, looking drawn, is eager to press on to Port Conget, get out of open country, and hopes to make it there before nightfall. Our line staggers together, passing the bodies of dead Wacagan, many of which still float a few inches off the ground. I ask Silichieh about it, and he points to the thick metal braces they wear clamped to their calves.

"They have some secret way they treat this metal. They make it so light, it won't stay down. All Wacagan, and some Yeseg too, they train to fight in those. That's how they move so fast. That's why we call them blackbirds, didn't you know? Because they fly."

*

Now the road is backed up, full of troops and supplies waiting for passes to get inside the town's walls. I can only vaguely make out the scene—a jumble of hills rolling down toward the far horizon, and somewhere out there a glistening breathing blue flatness that I suppose is the ocean. Port Conget seems to be a disc-shaped irregularity between it and me, planed down flush like a wooden peg into a dip in the landscape. We bunch up against the group ahead of us, a collection of carts, and wait. Hours pass, and no movement. There is talk of our being exposed here overnight. Makemin fumes and paces and cranes.

Presently a doughy corporal with a clipboard makes his way down the cue. As he approaches us, Makemin's diffuse anger condenses and he strides forward on the beam toward the corporal with me in tow.

"We have wounded and we've been waiting more than four hours!"

Without looking up the corporal takes Makemin's information and flips through his sheets. He ambles further along the line. Makemin, his face horribly drawn, calls after him. The corporal makes a sort of fluttering gesture at waist level, a hold on move, without turning around, which proves to be a mistake as Makemin switches him across the back of the head so swiftly his ferrule whistles and the corporal howls puts his hand to the new part in his hair and spins around his eyes popping. Makemin drives his fist into the corporal's face splitting his lip and squashing his nose. The corporal makes a choked sound, his knees buckle, and with amazing celerity Makemin's left hand shoots out to seize him by the lapel and slow his fall to a sag, the better to smash him again bursting the flesh along the left cheekbone. He takes the limp, squealing corporal in both hands and drapes him over his horse's ass, plucks up a company insignia from one of the casualty carts and claps it onto the man's lacerated cheek like a bandage. The corporal chirps and his legs flip weakly. Nikhinoch meanwhile has retrieved the clipboard and is there when Makemin reaches for him, calmly pivots the board into Makemin's hand the proper page bent back. The latter holds it before the corporal's streaming face.

"Now you're *one* of my wounded. Sign."

The corporal fumbles his signature and presses his seal ring into the document and Makemin calls "Piglets move up! Where's that worthless standard man?"

He mounts, and Jil Punkinflake, giving me a feeble smile only thinly veneering the fear that has sickened down into him now, advances to walk beside him. Using principally the minatory expression on his face, Makemin clears a path for us right up the middle of the columns ahead. I do not notice much because I'm trotting alongside his horse holding, as best I can, an ether sop under the mouth and nose of the corporal, who seems unhappily unable to lose consciousness for more than a moment or two. He gags a bit, and I clear a plug of red muck from his mouth. Bits of broken teeth come away, adhere to my finger.

Some officer strides up wigging his arms and Makemin without a word points his holdout gun in the man's face. Thrushchurl's people are exhilerated by the action and are raving all around us, out in front and on all sides. They gibber and gambol, and the soldiers in the road reel back appalled and avoiding contamination.

And suddenly the sky is interrupted by the arch of the gate passing overhead, and we're safely inside.

*

No one meets my eyes in the street. Fringes of dread hang in the lower part of the air, roll sluggishly down against the town's grain. Deserted buildings, houses and stores eviscerated by looters their innards spill from windows and doorways.

Looking around I see a grimy sweat like bitter metal soot on everything, gloom and nauseous headache that makes me wish for something really clean and frightening to happen. I catch myself the object of cowed and smouldering looks from hidden faces; they heat my uniform chemically. I want to escape, but even here there are Edeks. They don't come from the capital. They don't have to—they know.

A cry is rising all over the place—"The Redeemer's coming!"

I blunder along with the other soldiers if only so as not to be knocked down. When I can, I take my chance and slip up a stairway that tops out in a partially covered plaza, street-level with the slope on the far side, a few benches and tables where the town's old liars could sit drink and play pinochle, so I stagger over and officially commandeer one empty table. From here I can follow the pointing fingers to where something godlike is moving against the horizon.

That's the Redeemer, the Alak flagship. Even at least a mile away it rises high into the sky, towering over a fleet of massive Alak hulks; its immense, broad prow is shadowed beneath a winged steel colossus, his stern face nearly in the clouds, wings folded back along the lines of the ship, a huge shield in his left hand and his right, brandishing a sword, is raised four hundred feet above the waves. There are guns protruding from hatches in his rippling garment, and his legs are lost in their folds.

The Redeemer is unique, with so many engines and so many guns, all superlative numbers—its battery can, on one side, level a town in minutes. Its grapnels can drag enemy ships on massive steam winches; captured ships may be drawn into bays, or crushed between hydraulic rams in special compartments. Even from this distance, I can see the bristling, smooth-slabbed fortress rising from its midsection, and hear the fury of its engines, sullen and far away. Some of its forward bays are open and emitting barqots, which are not able to escape its shadow for many minutes.

I watch the barqots pull into the harbor and back their drawbridge tail gates to the piers with clamorous reports. Around me, gulls' wings glint like swords as they circle. In the streets now there are soldiers marching.

These are not conscript hicks. These are Alak regulars, the real fanatics. Now the larger barqots are open and disgorging a phalanx of Ministerial Ghuards. They dwarf the regular infantry around them, striding along the piers.

The armor worn by these Ghuards is worth describing in some detail. It is all or nearly all made of a special paper-light metal, the same kind Wacagan use for their legbands. It's an uncanny experience seeing the Ghuards in their armor—you begin to wonder if you've gone deaf, because, massive as it is, the armor makes almost no noise at all. No thundering footsteps, no clattering. Huge forms sail by you as quiet and easy moving as balloons.

The helmets are traditionally moulded to resemble the heads of berserk jackasses, with ears three feet long bolt upright on top them. The eyes are great blind concavities with a slit for each of the occupant's eyes recessed at their innermost edges, flanking the false-perspective nose ridge— actually a flat trench, not encroaching on the Ghuard's field of vision. In a perversely-inspired bid for perfect ugliness, the designers had trapezoidal openings cut on either side of the muzzle, and mail jowls hang flabbily out of these. The rest of the false face is a wedge snout with a horrifying if rather nicely-rendered snarl of projecting axe-head shaped teeth. A narrow, shaggy mane of needles runs in a tapering stripe down the rear of the helmet to the small of the back, rippling hypnotically like the scintillation of a wheeling school of fish.

When have I ever seen a school of fish wheeling?

Those manes must be fantastically expensive and time-consuming to make.

The chest, shoulder, and upper arms are plated over with two layers of armor separated by an air layer. There are two sets of hands—proper man-sized ones, in fine and elastic metal gloves, and colossal mechanical gauntlets that can crush a man in their grip. Strips of mail hang down from ledges at the tops of the thighs. From chains affixed to each armored groin dangles a pair of dull metal balls, bigger than a man's head and dotted with scratch-shined pimples, which clack meditatively together with every stride. The legs are thick pistoned trunks with ponderous hinges at the ankles, and incongruously prim pointed feet. They puff along in swarms of flies—their hindquarters and thighs are caked with excrement, as the Ghuards exhibit a marked disinclination to divest themselves of the armor once they've got it on.

Makemin watches them disembark with a sour, twisted mouth, and crossed arms. I know from his expression he has not been able to recruit more soldiers. I should go down to him, but I find I would rather not move. I sit and I watch. I will go down to him.

*

With aching legs I drift down mudslopped streets. No more whore's drums and pimps clapping their horny hands together on street corners. They fled at word of the Ghuards' arrival. I can see the camp of the Ghuards in the distance, through gaps in the buildings, where it lours like a chancre on the opposite side of town. Smoke, laced with seams of red fire and convolving bulbs of flies, hovers over the camp. Behind a rampart of chain-bound barrels they are smashing their screaming prisoners to paste in massive iron mortars, or pulling them apart in demoniacally gleeful tugs-of-war. I know there will be others, a rape ration is what they call it, brought in soon if they're not there already. A woman's, for example, right arm might set alight, or her face, for example, or his, might be mauled by dogs, as the Ghuard travails upon her.

*

The port's wall extends in a broad bow with both ends in the sea, encompassing an area in excess of the dimensions of the town itself. I can walk past the point where the houses peter out, and there's nothing here but dunes and ashen, sandblasted trees, all strangely deeply dark in the gathering dusk that layercakes the sky in fire ribbons. I'm gratefully still perverse enough not to miss even the beauty here, that flips adjectives and such around in my brains, as though this refreshing air, that seems forcibly to inflate my lungs and threatens to puff me up so I bob off across the sand, is stirring up in me a dust devil of whirling expository phrases. The particles tick against my skull's insides. I'm hoping any moment they'll blow out my far ear and inside and out my head will be all sliding wind, and I'll see my own shadow weirdly dark as well.

I'm simply too numb and tired to take in the ocean. I don't believe I can say I've ever seen one before.

After catching a few z's, lying in some romantic sand with a kerchief over my eyes, I wake up to still sun and breakers. The front of my face aches with the drying out of the wind, and nicely getting up there's a rill of pain shoots from my left heel along the back of my ankle. I hobble my tendonitis back in the direction of town.

There's a spot I faced as I slept, where a heap of stones receded into a jumble of details I didn't bother to make sense of at the time, and as I glance at them again I feel a memory come on, a dream of a black-streaked mouth in the stones, that spoke dream talk to me along the wind. I remembered the voice, but not in the way I normally remember voices. I didn't hear it in recollection, but my memory started making vocalities at me and it was the affect of the voice that it partially imitated; distracted, sexless, neutrally old, talking off at an angle and to itself, but I was meant to overhear. I only overheard it speak. A strong definite sound, but it trembled. It was a death's bed murmur, words maybe addressed to death, or through it, by a dying speaker. I get away from the beach fast, and as I walk the stiffness goes a bit out of my foot.

This broad bit of path seems to have lasted longer than it should.

*

Oh look another one of my outdoor cafés what about that. A handsome girl and brave asks me what I want and goes inside to get me whatever it is I've ordered. Everywhere, the same thing. I see mouths in motion on all sides. Incessantly in motion, on all sides. There's another; and now two more have joined us. They eat, and their jaws work the food around among the teeth, between the jaws, pressed this way and that so that the different kinds of food find the teeth specialized to destroy them. The tongue does this, and also churns saliva into the food, so that everything tastes like saliva. Although the tongue naturally tastes, while having no taste of its own to speak of, not that I'd notice. I watch this or that patron lifting a cup or glass to the mouths they come here to honor with this fine food and drink, and the mouths stretch themselves out toward the cups or glasses, reaching out to meet them before the hand has finished bringing it near, as the eye judges. These people, like me, are marked for death. But not entirely like me. They can run.

So much strain and muscular labor involved in absorbing food. I'm exhausted just watching it. But above all there is speech, incessant speaking, where the inflated edges of the tube are stretched and contracted, knotted and unknotted, ripped open or pressed shut, flued and drummed, hammered and gnawed. Licked. That tube has two ends. To the far end goes all ignominy, and to the fore end all the glory, hymns of praise. Her lips were lovely. The swollen ring at one end of the tube, fastened to rings and riggings of muscle.

All these sounds. It's exhausting.

I notice the upper jaw doesn't move at all, only the lower. You see the skull so clearly I wonder people don't think of death whenever they witness speech, or speak themselves, feeling that hinge flap up and down, and even back and forth a bit—how can it go back and forth? Is the socket that loose, or is it something else, like a leather hinge, like a book binding? A man sitting near to me is speaking emphatically. I'm wrong. He's reciting something from memory, either that or he talks like a book, and some of us do. I imagine a book that stumbles and blunders, um-ing and uh-ing and stop start again what I mean to say—well, put it like this, you see there's too or rather what matters here the emphasis ought to it's more productive of consideration it's more produ-producti thoughtfully produ it's a fertiler field of it's a more sophisticated it's a less crude it's a more sophisticated ... and so on.

I watch emphatic speaker's mouth, and I can't hear his

words really, only the strident tone. I am falling under the spell of that clipped speaking of his. There are moments where the mouth seems to take an entirely new position without any intermediate movement, simply jumping from one to another like a sleight of hand too fast to follow with the eye, so that the mouth actually seems to flash like lightning. I feel something like a weak panic at this man's unceasing, precise, emphatic mouth speaking those written words he has fanatically memorized. What other motion of a part of the body, and only a part, the rest still, so controlled, rapid, transfixing? But then, after all, it isn't hard for me to shift my gaze to the flame of the lamp on the table.

There it is, the flame. I will think, which necessarily means I will think obsessively, about this flame.

Is it there?

What is there?

Is it there the way an object is there every moment, considering that it is not exactly an object but a procedure?

Or an exhalation?

Are all things like flames, in that they only seem to be as it were stable entities because, after all, it's always the same name, more or less, more or less the same, used for them? I mean, it must be something stable because I keep on recognizing it and calling it that, this time, another time, over and over, but then again how can I know that I am recognizing, and not just sort of improvising with myself? Or repeating myself?

I won't write down a word of this. It's not history. Just nonsense, that comes and goes like this fire here. Although it's history that gives light and heat. So I pass the time in the evening, before, as I know will happen before it does happen, Jil Punkinflake claps me on the shoulder, and we go bottle-hunting as before, in a place where I can watch as a flame as before becomes a million flames through ranks and files of essentially similar bottles. If I were a poet I would say something about fire in the bottles, bottled fire, time is fire as before, bottled time, time is sand, sand in fire is glass made into bottles, hourglasses, fire burns time in me as I get drunk as before and forgetful; and I drink, and the drink burns my throat and slakes my thirst somehow at once, and I get dizzy and forgetful, and now—empty bottles. Splatter of vomit in the street.

*

I hear Jil Punkinflake's sharply intaken breath.

"That old woman there!"

He points to a bald old woman in a shapeless, colorless linen gown, emerging from the rubble that borders our little camp. A white band swaddles her neck up to the ears, and her intent, falcon face swivels this way and that, face cool and keen as a biting, weightless wind. Jil Punkinflake's face wears an awestruck expression.

"That's Nardac!" he exclaims. "She was executioner for the whole district!"

He makes a sweeping arc with his finger. He's almost forgotten to be pale and ashamed now.

The woman is making her way toward Makemin, taking long, back-crooked strides, slightly fragile, pushing her knees down from time to time with her fibrous hands.

"Did she come with us from the asylum?" he wonders aloud.

Thrushchurl shakes his head, "No. I saw her there once, but she was always free to go."

Makemin is fuming; we are stuck again. There are no boats that will take us to Meqhasset, not for a time and perhaps not at all. The transport he had been assured would be here isn't, and isn't expected. Diverted, maybe even. Plus, no additional troops. No additional supplies. Nothing.

Nardac and Makemin retire to his tent, and he waves Nikhinoch up to take her arm. I see her give him something. Then she's gone.

Jil Punkinflake puts his hand to his lapel, where the death's head moth had once hung—it must have abandoned him during the fighting. He has his dog now, instead.

I feel his hand in the crook of my elbow.

"Do you think—? ... Listen, I have nothing to give you ... but, couldn't you make another of those rolls for me, Low?"

"I suppose so, if I could find the right sort of books."

"Let's look!"

There's a wan, sad hopefulness about him.

We move out at random into the town, looking together for more books flowed in together. I feel half-ghostly and not up to the task, but Jil Punkinflake is insistent, electrified by the search.

This is the route those moaning carts of dead bodies take on their way to the Ghuards' camp, I suppose to be eaten or perhaps simply fondled and torn and toyed with. With which to be toyed. Or perhaps the dogs eat the ones who arrive dead? Jil Punkinflake's dog sniffs the air here, but he is a contemplative and unruffled animal whose loyalties are by now it seems ineffacibly established. He cranks his head around and I can see the nondescript little brows above his different-colored eyes. Jil Punkinflake squats beside the dog and rubs his knees, and I am standing there a moment confusing myself with my own haste to find the right way to get lost, away from here or any other byway frequented by the Ghuards, when Thrushchurl, who is beside me, lunges a bit and then starts over to the other side of the road, where something sizeable flattens down a bed of weeds whose fringes screens it from view. Thrushchurl carefully takes the body, a woman wearing only a ragged shift and some dust, and sets it by the road, holding her out at arms' length on the flats of his hands slowly without any visible tremor in his arms.

She must have fallen from one of the carts.

Thrushchurl arranges her, puts her arms on her breast, and smoothes her hair with the reverent attentiveness I knew from the Embalmer's College. He throws a glance at Jil Punkinflake, whose attention is drawn at once, but who clings instead to his dog, his eyes widening, staring. A Ministerial Ghuard has silently loomed out from a street abutting this one.

In a stride he snatches the body up by the arm and flings it jauntily over his shoulder. He reaches up one massive hand and flicks her head with his finger, causing it to flap on the limp neck. Jil Punkinflake gasps and cringes down trying to vanish into his dog, and even from this distance I can hear the hairs bristle on Thrushchurl's head. I open my mouth to remonstrate with him but his face is shuddering and his pupils fixed on the Ghuard's mask have closed to pinholes—he opens his mouth and the yellow teeth visibly yellow to polluted gold and from between them erupts a scalding effusion of curses that makes me clap my hands to my head. Jil Punkinflake's dog whines and cringes, and Thrushchurl chatters out each bitter syllable clear as a bell. Rotten, clotted blood black as ink forms in his jaws and streaks his chin, hanging in ribbons from his lips; these are curses that only a mouth that had moiled itself in foulest rottenness could utter. The Ghuard reels back and the body slips down his arm to the ground. He staggers against the wall of a house; I grab Thrushchurl and Jil Punkinflake and we run.

*

"Wake up! You must get out! They will come for you now!"

The voice croaks at me through mental slush, beating me awake from a distance. And something else—there's a bad smell.

I sit up blinking, and there are lights streaking by the front of the tent, and broadcast commotion, and Silichieh is sitting up too, rubbing his head.

"The Ghuards! Get to the piers!"

I go to wake Jil Punkinflake, whose upturned face is crossed by a beam of faint light from somewhere, and see he is shouting in his dream: this alien voice that is not his bursts from his lips and tongue without breath, without throat, splattering his coiled-up mouth and cheeks with ink brack, black decay ink like ink made from black sea-bottom muck, tarry bog ichor that stinks. His eyes flick open and he bolts up nearly striking his face against mine, begins gagging and making sounds of disgust in his usual voice. I hear him washing out his mouth, dangling his torso over the edge of the cot—but everywhere there is franticness. I stick my head out the tent and I see Makemin directing the others, packing up, some of the camp is already gone. Squares where tents had been. No sign of violence, but much fear. And I see something white in the waves, just opposite the camp, wallowing there side to side. As I pause to look at it, it drops its head in and is gone, a momentary white motion under the foam.

We get ready—why not? I'm asking everyone in sight what's going on until out of it all dimly emerges the suspicion that Saskia and Makemin have conspired to steal a boat and get us out of the Port.

We packed. We fly through the streets, all in confusion. We can't stay together. We are separated, flying along the streets and all around us now there are cries and shouts, horns, banging insonorous gongs. We dart around a corner a huge tongue of ruby-dark fire stops us, bellowing a tall point high over our heads and seizing furiously on the buildings flanking it. Ghuards are rioting in the flames, I see one right in the fire, his armor blackened and smoke seeping from within, through the eye holes, and he howls a high wailing raucous joy note of wildness and rage with nothing of pain in it, reeling drunk in the flames until he broils to death, and the others are crashing through the town on all sides of us now, rending it all out of shape and upset it everywhere in flames. Screams, alarms, dark shapes flit against fire, we are part of a general flight now toward the water.

Jil Punkinflake's dog leads us there. I see lamps rolling calmly on inky darkness ahead, interrupted by the dark regularity of a pier thrust out from the land. Piers here, and we are alone on this route. I can see the lights of ships pulling out to sea, but I can't see the Redeemer or the Alak fleet anywhere.

A shriek like ripping burlap and there's a Ghuard behind us, tearing loose from a blob of smoke, his scorched armor still smoking.

The Ghuard lopes toward us like a stricken giant; then he pauses as though lost in thought, and I notice a copious, dark juice flowing from his helmet's left eye. The enormous hands pat an invisible pillow and smooth a vast phantom bed, and the Ghuard falls on it on his face. Makemin struts purposefully forward from the margin of the road, and there is a sharp tching! as he snaps his visor-goggles back up into his helmet, snap of the bolt and the satisfied little ring of the shell casing as it springs from the breach. He waves us on, his arm crossing his chest as he points to the boat, which stands lit up at the end of this pier over here. We are among the last to board.

Makemin gives the order to cast off.

"Saskia's not aboard—!"

And I can't find Silichieh anywhere.

Makemin shouts again and the lines are cast off. I can see Nardac stationed in the prow. Gathered up into her robe she looks like a vulture. Her black eyes shimmer there against the stars on the horizon. She must have had something to do with finding the ship. The engines chug and we pull away from the pier and out to sea. Now Ghuards are spilling out onto the piers, and I can see missiles splashing around the other fleeing boats, and around ours as well. Running everywhere looking for Silichieh, now I'm on the bridge where Makemin stands by the rail shouting orders

down to the deck. Over me a star winks. I look, then clap
Makemin hard on the shoulder. He wheels and glares at me.
I am pointing, and he with furrowed brow traces my gaze to
something grey and small moving across the sky; he yanks
down his visor goggles, then waves his hand to Nikhinoch
who quickly puts his rifle into it. Makemin lifts sights and
shoots—grey form, a little Predicate flying to warn the
Redeemer most likely, plops into the ocean. Makemin jerks
up his visor again and nods grimly at me.

"Sharp eye."

After a while looking again I feel clammy nausea at heart
and throat as I don't find Silichieh. But he is there, after all.
One moment nothing, the next moment he and Saskia are
there on the deck not far from me and he is climbing down
off her back. She has those metal cuffs on her legs, she's
Yeseg, and trained, so she can fly along like the blackbirds,
too. It transpires they had been all over the Port. It's a good
thing she made it. Saskia is the only experienced sailor
among us, and she will be in effect captain of the ship. I
watch as she takes the helm from Makemin, who stalks off
to his cabin, pressing the heel of his palm to his brow.

From the butt end of the boat, we watch fire devour Port
Conget. Even from well out in the darkness the mammoth
forms of the Ghuards are visible bounding airily in and out
of black and red coils of fire. The reflected flames wave on
the still water of the ocean like tall clumps of grass in the
wind, upside down. In their sullen glow, a solitary Alak hulk
can be seen receding heavily up the coast, oblivious to the
destruction. Dark red lifts its bolts of red into black and grey
tubes of smoke, gobbled by the hot air below the moon's
thready crescent: buildings slump and crumple inwards

spurting embers, whisked away and gulped by the smoke too. There is movement everywhere on the shore, flight.

What about these others who were counting on all those burning boats to make their escapes?

*A Ghuard all in blackened, sizzling armor reels into an empty
street.*

"STOP!"

*The voice brings him all the way up and he turns toward it.
A uniformed Edek stands in the gloom at one end of the street,
her white-smocked aid at her side.*

"ATTENTION-UH!"

The Ghuard snaps to attention.

*He stands in a circle of cooling, blue white light that steadily
increases in brightness and in cold as the Edek continues seeing
him. The Edek brightens the light by darkening her own mind.
There is a cold inner suppression hollowing her, so that she
speaks and acts from her muffled face even as her awareness
still lives buried in a winter night.*

"SALUTE-UH!"

*The Ghuard salutes, his armor rattling. Steam plumes out
the snarling mouth of the ass. He is brightly illuminated now,
like a star gleaming amid all the red fire.*

"YOU WILL PUT AN ENNND-UH TO THIS ACT
OF FAITH-UH! YOU WILL ACT TO RESTORRRE! /
YOU WILL NOW / YOU WILL NOW ACT TO RESTORE

ORRRDER! YOU WILL PUT AN ENNNND / TO THIS
ACT OF FAITH-UH!"

The Ghuard turns at once and, his armor now bright and
cool, rushes purposefully back into the town.

You grope along the sandy bottom, bizarrely red and
flickering in the firelight through the water. There above you,
the aid leads the Edek onto the empty pier. The Edek keeps hold
of a pinch of the aid's smock, just above the right shoulder, as
described.

The Edek's black eyes pick you out at once, and the mouth
begins to work violently inside the cloth sack.

"NAR-RA-TIVE SPIRIT-UH! COME FORWARD-UH
AND LISTENNN! I HAVE SOMETHINNG-UH TO SAY-
UH! COME FORWARD-UH AND LISTENN!"

You climb one of the pilings until you are able to raise your
streaming head from the water. Heat billows over you from the
land, and you rise and fall with the water. The Edek bends
stiffly at the waist to stare down over the side of the pier, down
at you. She drops to her knees, thrusts a finger into one of her
black eyes, and brings it out all streaked with black.

Now she is writing with it on your face. You feel the light,
scraping sensation of her fingernail spelling TRUE TO OUR
MONARCH.

The Edek straightens up and points to where a few lights
dwindle away on the sea, toward the horizon.

"NAR-RA-TIVE SPIRIT-UH! FOLLOW NOW /
FOLLOW NOW AND ATTENND-UH! YOU WILL
SERVE-UH THE ONE MASTERR! FOLLOW NOWWW-
UH AND ATTEND-UH!"

Third Chapter

Daylight discloses land already far out of sight, blue profundities below, and a sky thickly striped with clouds that cross our line of travel at a right angle and high overhead. The clouds are curdled white and grey or fine black like dirty little heaps of slush, all in rows. Nothing all around but a mind-cancelling low hill of water sloping off to the horizon, its subtle peak travels along just beneath us. I can't tell if it is really peaceful or not. I mistrust it for its own sake and not as someone from the mountains.

I'll describe the boat, but I lack nautical language. It doesn't seem more than medium-sized to me, with a bridge up two or three ladders from the deck, that is the main deck or the one with the greatest area. There is a towerlike mast aft of the bridge, with a great profusion of riggings on it, but the ship really is powered by two impressive paddle-wheels amidships or nearly, covered in majestic sweeps of metal cowling. Paddleboxes is the word. These are driven by hinged pistons that periodically and in alternation thrust their acutely bent knees fantastically high into the air, rivalling the height of the mast; they look like the hind legs of grasshoppers taking slow thoughtful strides in alternation. The rhythmic churn of the wheels is lulling, the rotation of the frothing paddles is hypnotic, the meditative striding of the pistons is dreamy, the soft and fragrant air is narcotic. Across this reverence Saskia's voice often cuts as she barks orders from the bridge. We seem to go in one reliable direction, and we seem to move fast.

While some of the madcaps in the ranks are seasick or huddled below decks, terrified of all the open space, the majority are beside themselves with delight and excitement. They rush from one end of the boat to another with their faces wide open to every sensation, dangling from the ropes, yipping and cawing, their clothes flapping and sloughing often in defiance of decency. We're confined to the boat, smaller than the asylum was, with limitlessness all around us. After the first man overboard is retrieved at some expense of time, Saskia thunderously harangues the others:

"Go into the sea, and I swear to you you'll stay there!" she bellowed.

So far, no new splashes. Now we're pushing through a field of sea lungs, and the loonies are pointing and singing out and going ape. The boat is heavy and the strong engines lumber us forward so we seem to flatten the water as we go. The drone is oppressive. At first, I imagine I'd prefer to spend my time in the open air, but between the pummeling of the wind and the eyebrindling glare of the sky, I find myself staying inside. I can't open myself to impressions of the sea. Whenever I try, impressions of dying are what I get. Me dying. I dying. Among many others. As an officer—and that's a laugh—I am entitled to a bit of privacy. I bunk with Silichieh, Jil Punkinflake who is not an officer but counts anyway as a standard bearer, and a sleep-happy sergeant named Zept, who adheres to his berth like a clam.

The great monarch of the Alaks alone dispenses licenses to hunt the silver woodland lion. Whenever one is killed, only the head is taken. The body is carefully buried with a uniform draped over it. In exactly three days, an Edek will appear at the spot. Anyone unfortunate enough to witness this, I guess, sudden appearance, asphyxiates, and so no one can say exactly how it happens. Who cares?

Night falls, I go to the rail for some air. Up into the air, back down out of the air. Back up into the air, back down out of the air, always pursued by distaste. There is a ragged blue satin band on the horizon between the clouds and the black water. The ship is turning into a huge solid shadow, tricked out in a constellation of little lamps. Their light seems to twirl in the wind, and creates intimate, miniature islands in all the howling wildness. I'm not sick, only leaning.

I hear footsteps, and suddenly Saskia is beside me. Her hand drops heavily onto my shoulder.

"Don't be forgetful, narrator," she says. "You will remember it all, won't you?"

"Sure. Sure I will."

She's looking earnestly at me. I imagine she's thinks she's improving my morale. Has she been tapping each of the officers in turn?

That hand pats my shoulder twice, firmly.

"You will have the distinction of witnessing our glorious triumphs against the usurper, and the just punishment of traitors; and you will have the honor of telling all the world about it. And don't worry—" she raises a finger—"All are equal together in this great task. No one will hold your color against you. There is no room for bigotry amongst us."

She strides away.

I look out over the grain of the water, forgetting all about her, and a pang goes through me. I'm thinking miserably about the school, Twisse and Spiena, that each passing triangular wafer of water is separating me from. From whom each passing etc. I see the Edek's eyes glare like two cold suns—they dilate at me through holes ripped in the air, and I gasp with fear and unhappiness.

*

Jil Punkinflake tells me how Thrushchurl had been institutionalized after he set fire to a wing of the Embalmer's College.

"He kept seeing mice everywhere. Of course, there were a few. But the ones he saw were in the corners of his eyes, not in the rooms. I think he set the fire to get rid of them.

"I wasn't in attendance at the time," he adds. "Anyway, we should keep an eye on him ..."

He looks at me seriously.

"Just in case ..." he adds, and his face goes a little irregular. "I don't mistrust him—I'm just thinking of the safety of the unit."

Thrushchurl has taken up residence under some stairs; his

long knees and shanks protrude into the light. I'm looking, not watching. He's removed his silk hat; his backswept hair, split up the middle, is still pressed into a winglike pair of pancakes. The yellow gleam of his fluorescent grin is intermittently exposed, while he turns this way and that, his back to the wall, straightening out blankets, and pausing motionless from time to time, peering into a corner, or at the line where the wall meets the floor.

As Thrushchurl readies himself for sleep, he spreads his oarlike hands over the fabric of his blankets until they're perfectly flat, smudging the bypasser air with that somber rag of song that has taken up residence in his mouth. Often, he barely articulates the syllables; you get a melody of vowels only. I don't think he knows he's singing it.

"Little mice, little mice,
Even cats have got their lice,
Run-run, run get yourself away—"

"Dead as cinders, grey as ashes,
Cold as ice, now its eye flashes,
Too too late to get away—"

*

Who else has had anything to say about Meqhasset? Silichieh tells me the island's whole interior is haunted.

"It's supposed all to be ruins from another war, hundreds of years ago. Whole forests have sprung up from spilled blood."

Makemin has plenty to say, not about the island but

about the enemy, their tactics, his career. He deputizes me to copy out some of his financial papers—naturally he had no trouble taking them along—into one of the empty ship's logs, so he'll have all the information indexed, etc. The work is intolerably dull and draining. When I get the time, I set myself on Nardac, but she plainly avoids me, retires when I come near. She knows my narrator's star, maybe, and doesn't want to give her reasons for joining us. Jil Punkinflake made hesitant and breathless overtures to her, but he she spurns. At his approach, Nardac strikes the deck before her with a hand as numb and hard as a knot of wood, and he hops away in alarm.

Her preferred place is in the bow, where she has some shade and calm from the wild air. Once, as I sat waiting for Nikhinoch to give me something unimportant to do, and Thrushchurl was nearby, singing his ditty, I noticed she was looking at him, with no particular expression. With interest. But she sets herself among the idiots, who congregate around her in the prow. They mill and mewl and roll about on the deck with each other like huge, groggy kittens, as the wind dries the spit on their chins. From far away I have seen her lips moving, and I know she tells *them* things. Such a calm as hers doesn't need to speak, but she does speak, eerily.

So I eavesdrop, and hear her brief relations rapped out against the ocean's grain. The stories she tells have nothing to do with history. I provide a sample:

(An unhurried, slow inhalation.)

She was an artist (she says this in a matter-of-fact way, her eyebrows going up and her lips frowning a little). I followed her in that. I invariably begin by saying that she was an artist. I say that, but I mean that backwards. It's not that she made an art of executing, but that an artist is that, executioner. There's a kernel, a way of saying what I mean more simply than what I mean, which is that she was no functionary. The task was handed to her, but she did not merely receive that as a, as a task. (Her voice dropped there.)

Looking into her face, you wouldn't know that. You had to see her doing it, because I don't think you can imagine that. She did it with a look. She didn't look—her eyes saw everything from the inside ... when she was at it. That was like cold fervor, but no that wasn't. That was (she shook her head just a little) two things at once, you can't imagine. Enthusiasm, or mania, maybe, and dreaminess at the same time. None of it was not real to her, though. I knew that not one single thing about it was unreal. Or vague—or anything but sharp and distinct. It's ridiculous to say sharp but that's the word. When she was at it, her eyes were like black wells, with glistens all over them. (She caressed the air by her knees with stiff old hands, seeming to coax the guillotine blade out of the sparkling air so that I for a moment actually saw it.) All pupil, that seemed, staring, and seeing backwards.

And I saw her, or I watched her, you couldn't have observed her more closely than I did. I had my perches there to watch her from, that gave me a commanding view, unauthorized though. Never paid much attention to them, only to her. I saw them, naturally, but as she saw them. Or would have seen them, if she saw them from the outside, and she didn't, didn't seem to. No, she saw them inside, and I saw them outside, but I saw into her. She knew exactly how that was done, and she lived that through each of them, or that was her fantasy.

The door bursts open, taking the man completely by surprise, and almost at once the hooder claps the hood on him—they are superb at that, getting them right away. No amount of preparation on the man's part, unless he kills himself. And how can he? There's that explosive struggling. The sudden pinioning and muffling. The smell of the hood, and the brush of frayed eye holes. Pulled out in that hall, that moves forward like a ratchet one man's spot at a time. That stops. Starts. Stops. Starts. That hall has a long gap in the wall at the top, and they can see the top of gallows in the yard. They can see the chopper rise there. See it drop. See it drip. See it streaked and dripping. That smell from the door, the hall's full of it. The men struggle between their pairs of—helpers, as we called them. Cries, all of that tumult. Scraping feet. Now there's that unrelievedly plain metal door in front of him. He looks down and smells that puddle spreading out from under the door into the hall and he recoils from it. He wants that his legs would shrivel and curl up to his body in the air rather than touch his feet to it. And the smell is right up in his hood.

When that door opens, there is only the empty space between him and the gallows. All there is is that. The yard is empty. The gallows, spattered. The chill basket. It must be shattering cold. His knees buckle and his helpers hold him up. When that board indents the fabric of his trouser knees he recoils again without a sound. Or with not more than that strangled sound. They lay him down. They strap him there and stand away. He lies there on that board, his head turned on his cheek.

And now she glides across his path. She's tall and willowy, wears that loose, rough black thing. She's stately and calm, and he watches her shadow loom past him and he convulses, makes sounds. He struggles on that thirsty plank. She leans over him with the dreamy eyes and lightly checks his bonds with lean fingers. He won't hear the breath that darts swiftly in and out of her nose.

With a slam he is rammed forward, his head between the rails. His scream is all but lost in his mask. He is looking down through the mask into the sop basket. A balance is tipped—this is the part no one is ever told about—and the board spins him around face up and he sees at once that livid line and her, looming over with that well-eyed look. He sees her pull that lever. He sees the line streak down with a loud rattle.

A searing jolt. A blur. No sensation. One event. Frayed holes in the hood. The rim of the basket. That smell. Taste of blood. The light all seeps away.

She would always fling her arm around his shoulders the moment after it happened, pull that body back to keep the blade from spraying blood everywhere. Always listened eagerly then for that last exhalation of breath from the viscous stump. Then she stands back, and those two who brought him take the parts away quickly. Stuff blubbers out the cut neck, that always looked like a stuck pigskin, or wine skin, is that what I mean? The head is heavier than it looks. She takes it by the bottom of the hood, that's a bag now. It doesn't occur to her that she has blood on her gown until it cools; that's body temperature when that gets on. As you would expect.

And that's how they got her, during the fighting, when

many were brought there to be executed. She was at it all day. At night she sharpened. On and on. She started to tell them to hurry up, and crowded them together. All decorum went. For the first time, she became sloppy. She stayed, panting, by the lever. Then she climbs on that slick plank and reaches for the lever. Giggling. She was stretching her neck across that groove and groping for the lever. Stretching it out and stretching and stretching, giggling inanely. That's when they replaced her. She went to the madhouse that day, or soon.

After that, she wandered. Where is she now? (She shrugged.)

I go on eavesdropping after that, but my heart isn't in it. I don't like to listen to her any more. But, inside me, my heart is calm. Unaccountably calm. Wrongly calm. I'm remembering the fruit frozen on the trees back home; maybe there will be a thaw for me, but what will thaw me? I'm afraid of what it will take.

*

The loonies are beaming down at me from the upper deck as I stagger mindlessly to the rail in unsettling morning light. Not seasick, but I had a bad night.

"Did you enjoy the night air?"

"Refreshing, wasn't it?"

Last night, after I'd spent a full day of copying his damned papers, Makemin kept me up late telling me all about the exact nature of the enemy and their tactics and whatnot, all for the record he presumes to use me for, until my head spun. Despite my fatigue, I had a headache coming on and

I thought a wash might make me refreshed enough to sleep.

I remember starting ... dimmer and dimmer in a delirious fatigue ... and then nothing.

My throat now being completely closed, I can only make my way forward again in ignominy, with mockery at my back.

...

I see myself standing in the two hoops of my trousers on the floor, the top of my head foremost in my sight. I sink down into the boat like a ghost, until I'm through the hull and down in the water. I can feel a trivial bump as I penetrate the wood, and now I'm wafting with the errant, sluggish movements of the current, looking out into the dark fathoms. There are breasts beneath the waves, and ribbons of milk slipped in the brine, or so I think—I don't see them. Maybe a web of milk, so thin I miss it in the gloom, breaks over my face; I scent milk, and the taste appears on my palate anyway, not strong. She and I are walking down the hall.

The cloister is one section copied again and again. At the block, which overlooks a starry atrium, she is leaning thoughtfully on her elbow. I see her from a distance, and approach her reluctantly. I'd rather be alone, but the block is the only place I can go, even the spot I occupy right now is impossible, so I join her and she either doesn't notice me or accepts my presence there without any expression.

The fountain in the atrium is dry. The light in the hall is banded by strips of shadow from the stone lintels over our heads, and so her face pulses in and out of the dark, both soft in the depths. That and her hair drifts in the current and keeps falling past her face, interrupting my view. I hang on her every word, my attention riveted to her unfamiliar features. She avoids my gaze. The hall goes on and on without turning, like the same pair of doors, strictly opposite each other and both shut firm, copied over and over. There's no current, but I have to force my way through heavy water. I'm not getting tired, because I don't much feel my body, or perhaps because my attention is so entirely devoted to her, even though I am not able to follow what she says. I'm not following what she says. Her breasts brush the stone block as she turns to walk away, but the motion includes me and I know we are to walk together. The cloister has no end or turning that I can see. Only the same arches, striped dark and light, more dark than light, the same, one after another. She and I start walking down the flooded cloister, and while she talks talk I can't follow, her voice is so muffled anyway, I wait and watch as her body walks in and out of the shade. I'm trying to get a glimpse of her nakedness entire, or nearly, which is hard to do. I slip my hand around a supple waist as smooth as air, but she doesn't notice, or nothing changes, and this discourages me, so I'm no longer holding her waist anymore.

Following the ship's wake, now something in your mind bursts upward like a bird startled from its cover, to where thick clots of vapor batter the glowing and heatless moon. Now you are dragging yourself painfully, but with the weird strength of your emaciated arms and clawlike hands, across a broken crust of chalk, perforated everywhere with little cones that emit plumes of acrid steam. The landscape is like a fractured mirror, and dusty fires shake out their rags from its crevasses, scattering dust and cinders like beaten rugs. You pass a number of boiling clay bogs, and a place where scalding tar gulps in a long gouge in the ground.

We drift hand in hand down from the balcony to the floor. The ceiling here is immensely high, and that and the walls are utterly dark. In the far distance ahead there is dim moonlight, falling from high above on to a jumble of big furniture, like pews and upended wardrobes. There are windows around here somewhere as well, above and just behind me I think, that shed a blue glow with strict edges on the floor, the muted and worn scarlet carpet, plain and paper thin, beneath our bare feet.

My eyes travel up her legs. Her head is silhouetted against a window with a sill higher off the ground than I am tall. We're floating down to the floor. The water is dry and clear, with only a few grains hanging here and there. She leads me on to a suspended atrium where enormous halls converge. I think she speaks, without interruption; I hear her voice, but her words don't occur in my ear, rather I quote them back to myself as though she were reciting something I once had memorized. All the halls are dark, except the one from which we emerge, where there is a little light, and the one we face, which, after a dark interval, is illuminated with a glowing mist like the light of the full moon, shining down from what I imagine is an opening in the roof. There is a round window above us, or nearly, and off to one side, and this spreads a milky blue fluorescence around the floor here. There's a paper and glue smell, of bindings and dust, not much. The place is not in ruins.

She leads me, not especially urgently, to one of the capacitous tables, to set her bottom on the soft, brown wood. She has never once stopped her murmuring. The table is near one of this atrium's corners, which seems like the corner of a smaller, more intimate room, grafted onto this austerely magnificent one. Bars of shadow seem to hide the incongruity, the actual seams, and in the obscurity I can dimly make out a conical dung pile there. It all seems very domestic; I do detect a faint, barnyard smell coming from it. She walks a few paces ahead of me, heading for one of the tables. Now she goes around the other side of the table, and, as she turns her back to me for the first time, I notice a letter printed near the base of her spine. What's that doing there? She has another, by her shoulderblade.

From across the table, she talks to me with a businesslike, with a serious, look on her face. For a moment she seems to be spreading out a map on the table, but there is no map, and she has not leant over the table, or smoothed her hand across the thickly varnished wood. But her hand is all smeared with the brown varnish of the table. She's just talking to me, and as she turns to something behind her, some piece of furniture I can't really see except as a dark indistinctness, I notice a letter on one of her shoulderblades. It's too small for me to identify which one it is, but that it's a letter is completely obvious. Now I see she has letters all over, as neat as printing. They're small cerifed letters. As I wonder a bit about this, she is retrieving something from the tall cabinet or lectern behind her, lifting her arms and arching her back for it as the water teases her hair around her shoulders. I think about getting closer, to have a look at the printing, but I don't do it.

Just as you arrive at the lip of a crater you see a figure emerge from the pool of molten rock that fills it. The lava is hidden under a thick layer of fine grey ash, like the kind you knead in your palms here at its edge; the figure who emerges is someone you know, and who has already been speaking. You observe this figure walking along the brink, detestably talking without the slightest motion in his face; you know his whole body is a charred and brittle black mannikin. You are repelled by the heat of the melted rock, and by the stink of burning flesh this mannikin gives off; you must not be seen by this thing. You move carefully, but for all your strength you are awkward, and cannot move it seems at all without displacing tell-tale puffs of fine ash. Can it see? You were asked a question. You don't know, but it, he, just barely a he, is coming for you now. He has seen you. You are struggling to escape—he has you in his arms—

She looks at me haughtily, a sabre in her left hand. The opal, the size of a hen's egg, hanging from her throat, disappears in her bosom as she, having raised the weapon to shoulder height, sweeps her arm level, slowly across her body, until the tip of the blade points off to my right. I study the blade carefully, bending over the table so that its thick edge is like a bar across my thighs. I think she expects me to appraise it, and I find all sorts of information about it is coming up in my mind. I'm gauging its value; it's old, and well-made.

She is asking me something, if I know her name. I tell her I don't know it. She says tell me my name. Well, narrator? Give me a name.

I look up, and for a moment I can't find her. I hear the scrape of her bare feet on the dry stone flags, my eyes follow the sound, and I see the silhouette of a lock or two of her hair drift across a shadow boundary into the light. She's crouched in a corner, not far from me, facing me, and totally invisible in the dark. The corner is intimate, and seems too small to be the point of convergence for such massive walls and floors. It's like the corner of someone's parlour, or bed chamber, wedged into this larger structure. I can hear her catch her breath. She draws air in deeply, and then, after a long moment, lets it out again in a barely audible gush. Then another held breath, and another. I can hear a liquid, crinkling sound as well. There's a protracted, trembling, faint, fluid sort of noise, like a foot being extracted exquisitely slowly from thick mud.

I draw aside the heavy arras and enter the corner. She is standing in a windowed alcove lined with a tapestry. A woven man with tan eyes behind her seems ready to lean forward out of the fabric and drag her back into it. One of the windows is ajar, and the wind it admits lightly brushes her hair and the lace at her neck. She turns as I come in, locking me down with a glare of astonishment, and disrecognition.

You're the third person voice of fate, I tell her with certainty. She shakes her head, staring.

You struggle, and his body is tearing open, the brittle char is breaking up like densely packed snow, and the cooked and steaming entrails are dripping from his side, in fat, glistening white loops. You are shouting "Louce!" "Lou!" "Lulom!"—he is pressing his muttering lips to yours, and you burn and strangle, clawing wildly at him. He's trying to put words in your mouth.

Low stands naked at the rear of the boat, soap suds clinging to his skin, his right arm raised but not rigid. It's as though he were leaning it on an invisible bannister. Wind tousles his hair. The ship's wake smoothes out to nothing.

In the distance, a white something bobs on the water asleep. It slobbers and mutters as it bobs up and down. Its slobberings wriggle through the water like black eels. In a vision no one present can see, the ocean turns to fluid mirror, like mirage, where it crashes over the white figure, the mirror froth rolls away across the surface of the water like mercury and Low's outstretched hand draws the black saliva from the glistening antiseptic mouth of the sleeper to form elegant, calligraphic loops and ornate signatures of unreal sharpness on the reflecting surface. A down of phosphorescent ash spins from them as they move, forming glowing coils that sink into the black below the silver, whirring and snapping like whips. They seem to drag Low's arm to and fro.

Who is narrating this?

Hear the companion writing their reciprocal dreams made. Read the companion voice that is prosaically called the powers of the air. Conjure with them the third person, to whom this is addressed. Address the third person with *them*. Do it all as sniffed by a dead arm, as seen by a silent mouth, as heard by a stopped nose, as fingered by a deaf ear, as tasted by a blind eye, as undergone by a missing person nobody missed in the first place, and related by a ghost who somehow manages just about every time to persuade you that it presides over this switching operation between stories. Who is not dead and not alive, and who, the ghost, and this ghost was born a ghost not a living person, appears in Low when he does all its work for it, as the unknown knowledge of its name which remains hidden inside that knowledge, or as the owner's tag, hidden deep in the fur, attached to that work. These things are everywhere, one is speaking now, and its speaking is a writhing on the floor, twisting its lithe, sleek body this way and that, on its back and on its belly, as hands try playfully to seize it. It gambols. The third person squirts and slips from those hands like a lathered cake of soap, squirms like a intestine, one admires the gleam of its lushly oiled fur. And all the while it squeals out its speeches, revealing to you what it is, or what *that* is, as it is as sniffed by a dead moth, as kissed by a silent guest, as heard by a stopped charm, as fingered by a deaf parson, as tasted by a blind rose, as seen by an eye that was most often finally a ghost, and undergone by a tear or a tear who somehow happens to preside over this switching operation, if only because it can persuade you this operation happens between stories.

Pink light crimps the horizon, and there's a sudden wind. The white figure wakes and plunges out of sight. Low's arm drops. Still asleep, he walks to his bunk and pulls the sheet over his head. The third person cries out in terror at the sight of this sheeted form.

*

We'd left in a hurry, with many more on board than would normally be permitted, so we find ourselves inadequately supplied. I have to pick my way from one side of the boat to another, as the decks are jammed with sprawling madmen and soldiers with visors down on their noses. They get to rest; I have to copy. Nikhinoch pertly informs me we are making for Uithui, already visible a low broad mound in the indigo shade by the horizon, there to replenish our water reserves and lay in fresh and more copious food.

Thrushchurl is sitting with the loonies, Jil Punkinflake is puppy-dogging after Saskia, and Silichieh labors nearly every waking moment below decks, putting the forward batteries into better working order.

Makemin's fanaticism is nothing like Saskia's. She is a true believer; her way of seeing things is so abstract it's frightening. To her way of thinking, the other Yesegs, who simply remained loyal to Tewsetonta, as anyone would have, are traitors whose mere existence is an unbearable affront to her personally. Makemin strikes me as a man incensed to ruthlessness by a neverending succession of frustrations, disappointments, and thwarted ambitions. An intense, chronic irritability never quits him, and for all his collectedness and self-possession he nearly always seems only a step or two short of desperation. These are the people in command here.

In the mess ... I take in a traditional slogan, printed on a banner that sways a little on the wall. "I'm not hungry!" It refers to an old melodrama; someone must have dragged me off to see it when I was still at the orphanage. One of the asylum soldiers sits in the corner diagonal to me. He is neatly dressed in civilian clothes, with an incongruous metal gorget and a broken-butt pistol shoved in the band of a broad belt around his hips. His presence is discouraging, and I saunter dejectedly from the mess and back to my uninviting bunk. I have to take advantage of this brief respite from Makemin's papers.

Lying there, again I feel stifling warmth, just this side of making me break into a sweat. My hand drops to the floor, and brushes there a litter of books. I take one up ...

... the book slinks to the floor from fingers. I let my eyelids droop, and fantasize a warm round-shaped lizard or dragon, with a body like marzipan ... peach yellow and flame orange and dusted all over with powdered sugar, it slithers happily along a bank of fire grooved into a green mountain

... The disaster is that the end has already happened, and we have survived it, no one knows when or what it was, there was no *event*—over time, the world ended, and yet here we all are with no world.

*

The island is about ten hands' breadths wide now. I'm on deck, watching it grow; I smell petals, and moist green, in with the scent of fermenting brine and creosote from the ship.

Now my eye is drawn to something in the water, that's white but not brilliant, not a flash of reflected sun, and no piece of foam—and from where, when all is so dim and still? It's only just beneath the surface—it rises and falls in place with the current. And now it's moving, suddenly and deliberately, in a straight line, diverging sharply with our course, going off to my left, whatever that is—starboard I suppose. It's alive—is it getting itself away from us? I scan the approaching beach. A dark meltingness by the tops of the trees there at the edge of the beach, at the corner of the island. Now it's gone. I peer ... and there it is again. Black smoke. I stop Nikhinoch, who is smartly trucking to and fro as usual—he screws up his face and squints out past the tip of my pointing index finger through his glasses. He starts, and at once we are both, for some reason both, going to Makemin. He peers through his goggles—

"I see ships. More than one. On the far side," he says, turning to climb to the bridge.

I notice we are shifting course. Now the island, which had been approaching us a bit to the right, port?, is creeping to the center of the horizon ... now to the left of us. But we are not approaching—we must be going around to the far side ...

Here the shore is pinched out into a short tongue protruding into the ocean and as the trees that line it thin out our motion reveals a small bay with two steam launches at anchor not far apart. One's half our size, the other slightly smaller.

Saskia bellows at sight of them and our prow immediately swings hard upon their direction. Smaller steam launch is the farther of the two, and as we round on the bay its stacks gush smoke and it backs water. The other ship is slower getting started. Makemin gives my shoulder a squeeze and turns his attention to the other sharpshooters, arraying them with gestures along the railings in those places where the rail is solid. He clearly wants me by him, watching for posterity. The men charge the rail actually colliding with it guns already level, eyes straining down the barrels. They've been drilled to death for this kind of thing. Looking down I can see Silichieh through the open bow hatches, stripped to the waist and covered with grease he is loading the forward batteries with amazing speed. Thrushchurl above him on deck, holding the gun site; it's a brass thing like a tube with a wire across the glass. Thrushchurl's vision is keen, and I suppose they know it.

The bigger steamer wallows around away from us and a few puffs of smoke dash off on the wind as the guns on its decks fire on us. I hear a sharp crack somewhere behind me. Saskia is cursing them—her voice shakes the wheelhouse like a trapped animal. The loonies are capering and running from one end of the boat to another, except where the soldiers beat them and drive them back. Nikhinoch is trying to put up a barrier to cordon off the sharpshooters' area, where I am.

Thrushchurl sings out in a strange voice and the forward batteries explode, shaking the boat. I clap my hands to my ears and fall down, but I don't miss the big steamer buckling up the middle and then our ship lunges and a sound slaps my face, the water around the bow thrashes and the blow rips the big steamer's sides and topples its stacks toward the water. Makemin puts his goggles on his eyes and then ratchets down his visor sights, the next moment, he gives the shooters the command to open fire. I see blackbirds drop from the rails, another eruption that knocks me back to the deck so that I stay there—the big steamer is listing hard to one side exposing the hull below its waterline. Our bow is heavily grinding out to sea again, that's to port. Figures race along the beach and bound into the tree line. The sharpshooters are still firing and I see some dark figures drop on the sand, flop half in the bushes or half in the surf. The men are crushing themselves against the rails to get their guns closer. I see Saskia leaning out of the wheelhouse emptying her pistol at the shore—her mouth is pulled back but her lips are slack, her eyes staring and blank. A figure on the shore is running to and fro uncertainly and flings up its hands. Saskia lowers her arm and shoots it. Even from here I can see the tuft fly from its head before it sinks backward to bloody the sand. It seems impossible she could have hit him from so far away. They're all shooting wildly at the beach like they must unburden themselves of the mercurial killing power that they were charged with, and until then, no real words, spoken or unspoken. Only grunts and curses.

We are passing the big steamer—I can hear it groan as the timbers split, it is breaking in half. Cries of anguish rise from its flooding decks, faces sink into the sea.

Distant horns are audible now the shooters have stopped. Makemin drags me with him as he makes his way angrily up to the wheelhouse. Saskia is barking insults and random commands to an empty bridge.

"Make for their station!" he points to the island, to a pale regularity dimly visible through the trees. "Before they man their batteries!"

Our course is out to sea, our prow exactly in line with the fleeing, smaller launch.

Saskia flashes glassy eyes at Makemin over her shoulder— "We can handle their batteries!"

"Turn inland at once!"

"We'll be on them in two minutes! I won't lose them!"

"You will turn inland at once!"

"They'll go to the warships!"

Makemin stands nearly tiptoe and livid. Saskia turns back to the wheel, then flips her head at him again.

"Two minutes!"

And then—

"Why have one when you can have them all?"

Makemin thinks for a moment, then quits the bridge, his face white with fury. Moments later, we are back again among the sharpshooters. The small steam launch is nearly lost in its own wildly careering, wind-torn smoke. Thrushchurl crows again and the batteries explode. The smaller steam launch didn't even get out of the lee of the island. Its rear end vanishes in splinters and the entire fore end of the boat pivots straight up in the air and stays there. Now it is listing. Now it crashes on its side. Now it rolls over. Heads bob in the water. I see a two blackbirds uncannily sliding sideways across the top of the waves toward the island, veering like skaters. Makemin, his whole body palpably tensed, lifts his rifle and splatters them both. They drift—just above the waves.

Uithui swings in front of us again. Distant burps of smoke lift from a low level rampart embedded in the beach, adjacent to a pier and floating platform. Blackbirds are running here and there on the beach or fling themselves flat. Under Saskia's control, the boat plunges head on toward the station. With a sound that hits me like a blow to the stomach something strikes the water not ten feet from us sending up a thick fraying column of white water as high as the bridge. Another comes a bit farther away only a moment later. Though hopelessly out of range, Makemin begins firing mechanically at the distant station, and many of the sharpshooters join him. The clappers have finally gathered on the upper deck— how long has it been?—where protection is minimal, and have started their droning and knocking.

Some men emerge from below with two Bremml guns and are frenetically busy bolting them to their swivel mounts on the foredeck. Another crash of spray—now the boat shudders and I feel something pepper my back and neck—splinters—looking up, I see one of the forward booms or whatever they are has been sheared off, a jagged stump is left dangling on its sinews of rigging.

The level white station comes toward us, seeming to list like a drunken antagonist, spitting puffs of smoke at us, lobbing shells. Plumes of water proliferate all around the boat, crashing and rending wood and metal in a noise that never stops, and screams of men, continuous screams of men, a gullet-clogging stink of blood, stifling smoke ... The asylum soldiers are hooting and wailing—I can see one cringing behind a barrel bawling his eyes out and kneading his face with his hands. Others are shrieking imprecations at the shore, leaping up the rigging to get a better view, they bellow and gnash their teeth, cheer and masturbate and fall in fits, some flinging themselves over the sides, hurtling past our position on the middle deck, and swim frantically for the shore—some plainly in a panic, others with knives in their teeth or hatchets in their hands, I see one holding a frying pan above the water as if he didn't want to get it wet, wild-eyed and furious with violence, wanting to throw themselves bodily on the enemy. Somewhere in it all I hear Thrushchurl's chanticleer note, and our forward batteries fire—through distant clots of smoke streaking away in the wind I see the station is now ragged and blackened—although now there are more plumes around us ... another thud throws me from my feet.

Bruised and a little crazy I get up again and start looking around for injured to help, but I can't stop watching the station. The front of our ship blurs and throws a shotput of smoke up and out, and I see the top of the station flip clear off and back, the upends of huge black beams thrown this way and that. We are close enough now there's no mistaking the alarms, and screams coming on the soft air from the fragrant woods not two hundred yards away. The Bremml guns are clanking, the fire is continuous, men in regular movements breach loading shells the size of my forearm from lead boxes. Crash of thunder from the battery and the station seems to settle and subside like a collapsing horse—

faint, irregular and unceasing motion of fire inside it, visible through its gouged walls. Then a thump I feel more than I hear—their powder store going up—the walls race away on all sides and the remainder of the roof falls flat in, throwing out an ash cloud. Only then do I become aware of the ringing shots of the sharpshooters, and Makemin near to me, as they pick off the remnant, fleeing into the trees.

*

People are going over the side; Nardac stands clutching the rail, staring at the beach—the crumpled bodies littering the spattered sand transfix her. As the men go over, and the boats go out, she is tugged toward them irregularly as though a cable were yanking at her.

"Are you going ashore?" I had meant to say something a little different, but I can't think straight.

And she looks at me so that I feel vertigo; I stand on the brink of eyes like pits filled with crumpled bodies, and she says, "Yes."

Nardac moves a foot or so, leaning heavily on the rail going hand over hand, and the next moment she falls. Her dark garment glistens down the side that had been away from me. I kneel and pull at it, and the rent fabric slides apart to expose a red leg, torn open along the flank. Nardac is struggling weakly to move toward the gangway as I begin cleaning her wound; I withdraw many heavy splinters. Her flesh is smooth and flimsy with age. I don't know how long I work at her, but she passes out before much time had passed. A soldier and I carry her to a bunk.

The beach is cleared and the spoils of enemy stores,

crates of provender and casks of fresh water, are swiftly brought aboard. We endure some delay in retrieving the crazies who swam ashore; they took to the trees like apes or children released on holiday, frisking in the branches and capering on the sand, bits of asylum rag and uniform flung off everywhere. If anyone ever finds them, who will be able to guess how they got here, and from where?

I notice a scrap of regimental fabric at a cave mouth and thoughtlessly step forward to investigate when Silichieh catches me up short by the collar.

"Are you stupid? Enemy soldiers might be inside!"

As I glance back at him in passing alarm I catch sight of Thrushchurl, who stands nearby.

"There's no war here," he says flatly, squinting up into the grey glare of the sky. And in among the trees and rocks on all sides the crazies are crying and fleeing, foraging, straying into ambitious architectural political or cartographic projects ...

*

In the mess. Jil Punkinflake is going on about how she looked at him today. How should I go about telling him how much a fool he's making of himself? It's his right to, anyway—being sensible never did me *so* much good.

He leaves us. He's held back, or so he thinks, giving her time to I don't know what. He doesn't want to seem over eager. He doesn't want to importune her. We snicker half-heartedly behind his back, more in embarrassment than mirth once he's gone, but I find I love him better for that naive hope; and after all I don't know she won't take pity on him. At least he's not so afraid, or ashamed, as he had been. How did I come to think that *I'm* so old and sage?

I think of the one I left, back in Tref.

"I don't understand it," Silichieh is saying. "I can't get around her voice."

Of course we have nothing to do with it, and that's good.

"Just smile and nod," I say, feeling surprisingly base. "We smile and we stay always careful. So we happy people are shits."

He tells me about an engagement that fell through for him, years ago.

"So she goes to meet my superior officer and prevail on his noble sentiments to increase my commission, and she falls for him right there. She was a beautiful girl, he liked her too, and *he* married her instead. She thought she was too good for me anyway. So what's good?"

She's here, like an apparition before my eyes. I can feel her palpability in my chest. What is this—did I forget her? What is it about her that visits me now? It's as though her skin presses my mouth.

I go out on deck. The asylum soldiers are having an impromptu sabbat toward the rear of the ship, by moonlight. I stand alone up to one side of the bow, in the drone of the engines and the everlasting splashes and the relentless wind. Gradually I notice singing; like any idiot I have to see whatever it is I hear, so I start turning my head this way and that. It's coming from the bridge; Saskia and Makemin, it must be. They sing in unison one of those starkly melancholy songs easterners associate with the ocean. All about dying resolutely.

Suddenly I'm overwhelmed by a feeling, it's equal

parts fear and despair, choking me a like piece of sinewy butcher's meat lodged in my throat, and making me gulp involuntarily again and again.

First his voice, and then hers, sounds the more strongly in my ear, and each time, each one sounds crazier. They're both hermetically sealed, each in his and her own insane life.

*

The preoccupation of my other friends compels me to seek out Thrushchurl's company, and I'm getting accustomed to him these days. We're sitting together in the galley beneath a couple or three tilty lanterns, and we hit on the subject of dreams, or it is handed to us somehow.

I recount my dream of last night to him:

I'm at the rail, gazing out over the water, toward a horizon that's hidden behind a bank of fog. Suddenly, I'm afraid. I imagine the fog creeping by steady degrees to overflow us, of becoming lost in it. A disaster is rolling along in the fog. I almost seem to see it now through the fog, a colossal, humped thing moving swiftly, the size of a fist from here, although it must be at least ten miles away.

This is a legendary thing, I somehow know; for a thousand years, ships under archaic flags have ventured reluctantly through banks of warm fog. Then there is a muted rumbling. The ship turns and sails away from the sound; men rush to stoke up the engines or to ready the guns. In despair they know the legend is true, and they're about to see it.

"Bonant!" I hear a man cry. That's its name, utterly new to me in the dream.

Now it looms like a cliff, projecting suddenly above

them, too high to see. It's like a black egg with an opening in the front—it sweeps toward them, as oblivious to them as a passing god, but the men are suddenly quailing and dizzy. They vomit, collapse clutching their chests and abdomens. Blood drips from their skin, smears their teeth as the gums burst, and they die under the influence of that black ship's mere proximity. In its wake, boats full of corpses chug on into the fog until their boilers grow cold, sails fall in tatters. In the distance, the black dome is already far away, majestically descending the staircase of the horizon and shrouded in the fog it has worn a thousand years, patrolling for a navy now all at the bottom of the ocean.

I see the opening in the front of the egg, or the dome, from the inside. I take a spidery path across bare colorless soil, framed in dead trees, under the hood.

Now the floor bends upwards in a vast impetuous sweep. Gazing up, I trace its contour to where it eventually joins the curve of the dome at a right angle, and then off to the right, where it folds out to form a partial, tapering cylinder. Even the roughest reckoning tells me this is in the middle of what must be the rear wall of the domed area, opposite the opening.

I go into the wall. There's an incongruously intimate, round atrium in here, bare floors dusted with fine sand. Nothing to see but the same gritty, charcoal-colored metal. It has an earthy, metal smell. Unusual for a dream, to experience smells.

Climbing a spiral ramp, I can soon look out through square windows cut into the metal at the white window, which shines like a beacon up there. The switchbacks get shorter, the lower sill creeps up into my view, and I am able to peer in. My eyes are stabbed by the light. I wince and rub at them, blinking tears, so that my face begins to ache almost at once with the effort of seeing in through the glass.

Beyond is a bare, square apartment with a vaulted ceiling, crawling with transparent, glassy fires. Nearly everything blazes with an intense white brilliance that scrambles. The ceiling is streaked—it's streaking, it's a band of metal in continuous motion, every now and then a black gap appears in it, drifting back from above the window to the rear of the chamber, and from the gap a jet of gas escapes, scatters the fires and batters them into the extremities of the room. The fires scurry aside like rats.

There is a table immediately before the window; the table has a dark glass upon it, teeming with small, many-colored points and streaks of light.

Behind the table, the captain is sitting, and those cold, clear silver fires fitfully ensleeve his entranced form, seep and play in a trembling film across his skin.

He is naked, with long heavy white limbs. His massive body sits, like a sack of grain, on a marble cenotaph. His broad head looms forward over the glass, watching it intently, without the slightest downward inclination. The eyes have no irises, and the small, shockingly black pupils are craned down at the panels below his hands, which rest weightily on the silver. His features are pronounced, a long wide nose with flaring nostrils, strange lips, a strong chin, and buckling brow furrowed with muscles. His hair ripples back from it like peaks of white flame, down to where his feet are indifferently disposed on the floor. The glare seems to shine through him; his colorless skin seems tenuously thin, and his bleached muscle, wanly shadowed with a lace of veins and arteries, looks like parboiled horse meat. The regular pulsation of his blood is visible, and seems to coincide exactly with the light in the glass.

Now he moves his right hand to adjust a brass tab; it's his first movement, and it rattles me badly, though it is unhurried, unthreatening, and only his hand and forearm are moved. It's as though a statue were suddenly to adjust its position—without therefore becoming a person, you understand?

He is staring ahead, through the glass—not at me, but out to sea, through the distant aperture above the bow. Now I am him, staring down from his place as the prow rams a toy warship, and I remotely hear the crash as its hull cracks, the explosion as its engines blow up, splintering the aft half of the boat. A warship is crushed and sunk in a moment, but up here there isn't so much as a vibration. You could sleep through it. Bonant just does this, ploughing along through the waves, rolling over ships and sending hundreds and hundreds of men sinking to the bottom.

I am on the deck of a doomed ship—I see the implacable prow bearing down on us, Bonant towering over like a mountain—with a deafening blast the ship is struck, the deck flips and everything flies in all directions with terrifying abruptness, men and gear and pieces of strong bulkheads ... the ship is flattened almost at once into the sea, borne down below Bonant's keel, men and trash sucked down with the mass to drown under Bonant's keel that closes its coffin lid over men, ship, and all, in an instant, flattening warships like a foot flattens grass. Up here, perhaps that hand moves to adjust a brass tab, and some small matter of light changes on the glass, nothing else.

As I tell all this, Thrushchurl is sitting with his back to

the wall and his face in darkness. I can make out the slender glitters of light on his teeth.

"I had a dream!" he says, as though he'd not ever thought so until now. "I saw a warship."

"Ours or theirs?" Silichieh asks conversationally.

"Nobody's," he says.

He sketches it hastily and hands me drawing after drawing, as soon as he finishes them. With a cold spatter of rising hair all over me I recognize it.

"I stood on the deck and I watched it," his shoulders raised and lowered in a sigh. "I knew that it was older than the Limiters. I simply knew it. It has watched over this sea for thousands of years. And when it first embarked, there was land, and an important city, near here. This was the coast. All under water now though. Just empty waves now."

He smiles for an instant.

"That ship kills with its light. It can't be seen. The light is invisible."

Silichieh looks over my shoulder at the drawings, takes them in his hands and switches aghast one to another. In astonishment, he says, "That was Bonant."

Thrushchurl stares intently at him.

"Don't you know its name? You must have heard about it somewhere."

Thrushchurl shakes his head a little, more in confusion than negation.

"Well, 'banaut' is Wiczu for 'enemy,' or 'monster' ..." I say.

Silichieh shrugs expressively.

"It's all forgotten sooner or later, anyway."

He thinks for a moment.

"You didn't see its captain?" he asks after a moment.

Thrushchurl's face kindles with memory. "Yes I did!"

He closes his eyes, turns his torso, his hands in the air before his chest as though he were playing a piano, showing how he turned.

"I saw a star far above me and ahead. There he was. He was in the light. It can only be seen there, on the bridge. It shines all around the ship, though—" he cups his hands in the air as if he held the ship like a ball, "—and kills whatever comes near."

"And him?"

"The captain ...? He's part of it!" Thrushchurl is excited. "It shines through him, and he inured to it. He *has* to stay in it—he can't leave it and live—he stays in it to *stay* alive!"

"Did you get a good look at him? Did you see his face?"

Thrushchurl thinks, and nods, not looking at Silichieh.

"I saw him! I didn't come close, but I saw him through the light, and it was as if I stood right by him. He was sitting at a table by the window, looking down over the trees toward the mouth, from high up. He was all washed out, and naked. His skin was like powder; I could see the muscles, everything, through it. His muscles were grey, like parboiled horseflesh."

Again Thrushchurl smiles. He shakes his head admiringly, and gasps a little.

"Did he say anything?"

"No," Thrushchurl looks disappointed. "I don't feel he could speak."

*

The giant, the slovenly glutton who has his straw stuck

down into my chest, sucks idly at me with a rattle in the tube, and my whole body is weighted down like under a lead blanket. He swings his tassles back from his head; he has a mouth of fishhook teeth in swollen satiny gums, an unearthly inhuman voice, the haunting, disembodied third-person talk that never stops slobbering. "The book of life." It always needs an avenue like that.

He eyes me sadly and explains, with hopeless malice, "This isn't my true language, or even the language I'm speaking to you now, you know. My real language is fo di spurdzem mo mon fi litourn ap—"

And where I had lain paralyzed all this time now I struggle wildly to escape this gibbering, as if it were the quintessence of all horrors, all my strength rising in me only to be consumed instantly ...

A blizzard—snow falls from my face like soap bubbles, as though I were fizzing away—and everything screams memory memory at me, but it's as though memory doesn't work unless it's all in one piece, so that one memory depends on all the others like a house of cards. This one, now, doesn't. This is somebody else's memory—it is someone else's memory of being me.

The snow coils and bounces as it falls, the whole mass rippling gelatinously in a beautiful, sourceless snowlight. One—not me exactly—imagines a snow world saturated with limpid lightsyrup and light shining through light. Imperturbable trees in a swarm of light shed by a milky low sky. Buildings seen from the train emerge and vanish in intensely calm, shimmering white ... in a silent activity I'm being hollowed out. It's a village. Silhouettes, anonymous and uniform, stagger by the walls, stiff arms swinging in streets the snow has erased. I wake and escape through the door into the dim day; cross to the rail, and see a patch of slush, or some white thing, on the waves.

This brutal sleep pushes everything else aside, bullying me with its demands. A soul in this body, or is there only body? Once a crisis, but now that I'm older, these two ideas lie locked together in an iron sleep. Back in my bunk I can't get away from the heat of my pillow and my blanket, and I can't tolerate the touch of the air. I shake out of my skin and back into the darkness, close, hot-and-stifling. I hear the dark; it drones at me.

Alarms jangle me awake even though I wasn't asleep and I stagger again to the door. Soldiers streak this way and that, crane over the railing and then dash off frantically. A woman I don't know pulls me from the doorway and propels me a little along the wall, saying "Come on."

Her level voice kicks away the last drugs of sleep—"My medic's bag—" I mumble, rushing back for it.

She's gone when I return, and I proceed in the direction she took. Through the alarm I hear faint thuds and now my heart is pounding. I come round the paddle wheel cowling and out to the foredeck—a warship in the distance. Crash of spray as a ball gouges the water between us.

I look up. Cold air, white fog, white dark sky, dark and bright at once. Soldiers near to me pointing and shouting in alarm—past their pointing fingers spots are moving deliberately on the horizon. Two far off and one in the middle distance and we're heading nearly straight into them. Angling away from us, a steel-flanked cruiser larger than our ship is trying to bring its broadside to bear. Its outlines shiver a moment and now crashing erupts on all sides, gouts of foam as the sea face is mauled by their shot, rags of spray all over, but no jar, no hitting. I dash for the steps trying to find my usual refuge with Makemin, running half doubled over—as I climb, a flapping mass flies past the top of my head arcing down over the side. Saskia strikes the water feet-first and sinks only as far as her waist. She kicks her feet vigorously and begins to rise and move weirdly along the surface as I look down on her from nearly over her head. She has on her Yeseg legbands, and she bounds sideways across the water in a long arc, swinging her out toward the nearest enemy ship.

A couple of soldiers are trying to force or unhinge the hatch to the wheelhouse, and another looks speculatively around to its front windows, meditating an attempt to climb in? Saskia has a loyal following among the former asylum inmates; she's set one of them at the helm, and he has locked and wedged all the hatches, sealing himself in. He stands singing and cackling gaily as we streak in toward the enemy ships, cannonballs splattering all around. Every now and then he seizes hold of the clapper belonging to the brass bell that hangs near the wheel, jangling it and screeching. A ball rips the froth within ten feet of the bow on our side and even Makemin jerks. I see Nardac scramble crabwise from her bed, crawling and keeping the weight off her injured leg, to duck into the mess.

The hatch gives way. The mad helmsman spins, a knife in his hand, his eyes glassy, his mouth a line. He looks back and forth—a thud I can feel in my gut and the boat wallows from side to side.

Makemin shouts, "Bring us around!"

Saskia's man steers us hard on the enemy. From the

window I see Saskia herself darting across the water. The blackbirds are shooting at her. She zig-zags with astounding speed and in the next moment is right alongside them. She whirls around toward the rear of the boat, gesticulating wildly, then suddenly hurtles back toward us in fantastic back and forth curves, her legs pumping. Blackbirds on the deck behind her—sharpshooters' guns crackle from our upper decks. I see silent bodies drop on the distant enemy ship. Then an eruption in the back of the ship, and a second and third—grenades she'd thrown. She's halfway back now, and in all the grey and blue and tossing white froth there is a shock of livid red, fire snickering up from the battered rear deck of the enemy ship. Something whips down in a short arc and the collision throws me from my feet—I grab the wall. I scuttle away from the window. Loony at the wheel is jumping up and down hooting and laughing and ringing the bell. I still haven't heard the forward battery. A rattle on the roof, Saskia drops in through the broken hatch slopping with water, is nearly flung aside as another jolt bats us in a roll to port. She strides haggardly to the helm and peels her man off of it—

"Tell them to get stoking down there!" she rumbles, her voice tired, body sopping.

Another bang—this one hard, I can hear splintering. I cower by the floor, clutching at a pipe in the wall.

Makemin's face in mine—"Get down to the battery!"

I know I'm looking at him as though he'd asked me my favorite dance, but I go, scrambling down the steps and the boat that had been so steadily solid yaws freakishly under me. Panicked faces and the leers of the madmen screeching imprecations from the deck. Silichieh's head and shoulders plunged into the gun truss or whatever it is—an X-shaped brace with a gun at each extremity and a pivot thing in the middle and that's what seems to need work at the moment. He pulls his head out to switch tools, sees me, and tells me to hand him this and that. The ship jerks violently to the side as though it weighed nothing and I hear his head knock on the metal. He curses. I help him work. Suddenly he snaps the compartment closed and races past me.

"Help!" he says, his breath fast, his eyes glassy.

We're loading shells into the gun. I'm to toss the shells to him from the box they come in and he'll put them in and shoot the gun. He jams two lumps of wax in his ears and hands me a pair—I do the same. There's some business with a lever and a kind of trolley-cart that carries the shells over to him and I have to pull them down by hand from the cart, keep the next cart ready etc. The guns are loaded, and he springs up on the X his legs spreadeagled standing on the guns, back bent, aiming somehow. The barrel ends protrude from the deck, but we can't see anything outside the hold—a targetter has to direct the fire from above. Thrushchurl is up there, not looking especially alarmed, staring through the site, and Silichieh is breathing with his whole body, his thick arms hold him in place over his head as the boat rocks. Another stiff one and the ship groans loudly, feels like it's listing back.

Thrushchurl sings something and Silichieh instantly yanks a lever firing the first gun—the crash deafens me my ears ringing. He is whirling wheels and adjusting his aim frantically, his face drawn, grinning, his movements electric—the second gun fires, then the third—I am clutching my ears—but I remember to ready the next shells.

He fires all four guns, then reloads all like lightning and pulls the one trigger that will set them all off at once, the chamber dips—like a demon Silichieh is laughing reloading and firing all four guns at once again and again, standing right in the crossing of the X as they go off and shunting back with them as they fire.

*

... He's sitting with his legs out, his belly rolling in and out, his eyes staring, his back to the greasy base of the smouldering guns. I stagger out, shaking my head. There's cavorting on deck. Feet dance among motionless human forms. The enemy ship is a clot of flames and smoke. I'm splashed with brine as I pass the men dumping buckets to cool the Bremml guns. Numbly I respond as I am waved over to help an eviscerated man who dies under my hands. His eyes are white as snow, in a face the color of grey felt. A few other injuries to see to. I can hear again, mostly. Overhead our stepping grasshopper legs are still unscathed, and lunge and soar driving us forward at our top speed. Saskia is gripping the wheel, her face ashen, her mouth tight, confronting Makemin who lours down at her. She steps toward him raising her fist and he seizes her under the arms and shakes her so hard her helmet flies off.

"*We can't fight them all! at! once!*" he roars.

The other two ships are much closer now—it's not over—they're coming on with a speed that's terrible to see, and both of them warships. Already they've begun firing their bow guns at us.

Makemin thrusts her back, and she turns angrily to the

wheel, gripping it so tightly I can hear the wood creak in her hands. Her head is down.

"They *will* die some day," I hear her say in a bitter undertone. Makemin stands in the middle of the bridge like a post.

"We aren't fast enough," Jil Punkinflake says—I hadn't noticed him. He's been hiding by the other hatch, and watches out through a loophole toward the aft end of the ship.

We all turn our heads at once to him, and I think we all realize he's right at the same time. No sound now but the groaning of our engines, and the distant, irregular but constant effusions of the gaining guns behind.

"There's that fog bank over there ..." Thrushchurl says, softly through his grin. He points with his long duelling-pistol of a hand.

Again all our heads turn—a fogbank ahead and to port, with a black thread underlining it. I feel something nameless and freezing blanket my face and front like a chilled mold. This is a fear utterly unlike the fear of battle that I've been getting used to not getting used to. Makemin takes one step forward—

"We'll make for it."

Saskia angles the ship into the bank. I watch, paralyzed, as the point of our bow turns, and that black underline begins steadily to approach, to broaden, to extend toward us.

The fog closes around us with a flap. It's dense and warm, with a heady, iron smell, nothing like the sea. We churn forward, and in the greater silence of the fog, the reports of the enemy guns are muffled.

"There," Thrushchurl says, starting forward suddenly

and pointing again, his face rapt, "Look there!"

I would have thought it was a thunderhead sweeping low to the water if I hadn't seen it before. Through sheets of vapor my eye discerns the faint silhouette of a dome the size of an island, moving in the fog. It is going across our course.

"Call to it ..." Thrushchurl murmurs.

Nikhinoch is in the hatch, his eyes enormous in his glasses.

"It's veering toward us," he says flatly.

"Turn," Makemin says in the same tone in the same instant and Saskia's turning is simultaneous. The fog before the bow lightens; we are turning out of the bank.

The fog thins. The engines are still pumping all out, though the planks of the decks are smoking. I stare down the length of the ship. A round blackness is there in the fog behind us, and suddenly I'm dizzy ... I have to get back inside, step over the threshold stumbling, nearly falling, but Thrushchurl is there, my arm in his sinewy hand, holding me up. His breath is a little short, his grip slightly trembling, his grin wavering with billows of an overpowering feeling.

A confusion of cannonfire from behind us. We emerge from the fog as the sun is setting, a brilliant silver scar opposite the cloud in our rear. There are no more enemy shots trailing after us. A ragged chuckle escapes slowly from Saskia's unsmiling lips.

"I told you they were going to die."

Fourth Chapter

A voice is calling to me. It shouldn't be so still that I could hear such a soft voice, calling out so quietly, but just at the moment things are truly still. I step onto the deck.

A wall of water is coming. I can hear it absorbing all sound. I turn from it, with no feeling or thought at all.

Halfway on the stairs to the upper decks I am slapped to the bulkhead churned up in darkness I spin and a great sucking indrawing pulls me back—air and light burst about me again as the water sluices away in recoil from our alien boat leaving me where I cling to the twisted handrails, a hacking in my throat like a hand chopping and chopping at my neck.

The ships rocks and shouts out from everywhere. A hissing mass of infuriated water seethes up onto the deck again breaking its teeth against the metal and the deck—Tabliq Quibli's drawn face flashes by in its suction his hand reaching for one of the railing's slender posts and fails to grasp it I lunge through the railings and seize a fistful of his jacket yanking him back, watch his frantic hand snap tight on a bar and together we pull him onto the stairs and up toward the bridge as the next wave wells up from the lower deck to engulf us in its weight—we are buoyed up a moment, then hauled down. My body is half in the rails and the rail is cutting me in two. I can't think for the racing along my head, the icy fingers of water raking my face—Thrushchurl's long-wristed reach has me as the wave gathers itself in again and he pulls strenuously, helping Tabliq and I up to the bridge deck.

Sea wrack and foam flock in the air around us up here. The sky is calm, but the sea around us is suddenly insane and the ship is wrenched and buffeted. A report like a cannon shot and I turn in time to see the mast break off and drop sickeningly overboard. We huddle together against the sealed bridge, bracing ourselves against the boxes welded to the deck and spray barks and sizzles at us from the brink and rampages on the steps we'd just escaped, but little of the water as yet can make it this high.

The bridge is filled like a basin with seawater. Suddenly Saskia rears up out of the water—I can hear her hoarse and straining breath rasp deep in her chest. She plunges braving water and tilting unlevel boards beneath her feet throwing herself on the wheel and turning it wildly into the waves.

The next blast of water throws us nearly sideways and Tabliq's knee bats my solar plexus. We roll back as the water recedes and now as I gasp for breath I look down at black anger laced there with white steam—the next wave strides beneath us and the ship lurches revoltingly but with less violence; we are hurtling along now against the grain of the waves—Saskia will hold us there.

The bow slashes open the waves like an axe and the shreds are bashing back against us on the upper deck. A wallop swats me against the bulkhead knocking my head angrily against the metal. I cry out, and gesture to Thrushchurl that we might try to get into the refuge of the wheelhouse. As the prow dips into the gulf between waves we drag ourselves over the sills and are immediately tossed to the rear of the compartment. Saskia has her feet planted forward and is holding the wheel braced there, snarling half-choked curses at the froth that belabors and bruits her to her face as she holds the bow into the ridges. The deck suddenly jerks to one side and I hear a cry near at hand—Jil Punkinflake is cowering with his dog in the corner, sobbing uncontrollably, his arms around the dog, who looks up plaintively at us. Thrushchurl moves at once to Jil Punkinflake, crossing the flooded bridge with apelike swings of the arm grabbing pipes and struts whatever will keep him. The ship pivots down into another trough.

In the light flashing between tufts of flying water I see Jil Punkinflake has a bad gash in his forehead—I make my way over to Jil Punkinflake and lash my kerchief to his wound. He calms a bit more at my touch, but he is cold as ice and trembling. The ship bucks forward and I am flung headlong toward the bow, water rummaging in my eyes ears nose mouth—my outflung hand finds a purchase on a windowsill; I pull myself back into the air with gushing sinuses and streaked eyes.

I am looking up and along the ship, aft. As my ears drain I hear explosions, shouts—I look for fire, smoke, wondering about the boiler. Makemin is up there, lashed with lengths of chain to the rail of the bridge deck. Below, I can see men roiling on the decks in confusion and some of them are making movements toward the lifeboats on that side.

"Cowards! Cowards! Get away from there!"

Shied to and fro by the motion of the ship, and rammed against the railing again and again, Makemin is screaming at them and blasting holes in the lifeboats with his pistol. My grip fails me—for a moment the water is in retreat and I am bizarrely weightless. I scamper back to the rear of the bridge and am forcing myself down between the radiator and the wall as the next blow pounds the ship ...

*

... One by one, things gradually are falling, fall back into certain places. I am one of these things. The story will have first no person at all, and now a person is coming back.

That I will start with the unhurried, the casual, pausing now and then to reflect or to collect itself, approach, of a visitor: a pain, which is drawing nearer by hasteless degrees.

It is with adjustments in my midsection, so *there* I am. Coming back into it, out of some other place of stifling closeness and oppressively contained body heat.

A pain has drawn near, not too close to be serious. I can hear water dripping into water. I am slung forward over the radiator and the pain in my midsection is evidently the result of this. Unhinging myself with shoots of new and distracting pain at the base of my spine, I extricate myself. I am in sound condition, I decide, slump to the sloppy floor in an inch of brine, and just breathe. My eyes and throat are swollen, my body is thawing from cold to pain. It is a relief to lie here.

I make myself get up. Tabliq Quibli is in the corner, not conscious. Jil Punkinflake, pale, eyes fluttering, is prostrate across Thrushchurl's legs, and Thrushchurl is slouched against the wall with his arms still locked in the struts to either side of him, gazing calmly on vacancy. I can dimly make out the motion of his vest. I blunder over to Tabliq Quibli—concussion. Glancing up—

Glancing up I see Meqhasset's charcoal bluffs within a hundred yards, dwarfing us. I shout.

Saskia lurches from where she lay slumped to one side of the wheel, water dribbling from her slack lip, pulling her body upright with her hands on the wheel. I am going back and forth. I suppose I'm blubbering, panicking, although I'm almost too tired to. My eyes smart and there are hot streaks eating their way down my cold face. Makemin is crumpled by the rail slumped in his chains. I release him and drag him back to the bulkhead. I fetch fresh water from the cabinets in the upper decks and bring it to Saskia first. She drinks it dazedly and retches down the wheel, turning it to steer more strictly into parallel with the coast. The waves about us are becoming agitated, and now she is hoarsely at it with bilge me this and batten you that. Her voice is strange and high, a woman's voice. I am careering around the deck uncertainly, feeling very much unable to think, and somehow the deck itself is there to hold me fast to it, teasing me in my weakness with spurts of seawater in my eyes.

*

The island is rolling by us on the starboard side. The bluffs screen the interior from view, but there's an odd smell blown off the land to us, earthy and metallic, a little rancid. Saskia has turned from the coast, to swing us wider out and give us a broader view of the shore. Her voice crying orders from the bridge down to the lower decks, is deep and thrilling again, like a baritone bell.

After an anxious counting and recounting, it appears no one was lost in the swells. Makemin brings the Clappers forward again, drubbing them on the shoulders and setting their complicated gear rattling, brusquely orders them to mount their song of thanksgiving, and they break into their music like a clock striking the hour. I suspect he is less interested in giving thanks than in diverting us, so that we won't be abashed in sight of the island, but the song, that used to stir uncertainly deep feelings in me, seems weirdly thin and preposterous now, as though a number of dignified men should roll around on their backs uncouthly, sobbing and simpering like babies. We are further distracted by our work, setting the half-wrecked ship back in order. And as we work, the island is still sliding past us, like an irregular, black rampart.

We swing gradually around a promontory. Wreckage in the water by the breakers, and two vast dun red-laced ribs sticking out of the waves like fingers pointed toward us. The ship must have been far larger than ours. Fragments of it are spilled out along the rocks—I imagine a ruptured hull slopping its contents onto the studded shore at the base of the cliffs like a disemboweled whale, and shreds of bulkhead sinking out of sight. The ribs are motionless. They might be part of the island. Looking at their uncannily clean lines, the rust scoring them, and the paltry few clumps of foliage or sea stuff that have managed to attach themselves to the metal, a resounding accumulation of time thrums around me, and without being told I know this is an ancient wreck.

I feel Thrushchurl's hand engulf my shoulder, and he points to the water in what strikes me as a classical sort of gesture, one of the things only human beings seem to do. There's something white coming up in the gloomy water by the wreck; I recoil for a moment, and would leave the rail if Thrushchurl weren't unwittingly blocking me, but now I see I didn't recognize something after all. I don't know what I took it for, but as I shrink away at first sight Thrushchurl says, confiding and explaining and grinning,

"Bones."

It's a humerus. An upwelling current, tumbling shipwrecked bones here round and round from bottom to surface, for how long? There's a fountain of small bones, from the hands and feet, and back bones in with them, spinning there in that spot; a pelvis makes a long arching pass away from us, up from the dark and then down into it again, like a white ray; I see a witty mandible spin there for a moment, and then an actual rib in the shade of the metal ones. Thrushchurl doffs his hat and holds it meditatively to his chest.

"Bones," I hear Jil Punkinflake say softly beside me. I peer surreptitiously into his face. For the first time since we embarked, I see there a resurgance of his old self; maybe the bones are calling him back, or perhaps it's the land. His dog sits pragmatically down beside him and pants, looking relieved. Together we watch the wreck go. It takes a long time for it to fall away. The day should have ended hours ago.

Saskia is navigating more confidently now, or I get the impression we have a decided course. The bluffs give way to sprawling, basin-like green banks under a skyline turreted with indigo peaks. The land grows flat, as though it leaned away from us while stretching itself thin. We pass lacy shelves of barely-submerged stone; they extend out from the coast creating mile-wide shallows, before dropping deeply away as though sheared off at the edges. The water on these shelves is no more than a few feet thick, and the surface shimmers silver with black angles. Thrushchurl stares at the island mirrors as they go by with rapt attention on his face. They do reflect the sky, a long look discloses.

This one is the shallowest yet; the stone here is more of a ramp than a flat plate, and the water flings itself in long corded arms up the slope, and topples back all ramshackle again, at incredible speed. Monstrous boulders big as houses, and a few are larger than our ship, lie on the ramp, and the water rolls them up the ramp a few turns as it comes in, and brings them tumbling back as it recedes. Saskia turns us further out from the coast and we watch in silence as black blocks reel and slam with thundering noise. Gouts of white ocean cream glow against the black of the water and the rocks, the thudding of the blocks cracks and mumbles in the distance as we pull away.

A sharp cry. Saskia turns the ship quickly to port. We've narrowly missed running up on a huge, submerged stone. The alarm began with Nardac in the prow, her long arm extended remains pointing unerringly at a cubical black stone under the surface only a dozen or so yards from us.

Makemin consults with Saskia, showing her with his finger how the coast is forested with mammoth stone blocks, strewn down from the land and protruding everywhere in the water, some visible, some low in the water, and certainly more of them completely submerged. Ahead of us, the land folds in on itself in long, low sweeps, like two arms dragging in the water, one bent in within the curl of the other. That place is evidently where we are bound.

Grape-colored dusk gathers around us as they talk together in low voices. We will anchor here, to wait for the sun's light to steer by.

*

From here, it's possible to see some way inland. The bare slopes alternate away from me, back and forth from left to right, and ascending toward invisible mountains, now that even the clouds have bled out their light. Only a few glowering scars here and there in puffed blackness fuming overhead. The water ruffles by with no strong current. The land is beautiful; I want to admire it, but the wind sucks the breath out of my lungs, making them ache, and I just can't catch or keep my breath. I'm drying out like a salted fish, and I have to make my way to the mess. The inside of my head feels like it's been scoured with sand.

Silichieh is there at one of the tables, his head on his fist, emptily stirring tea in a tin cup, and Tabliq Quibli is on the floor up against the wall with his head on the insides of his elbows and his forearms on his bent knees. A bandage under his turban. I get some hot water and sit. I'm so dried out I'd upend myself into a rain barrel if there was one handy. Silichieh keeps rubbing his red eyes and I know he feels it too—he's not smoking. Looking out at an all but undetectably rising and falling shoreline in the dark, the steely phosphorescent blue night, the layered slopes left to right like slabs of silver fat, the dry air stealing in to scrub the corners. The mess is a bladder of orange light in a world of blue and the only place on the ship we didn't all look like ghosts or statues of blue lead.

I'm trying to collect my thoughts, but I can't compose my mind at all, my face is smarting and my eyes rasp in their sockets as though they'd rusted there. I turn away from the door for relief, splash water in my hand and squeeze it into my eyes. I feel that unaccountable feverishness again.

Outside, Thrushchurl is pacing the deck. Maybe Jil Punkinflake is with him, I don't know. Silichieh staggers off to his bunk, looking beaten. Now I follow, not tired, not alert. Lying in my bunk, I can hear flakes of air rattle against each other.

Someone whispers something in my ear and I bolt upright out of sleep. Silichieh is gone. I'm alone. It's night. The island is still floating outside the door.

I lie back. I sleep.

Someone whispers something in my ear and I start out of sleep. There's nothing but the wind in the cabin and the island at the door. I lie back and listen. Gradually, I begin to make it out. There is a sound like speech in the wind blowing from the island, a whisper, without words, but with an addressing sound of speech. I imagine the island is haloed with that sound.

I lie back in my bunk again. The sea laps at the hull, the wind grates gently on everything, the island gazes in through the door at me. I dream of the dark water beneath us; I'm a spirit moving effortlessly through the coolness down there, the water moving through me, my calm mind settling as though I were only sinking into a bottomless bed. There is a white mass of paper in a rude body, pulling itself along the bottom with its reedy arms, sliding itself in among the rocks. A sudden impulse makes me want to drag myself down, to stare into its face, because the sight will terrify me and realizing this is like acquiescing to the impulse—I divert myself toward the bottom and watch from behind as the two pale arms float out and it lays its hands on a polished brown brass-framed counter top like a barman. I snort with laughter and wake myself up.

*

We'll depend on Nardac's keen eyes to guide us in. She is set out with a couple of sailors in a patched lifeboat, haunched there in the bow, over the water and swinging the boom of her bony arm, in line with her beak, this way and that. There was no keeping her to her bunk, although her wound is still not healing. She seems almost not to notice it, and to be insensible to the pain.

With the coming of the wan morning light, a survey from the mast has disclosed an end to the field of blocks where the land opens up, and that there is a passage through. All hands are on deck watching anxiously; at the rail someone I don't recognize is impatiently taking it all in. Saskia arrives on the bridge. She puts her hand on Jil Punkinflake's shoulder as she passes him, no differently than she would have gripped a post standing in the same spot, and he's just beside himself, his face mingling pink and yellow with pleasure.

We begin to glide tentatively forward; Saskia is unbelievably deft at the helm, but one strong swell could ruin us within sight of the shore. Not all the lifeboats have been patched—some still show daylight through the holes Makemin made. A little after noon, the sun is a snowy coin above us, and with a gasp of relief we drift forward into clear fathoms between the two arms of land. Nardac is reverently lifted from the life boat back to the deck, and, resting her meagre weight in my arms, permits herself to be carried back to her bunk, clucking once or twice to herself in satisfaction. This is as close as I've ever been to her, her eyes do sparkle like diamonds, as though a cold fire were caught in them.

Our eyes peeled for more rocks, we are making our way cautiously up a wide estuary. The wind dies away nearly to nothing as the land closes around us, and, in the raw new stillness, the noises of the ship seem excessively conspicuous. Above us, on the port side, are high grey cliffs with black bangs and gaunt, shaggy pines that stand out, dark and insubstantial, against the clouds. The opposite shore is lumpy and sere with blistered yellow-grey stubble, lunging up toward the mountain line. Ahead, the land bells out like a vast low amphitheatre, the river curves away behind slopes and, still far off, in the crook of the river's sweeping curve, I see an enclosed sprawl of buildings collected there like mine talings. With care, Saskia brings our prow to bear on it.

The water here is as calm as a lake, with an indifferent current. Deep chasms are tearing open and grinding shut again in the clouds above us. We pass a ruin set in among the cliffs, its foundations half submerged; I can't make out the contour of the building. It seems likely to have been a square tower, with its feet in the water and its head up in the pines. Its exposed grey bricks are insanely uniform in shape and size; a tangle of pipes sprouts from the wall like a trunk of thickened vines, and their ends shiver in the air.

A dream pulling up alongside another dream, each measures the other. The war is up there on the island, where we're going to meet it, but there's no war there, nor could there be. War is dreamlike, but war *is* a dream ... Where is the war? In the guns and helmets and uniforms? Is it in the rock from which the ore to make the gun was mined, the grass that fed the sheep whose wool went into the uniform, or the sun that lights the battlefield? Not impossible to escape but it tethers as unsubstantially, as lightly, as a dream, the bonds binding me inside. I go on with it; I'm not bound like a prisoner, but like a sleeper. Two men meet, and one will give his life for the other, or they will each try to kill the other, while the day is still blandly unfolding around them. The violence I've already seen has been as random and abrupt as a dream, always ending in death that seems only to become more and more impossible. I always know that I'm no more than one sharp breath from waking. It's a breath I can never manage.

We're drawing nearer to the city now. Makemin is peering at it with his goggles and looking glasses, Nikhinoch stands by him with his hands behind his back. Makemin points suddenly at something in the air before us. I can't see anything but some streaks. As I watch, an uncouthly flapping near-invisibility vaults over and around the ship with a sound like a leather umbrella being shaken out.

"A Predicate," Silichieh says.

"It's an ungainly flier," I say, as it wobbles away from us and back toward the city. So we come to know the city—Vscriathjadze, they're telling me it's called—has not fallen into enemy hands, and we may approach without fear of attack.

The steep brae shawls itself around us; the grade is only just recumbent enough to prevent our calling it a cliff, and covered in a blazing new green, right down to the water. There are no waves, and the surface barely heaves against the shore. Mountains with green sides, and Vscriathjadze sits in a narrow groove between them. I'm glad to see mountains again, surprisingly glad.

The harbor is like a huge loophole in the rock; we must pass through a narrow gap like an inverted triangle to enter it. Drawing near, I see the stone is unnaturally smooth, with many small marks of human work there, peering out from fronded mats of fern and quivering vines. On top of the outer enclosure to the harbor perch two towers of heavy gneiss with elongated eaves, and a man emerges from one of these waving small flags. Saskia's voice resonates from the bridge. Our ships' huge grasshopper legs slow, nearly stopping, and the stacks begin to vent steam. The man high above us goes away, and presently a small launch chugs out of the gap and pulls up alongside with the pilot. He's a boxy yellow man in a quilted jacket, who tugs his cap's visor at us, eyes flitting from face to face in search of the one to whom his deference is chiefly due, and bows a little at the waist. Nikhinoch accompanies him to the bridge, and in time we begin to advance smoothly through the gap. Why didn't he come out to meet us earlier, when we were threading that maze at the estuary's mouth?

The harbor is as steep as a chimney, and completely paved. We're in a vast mortar cone, hundreds of yards across, with straight and switchback stairs cut into the sides. The circle of sky over us is confused by a jumble of crane arms, dangling chains and ropes. The docks radiate from a curved platform against the wall opposite the opening. As we pass through the gap, I look up at a narrow strip of satin blue, and little curds of dense cloud racing across it.

There are many small boats moored to the piers, but only a couple or three of any size, and nothing approaching our ship's dimensions. The pilot guides us toward an empty dock just off the center. Already a number of people stand there, waiting for us in silence. They do not move, they make no gesture, nor do they speak to or in any way I can see acknowledge us or, for that matter, each other. They are like statues.

The pilot is taking a long time angling the ship in toward the dock. Still, no one moves. The upturned faces blink, but they do not vary their position, they are not passing their eyes over the unfamiliarities of our ship. Only when ropes flop down toward them do a few of them move, without any particular speed, to retrieve and tie them.

Makemin strides up and down the pier giving orders; the locals totter out of his way like mill horses, and meanwhile many of the loonies are capering off the gangplank and scooting up the stairways toward the town permission or no. I'm asking Makemin about Nardac, specifically what I, as *her physician*, should do with her.

"We might leave her in the boat. Do you think she can be moved?"

"She's not in any danger, but she'd be better looked after on land."

"Well, fine, fine," he is looking away, watching as our ship's laden cranes swing out over the pier. "We'll make arrangements."

He wants her out of the way; he seems to want to avoid her now.

"Tell them who we are," he says.

I climb up the gangplank and address the crowd in Lashlache.

"Aw hawdemin-herleken! Hawr s'dan s'dess! Aw d'hadr s'dess! Aw w'hodet s'hodet hodet woi m'set! M'swedet sherd'dhemeto, m'dqess ..." and so on.

This kind of formal speech in the vocative mode is nothing like the written or formal Lashlache upon which my studies concentrated, but as often happens with this sort of thing, I find my memory serves me better than I would have expected. I enjoy unshackling my voice like this. The people on the pier plainly understand me, although they do not attend to me.

The steps leading up to the city are steep and narrow, slotted into concrete like hardened custard. Ascending one by one, we gather in the open area above the harbor, where there is a profusion of water tanks, coal hoppers, rails set into gravelled scars, scaffolds thickly painted with creosote, barrels, carts, and warehouses with arched mouths standing open. The air here is still. The city doesn't embrace the upper ring of the harbor, but only touches it, gingerly, at one point, where we are gathered now. The buildings here are tall, lean, and close together. They fill a narrow alley between two steep slopes of coffee-colored rock. The port is at one end of this alley; the city is at the other, where the slopes fall open. Apart from a few paths, there are no buildings or terraces to be seen on the sides of the mountains.

A messenger in Alak uniform has appeared, and Makemin is interrogating him sharply. The messenger dashes off again; Makemin says something to Nikhinoch and begins pacing with signs of disgust and impatience. Nikhinoch presently comes over to me and instructs me to bring up Nardac.

"Well, but how? I can't carry her up all those stairs."

He tosses a glance of withering indifference over his shoulder at me, and returns to Makemin.

Jil Punkinflake and I contrive to bind Nardac to a stretcher. We find her in the bow, lying on her back, her head craned round and her glinting eyes peering steadily up toward the island. She lifts herself onto the canvas, and mildly submits to our snugging her in. I'm the stronger, so I take her feet. With some puffing and straining we convey her up the steps, hurrying, lest we be left behind.

We needn't have bothered. Nothing has changed. Makemin is apparently still waiting for the arrival of the envoy of the local officials, or what have you. I look around in vain for a cart in which to transport my patient until it occurs to me to find Tabliq Quibli. He unerringly locates or emanates carts. I find him already seated on one already, directing the installation of our cargo, and we add Nardac to it. She is still staring at the land.

Fed up with waiting, Makemin orders the columns to take form, and, with some commotion, we enter the streets. The city is grey, damp, and built of strange materials; there are pipes running everywhere, along the streets or up the sides of houses, like clumps of noodles. The main boulevard is a wide slab of silky clay with meagre, chute-like lanes sprouting from its sides, most of them narrow, covered, and as sharply inclined as staircases. Where the slopes draw back, and the city, no longer corseted by mountains, expands to fill the basin beyond, we begin to see side streets that are more proper-looking, but they are still disproportionately small in comparison with the artery we follow now, like a snake with centipede legs. Shallow puddles everywhere reflect the sky, like cold dollops of mirror. A thickened fear, kind of a miasma, is thrown over everything like an oppressively heavy blanket. I feel exposed, although I can't say to what. I notice the inhabitants now, at their windows, in the doorways and alley thresholds, always half in hiding and I suppose ready to flee, even if it seems as though such exertions would be beyond them. On all faces I see weariness, and velleity; a quiescent mistrust.

Vscriathjadze means "thousand waterfalls." The broken slopes against which the city crowds its seaward edge are draped with waterfalls, many of which are used to run mills, and the water is collected in a ring-shaped reservoir encircling much of the city like a moat.

Jil Punkinflake is marching near me, holding the banner, looking visibly firmer now he's back on land. I turn my head. There are many familiar faces around me. I don't want to part from them—away from them, I imagine I will begin to feel less real myself. I am imbibing small draughts of confidence and substance from being among them, and words half-form heroic verses in my mind telling me that my destiny does not lie apart from theirs.

We're approaching an elaborate, composite noise. Here,

on the far side of the city from the port, the buildings trail out onto a broad plain, and a sprawling camp has been laid here on the uneven ground. Voices in our ranks relay information—this is a battalion from the First Specialist Army, sent to reinforce us, mingled in with a Yeseg militia, who came to the island on their own. We stop and wait at the border of the camp, imagining ourselves to be a reassuring sight, while Makemin consults with the other commanders here. Presently we receive the order to set up camp.

A tall man is leaning against the tree, and another crouches at its roots. Suddenly she rises and snaps around— an Edek, fixing her sucking, blind gaze on me. I stiffen and lean back.

"You can't touch me. You can't touch me."

I say it softly, to no one.

The Edek taps the crease of the last joint of the middle finger of her right hand against the pad of her thumb twice as I go by, her head swivelling as I pass.

*

Time wasted on my cot. I turn in my blankets and my hands reach up to my face—I idly cradle my head in my hands, turning it this way and that, and feeling its weight as an object. So this is all I suppose I am. I try to realize it, and imagine handling this head severed. I'm too tired to sleep. I'll go into town and look at what they sell here. A billow of incredulity when I remember money, and how important it is. I am moved to hilarity, not too strong, in contemplation of the pomp of money, laurels profiles lofty slogans and the like. Our scrip is funny stuff. I lie there and tremble. A wave of fear rolls over me like a heavy rolling pin.

No one is available so I wander in the streets alone. I look about me with numb disinterest that I feebly stretch and try to break, but I lack the will. The people here seem to have no will either. They walk heavily. I expect at any moment to see them collapse on the ground in heaps of bones and flesh like wet cake, oozing from shapeless clothes. They avoid me, and it's a relief to catch sight of Silichieh sitting with some of his countrymen, drinking on a raised platform. I am waved over and sit among them in a dully jovial chorus of greetings in Deme. I try to drink but a cat jumps in my lap; a burly young one, with thick grey fur, and his beefy tail interferes with my glass a bit.

*

It's late in the day. The other soldiers are carousing noisily. I stop to examine Nardac, who lies breathing shallowly on her back, her eyes sparkle like black jewels in the gloom of the tent. Her wound is closed over now, looks like a coal-colored patch of bark growing on her flank.

Makemin is in his tent. Incredibly, there was a new stack of legal correspondence already waiting for him when he arrived. Sitting in an orange globe of lamp light, his table with the folding legs in an X, the regular motion of his pen pauses from time to time as he inhales a pinch of his stimulant, one nostril at a time, from a small pewter vessel beside his inkpot. I won't be needed until tomorrow, and I rather hope some other translators can be found in the meantime. Nikhinoch whisks past me, bringing Makemin a pitcher of water, his hand on the bottom. He carries its weight through the air as smoothly as though it were on rails. We all seem to be hung here at our different levels in the night, each in his own station, and I'm like the little cat who goes levying or begging from one to the next, lapping up the cream I'm offered as if it were all my greed had had tonight. I don't like to sit still. None of us knows what's going to happen next, and none of us wants to dwell on that uncertainty, on the fantasies of that uncertainty ...

My cot receives me with a shrug. A moment later I am joined by Jil Punkinflake. Saskia has gone off somewhere among the other soldiers, most likely grilling them or sorting through the other Yesegs for spies. I can see he's decided they've had a falling out, and is punishing her by withholding from her his unwanted company. This will end whenever the realization that she doesn't notice stuns him, and I don't want to be present to see his perfume cathedrals drop in rags. He greets me with a sound and lies on his cot, letting his hand sink down onto his dog's head, the other cocked behind his own. Someone has pinned a scrap of printing on the tent's center post, and I am staring at the two princes on it, Tewsetonta, our enemy, and Tewsetonka, in whose cause we fight, confronting each other in oval frames.

How is it possible no one sees the mania?

I see her distraught on her bed, the straps of her nightgown slipping from her shoulders. An ember sinks into me. I feel its heat against the backs of my eyes.

As night comes on, a wind emerges from the interior of the island and crumbles down out of the mountains into the damp air lining the valley, compressing it to the ground in the center and pushing it up along the sides. The dry wind runs off without mixing into the damp, divides into limbs that reach into the city, stirring the cool humidity they find there. Soft breaths sigh along my face and down my body wrapped in its uniform, and then a rough trunk of parched wind will strike and suck at me a moment, raking in my nose and throat the glittering dust it's laced with. With which it is laced. I stretch my legs in front of the tent, the wind pouring eerily over and by me, and something is transmitted to me. The idea that this is a magical place, why hadn't I felt it before?

There's a fixed constellation that wheels directly above the city, not visible from anywhere else in the known world, and must therefore not be made of stars but of smaller, nearer things, at least according to some. My explainer here is obviously not impressed with this idea and I think it likely this is typical for natives—others, she goes on, and I know at once that this is her own opinion, believe them to be proper stars. Thrushchurl has appeared before us, his head against the starry sky busy with clouds, the constellation reflected in his fixed grin. He wants to look around, and me to join him. I turn to Jil Punkinflake, whose sullenness, after the briefest struggle, melts.

"God, I will," he says, and instructs his dog to stay.

My grogginess evaporates; I am instantly bright and vigorous. We leave the camp, slip into the streets hastily, then slow our pace and begin our promenade with hands in our pockets. I amble in the direction of the well, but Thrushchurl whistles gravely at me.

"No," he says, "Edeks there."

We step back and remain in the line of the shadow. A moment or two later, a man drifts briefly in and out of view, his head back—unmistakeably one of their helpers. I retreat with Thrushchurl, who is leaning in a doorway, idly prying at the dry rot in the lintel with his finger. He tells us when it's safe to go. He seems to shine in the clear air under the night sky, as if he were in his element. We make our way toward the outskirts of town, where it winnows back into a separate canyon. The buildings are no smaller or farther apart, but the streets are empty, and there are few lights.

Thrushchurl stops in front of a lit window, then steps up to the building, resting both hands side by side on the sill before his chin. A light burns on a table inside.

"I want that lamp," he says softly, and rises off the ground, pushing himself up on his hands. He steps over the sill, cocking his knees. Jil Punkinflake steps forward with enjoyment and pulls himself in deftly, and I follow, straddling the sill sideways and ducking in my head.

The room is square, with doors opening on a hallway and a narrow flight of steps. A tiled fireplace, wooden floors with matting, two spavined chairs, dingy portraits. Thrushchurl creaks around the room, breathing it in more than he looks at it. He examines the lamp very critically, but it no longer seems to interest him.

"The fire's all wrong," I say.

"Fire is fire. All fires are the same, surely," I say, blustering and disliking the false tone in my voice.

Thrushchurl glances up from the calm flame to me, "You're ignorant," he says plainly. "There are all different kinds of fire."

There are plates on the table. Thrushchurl takes up one plate with thumb and forefinger and gropes overhand at the heap of peeled grapes it contains.

"Eyeballs," he says.

Jil Punkinflake takes up another plate and similarly gropes at its tangle of noodles.

"Intestines," he pipes.

They begin to dance around me like balletic waiters in a musical number, plates balanced on palms. Jil Punkinflake looks up toward the mantlepiece and Thruschurl looks round at the hallway. He gives a sudden, convulsive movement, as a puny grey shape darts from the room and into the hall. Like a gawky cat, Thrushchurl is after it, his feet clamouring on the floorboards. I run after.

Thrushchurl has it trapped in a corner between two doors. He is crouching with his face bent down to it, his lips stretching back from his teeth. The mouse is a tiny bundle of shivers—Thruschurl is staring into its round eyes. He seems to say to it, you are paralyzed, and the mouse understands, it does not move. Thrushchurl slowly brings his face in closer. The mouse is palpitating, and I wonder if it will die of fear. Something white is oozing from the corners of its eyes. Its terror is so intense I see the thick hair around its eyes is turning white.

The white forces its way along the length of each tiny hair from the skin to the tip, and now both its eyes are ringed with white. The white spreads, joins between the eyes, runs down the snout, up to the ears. Now the entire mouse is white, and its eyes I notice are turning red. I keep thinking it will burst apart for sheer fright, it's trembling so violently—and I think I might see a trickle of blood run down from one ear. I'm wrong—it isn't a trickle of blood. It's strange: a vertical, dark line segment. Now the mouse's head weaves slightly but the line segment doesn't move with it, and I realize that I am seeing a line in the moulding of the wall *through* the mouse's head. The mouse is plainly turning transparent—I can make out its tiny bones, and I can see the shadowy throbbing of its viscera. The heart is a flailing blot darker against the darkness of the floor. Suddenly the mouse bends itself in half and springs past Thrushchurl and through the door. Whisking along the bottom of the wall, it disappears through a gap in the floorboards. Just before it is gone, it passes through a bit of light, and I see the working of its hind leg bones through the transparent integument.

Thrushchurl is sitting up on his knees, his head thrown back, a look of wild triumph on his face.

"How did you do that?"

"I don't know!" he says, his grin furling wider, "It never worked before!" He raises his trembling hand to his face, fingering his upper lip and teeth.

*

We are standing on a streetcorner in the wan light from the windows above us, glowing through dimity curtains.

"Do you smell that?" Thrushchurl asks suddenly, turning his head and raising his nose.

"It's bodies!" Jil Punkinflake says, sniffing.

"They expose their dead, you know," Thrushchurl says, coming a step towards us. He turns and follows the scent. Jil Punkinflake sails out after him as though he were tethered to Thrushchurl, and I come too, behind. Their heads go one way and another, like bloodhounds combing the air.

The street we follow is dark blue, all the windows are dark except where pale curtains glow feebly like clouds at night. There are light clouds wandering the sky now; stars in the strait between the buildings overhead, no moon. We are approaching the end of the street, where it does the splits and folds right and left in what looks to be little more than a pair of trails, and directly before us is a silvery ridge not quite as tall as we are, sparsely quilled with rattling white weeds. We take the left split; the trail is dust, overhung with half-fossilized branches, the ridge on our right and brick wall on our left, seven feet apart or so.

Why are we stepping lightly, not talking? Thrushchurl's magic embarrasses us. Maybe magic works here. I should try making myself disappear.

No sound but the all-surrounding stir of air. The trail veers away from the wall and into a tunnel of laced boughs fragrant with resin, so low we have to duck as we pass. The path is a shallow trench; I catch a few snags. The roof drops away and the path sinks in between stones and follows an incline up and over. Weeds bow in the wind. The path widens, the land opens, but now there are trees around us, corkscrewed and bare, separated like trees in a park. We walk among these trees, which grow sparser and older, more enormous and spreading. The ground between them is a porridge of blue and silver soil, grit, stones, bleached weeds, into which the path has faded. A little aspirant noise from Thrushchurl and he points to a scaly wall. We trace it to a corner, double back and, further in the other direction, we find an iron gate. Thrushchurl pushes the gate, which is bound shut by a length of chain, in as far as it will go, and, his grin out of place with the concentration of his features, he squeezes himself through under the chain. Jil Punkinflake slips in as readily as he might through a half-open door, but I have to take my time, turning this way and that, the disagreeable smell of iron smearing on my clothes and hands.

There is a path here, flat between humps and trees. We stand peering into the blue dark, and I can see white forms standing around us. Statues. Silence. Excited looks. Jil Punkinflake's face settles further into its old color, the pink bleaching away, his face yellow against the blue night. Rotten egg smell, or stagnant water, and beneath it a familiar odor. Out of the trees to the base of a tower—one of many. They loom up just above the tops of the trees on either side. I can't say whether the tower before us is stone or wood, it seems as though it were all one flow of stuff, like wax, or a wasp's nest. The surface is puffed and cracked, chips hang peeling with faint shadows behind them. Thrushchurl disappears into the darkness of the rounded doorway; a chain knocks on wood. Sound from nearby of wind shifting broken glass. I examine the ground and see bits of glass here and there against the bottom of the wall. Thrushchurl holds the heavy heart-shaped padlock in his hands, turning it, then he takes it in his fingers like a sandwich and carefully sinks his teeth into the keyhole. His head works back and forth as though he were gently worrying a bite free of the metal. The lock clicks, and Thrushchurl sets the crinkling chain against the wall, pushes the door open with one hand wiping his lips with the other.

There is an atrium with an alcove, tenanted by a brass vessel full of dark earth. To the left is a stairway curving up out of sight, glittering with tiny square and rectangular tiles of cream marbled with blue. I smell decay.

Single file, we climb—the stairs end at the bottom of a shaft. There's a stink of rotting flesh. Dusty, misfitting floorboards, trestles, a rough walled tube open to the distant sky, niched with alcoves and ledges. Pale figures lie in them, on the trestles, and some are scattered on the floor and against the wall. Fragments of bodies litter the floor. Thrushchurl sighs and clasps his hands, and Jil Punkinflake gives an awed "ohh ..." They pick their way reverently out onto the floor, and Thrushchurl strokes an arm that lies outstretched on a table.

The corpses are set out for vultures and ravens; the practice is known as "air burial." A carcass lies near me, the chest open, the wind-stiffened skin pulled up in rags like hard leather. Looking closely, I can see phosphorescent, thin sky-blue V's, regularly spaced, along the edges of the wound, fine as calligraphy. The cavity is plugged with black amber. I know the body was not prepared this way, but set here unembalmed shortly after death. There are a number of them, in this condition. Thrushchurl bends over a body examining the marks, takes its face in his finger tips, turns the head this way and that.

"Someone's tampered with this one," he says, a soft horror in his voice.

"The Predicanten have fed here," I say, pointing to the prints of clever little paws in the dust by the remains.

At the mention of the Predicanten Thrushchurl quickly glances up at me, then peers down again into the face in his hands. Jil Punkinflake brushes up next to me, ducks to finger the amber. I can hear Thrushchurl's breath catch.

"You're right!" he whispers, tenderly drawing the eyelids up with his thumbs. "—they've been busy here inside ..."

He comes toward us, stepping into the capacitous shadow of a beam overhead.

"They replaced what they took out—"

He stops in the shadow. His speech stops.

I turn. Nothing behind us. Nothing to see. I call Thrushchurl quietly by name, but he remains stock still, as he is, in the shadow of the beam. Jil Punkinflake and I draw nearer to him. In the dark, I can barely make out his face; his smile is gone—his eyes are round. I take his shoulders in my arms—his body is rigid as wood.

"What is it?" Jil Punkinflake asks. "A fit?"

"I think it is."

I touch his face—it's cold. I give his shoulders a tentative shake—he tumbles forward into me, body toppling like a stack of boxes.

"—with memory," he says, swaying onto his feet. He puts his hand dizzily to his head and leans on me.

"We should go back," I say, trying to find his gaze.

"You're right," he says, "We should get out now."

Jil Punkinflake takes him by the hand with a complicated expression and leads him to the stairs. Thrushchurl seems in a hurry to leave. Going last, I see my shadow condensing on the plaster before me as I turn to descend the steps, look back at a frail, yellow-gold light, a little brighter than a patch of moonlight would be, pooling in an alcove opposite me. A body sits there, its head tipped back into the alcove, and the glow gathering around its head in a circle, growing steadily brighter.

I'm afraid. I hurry away, and say nothing about it.

"What did you see?"

He is silent for a while. "I was falling ..." he says uncertainly. "A voice sang out low, on and on without pausing. I heard Makemin say 'fire.' I fell then."

Escape through the trees now, as though something were coming. I keep looking back over my shoulder, and my fear doesn't leave me. I get out ahead, am first into the road, glance up in time to see something whirring high in the air and recoil back under the branches hurling out my arms to stop my companions. We watch from the shade as two Predicanten crawl by overhead, flying in the direction of the towers. When they're gone, we stride quickly down the road, keeping to the farther side.

"Who's calling?"

Now I hear a howl—it starts low, and then rises, and grows louder as it rises. It outlasts itself, remaining in the air when the sound is gone.

"Predicanten don't have voices like that."

I think of the haloed head.

Grown gigantic, a Predicate passes in complete silence, its shoulders loom above the tops of the trees; I catch sight of it just as it begins a slow turn, melting into the gloom.

Predicate heads are bobbing among the trees on long, limp, stalk-like necks that trail off into nothing, peering this way and that with eyes swollen to slits, swinging all together in the air like a cat-o-nine-tails as though all those necks were gathered to one trunk.

We move swiftly to the nearer edge of the road, to hide behind the trees, go quietly, all of us breathing together. With a recklessness I can't understand I sweep out onto the road again after a few minutes. I see no sign of the Predicanten, and we are a bit away now. We stop, looking and breathing. The night is very still.

"They put memory in the place of what they ate," Thrushchurl is speaking a little as though this were obvious, but his uncertain tone might be a sign of astonishment. "Not memories, you know, of this or that, but just memory."

He pants once.

"That's how I know—I remembered it."

"Without seeing it first?"

"Yes," he beams, but with some fear knotted in his brow, "I remembered it *first*."

His breathing grows more pronounced, through his teeth.

"I want to go back!" he says, and turns. Jil Punkinflake and I have him in a lunge, and we restrain him with effort.

"I want to know what they know!" he cries.

"No you don't!"

"Please let me go! Please let me go!" he implores as he struggles.

"They don't know anything!" I shout. "They don't know anything!"

He stops struggling, and looks diagonally down at the ground. Warily, we unclinch him.

"You don't know that ..."

Thrushchurl looks probingly at me, the yellow glow of his teeth like a banked-down fire there below his eyes.

"I wish I knew ..." he says, and I relax. I had thought he was going to ask me something.

"Where do they come from?" he asks, looking directly at me.

"I don't know!" I shout, jerking back.

I'm flustered—why am I flustered?

"I don't know! I don't know!" I keep shouting.

Jil Punkinflake joins in, staring at me, his eyes harder than I've ever seen them but once but once before.

"Do you know something, Low?"

"No!" I shout.

A panic is eating me.

"They're like Edeks and everything else. That's all I know, like anyone knows! What everyone knows!"

"What's the matter with you?"

"You know something," Thrushchurl says, pointing gently at me.

"But I don't! I don't!"

I don't.

I don't know anything.

I see an idea in Jil Punkinflake's face, his nostrils quivering, and he shrinks almost imperceptibly from me—

"You're a *dreamer*, aren't you?"

Between their two heads I can see the staring paper thing between the trunks of the trees—

"No! No!" I shout again and again.

"You're one of *them!*"

"I'm not! I am not!"

I feel like I'm dying. The world is just breaking ice floes spreading implacably apart over black killing cold water, ice water.

—Somehow I'm there, as though I'd been nodding off into an instant nightmare and now snap awake again, right into those denials still streaming from my mouth.

"I'm not! I'm not! I'm one of you! I have to be one of you! I'm the narrator!"

I am persuading them.

I see the suspicion slacken and fall from their faces, and they're not leaning away from me anymore.

Jil Punkinflake actually takes me by the arm.

I still my voice and put my hand to my face, bringing it away slick with cold sweat.

Everything's all right again.

We are *merry comrades* on the road together.

*

After a paltry morning mess I cross the camp and find Makemin in conference with the other officers. Saskia sits beside the leader of the Yeseg militia; a small man with a pale face, fierce without strength, red-rimmed eyes glassy with will. She looks obdurate and stony beside him, but she doesn't seem like one of them, the Yesegs; from the way she keeps her eyes trained on Makemin, she declares herself still a part of our contingent. Jil Punkinflake's face stiffens at sight of her and he also fixes his eyes strictly on Makemin.

The commander of the First Specialists is a gangly raw-boned thicket-faced man with freckles all over him, overbite through his moustache's long threads. He's speaking with Makemin in a low voice, waving his hands incessantly. No one has been here long and there hasn't been much time or opportunity for organization, though only a few deaths since camp was established, luckily, so Makemin, who is evidently and to his obvious if undemonstrative satisfaction in charge, will handle the organizing himself. Commander overbite hands him the brevet notice in my presence. The First Specialists have accumulated a number of locals, some of whom speak Alak, and now they are called upon to help arrange a meeting with the city authorities.

These local people, a few men and women, talk among themselves, and one is dispatched up the street with the words—

"Go get Wormpig."

Wormpig, it transpires, is a round, smiling man in a quilted jacket and felt boots, with a brick-colored sash round his waist. His grin folds around a twig of licorice in the corner of his mouth.

"The mayor?" he says immediately, his pronouncedly curved eyebrows scaling his forehead. "I'll show you," he turns in place, flicking his index finger by his shoulder, so that we would follow him.

Makemin looks about and catches sight of me.

"Narrator, you come along."

Wormpig leads us through streets as tall and narrow as mine shafts; the towers are open in spacious verandas at street level and I wonder how these insubstantial lower stories can support the upper ones. Lamps burn everywhere even in the middle of the day, because the huddled buildings shut out most of the daylight. Wormpig stops before one of the verandas and gestures to it. Makemin takes to the steps and pauses almost at once, astride two stairs.

The mayor, for such I take him to be, sits on a cushion on the carpeted boards, slumped nearly altogether over a low table. Illuminated by a flannelly-looking fire in the compact hearth just behind him, he is sodden and irregular, like a half-molded clay figure. He laboriously turns his whole head in our direction; his face looks like he's slept on it, his eyes clouded from drink. Makemin joins us in the street again, disgust on his face.

Wormpig, still smiling, says, "Now I'll take you to see Pepedora, if you like. I think you'll have more to talk about with him."

We follow Wormpig to an open space below the steeps, where the land rises to form a tree-scalped shelf that curls like a cat against the feet of the seated hill. A few modest homes, octagonal towers with small-paned windows and elegant trim, gaze out mysteriously from the black hedges and branches here. The walk is brief. Before us rises a windmill. There is a low picket fence around it. The front of the mill is raised a little on pilings. Wormpig approaches from the side and I see there is a broad sliding section of wall, like the door of a freight car, I assume for the loading of grain. As we come to it, Wormpig takes a sudden additional step forward, rotating to us and raising his hand, pudgy fingers outspread, to make us stop there.

"Leprosy," he adds, and then goes to pull the loading door aside on roaring, well-greased runners.

We peer together into the spacious room, a shuttered window's bright regular lines opposite us. To one side is the grindstone and all the mill works, barrels and bulging sacks. A carpet of unground grain evenly spreads over the floor in big gleaming kernels, like little beetles, but a weirdly precise circle has been cleared of them entirely. At its far side, below and slightly to one side of the window, is a man Wormpig points out to us as Pepedora. He puts his hand on the door and leans in, speaking quietly for a few minutes. Pepedora sits cross-legged on a mat, the foot at the end of his exposed lean brown calf is misshapen and incomplete. His hands rest invisibly in his lap, and I can see the oily glint of light on his bare scalp, and the shades of a few disheviled locks wafting filmily around the sides. There is an awed hush around him that suggests power to me, and I imagine he is the real authority in Vscriathjadze.

Wormpig makes an ushering gesture to Makemin. "Tell him."

Makemin glances at me and strides bravely to the spot. Through me he explains our presence here. Pepedora does not fill in the occasional silences, but seems to be paying attention. When Makemin asks him,

"So, what cooperation can we expect?"

... a sepulchral voice, soft and yet resounding, comes from the man inside. I translate.

"He says we will have the help of their Spirit Eaters."

Wormpig dispatches a boy, who seems attached to the place, up the hill with the message. Leaving the mill wall open, he then leads us across a bare space to the adjacent house, not twenty feet away, and knocks vigorously on the door.

"Open up!" he cries gaily in Lashlache, "Soldiers are here!"

We are seated within view of Pepedora, on cut up logs and barrels, and a woman brings us all cups of tea, one at a time, from within the house. The tea is surprisingly good— the water is very pure. We wait for the Spirit Eaters to come down. Wormpig and Makemin talk quietly together. I sit alone, resisting the temptation to stare at Pepedora, who seems to stare unblinking at us, and watching the breeze toy with dry weeds.

A steady rustling sets up around us; the boy thumps down the slope holding out his arms, hopping and bounding, erupts panting into our midst with a smile and darts out of sight behind our host's house. The Spirit Eaters file down toward us along a rocky groove. As they pass a certain large stone on their left, each swings out his leg and claps the top of the stone once with the sole of his foot. They do this in a perfect rhythm, and flash of white fabric, although only the foremost seems to be wearing white—it's the same gesture, repeated again and again with what looks like the same leg.

The Spirit Eaters rustle down in a knot, coming among us, seeking Pepedora and Makemin alternately. I can't count them. There are more than a dozen; all roughly the same height, about forty, all in quilted jackets and trunks with puttis. Wind chapped and burned hands and faces, loose black hair lightly salted with dandruff or white hairs, a few approximately conical hats. They are muttering together in hoarse voices, milling and smoking. Somehow this all becomes a discussion involving both Makemin and Pepedora. I am privileged to observe one of the sublime transactions that form so much of the essence of our kind.

We return to the camp with the Spirit Eaters, who keep in their knot and talk low to each other, I think more to prevent us trying to address them than otherwise. Makemin calls out our Clappers, and immediately the Spirit Eaters and Clappers are embracing and hailing one another, forming a single mass. They arrange themselves and begin chanting aloud and clapping, raising their faces to the mountains, the clouds, the wind, with funneled lips.

*

I wander off to get a bit of lunch, then return to my cot. Shadow across my face, voice speaks my name. Zept stands there, holding an envelope out to me.

"This just came for you on the packet," he says.

Now I'm alone. The letter is from her.

My darling, darling Low—
My precious Low,

I simply had to write you immediately. The idea that you might be worrying yourself about me weighs heavily on my mind, and I would place upon you nothing, no burden, that might distract you from the all-engrossing work you have nobly consented to do. Think only good and happy thoughts of me, with the fullest assurance that such thoughts reflect only the truth!

Your absence is the only imperfection in my happiness. Remember me—let your confidence in the constancy with which you shine in my thoughts be a comfort to you in the difficulties you face and please, please be careful. I am yours and, I believe, entitled to stand on my insistencies!

How empty my days are now, though my heart is full. News reaches us swiftly, and Orvar is so good at gathering up all its pieces to bring to me. I am thankful to have his help.

Yesterday I visited the tower by myself. I wanted to stand again on the spot where we first joined hearts. It seems the height of poetry, so to speak!—that it should have been there, at such a great elevation, and with such a free and open view of the world below, that it should have happened. You really tell me so little of your feelings, but that is customary for men, I suppose. I know that, for me, it was as though I had been rescued at the last possible moment, as I had been floating away from the world, off into the air, like a piece of dandelion fluff, when you took hold of me, and kept me from going.

How I wish I could go on, but I must get this at once into the post or it will not go at all. Orvar has just been here, and sends his "hearty hello." Do not be too jealous, dear. I would not have you distracted on that account!

I send you all my love, and many many ardent embraces, many kisses—how hard it is to stop writing! Do write to me as soon as you can, you cannot know how I thirst for even a word from you! How well, how like paradise, it will be when you return—do think of it, it will be the very summit of joy for both of us!

Time will not wait—
cruel!

All, all my love to you—
your own, adoring,
Ohra

What I smell sifting up from the page makes my head spin. It's insane. I can't smell that smell while I see what I see around me—I feel like I'm in a dream as it starts to dissolve.

At the bottom of the page, I find what look like hastily added words, a little smeared, the letters less perfectly formed—

"please please you mustn't believe what they say about me"

*

The Spirit Eaters and Clappers are still at it, and the day is wearing on and on. I'm outside the tent with the others, not really listening to what Silichieh says to me.

"He's not listening," Jil Punkinflake calls nastily to my turned back. "He's just had his first love letter from the Cannibal Queen."

Waves of fatigue billow over and anger me. Without a word I cross to Jil Punkinflake seize the front of his uniform and pitch him to the ground. I don't know why everyone assumes I'm weak; as if a man could spend his life climbing rocks and hauling bags of books in the thin air of high mountain roads and not have some strength to show for it.

Jil Punkinflake tumbles down laughing, smiles up at me from the ground.

"All right all right," he chuckles. "No tapping Low's sore spot."

"He gets grumpy when he's tired, doesn't he?" Silichieh asks.

Jil Punkinflake's death's-head moth flutters around my head and settles again on the lapel of his uniform. Where has he been keeping it?

Now a group of the Spirit Eaters approaches Makemin and Wormpig, and I hear them say, in clear, clipped tones,

"Now we should consult the Oracle."

Wormpig translates that one. Four of the Spirit Eaters guide us out to a listing wooden tower with a badly cowlicked thatched roof and warped clapboard siding, to which are clinging a few intransigent, colorless scraps of paint. The Spirit Eaters gather in front of the tower, facing us, with dark expressions on their faces; disapproval, distaste, indicating to me that we are in the presence of some kind of delinquency. One of the eldest points at the gaping front doorway, in which a black rag curtain is currently floating, looking nearly into the eyes of a few of us in a row. He also mutters something I don't catch—"In there" most likely.

Makemin dashes the curtain aside with a bold gesture, disappearing at once into the building; I hear a cry within almost immediately. A clear tenor, alarmed.

Now a crouched man comes barrelling through the curtain, across the porch and tumbling, nearly falling, down the steps. The Spirit Eaters fastidiously recoil to avoid colliding with him, and the man stops himself short and straightens, just as Makemin, who pushed him, emerges from the doorway. The man is surprisingly young, dressed like the rest of them in a sack suit. Short golden stubble covers his head; his wan face looks as though it had been carved out of an enormous scallop: white, cold, wet, and rubbery. He has a cleft chin and large, blue eyes, and he wants to escape, looking desperately from face to face. The Spirit Eater who pointed at the door takes hold of him by the collar and shoves him forward on the path, and the others cuff his head as he darts past with his chin down. We begin walking together; the Spirit Eaters keep close to the man and hold him in place with their censorious presences. Their hostility seems more or less formal; I don't get the impression this man in particular has done anything to merit it.

The path takes us further into the foothills, through sparse foliage and rocks. We climb a ridge and move among many low peaks. Before us opens a broad arid space perhaps a hundred feet across and surrounded by steep slopes. The flat space is not marked by anything but its bareness; obviously all rocks have been cleared away. The path collides with and spreads along the circular rim of the space without touching it, forming a random, roughly triangular region between the circle and the slopes, with stones arranged in rows and sheared off across the top to serve as seats. We gather as indicated in these rows, although there are more of us than there are seats, and Thrushchurl, Silichieh, Jil Punkinflake and I end up standing in a milling bunch of other soldiers and tag-alongs, craning to see. Opposite us and a bit to the right what I take to be a natural channel extends across the slope and then breaks, sending water tumbling down a many-forked notch, in the form of many waterfalls, some frothing and some clear sheets, all collecting in a stony basin half-hidden from view on the far side of the circle.

The young man is standing despondently by the ring's edge. I can glimpse him through the crowd, his shoulders rising and falling. A hand shoves him in the center of his back, and he half-turns thrashing the air with his forearms, anger and fear in his look. His lower lip protrudes a little, and as he turns back to the ring I know he is picking his moment to enter it.

Finally he steps deliberately in, walking toward the center briskly, in a businesslike way. Hush. He walks loosely, turning his soles up toward us, and swinging his hands past his hips. He passes the center of the circle and slows, then stops; I can't see what's happening to him. He drops onto his knees, and then, after a moment, forward onto his hands. Now he just stays that way, on all fours. Our mutter begins to return as time passes, and I wonder if the oracle will come out of that muttering, and not out of the empty circle at all. The light of the day is irregular with the drifting clouds, and now it grows brighter, as though a blind were being lifted in a corner. It shines on the falls and makes them sparkle, brighter, brighter, and brighter still. The water is dappled over with lights that turn as they gleam like gems, and now like stars, and now like suns—

—your enemy has landed—

—they're here—

—they are coming through the mountains toward Cuttquisqui—

—as though a blind were lowered, the light goes. I have a rock at my back trickling grit onto me, and Thrushchurl is to my left, his hands pressed to his ears and his teeth chattering. Jil Punkinflake stands down the path with shock all over his face. He ran a little, I guess. We all did, or something waved us back. Silichieh is peering intently into the circle with pursed lips and his brow screwed down. The shamans, Makemin, Saskia, Nikhinoch, and other soldiers walk past us, heading down the path, discussing. Makemin turns halfway between me and Jil Punkinflake and calls out sternly to us—

"Hey! No dawdling!"

—and Nikhinoch nods, peering at us one by one.

We straggle together and begin heading back, in a mixed silence. Some of us are rattling more than we might, maybe trying to stir up some familiar sound, and there's nervous laughter. I glance back through the men and get a glimpse of the oracle, sitting on the ground, his head bent on his knees. We are going to go meet the enemy. Silichieh is telling us hoarsely about Cuttquisqui.

He clears his throat.

"They worked a silver vein there, a while ago, until an influence came out from a ... mineshaft and made people sick, killed them. So they said a god had come there, and they left."

The voice of the oracle hadn't been so loud in his body, in his open mouth—the instant it flashed from his mouth, it spread in the air, like a pinch of dust dropped on to the surface of some water. I could feel my cold heart beating against the heat of my muscles. A deafening voice in a brittle sheet of sound, sweep and break over me again and again. Thrushchurl giggles vapidly. What language was that? I turn my eyes out over the ground to the side of the path, and I can hear the churning of waves, although the surf is miles away.

*

Clapper racket in our ears we begin our march to Cuttquisqui, which it has taken me most of the morning to discover is a little less than ten miles away. We have each received a kerchief of a dirty white color, peculiarly dingy and shiny at once, to put around our necks. These have been specially prepared, boiled in something that has made them stiff but imparted no smell to them, to protect us against "the influence." It is likely the enemy have these as well—they have spells of their own.

Practically no horses to speak of on the island, in the end we are all, even Makemin, going on foot. Here and there we encounter rough spots where rock slides have cluttered the road with stones, but the route is mostly clear. An advance party of Specialists falls in with us two or three miles into the foothills, swelling our number to a little over a hundred, drifting down in sociable groups from a stand of trees where an elbow in the hills makes a shaded nook by the road. Silichieh immediately takes up with a pair of aristocratic officers who seem to float along in the dust, coming down arm in arm to meet us. The captain is an elfin man with tow curls and an excessively refined pink face. The lieutenant is more ruggedly built, with straight limbs and a broad flat body; he has brown curls and a slightly sallow complexion. Between these newcomers and Silichieh there is an insubstantial familiarity of incomplete acquaintance; they have served together, but had not had the opportunity then to become friends, so perhaps they will take another now. They converse in their own language, which I understand only imperfectly.

I can't hear anything but the sounds we make ourselves. A sick, frightened feeling begins to seep into me. We march through silence, a smell of wet green plants, and something fainter beneath, like rust. The grass and scrub grows thinner as we proceed, and now we are in a place where there are only solitary trees, although the slopes are acrid with rich-looking black earth, packed firm. Where the soil is torn open, pale limestone curds bulge into the air like warts, but the exposed rocks along the path are ferrous, sparsely spotted with lichens and abrasive to touch.

"I wish we had a bit of a breeze. I'm starting to feel stifled," Jil Punkinflake says.

"As long as it didn't blow any of this grit into our faces," I say, and Silichieh nods sagely at me. This brings me back into the circle of his companions, and as I look at them I keep seeing them coming down the declivity to us, kicking out their elegant legs, their heads flung grandly back.

The captain resumes his conversation with Silichieh, now speaking Alak. The lieutenant meanwhile has been asking Thrushchurl something, and now I hear him say "It's the interior they're really scared of."

Thrushchurl turns his head in that direction, away from

me. "The interior ..." he says softly.

"What have you heard about it?" Silichieh asks.

"That's where all the ruins are, and the wilderness and the war. Something else there too, like gods, are there. No one goes in there. The people in town are frightened all this—" the lieutenant makes a vague gesture including us, the war, "—will elicit an answer from it. There's already stirring inside, and any killing will stir it up more."

"You really think so?"

"Oh sure," he says. "How could that not attract attention?"

A cloying, flavorless dampness fills my nostrils. Only now do I notice the fog, dark as twilight, erasing the land. It's so thick I can't make out the end of our party.

"I have a riddle," the lieutenant says. "Want to hear it?"

"I'd like to," I say.

He bends a little forward, past Silichieh, to have a look at me.

"All right," he says. He is smirking a little, and now this expands into a proper smile that suits him better. He holds out his hands to the road, and raises his eyes brightly up.

"There is nothing in this world you love like you love me. You would part with everything else you have before you part with me, though you need never worry I will ever forsake you. More than love, more than life, more than death, you love most of all. *What* am I?"

"Can I ask questions?"

"Until I say stop!"

"All right. Are you always with me?"

"Always, though you don't always know me."

"Are you a part of me?"

"You are a part of me, and I am someone else."

"Are you a spirit?"

"I am a spirit, but all spirits are part of me. And gods."

The captain rolls his eyes, grins at Silichieh.

"You're not *time?*" I ask.

"I grow with time, and time often strengthens me."

"Are you beauty?"

"I think I'm beautiful, but that's not my name."

"Virtue?"

"... That is not my name." Very grand the way he refuses the contraction there.

"Honor?"

"All wise people do me honor. But I'm not wisdom, either—and you're just running down a list, so stop now."

"I give up."

"My name is *fear.*"

*

Rattle of our gear against the quiet; Thrushchurl's anthem, and unsmelly smell of the fog, not a trace of salt air in it, and suppressed under it is the smell of cakey black earth. The swaying shapes of marching soldiers, blue shadows against a low ceiling of fog and the dark crescent of the hillside above me. The captain, speaking in a clear ringing but not loud voice, is describing his great patriotic epic to me. Sounds awful.

"A complex book," he says, "a sorcerer's-apprentice book. A book of loneliness," he adds with a wistful note. "It's about a young man who is sent far away to a sanitarium in the mountains; he must learn there how to cure the plague that is destroying the people back in his home."

He lapses into his original language, addressing himself to Silichieh, and then runs out of words. None of us has much attention to spare. We are less and less able to combat our awe in this still country. Even the loonies are. Thrushchurl's singing has retreated under his breath.

Our muffled noise. An extensive white swatch of dim scales on the slopes ahead, looking like splashes of spilled milk. Presently we draw near, and the patches of white come down to the brink of the path. Even close up, the white is confused by the cloud of fog we're engulfed in, so I have to step to the edge and stoop. Suddenly I can see clearly—tiny, incredibly regular flowers, growing low to the ground, each with six diamond-shaped petals. They aren't white, finally, but a colorless, mother-of-pearl silver, like polished chips of fog. The petals are inflexibly hard, and when I reach to pick one, the thin stem bends stiffly in my fingers like wire, and won't break.

"What's that?" Jil Punkinflake knocks my back and points up the slope at something dark tumbling in among the flowers. I peer through the fog, and I can see a little almond-shaped head up there, and a few others besides.

"Those are hares," I say.

"I've never seen one," he says.

I wonder if, and if so how, they eat these mineral flowers.

"Look there!" and no sooner has he said this and pointed than Jil Punkinflake darts from the path, following the rocky bed of a shallow brook. Thrushchurl follows him avidly on his long legs. I hadn't seen the brook at all, and now I can hardly believe it's there. It flows without making a noise.

A rounded arm lies in the stream, the water bulging around it. The dog stands attentively beside me. Jil

Punkinflake says something I don't catch, facing away from me and still advancing toward the arm, then repeats it over his shoulder.

"It doesn't look real," he says.

They both bend and loom in, faces first. Jil Punkinflake picks up the arm, and then stands, holding it by the elbow.

"It's fake," he says in a loud voice, looking back at us.

Thrushchurl, grinning or squinting, looks to us and echoes his words. "It's fake."

Jil Punkinflake shows me the arm. The flesh is spongy stuff over a hard core, neatly sectioned at the shoulder, with a white bulb of bone protruding. The bulb has four identical, deep grooves cut into it. I turn the hand over and examine it. The slender, womanly fingers close on mine and hold me with gentle pressure, frigid from the icy water of the stream that still trembles in droplets on the blue milk skin. The sensation shakes me. There's something frighteningly enticing about it, and at the same time I want to drop the arm or fling it away from me.

Silichieh begins looking at its articulations.

Ahead, Makemin's voice, flat and strict.

"Come on. Leave it."

"I think they used to put artificial people near crossroads markers," Silichieh says, and his voice seems to plummet in strength during the brief journey from his diaphragm to his mouth. "We should look for markers."

Makemin nods and turns into dark fog. Scouts are sent probing around in the silence ahead. The road here is vague in the shallow breadth of a dip between hills and it isn't entirely clear which way in the fog to go.

Hooting from one of the scouts, an asylum man.

Silichieh dashes forward to examine a small shrine that stands above a V in the ground as thin and meager as a fold in a linen top sheet—the fork in the road, it seems. The shrine is a metal cage on a squat, undulating pillar of the same material, about three feet high. The cage is square, with flat bars, and topped with an acute dome. Inside the cage a polished steel ball rolls back and forth in a groove with pinched-up sides, making a grating stone scraping sound. Why hadn't we heard that? Makemin bids me look for writing. I find none. Silichieh is fascinated by the movement of the ball. He thinks it is not perennial, but starts when someone approaches, and that its movement or sound are articulate in some way. Drawing a knife from the pocket of his sweater, Silichieh tries to probe at the ball, but his knife point stops with a click in between the slats. He taps there twice.

"Glass—so clear I couldn't see it at all," he says.

I'm the last to take my turn peering into the cage. When I look at the ball, which is clouded over with a scoring of fine scratches, but still reflective, I don't see my face. The ball reflects the hills, the landscape behind me, but there is no face staring where mine ought to be. There is no one on the road.

*

The scouts report the lower peters out after only a few hundred yards in heaps of broken glass and rubbery black slag. We take the higher fork.

After not more than forty minutes of climbing, our heads begin to turn and scan into the blank—we're hearing a sound, the first we haven't caused in a long while. What is that steady groan?

A metallic odor, sharp like vinegar, is woven in with the fog here. The groan and the scent come out from a crevasse in the seam between two hills. The opening is sheer and narrow, and the chasm shows no bottom. Its sides are smooth, and faceted in narrow vertical strips, all angles with no curves; the surfaces are all unnaturally flat and smooth as pressed steel, the color of glass smoked almost opaque. Light seems to penetrate it a little, to gleam in the edges of the facets, and there is a sullen glow down deep inside, creeping up but without even slightly illuminating the black center of the pit, from which the groaning comes. The sound is like the legend of the mines. One side of the crevasse is higher than the other, and separate stones ranging in size from pebbles to rocks half my size cling inexplicably to the faceted surfaces, as though invisible hands held them there. Silichieh volunteers to clamber down to the crevasse and pry loose one of these hovering rocks, and Makemin turns him down only after a long thought.

We make our way past, and as one man we tend toward the opposite side of the path.

Now there's grumbling coming from up ahead.

"What now?" the captain asks irritably.

A rockfall—a detail gets busy at once clearing it. I'm not in the detail. Silichieh is poring over the face from which the rocks fell, looking to see if anything interesting is exposed, and I drift past him into the brush for reasons of my own.

Something drags at me—the sensation is impossible to describe—it's as though hooks have snagged all over the front of my uniform, and a single even strength pulls on them all equally and steadily. Despite myself I stagger with the pull, and now my eyes pick out a seam of bright blue silver in the shade of the stones. I allow myself to draw nearer, leaning back now against the pull.

A piece of lightning lies on the ground where the rock face bares itself out of the soil. It gleams with reflected light: a hair-slender forking line. The clay around it stands out dark and broken, so this must be something the falling rocks exposed.

Thrushchurl gasps at my side, gazing at it. He kneels, taking up a stick, and cudgels some of the loose stone aside. The pull strengthens so that I double forward—then fling myself back and push with my legs. It's the metal I'm carrying that is pulled. Thrushchurl's tentative digging has exposed a thicker limb of that same blue silver from which the forks emerge. It looks like the blades of ice that are first to form on still water in winter. Thrushchurl carefully extends his stick to prod the thicker limb, and to my amazement the metal yields like water. Thrushchurl makes a strangling noise, and I take hold of his shoulder and start dragging him away. His astonishment seems to have made him inert as a doll. I don't like this blue silver's unwholesome aura or its insistent appetite for my metal. I tell him and myself that we ought to find Silichieh, but the way is clear now and we are brusquely ordered to fall in.

*

After a time, walking mechanically forward with my eyes on the ground, I glance up and stop so abruptly that Jil Punkinflake collides with my back. A shiver transfixes my whole body from the top down, and my jaws clench so hard I can feel the muscles on my skull push out. A hollow in the mist, like a floating tunnel, drifts past, and through it I see the blue slopes of the mountains, blue as cobalt, seeming as though simply standing there were a shimmering action they took.

"The interior," Thrushchurl grins at me, nodding, passing, his hands thrust in his pockets and his carbine high on his back.

Jil Punkinflake is shoving me forward high-handedly, as though Saskia were watching.

The sight is gone, and now fog and swaying backs fill my eyes again. I breathe out through my mouth; the mountains I saw there, so briefly, were the mountains of home.

*

Dark bluffs of that iron rock lift up above us and boulders line the road. The rocks are fanning our line out and Makemin is concerned; he is continually calling to his officers to keep everyone together. The bluffs seem to wall off some of the mist.

The path tapers down to a flat clear spot shored with talings and boulders. From there, it angles in forks to the right where it descends, diverted around the high iron promontory facing us. The shoulders on all sides are fringed with enormous basalt rocks. Rounding the shoulder there are other men walking towards us and into our ranks shouts rise on all sides and I see blackbirds' shocked faces uniforms and the world blows apart in explosions of gunfire as I turn see one of our men run twist in air head whirl on his neck and fall in a heap I scramble to one side ducking my head. The lieutenant is just ahead of me pitching headlong behind the rocks. I shove in behind him and lower my head nearly to the ground, shots rebounding against the stone, spatter the higher boulders behind me, their noise punctuating the more continuous howling of the men who cry in surprise, alarm, dismay, pain, sudden fright. A spray of gravel patters on my back I turn and see Silichieh, who had been relieving himself in among the rocks, dashing forward between them in a crouch, holding his trousers together with one hand and homing in on the lieutenant. Looking about me, I see the captain standing impossibly by the shoulder in firing range posture, left hand on his belt buckle, shoulders and hips following the arm, legs akimbo, aiming firing and aiming his pistol with a kind of shining boldness, golden hair and regimental uniform. I fold myself backwards as the lieutenant continues to crawl for cover and I am on my side, in the dust looking out at chaos of fog and jets of gunsmoke I have for a moment the bizarre thought that I see dawn haze over high tiled roofs, a willow tree glazing with the pale light of a chilly winter sunrise. A moment ago we were simply walking along together—now my friends and companions are lying dead on every side—not ten feet from me a forearm lies spreading blood—I hear screams from forms dashed to the ground, while over me the sky is cool, the day made beautiful by the fog, the hills roll placidly off into the distance. I lie here in a nightmare while all around me the world continues tranquilly.

Saskia races by, barrelling toward the enemy and one of the Specialists staggers forward out of the fog and collapses with a sluicing wound in his thigh—a moment later, his screams begin. I go to him; he lies on his back. I'm bandaging his leg but the blood flows out of him even when I lean forward with all my weight and press both hands to the rags of his thigh even as he is screaming so loud I can't hear the shots crashing all around me. Now I'm stopping the blood—no, the flow has stopped because his heart has. The ground under my knees thumps like a drum. One of the Expeditionary soldiers lies on his side not ten feet away clutching his arm. I crawl to him he jerks as a bullet ploughs up his body his abdomen splits and I seize him the next moment, holding him as he screams and flails I try to stop him, he's spilling and spreading his scarlet entrails around. A hammer smashes me on the hip and his body jolts, I am knocked backward. When I rear up again into his abrupt silence I fumble at his neck, he's dead—my pelvis aches at my left hip—investigating I find the bullet that struck and killed him passed through his body and deflected off the heavy steel holster clip on my belt because fate loves idiots. From everywhere come cries for help. I make for a low rock that's near and slump behind it stupidly, bullets buzzing on all sides like heavy midges and surrounding them the noise of the Clappers high up on the path in our rear. Men are crying to me, for *my help*. I see another wounded man near me. I'm the only medical officer here and I go quickly to him—

"Wait! Stop shooting!" I scream nonsensically to no one as I flounce on all fours to his side. I am listening to the rhythm the Clappers make up and about the shooting; I look down to bandage my casualty and find I've already done it. I follow screams to another man, wafted along I feel light as air, I attend to him and pull him behind the rocks.

My head feels turned to light. The world cries "help" to me, and I say to it "I'm coming! I'm coming!" as often as I can, as I dress another wound, as I pull a man to cover, as I catch the next man to be hit before he touches the ground he is in my arms and receiving my help.

The horns of the Clappers blat out loud. Now I see Makemin in a knot of sharpshooters firing from a heap of rocks an explosion from the path ahead cuffs me with its noise and I lunge for Makemin's cover. I see one of the blackbirds pick up and pitch back one of our bombs, and it detonates close enough to me to shower me with particles of stone. Makemin orders the grenadiers to stop throwing. I'm looking around this way and that—I see Jil Punkinflake flat on the ground with his hands clutching his head and his dog tugging insistently at his coat tails. Going to him I find him unhurt, sobbing and rigid with fear, drag him to cover. Now I see Thrushchurl high up behind the rocks, grinning and methodically loading and emptying his gun without pointing it at much of anything. The fog is lifting a little. Silichieh comes from Makemin's direction and slides in beside me in a hail of gravel, his face drawn, eyes dull and blank like a doll's eyes.

"They're falling back. Makemin wants us to regroup."

He bustles on past me his sweater brushing over the dog's head. I don't know what to do so I stay put and watch. No sign of any regrouping. Another fusillade of shots spatter all around, one of the loonies falls a few dozen yards from me, face down in a mound of black earth. He's dead when I reach him. I run again for cover, the same stones that sheltered me at the start, years ago. I can see the lieutenant is still there, the whites of his eyes as he peers at me, rigid, breathing hard, face in the grey.

The ground around me stutters with shot like cracking whips and I'm pelted with grit. There are enemy rifles sparking from stones just down the path from me. Saskia is suddenly there between the riflemen and me; she bounds up on their cover and kicks one of the blackbirds in the face the pistol in her left hand is pointing and firing and the sabre in her right swings up and down. She's leapt right among them—I can't see—one of them backs into view with his rifle flung up her sabre shears it in two and hacks him so that he is driven back, tumbles over a boulder and falls sluicing blood to the ground. Another is coming up the path rifle level she bounds over the barrier thrusting out her legs and kicks him in the chest. He lands prone and spins but she swifter than thought is upon him and spits his throat, pulls the blade out and chops him across his adam's apple. Never stopping she flies up the opposite declivity of the path following a broken defile along which some of the enemy are retreating. Up the slope weightless she goes and slices a man's legs out from under him from below, impaling him in the chest when he falls. The soldier ahead of him she shoots as he crests the grade, the bullet blowing his hat up and off his head. She climbs to him and stabs him, then vanishes over the declivity, firing her pistol. Last I see of her, she is charging down after them, now both hands on her sabre she lifts it over her head again and again, hacking at them like a crazed woodsman chopping logs.

The Clappers suddenly call *congregate*. The shooting has stopped. Only now do I realize it has been over for a while. My ears are ringing.

Men are timidly emerging from cover and gathering in

the flat spot where the road forks. Makemin and Nikhinoch stand there impatiently. As I approach, and the lieutenant, looking grim, comes behind me, the captain strides up lightly but out of breath and reports to Makemin, pointing down the path. Makemin nods. Presently I hear him asking after Saskia. I point down the path myself, explaining where she went. Makemin frowns and pulls the havelock from his helmet angrily wadding it in his hands. I can't yet follow entirely what is being discussed—I look back and see one of the blackbirds scrambling at the top of the declivity on the path ahead. Before I can cry out, I see him slip and drop. When he emerges from the stones among which he fell, he is staggering in obvious pain and clutching his right arm. Saskia appears at the top of the declivity and shouts. The enemy soldier sees her and flees, heading down to the base of the slope. She is on him, but ungainly, colliding with him she knocks him to the path, where he falls on his side. Saskia, regaining her balance, strides up to him and kicks him in the stomach hard enough I can hear it all these yards away.

She kicks, kicks again. I am running toward them. She kicks him mechanically, and steadily. With each kick I see blood spurt from his lips two feet. I call to her to stop, but nothing changes.

Now she stops, and walks a little down the path, picks up his hat and tears the emblem from it, pockets the emblem. I am at his side now. His ghostly pulse gives out beneath my fingers.

"What's the matter with you?!" I shout at her as she walks to Makemin, passing me. No sign that she hears me. The features on the ground are so badly broken no amount of mental effort could reassemble them into a face; not a real face.

I follow her back.

Makemin is fuming.

"That's the last time you run off on your own!" he says harshly. She seems not to mind him. Her front is butcher-bloody from her head to her feet; she seems winded. Makemin inclines his head and seems to gather up her gaze.

"And we need *prisoners*, you understand?"

Saskia purses and unpurses her lips and nods wearily, putting her hand to her head. Makemin sends scouts forward and continues to gather the men; I gather the casualties.

"How many?" I am asked.

"Sixteen dead, eight injured, don't know how many minor hurts yet."

"We leave the injured here with two of the asylum soldiers to tend them. Silichieh will erect the tent. You select the two attendants, tell them what to do and supply them. Make certain you strip the injured and give their supplies to Nikhinoch. Get your funeral friends to strip and burn the bodies."

Crossing the flat area, my face feels intensely cold as the wind comes up. I have to keep helplessly dashing tears from my face.

*

Faint cries of enervated surprise break our monotonous rattle; on the slope rising in an acute curve to the left a black piglet stands watching us sidelong. It soon trots away beneath the rise.

Now, as the slope levels a bit, a house is coming into view

on the left side. It stands out, a peaked blue angle against the high arc of the horizon that no other thing breaks. The hill is all packed earth, and I can't see a single stone or so much as a pebble on it, not a twig or blade of grass. This is the first house we've come across, and after bringing it a few dozen feet further out of the mist I see a dark activity flurry the air above it. The gaunt stone pipe of its chimney dribbles smoke into the fog. As I hold my gaze on the house I remember a line of verse, "an orphan fang in gums of clay." Terrible. I wish I had forgotten it.

I can't run. Where would I go? The land is barren, and I don't know it. Makemin would shoot a deserter. What do I do?

The path will pass close to the house. Two or three black hogs are drowsing in a stone sty adjoining it. Makemin halts the column and beckons me to accompany him to the house. As we plod up to the door, he informs me I am to identify him to the occupants if any by the rank of brevet colonel. He is less peremptory with me than usual and I am ashamed of the idiot child of pride this stirs in me, as I imagine I have acquitted myself well in his eyes.

A confined, level spot has been cleared before the front of the house, which faces the path. Two windows with big shutters now shut, and another set of shut shutters directly over the sturdy-looking front door. By their regularity, I can tell these fittings are made of metal, not wood. The house is black brick with coal colored mortar, and a slate roof. Makemin raps noisily on the door with his knuckles, stands back and waits. After a moment, the upper half of the door is swung back by a lackadaisacal-looking woman with poached-egg eyes and her black hair is a little frizzled.

Her sleepy face is sallow and vaguely made, but there's something even sly in the way she takes us in, resting her forearms on the lower half of the door casually.

I greet her and reveal to her our amazing identities. Behind her, I can see a strangely inviting, limpid darkness, through which a fire sends flitting rays like the setting sun streaking thick and agitated clouds. Two old men are irrigating soup into their beards at a burnished wooden table with a single empty seat and a bowl waiting. Tin tram signs hang from the walls. Makemin asks me to ask her if she's seen any men in black uniforms or groups of Yesegs pass this way. She addresses her response to me, her voice is caressing, shrill but quiet.

"She says she saw them pass by here a few hours ago, heading in our direction, and then saw a few of them returning in haste more recently."

I am asked to ask how many there were. I ask, she answers, I tell Makemin—

"Far fewer than there had been. Three dozen or so, she thinks. She wants to know if we fought with them. Shall I tell her?"

"Yes."

I report this, and she blinks slowly.

I am asked to ask if she saw where they went and if so where they went. We proceed.

"They left the path not far ahead and went in among the hills. She thinks they avoid the village influence."

...

"The village is not ten minutes walk from here. One practically can't live any closer than this."

...

"They say they are the only people remaining here. Everyone else died, or left. Most went on to Verauar."

...

"Are there supplies in town? No we are not afraid of the influence we have these—" he shows the kerchief, causing her to cock one eyebrow slightly.

"She says there are probably some stores left in town. The wells are bad, but there are cisterns for catching rainwater. That should be all right."

...

"She says she has seen no other soldiers here."

...

"She did not see the effect of the influence."

...

"The old men did not see the effect of the influence. No one who went to see came back to tell."

"What was mined here?" Makemin asks through me.

The woman smiles loosely and holds up an arm bangled with bright gold, thick bracelets and engraved rings fretting her fingers and thumb.

Makemin looks up as magenta grains appear in the fog. I see his thinking—sunset coming on, we're safest camping in town. I am instructed to thank the woman for her information and to offer her some reward. She and the two men behind her are like a kind of trick picture, appearing to move but not moving at all.

"She wants a gun."

Makemin calls to Nikhinoch, who goes and comes with a rifle. Makemin takes it, gives it to me, I give it to her. Her fingers brush mine lightly as she takes it, her eyes invariably on the gun. As we return to the column with our gratitude still hanging in the air her gaze remains with us like mist resting on the water.

"Do you believe her?" I am asked.

"Of course I do. They always use a particular inflection when they lie."

"I can't say I see the use of that."

"Oh," I sigh, "it's conventional. You use it when you want to seem to be lying, and so then you can tell the truth."

The men abandon their resting postures and though they are tired I can see they are very interested in getting to safety, like Makemin. Descending with the path away from the house on the slope I feel oddly clearheaded as though my mind were a wiped-clean glass. We pass between two hills and into an exposed place. Its openness eyes us unnervingly. The grey ground is dimpled over with puddles that reflect the sky's moving seams like a mirror pelt of milky spots. As we venture out onto it, like spirits answering an incantation the first buildings appear opposite us, looking silver and blue as pink radiance percolates down through the fog. As I walk, my eyes on these foggy buildings, I find I cannot make myself step in a puddle—no one can. I hear no splashes. To my right, ahead, I see an arch standing alone, two slender columns and a delicate span. There are many, maybe too many, lined up here in rows, as though someone wanted to make tunnels through the air. They are too attentive to us to use for cover.

House coming up ahead. I feel a knock against my boot and there's a twang of metal fleeing me on the ground—as I look down to see the rusted can I've kicked the house turns and disappears into the fog—I stop. There is no house in sight. Was it an animal? There are no animals as big as houses, not on land. Fog magnifies things.

These structures are gathered here in isolation. We do not draw near to them but march instead between huge mounds of displaced earth. The light, or the air, is soft, grey shining through grey. Icing the odor of damp stone and the breath of the clay, a smell like onions. No nothing like onions—a chemical smell, like waterproofing chemicals or bookbinder's glue, musty as old hair, but with something reeking in it that puckers my nose.

Thrushchurl points. "The mines," he says faintly.

There's a long shallow scar immensely chiselled into the ground. In one of its sides is a series of low arched openings in a canted wall extending away from us. Each opening is lined with stone. The rails for the ore carts glimmer unrusted in each arch, like bright-sided fish in a row of black wells. Before these openings a scurf of white powder, like wheat flour, lies tamped in crescents. The excavated floor otherwise is meticulously swept, unlittered and without so much as a single stone. Not even an irregularity or crease in the surface. The ore carts that ran on those rails are lined up neatly against the low far wall and the side facing the openings; their wheels still glint showing white strips of reflection. These points of light, the wheels and the ends of the rails in the openings, are the only intensities my eyes trace. Around the steel of the rails and the wheels a transparent light trembles like water.

"Masks."

Hurriedly we pass the spot, and the town is not far beyond it, materializing building by building out of the fog, behind many lower mounds of earth, so that I am walking a cobbled street before I know it. Everything is made of tiny ash-colored bricks, like metal ingots. Dusk, and these black doorways and small-paned windows, one precise edge after another as we walk up the street. Houses and low-walled square yards, a shop on a corner. The street is bare, though many of the houses show doors fallen in flat and broken glass in the panes. I don't feel sheltered by these buildings, they have only added their dead stares to the dead stare that might as well be the fog, all around.

From somewhere above me and to the right a sound like the glass chimes that used to hang from the eaves of the old narrator's house, and something else, like the noise of coins poured out spattering in a heap. It whirrs and peters out almost at once; an alarm phantom.

We are to break up and take shelter in the houses, as though the pretext of our being soldiers were abandoned. My fingers reach out and touch a piece of metal that has been welded to a window frame, as a patch or crude decoration maybe. Unlike the frame, this metal is unrusted; I brush irregularities on the surface and, bending near, I see stamped there characters I know are ancient. I touch the metal again, thinking this was made by human hands since turned to dust, before the Limiters. In the metal or in the fingers I feel that age feebly answering my thought; it stirs, then sinks too quickly away again.

Black doorway before me and I have to force myself to cross the threshold. But I am stupid and weary, not my legs they never tire, but my mind is too tired to sleep but then I will. I enter, my feet scraping loudly on the floor, and lie down not far from the door. My gaze wanders out over these tiny, carefully laid tiles, leaves and fishes; I wonder about the hands that laid them, what a waste now. Thrushchurl tosses and lifts his matted head looking for mice. A wind I don't feel makes the metal casement creak, the window sways. I close my eyes and feel a familiar rushing sensation, like canting forward down a steep hill, just begin to.

Now I am asleep. My breast rises and falls, pulling and tossing little mouthfulls of this spellbound air. My face has slackened, and the night's lustre confuses my face and makes it a corpse's—if I could see myself how horrifying I would find this sight, I look like someone who's been broken on the rack.

The sound of my breath, stealing in and out of my empty nose, is the same breath going over itself without stifling me—but I do sink a little each time—the breast falls deeper, rises lower; not dying away, but almost sinking into the ground. What I am is seeping up like wisps of vapor—remember placing drops of alcohol on small pieces of ice, watch, the viscous steam ooze from the alcohol bead ashen with frost and just so the essence of me climbs in a suppressed breath from snow white writings and flows among the marks.

You are made of the strongest stuff, icy matter and black ichor, and as a follower you are always the first to arrive. You were summoned to be an eyewitness, but in being summoned you were cut off from the underworld that is the only place you actually can live in, that allows you to enter any place and see any scene. Some witnesses are called to see and testify, and others to be watched and kept, although it's not always only the one way or the other.

Now he's asleep—draw near—your life is in him—draw on it, with rootlike fingers outstretched, and the wrenched crescent of your sickle mouth slopping ink down a scored face.

A hand on my shoulder wakes me and I gaze madly up into the lieutenant's quizzical face, sallow and blue in the dark.

"It's only me," he says a little irritably, some sleep still in his voice. "We're on duty now."

No Thrushchurl there on the floor as I collect myself—where has he gone?

Back out into seeping chill, soft crush of our feet on the clay between the houses. The lieutenant seems to know everything, leads me to a thin track that runs along a broad river of clear water lined with streaming, almost glowing fronds of green. Despite their luxurious growth I can still make out the rows; the only plants that grow around here grow underwater, and these were cultivated. The current is swift and lays flat the vines, but the riled surface is silent. Likewise we are silent, baffled in sleep and fog.

Our path takes us through an enormous brick building with empty arches and a vast floor of tamped clay. The roof has vanished without a trace, if there ever was one, but the fog respects the walls and remains above them. These bricks are red, and of the usual size. The place feels imported. The lieutenant looks around avidly, but he and I both are awkward and nearly stagger against each other so that I can make out the sparse bristles on his cheek, the little circular scar on his forehead. He chuckles a little.

"How stupid we are," he exclaims softly, and yawns so that I can hear his jaw creak.

We emerge on the other side the building, the lieutenant curves back toward Cuttquisqui, and something white drags itself out the mouth of the second mine shaft there in the distance. It pulls its bulk on long spindly arms, stops, straightens its arms pushing its shoulders and rearing head up. Far-away black eyes stare at us. It holds this posture as it sinks into the ground no more rapidly than a candle burns down. It tilts back, so that its face is the last of it to disappear.

I can't see the lieutenant's face. He is not moving, looking back toward town, and he sounds like he's choking. I take a step toward him, and he swallows and says, "Is it gone?"

I look unnecessarily.

"Yes."

"Where did it go—into the mine?"

"Yes."

He pauses. Perhaps he turned away after it started to sink.

"Let's get back," he says.

Back among the brick houses, the small-paned windows swing just a little in the fog.

*

Yours are the eyes I see open wide. Nothing in these images of you touches me until the moment I glimpse you from the side and a bit behind, and see a little fold under your chin; that melts my heart. I hear my voice speak before I know it is my rolled jacket whose folds my eyes are searching, "How do you feed stone fishes?"

Thrushchurl rubs his head, sitting up grinning as always. The long stringy hair he keeps under his top hat is pressed into two mats that sweep back from the peak of his high, narrow brow.

We sit gloomily in the street, straggling in and out of buildings, forking food out of cans. The light here is silver, haggard as rain and retarded by the fog. I join Thrushchurl as he slips into a narrow alley. He stands himself on top of a sizeable rock and gazes off toward the mines.

"They're so still," he says. But everything here is still.

Makemin stands with the Clappers around him, conjuring us to gather and hear his orders. This is not something I am eager to do. The loonies are there already—they seem cowed, and dislike to leave Makemin's vicinity. They sit together in rows, looking around with mouths open and slumping eyelids. The Clappers' tattoo struggles to make itself audible in the muffling air, and the rhythm begins to click and patter, its regularity to break.

Only now, as they start to their feet, do I realize that it's bullets that click and patter around us. I turn and push Thrushchurl into the nearest doorway with both my hands on his broad flat chest. He turns suddenly and plucks at the latch, teasing it with his fingers, his other hand flat on the calloused wood, and then the door subsides and we are covered—I hear the bangs against the wall. Do I go to the window?

Thrushchurl fingers the air, saying "It won't last long."

My thoughts are all out of order; I numbly ask my eyes on the light from the window to restore me. The banging has stopped, come and gone like a summer shower down in the valley. I turn to the open door. Voices in the street, men emerging from cover.

"How did you know?" I ask.

"I didn't," he says, going out into the street.

They hit one of the loonies, who had generally needed someone to lead him by the hand and had not had that someone just then, when the shooting began.

Makemin gathers us in a few buildings at one end of town, where the land rises. We can't all fit inside one. I am present when the scouts report signs of the enemy moving back and forth on a spur of high land thrust out from the foothills and overlooking the town. Twice I hear the ping of bullets again, and now I see, in the fog, a blur here or there, that flits from rock to rock, or sways as light as a ghost swinging to and fro, guns banging far away ... Saskia wants to go after them—Makemin won't hear of it in this fog. He takes my arm and tells me he is suspicious, he has intuitions, and doesn't wait to see me nodding obediently. As the afternoon comes on, and there's been some time with no shooting, the scouts go out again. Signs the soldiers have withdrawn—dusk is coming. We stay together in the houses until darkness falls, and leave our lamps unlit. We crane our ears into the silence, knowing the enemy is there in the dark and the fog, hidden in the rocks, high over us.

*

On patrol that night, again with the lieutenant. We fall in step with few words, following a street on the thin town's thin edge. The houses loom larger than they are.

He's looking away from me, at the windows we pass on his side.

"Any more riddles?" I ask.

"What?" he turns. "No," he smiles faintly, looking away distracted.

I can go on walking these streets of fog for eternity. I look at the lieutenant, so when I hear the distant snap from above, when he stops and I hear him abruptly make that soft, sad "oh" as though he'd just blundered gently into something in the dark, I also see: his head dips, his face splits, his mandible swings wildly from his head on a strip of ligament, like a helmet's loose chin strap, and blood cascades down his uniform to the ground. His feet take two little steps to the side, in the direction of the force, toward me, his body shudders and with it the jaw hanging by a scrap of left cheek, and now he makes and indescribable sound his eyes starting from their sockets, raising hands around a wound he dare not touch. Flinging out his arms he disappears into the house to his right.

I call and run after him—his shadow before me arms flailing, jaw swinging, the shape of the doorway as it runs feet loud on planks. A raw voice whoops out from the cavity, flying back to me from every wall in the dark as I've lost sight of him, the voice riots from everywhere as though the night were belching out its entrails.

A crash of water directs me and in a moment I am outside again, and there is agitation, a writhing black thing crosses the river away from me.

"Come back!" I stand on the bank. Where do I go?

Not even a streak in the water shows where he has been. I run in the dark, following the water's edge; here a gravel mound spans the flow and I can ford across. My splashing legs make a great noise in the dark. I climb the opposite bank peering in all directions. The bank levels then swings up again. Moving from one boulder to another I gain height, hoping to find a good place to stop and look around. The slope is fractured ahead of me—a path. I head toward it.

I stop. These are the heights, where the enemy is. Dropping to a crouch I start dithering sideways below the level of the path, kicking down thick earth but not too noisily. This is a kind of spontaneous compromise between going on and going back—I think in confusion I will arc down toward the river, pausing along the flattened apex at intervals to search for the lieutenant. The path should be avoided, but it seems to draw me, and all the obstacles displaced to clear it now lie in my way. A rocky space like an ingrown wart comes up to me, and, still defying the path, I begin working my way down in among the rocks, holding on with hands and feet. It's important to keep an eye on the path; it wants to trip me up, but it is the only landmark I have to gauge my height and position from here.

I look up to the path, and see barrel and gun, hand and half-hidden face … the enemy uniform … the eye at the sight.

Fifth Chapter

The rain hides them from me. I have to walk with my head down. One goes ahead of me on my right, the other behind at my left, about six feet away. The one behind me took my gun and my pack. I don't like the disembodied, light feeling that being disburdened gives me. I'm afraid, and there is no ballast of gear to hold. The path is satisfied, its personality is gone.

I don't want to move my head, let the one behind me know I keep glancing about me, and at the one before me. A filled black uniform shiny with rain, a pale hand waving by the left hip. They are taking me toward the heights. Stuck in a vice I can only stare helplessly at my profuse and hasty thoughts none of them any good, they're only making me crazy with the rain driving down on top of me. Will I panic? A sure way to die, how wise. How can such inane thoughts be possible now?

They conduct me between two large boulders as the path begins to curve around to the high place overlooking the one end of the town. I see a few tents bowed by the water, and the rags and ends of many others there; the camp is littered with trash. Enemy soldiers look up from their shooting places among the rocks, where most of them lie flat under grey sheets. Rain is gathering in a broad ribbon, widening to sheathe the end of the path before frothing over the edge and down the slope through a rough, fresh notch in the rim. The soil is crumbling as the water saws away at it. A bit of surprise keeps the fear from flashing too strongly over me as we come into camp—there are no more than a dozen or so of them. The rest have gone—I can see their tracks, the flat grooves the cartwheels left now bubbling with rain. These skirmishers remain to hold us down and convince us the enemy are massed on the heights, while the bulk of their number are already on their way and are now between Vscriathjadze and us.

Inside a spacious tent the rain has made into a drum, a man lies groaning on a cot. One of my guards talks to me and points at the man. He turns and puts my pack on table, sifting roughly through its contents. After a hasty inspection, he pulls out the sharper implements then shoves the pack into my hands and points to the wounded man. I don't want to have to put up with his injuries or his weary suffering any more than they do; I set to work at once.

They must have no medical officer: they won't kill me. But will they drag me away with them?

I finish, I do a good job. The guard who handed me

my pack is gone. The one I presume to be the one to walk behind me sits now on a box by a lamp, elbows on knees, tired eyes on me. Pale-sallow, with a high square forehead tucked into the black visor, honey-brown hair, aristocratic looking nose. The first soldier returns and roots around in some boxes, festoons of water gushing from him. He's removing bundles wrapped in rough fabric and tucking them under his arms. Suddenly he turns and crosses the tent in three strides, leaning sideways from the waist to peer down at the injured man, whose groans have subsided. He stares at my eyes sticking his finger into my face and speaks harshly to me, his voice so hoarse he can't stop it breaking. He speaks Tauride, not Yeseg, but there is one word with a shock I know. It's "narrator."

The first soldier storms out with only a glance at his companion by the flap, who has not moved nor shifted her eyes from me. Naturally, they will have their own narrators. Soldiers come in and out for blankets or rain gear, as the water begins to fall hard again. They are not hostile, and pay me no more attention than seems necessary. Drawn anxious features stretched over their skulls is all I see. I'm a nuisance to them.

Relentless dripping, tapping on top of the tent.

Now I am compelled to rise and taken to another, half-collapsed tent, close to the rim. There is not much space in this tent, only enough for me to sit on the low stool that occupies it. The irregular flap has a view of the town below. The soldier walks away; I can see the others before me, huddled in among the rocks, scanning the town.

With nothing to do I have a harder time keeping the fear from gnawing—I've already begun to shiver, my uniform is plastered to my skin with sweat and icy rain. A wave of sharper cold blisters over me from behind ... out of the drumming of the rain comes a whispered roar, like the hooning sound of breath being blown into a bottle. It approaches the tent with steady deliberation—I can't turn to look. It's high up ... Nothing I could see anyway, without leaving the tent.

The roaring stops as something thuds on the canvas right above my head—two puckers where talons clutch the fabric.

I hear its respiration, regular, painful out of water, a protracted lowing, like a stricken animal moaning out its life in a deep cave. I look forward out the flap, my hands beginning to tremble on my knees. The presence soaks into my back. I can guess what it is—Wacagan have Predicanten.

The tent creaks. The thing lows just on top of me like a harbinger of doom.

The rain falls harder still. Though it is louder, it does not overwhelm that other sound ... As it eases again, my eye is drawn to a sprawling activity before me. The grey slopes to my right flap turbid with mud, I see the fumbling, cream-fringed edges of water tumbling over each other in layers as they grapple over rocks, down to the levels. Motion on lower ground now—the water climbs the walls of the houses in Cuttquisqui's streets—all that landscape we explored and found swept clean of litter and this is why—the mounds of earth at the town's edges were dykes, abandoned half-built.

The Predicate's presence drops down out of it, enveloping me in a pillar of sway and suddenly every muscle in my body strains against itself, my jaw trembles and I am rigid. My spirit leaps against my frozen body—

They'll be driven out into the open if the waters keep rising. Something drains out of me as I sit fixed in place watching.

The water goes higher. The streets are a grey slough.

Higher, higher—seething ashenness rushing in the doors. It climbs toward the windows.

Now I see them, dark spots emerging from the town, feet drag and slip and fall in the flow and now the careful enemy aims fires aiming and firing—some of those struggling shapes stop, weave, some fall; they are making for the mounds of displaced earth by the mine. Figures shapes move on the rooftops—with sick impotence I see them picked off, my eyes darting around and finding nothing, nothing, I can't shout or fling a stone to jog their aiming arms. The breathing grip on me is driving its cold into my body harder and harder and I can only sit, my fingers crimping my knees—bodies of my friends bob and spin, rushing along fast enough now—or they fall wounded and struggling, and drown—and the horror of this thought is enough to wrench me an inch forward on my seat.

Above me I hear a studiously adjusted clench on the canvas. That breathing makes the canvas sputter as it rakes it with its grip—I will make that thing move drive it off strike it—I've seen mountain snow and I call that snow to mind as I drop my eyes to the fist-sized flat stone that weighs down one corner of the tent flap near my right foot—tears burst like acid from my eyes.

Still, white-clotted pelts of shaggy evergreens on the far side of a field of blue snow.

And then night, the flakes spin bright past my face and vanish in the gloom, fluffed and weightless in filmy air and a cold that polishes me.

My fingers have opened and my hand slides heavy as a millstone from my leg my arm drops to my side nearly numb.

Lighter than feathers, the snow flakes dance to the ground, weaving and looping with no breeze, no palpable influence, with only their own native frivolity. My hand stretches toward the stone with a feeling like the grating of rust on rust in my elbow in my shoulder. I am pulling madly against my lower back that is rigid as if I wore a corset, but I say I. am. in. the. snow. which scatters in high plumes with one half-hearted kick of my foot, which wafts back up from the ground like it's not done playing.

The rock presses my palm and my fingers snap shut around it I swing straightening my legs and strike at the puckered canvas. The tent roof plunges violently, a hoarse indrawn moan erupts, breaking the breathing and that yawning roar takes its place again. The blow felt weak, useless. But perhaps it wasn't.

My body snaps out of its confinement and in my tremor I lurch against the wall of the tent, bringing it down on top of me. I flounder there, pulling the canvas this way and that, struggling to free myself.

Now I am kneeling in the wreckage of the tent, facing a soldier who stands with his knees flexed before me bayonet levelled. He charges me with a high wail like something out of a madhouse and I throw my arms in the air. He stops short the bayonet only a foot away from me, but he wails again and again, glaring at me eyes white, his howls more terrifying than any attack.

Voices speaking normally—men walking along the height—the shots have stopped. Their assault is over, and whatever I was just a moment before, I am only a captive now. The first soldier to take me comes up, looking sternly at the ruined tent, but he says something to the other, who stops voice at his approach. With a start I hear the man who nearly bayonetted me exchange words calmly in a voice that is even rather beautiful with the other. They turn to me at once, and motioned me to stand.

The rain abates. They march me to a small clear spot by the top of the slope, hemmed in with big rocks. I am made to sit with my back to one, by the very top of the slope, and bayonet will stay to keep an eye on me, sitting on a stone by the aperture in the rock ring where the path threads.

I hear their voices move off, and then nothing but the crumpling sound of water draining among the stones, down the slope. I sit on the wet ground numb as a stone. Bayonet seems preoccupied, his eyes remote. Suddenly all my vitality is gone, and I nod.

A hiss explodes my sleep—bayonet bolts white faced to his feet barking out with fright as the lieutenant steps into the circle ... dew dropping onto the front of his uniform from his dangling end of his jaw, his own blood.

"Xupí!" the guard breathes, and runs away, footfalls scraping on the ground.

The lieutenant is walking away from me, arms at his sides. He dwindles into the shade at the edge of the circle. Unshackled, my life leaps into my legs and I get up, scramble down the slope from one rock to another my feet slip crazily but I keep my balance—now I'm in the passageways between the boulders—now flying down the mushy slope somehow keeping my feet beneath me and not behind me.

Ground flattens and my legs bend—I run for the mounds, splashing across the distance the water already subsided into the myriad puddles reflecting the sky as they did when we first arrived. Xupí is their word for ghost, isn't it? How do I know? How do I know? I'm drawing near, and shots thump into the ground by my feet, a stone chip flaked off by a bullet cuts my cheek—

"It's *me* you idiots! Stop shooting!"

I stand in my place holding my head in my hands with my elbows in the air shout my name again and again— the shots have stopped, hands on my shoulders, I am being brought forward. I see Jil Punkinflake's glowing face, smiles and shakings. So I'm back, I'm safe, self-saved safe.

*

Makemin's face shifts and then hardens again as I tell him about the skirmishing party, the signs of general withdrawal. He turns from me the next moment orders already shrilling from his slot-like mouth. We march back the way we came, at once. Daybreak is mired in yellow fog, and the sun's heat does not penetrate the chill rising from the bare black earth of the hills we pass.

Vscriathjadze is too well defended a port to take by sea: the difficult passage into the estuary, impossible by night and slow by day; the city's defenders have ample time in which to spot and prepare for a seaborne enemy. The port itself is high-walled, and really can only be entered either very slowly or with the assistance of a pilot. Once within the confines of the harbor the enemy ship is vulnerable to fire from above, and so are the troops as they ascend the long steps to the level of the city. Impracticable. But Vscriathjadze is strategically vital as the only proper port on

Meqhasset's southern coast, where troops and supplies can be deposited in any quantity. It is also the island's only city. So Wacagan set their troops down elsewhere in small groups on strips of empty stone beach and direct them to travel inland. Their Predicate tells them to go to Cuttquisqui, where they may dig in and wait in some security as these smaller bands come together to form a body of soldiers large enough to take Vscriathjadze.

Makemin speculates that the first band, their Predicate being away providing guidance for some other newly-arrived group, misnavigated and overshot the town. They pressed on down the road, ran into us, were routed, and fled; their only hope being to find another group of their own. A Predicate most likely arranged such a rendezvous and it was from this mass of Wacagan troops that the skirmishing group was selected, set to mislead us into remaining in Cuttquisqui. Makemin had hoped to find the enemy remnant there, and finish them.

A runner, a drawn-faced boy trembling with fatigue, meets us on the road. Makemin gives me the message to keep—Wacagan have attacked Vscriathjadze and occupied the outskirts, but they are momentarily in disarray. The assault came, not from the slopes, which would have given them an immense advantage although at some expense of time, but from the flat open land on the far side of the city from the port. It appears they underestimated the number of defenders, assuming Makemin had taken most of the army with him to Cuttquisqui, and had decided to take advantage of his absence for a rapid assault.

"But wouldn't their Predicate have been able to make out the strength of the city's defenses?"

"Our Predicanten would have interfered with that, and the Edeks can mask the numbers. Perhaps the ones we met on the road exaggerated our strength, to cover their own failure."

Wacagan casualties were not heavy but apparently far more than were expected. In the time the enemy lost reorganizing themselves, the city's defenders were able to take up positions on the slopes, from which they might survey almost the entire city. Now Wacagan are stalled; their attempts to dislodge some of the defenders from the heights were all repulsed.

"They'll know we're coming. If I were their commander, I would pull out, head into the mountains, and come down on the defenders and the city from above. It would be best for us to arrive before they can try this."

We take those paths that angle up into the mountains; voices peter out as we climb and soon there is only the sound of heavy breathing. Jil Punkinflake is looking a little greener than usual and wheezing with his tongue against his lower lip. I watch this transformation with complacency; the lighter air here refreshes me, and may account for the giddy, brittle hilarity I feel. My capture seems like an accelerated dream.

Even Saskia seems out of sorts. She looks at me, her brow bunched over her eyes. Her face seems to conceal something crude, like an elusively roving phantom feature disrupting the harmony of the others from behind.

Makemin calls me forward and points to the conical peak adjacent the path. For all his stamina even he is a little short of breath.

"Someone must go up there and get a good look. You

don't seem affected by heights."

"Affected?" I laugh. "Certainly not! I've lived my whole life up twice as high as this!"

I leave my wan-faced lowland companions standing lopsided on the path and trip lightly up the rocks to a high spot where I can survey the mountains and the sweep of the far edge of the city, beyond the lower folds.

"Now if only you could fight!" Makemin calls thickly to my backside. I suspect this is his idea of being friendly.

The sun shines there more strongly, on the water and on the town, so that I can see some smoke trickling against the shadows. But here even the light is thin. I report back to Makemin.

"Both paths will take us to the city."

"Which is shorter?"

"I'd say they're both about as short. But the lower one looks slide prone to me."

"Which will put us nearer the enemy?"

"The lower."

"Then we take it; you will go with the scouts and alert us about slides."

"It's more time if we have to double back."

"Yes but we're not mountain goats like you. The men need to get down soon or they won't be in condition to fight."

I am paired with two of the more reliable scouts, a terse, dark-skinned man from the asylum, and a brisk woman from the Yeseg militia. We go ahead, picking the path among the rocks.

By nightfall we traverse the short pass that brings us out onto the slopes above Vscriathjadze's paltry few lamps. We begin our descent, using a switchback path among boulders. I perk up hearing an unfamiliar sound, like insects, heavy beetles flying by on thick wings that wouldn't be up here it's not a kind of place for beetles—a far away pinging noise like tiny metal hammers—Makemin's voice booms out—

"Under cover!"

—as a bank of shot rolls in over us in the dark. I throw myself on the ground and drag sideways toward the rocks— peering up eyes against brows I see the fleeting shapes of the enemy soldiers sweeping pendulously from side to side. They form a whirlpool around us; Makemin is doing something, calling his men together. A sweet-heavy fatigue is pouring down on me like a stream of sand weighting me to the ground. With effort I get myself under cover and let my head droop against the stone. In among the noise, now compounded by the sound of Makemin's thunderbolt and the rifles of his sharpshooters, comes a concatenation of raving and sobbing, mournful and mirthless laughter from the asylum soldiers. They are floundering in helpless panic. The noise grates intolerably on me. I try to rouse myself, but even from here I can see the enemy circling, one rank flashing between me and another, space opening and closing between them as they dance past, guns cracking without a single flash, nothing to make anything more than silhouettes out of them.

... A voice repeats the same phrase, moving from place to place. After a while I make out the "All clear" and so out I come, numbly scanning the ground for bodies. I walk neither quickly nor slowly to a crumpled shape—dead. Another, also dead. There are at least a dozen. Who knows how many, if any, lie dead up there and around us, where the enemy were. Our number is patently less again.

Makemin urges us together, to regroup and proceed, get out of the open before another attack. Behind us the asylum soldiers make a terrible sound of lamentation in as many ways as can be imagined; loud prayers, sobs, a motley demoralizing sound. Makemin is earnestly badgering the officers to quiet the noise and calm the asylum men; the noise only begins to ebb and surge as they listen only to break out again, listen and break out again. It isn't stopping—the sound is nettling Makemin—something serious is happening to his command.

Makemin calls the officers together and we hurry forward to a ledge from which to survey the field. In my rush to catch up with him, my pack slips from my shoulder and tumbles into the bracken fringing the ledge.

"Get it later!" Makemin says impatiently, waving me forward.

Below us, I can see a number of fortified positions, small ledges fringed with heavy rocks and sandbags. In the one nearest us I can see two men in civilian clothes huddled there behind their cover, occasionally lowering a lean barrel level and firing toward the enemy. Makemin makes a quick survey and then dispatches each officer to some task taking them away until we are alone together.

One of the defenders below us calls up, waving furtively.

"Help us!" he calls.

"There are still a few injured men back there, among the asylum men," Makemin tells me. "Go see to them."

"I'll need to move them. If you could spare me a few hands—"

Makemin turns and slaps me.

"Why don't you act like an officer?" he snaps. "Attend to your patients!"

He turns away.

*

The loonies moan and cry behind us. Makemin stands in the little enclosure of the fortified spot. The two men I'd seen earlier, one of whom called to us for help, both lie dead. One is sprawled on his back, draped over one of the stones of the rampart. The other is curled into a letter C on the ground.

Makemin has turned to speak to us. The men are livid with terror, and seem ready at any moment to dash back up the slope. The asylum soldiers, or I presume they were, are moaning and wringing their hands.

"Get back to your ranks!" Makemin screams, his eyes flashing.

"I will not have it said that we cringed here on the heights while the city was taken right under our noses! We have a Narrator here!"

He points at me, and now I am leopard-spotted with their eyes.

I'm paralyzed—I look from face not knowing how to tell them the truth.

"All of history looks at you through him! Now are you soldiers or not? *I* am a soldier."

He points to the two dead men.

"Are you going to allow this? These men had less chance than you!"

I weave a little. I feel violent illness coming over me. As

he talks, a wild light begins to glimmer in their eyes. I can see the contagion spread.

Makemin is a good narrator. He has his own story, a revenge story, and its power has revived in the men the will to fight. He will get his way. They will fight. They believe him. I failed. I failed as a narrator, because I didn't tell them that I had had to get my pack from where it fell and was tangled in the bracken by the path, and that Makemin was wrong to believe himself alone in the moments after he struck me.

I was still there, and I saw him carefully aim his rifle at the bent back of the first one, the one who had called to us from below, and fire. That one spun in place as his back erupted. I caught a brief glimpse of his shattered ribs. He'd given a belching cry, blood fountaining in his throat, and his knees had buckled, dropping him onto the rock. I saw Makemin shoot the other one right after—that second one only half turned when it hit him, and then slumped to the ground, his outstretched leg fluttering. Another bullet nearly split the first one in half. His abdomen exploded like a marrow bone being burst open. He went limp at once. I saw the head of the second one leap. The fluttering of his leg stopped as Makemin's fourth bullet lanced through his brain and spread the pulp against the base of the stone.

Today, Makemin is teaching me a *good lesson* about narrating.

Have I explained it? It was murder.

*

We left the path once the rocks thinned out and we were

within the ring of fortifications on the slopes, plunging headlong down toward the city. Makemin is determined to get down among the buildings before daylight reveals our presence there, or at least exposes us and our position.

I am determined to get away from Makemin. I can't run from the Predicanten, but I might hide from them in town. Maybe find a different unit—they wouldn't care about that, would they? There is no way away for me on land or in town, but the town gives on the sea, and that way I might escape.

I hear a moan ripple through the soldiers around and ahead of me. The grey smoke and the buzzing shot fold around us again. We fling ourselves headlong down the slope. Cries all around me—men flash by in the dark, falling or tumbling down the steep—a confusion of shots—I am running, pass men kneeling and firing off to my left. I still have to attend to any wounded man I find, but I am not searching, only running, looking only along my path. Snap of a shot against a stone not two feet from me—the Yeseg woman who scouted with me coughs once, a stout vocal sound—I hear the thud the bullet makes when it strikes her—my hand comes away from her uniform darkened. Her blood-striped face eyes closed mouth agape receives knowingly the news that she is dead as I tell her you are dead, pick up and go on running as she seems to say save yourself, nothing is worse than this, nothing is.

Flying slope beneath my feet, movement all around me, screams and shots—I am racing toward a few wan lights that illuminate a window with printed gingham curtains, a homely sort of porch with a box planter, pale flowers in the lamp light the petals throwing shadows over their own blossoms. A shriek as a man swings to the ground not far from me his knee blown out. Without a mind I run over haul him up with his arm on my shoulder and propel him down toward the planter and the gingham curtains. He is screaming in my ear so loud I think my head will split. My hand cups his ribs I can feel them pump—he passes out and we both plunge forward. I splint his leg but he remains unconscious—someone ploughs into me from above and we tangle head over heels rolling down the slope. This person kicks loose from me and I am left rubbing my bruises and craning my eyes up.

I try climbing back up to the man I left but bodies whip past me I can feel the thud of their air go by—I can't see anything. I turn and look again to the porch light, put it due behind me and climb up. I can't find the wounded man. Hands take hold of me—Silichieh is bellowing in my face, calling me names—I try to explain but my voice is coming out of me by way of the ground and I can't make myself understood and he is dragging me down the slope toward the city. I am not released.

Now I am sent staggering forward on level ground, I feel cobbles under my feet. I look up at the lamp, the planter and the curtained windows above it; I see two horror-stricken faces there in the glass, staring out at me.

*

The camp is still where it was, everything though is scattered. I look in on Nardac, whom I had entrusted to a trained attendant before I left. Evidently, she has been unconscious for days. Her wound looks like a charred spot in a pile of rags, but it hasn't festered. Gazing into her eyes I see she is a living corpse.

...

"If they capture you, they'll kill you."

"You think Makemin *won't?*"

Thrushchurl sits nearly knee-to-knee with me back in camp, in our tent, on our cots. I've told him what I saw.

"But by sea—if I could get a ship, would you come with me?"

He lies down on his side, two black crescents still looking at me.

"They'll kill you, you know," he says conversationally, softly. "If you haven't a pass to leave the harbor, they'll stop you."

A scrape on the ground outside and an Edek bursts into the tent, her attendant reelingly visible outside and behind him. She seizes me by the front of my uniform and drags my face near to hers—I hear the faint, quick breath through the fabric—the pits of her eyes bore into me—in panic I feel myself become weightless falling in all directions—the grip on my clothes is gone, and everything else.

I am blind—

This blindness isn't mine. It occupies me, and gazes unbearably at me from everywhere—the whole world is looking at me. I'm disembodied and struggling like a ghost paralyzed by a charm or trapped in a looking glass—my sense of being stared at is the only one that remains to me and the stare has a *meaning*, I know what it's saying without speaking, without my hearing it.

Say you'll go.

"I won't say it!"

Say you'll go.

"I won't say it! I won't say it! I won't say it!"

It repeats itself without the slightest alteration. The repetition is or wants to seem simultaneous, one utterance said once and an infinity of times at once, and that repetition also says something of its own in reply to me.

"I won't go!"

Then this will go on.

"Then I'll get used to it!"

The feeling lasts and lasts—it's going to break me, but I am pouring myself into my own words and thoughts for refuge.

I feel myself drop onto my cot. The gaze is lapsing. This is the retirement of a resourceful enemy, who will find another way. It wants to wring something from me, even something easy, an acquiescent appearance will do. Will do what?

Thrushchurl is sleeping across from me. The tent flap unscrolls lazily in an empty breath of air.

*

Trumpets wail.

Day dawns.

Drums drum.

Feet drum.

Guns wail.

The city groans.

Movement fills out scurrying legs and hands.

Eyes dart.

Saskia has smeared her eyes with kohl.

Orders are barked, or sonorously called.

The captain directs me to go with a group of militia men toward the slopes; I am supposed to climb with them to a fortified place.

"But, my medicine ..."

"There are other medics here," the Captain says, putting his hand warmly on my shoulder, putting his eyes warmly on my eyes, putting his voice warmly in my ears and even my mouth. "Don't worry about that."

I follow the militia men toward the fortified place. The buildings subside and we leave cobbled streets for packed clay and heaped rocks.

When I get to my feet again they are lying all around me—

I rush to one who screams and claws his abdomen, dies under my hands with one last cry. The others are dead as well. I alone escaped, because I was hindmost and only just emerging from the rocks. Dancing forms veer away the bright sun gold on their black shoulders and hats. Though uninjured I moan as I go forward uncertainly to look round me because I am ringing through and through as if a huge hammer had just banged me like a bell. No fear, nothing but a stupid animal with a silly name distraught and puking in shock. I stand over my reeking vomit and dash the water from my cheeks, cold dawn air harsh on my face, hearing shots from all around, a gathering bellow that seems unreal like a memory in the mind against the unchanging calm of the slopes, the dawn.

There near me is Thrushchurl scrambling like a stick insect; he disappears with a few powerful strides. He looks unreal. There's an apron of mottled white and black stone flakes emerging from some bracken near me; that means a trail or dry streambed begins there—I'm right. I push through the brush and climb away from the noise. As though a voice called to me from it I glance up and see a shallow depression lined with stones: a good hiding place. I hide there. I keep my back to the rock and huddle there, feeling chill and watery inside. But the noise from below forces me to turn on my knees and look down. The grenadiers rush out from cover, heading for the slope and suddenly the blackbirds drop down on them in two flying ranks catching them in a dip in the ground. The grenadiers draw their pistols and fire. Wacagan swirl around the rim of the dip mowing them down, and Saskia streaks out from the walls like a comet—

She's not fast enough—the grenadiers are blasted to bits in the bottom of the dip. Saskia flashes in among the ranks of Wacagan now and even from here and through the shooting I hear her voice—she catches three of them from behind firing her pistol as she comes and weaves in among them hacking wildly, using her sword like a meat cleaver. Some fire at her but the others are startled back—she drives her knee into the chest of one who levels his rifle at her pinning him instantly to the ground she takes her sword in both hands and stabs his face again and again, leaves his body gun drawn again firing at the others who curve around her, charging them—one raises an arm in fear and she hacks it off, another she seizes by the uniform and chops at randomly across the chest and shoulder.

A Yeseg fires at her and she spins to the side—she is getting up again, the Yeseg who shot fell backwards onto her backside when the gun went off and is getting to *her* feet again. Saskia, without straightening up entirely, veers on her lightened feet toward the Yeseg woman Saskia strikes her in the chest with the hilt sending her sprawling, flailing out her arms for her rifle. Another soldier fires at Saskia and she turns and shoots him—I see her pistol jump again and again in her hand—the soldier falls like a sack of meal—Saskia turns to the woman on the ground who has her rifle and flips onto her back to fire it—Saskia kicks her in the face so hard her head snaps back the crown striking the ground. Saskia kicks her in the abdomen twice more and Saskia slashes her throat.

One of the grenadiers pulls himself out from beneath the bodies of his comrades and runs back—coming this way.

Blackbirds swing down toward Saskia and the dip. I hear cries from men on rooftops—Makemin is there among them and with a loud command they open fire. The blackbirds fly apart and scatter, tumble down the slope, others rush for the fortified rocks. Saskia charges after them alone—she flashes over the stones and down behind the fortifications as a deafening shout rises in the air and a numberless wave of enemy come crashing down the slopes like an avalanche. One wave descends toward the city and two others swarm and proliferate to either side along the slopes like a pot overboiling down its sides and along its rim at once—I see it all from here. Wacagan swoop, bobbing on many legs, the terrible shrilling of their guns tears loose in a seething ring.

A mass of our men, the asylum soldiers, rushes out to meet them, clotting up along a line formed by the foundations of a ruined aqueduct, now just a low strip of black stone and mortar not a foot high. They gather there firing into the encroaching enemy they are jumping in place waving their guns hooting and firing they are being shot down on all sides but they don't waver, they don't move, they stand and fire reload and fire barking with murderous ecstasy roaring from swollen throats, and the enemy, so much more numerous, shrinks from them—they are being blown to pieces on all sides but they do not move, they do not pause in their firing—they fire, and the enemy scatters in front of them. I see half a dozen drop at once nearly all in a row—I see another standing by himself surrounded by his dead comrades howling wildly his gun butt braced against his stomach wheeling this way and that shooting and reloading and shooting. His head twitches as though he'd sneezed, and he collapses on the spot—but more asylum soldiers rush to the front with terrifying cries. They can't retreat, they can't move, they are held there by madness that teems through the air turning men into shrieking—they can only stand and shoot their eyes streaming with thick tears of rage.

The onflow of the enemy reverses and they are regrouping now out of range on the heights not far from me—fast!—and the single remaining grenadier hurries by below my position, heading toward them. As I look in the direction he's taking I see Jil Punkinflake there ahead and below me; he's in a wide hollow hidden from the enemy, slumping down in my direction so I can see him there. He's dithering back and forth, maybe wondering whether or not it's safe to come out. The grenadier enters my view, rushing awkwardly up along the ridge above the hollow, leaning nearly double as he tries to get up among the rocks. Jil Punkinflake puts his hands to his mouth and calls, the grenadier pauses and looks down and the back of his uniform emits a single sheet of dust in a plume—he flops to the ground where he is and I hear Jil Punkinflake scream. He drops to his knees and onto the ground, curling up. I can't get to him from here. He is lying on his side in the dirt, shaking. His face, chin down on his chest, is almost unrecognizeably distorted with terror; sobs expand and contract it without let up.

The dull booming on the heights grows louder, the blackbirds are gathering and I see them swinging back and forth there as though a huge invisible pendulum were throwing them this way and that. The grenadier's weight has been slowly shifting since he fell, and now his body slides down toward Jil Punkinflake on its back, turning in circles the arms and legs limply spiralling. It stops only a few feet from Jil Punkinflake, who stares at it.

No point in calling to him, though I do, unheard. He is reaching for the body. He takes the bag. Jil Punkinflake sits up slowly, puts the bag in his lap, holding it open and peering down into it. He is shaking again. A ragged opening in the noise flits past, and through it I hear his laughter, that makes his head jostle back and forth.

He's on his feet, dashing up the side of the mountain with the bag in one hand swinging wildly back and forth. The movement is so swift and fateful I shout uselessly after him. A moment later he's out of sight among the boulders.

The mass of enemy soldiers stretches, making a deliberate lunge along the length of the height and readying themselves to come crashing down on the city. Jil Punkinflake appears from a stand of trees far off, sprinting fantastically for a long, half-ruined wall that runs the length of the ridge for many dozen yards, above the mass of the enemy.

Now a grenade claps among Wacagan below the wall. Explosions erupt in a line, one after another—Jil Punkinflake must be running along the wall hurling grenades one after another over the top. They fall past the bottom of the wall down the ridge and land among the enemy—the explosions are driving them from their positions, further down and into confusion. They flee the explosions the only way they can: toward the city.

At once comes Makemin's clear shout—"Slaughter them—shoot them!"

—The city is topped immediately with flash-tipped barrels, a crackling that breaks out into blasting like one thunderbolt after another and whole files of the enemy are falling. Makemin is in the middle of his sharpshooters, firing and working his bolt and firing again faster and faster his men shooting and rearming faster and faster some kneeling and some standing over them the better to collect their fire so that their rooftop begins to look like a smokestack or a volcanic vent of fumes and flames—the Yeseg militia has advanced on the ground and their guns level at the enemy as well, and everywhere the same roar shakes the smoke like one disembodied voice of war from every throat. From a broken place in the wall Jil Punkinflake has thrust out his head, laughing like a maniac at the dying blackbirds, his face shattered by laughter.

Exposed in the open, the blackbirds are too crowded together and they are cut to pieces, fingers ears shocking white fragments of bone from splattered heads forms topple down from above throwing those before them to the ground—the sharpshooters are firing faster still and each shot rips a soldier open splinters arms legs so the enemy are wallowing in a slough of human pulp trying to escape. I watch as they claw at the ground trying to pull themselves up and away from the guns, and as the guns split their backs, as invisible hammers smash their arms legs and heads, as swift invisible force plucks at them pulling away fingers toes ears cutting grooves into their chests and along their faces, invisible talons slip along them in convulsions their body cavities open up their tender entrails slither out to be trampled by their routed comrades.

Those who are high enough, or far enough over, swing in their crazy arcs back and forth and escape like ghosts. They leave behind a carpet of screaming men and women.

Later, I see Saskia stride deliberate and cool among them, everywhere extinguishing life with her sword.

*

The outskirts of the city and the heights are blanketed with flies; their buzzing is so loud it can be heard in the harbor. Looking up from the streets I can see, through the buildings, the bodies on the slopes. The slopes look as though they've been daubed with tar, so much blood is there. I can't find a clean spot.

The Edek found me, dragged me to my feet and glared my will out of me, brought me back to the camp. From the city come monotonous bells, four notes, four lower notes, one of the first and one of the second twice, then a final low note before resuming again from the beginning, all the same lengths and intervals, endlessly repeated. To their noise I saw Saskia returning, so weary she barely could walk in a straight line, so drenched in blood that only the whites of her eyes broke the red that covered her.

I hear raised voices sing out in Yeseg. They praise Saskia's beauty and ferocity.

An Edek's gaze emerges from every dark spot, like a mask of insane hate, riveted to me, as though the hate were mine.

No reasoning with Makemin is possible—this wasn't a *mistake*.

There is a bellowing bull-like insanity striding up and down here that I am desperate to escape. Its every step lands in blood, crushes out life. And I didn't tell them Makemin is a liar and a murderer and I don't know why. Did I accept the false idea that it was necessary, too?

I can only escape by sea. Looking down I see my hands are shaking. Now I feel the tremor. It's going to shake me apart.

*

In these few hours I see the soldiers are changing and becoming hostile to the natives, brutal and domineering. That I know the language seems to make me a lesser being myself. They are becoming machines. I saw one of my unit dash a local man to the ground with the butt of his rifle to the face. The more heavy-handed my comrades get, the more deferential and even fawning the natives get. Will that last?

From the attendant, appointed by me, I learn Nardac had dragged herself from her bed during the fighting. He frankly admits he abandoned her and fled toward the harbor; he left her unconscious, near death, and on his return saw the traces—he points to the sheet trailing on the floor where she'd left it, the crablike drag marks written in the dust. How did she pull herself out through the window?

"Did you find her?" I ask.

The attendant waves at the doorway and a compact

woman with red-brown skin steps in seriously from outside. He points to her, and she talks to me.

"I was up on the slopes gathering casings. I saw the woman crawl out toward the bodies. The flies began landing on her leg. More and more came, and covered her all over. She took no notice of them but kept on crawling to the battlefield. There were so many flies I couldn't make out her arms and legs. Even more came, and she was like a hill of flies. But she kept going. Then I didn't see her any more."

I quit them and walk a little way to a place overlooking some of the battlefield. The flies still inundate it like a pitching mat, dense on the ground, undisturbed and busy in windless day under an egg shell blue sky, a phrase I've never understood.

I have heard that there are blue eggs, but I've never seen one.

Makemin even now is in his tent, still sending back punctual bulletins to his lawyers, full of meticulous instructions as to precisely how he wishes the most recent phases of the suit and the divorce to be conducted. I stare at him, through the mosquito screen. I think of the enormity this man, who now sits before me, efficiently writing documents, committed in my sight, and a spur of detestation drives itself into me.

Getting away from the battlefield I see Saskia lying asleep in her tent. The peace that hovers over her sleeping face is so strange, and the streaming, flat hair, like silky brown straw, that I've never seen undone from its braid, draping over her shoulder, and across the bed to the edge, looks somehow impossible.

Later I lie down and look into the fire.

I tremble with hatred.

I think the expression of grief that would come over my parents' faces when they would get news of some crime, no matter who suffered it. They seemed to take a measure of shame on themselves whenever they were forecefully reminded of the base acts people are capable of. Burning shame is being forced on me now, by this situation and by that man, if that's what he is. I wipe my eyes. He has to be killed.

Did I think that? If you hate him and kill him you—who am I to think that? If you hate him because you kill him he killed because he hated and you will be no better. That's not true. He killed two men. He killed them with horrible coldness and all because of some scheme or other. If I kill him I will be doing what's right because he committed an atrocious crime and he must suffer and die for what he did. It isn't the same. But there's no crime in war there's no crime out here, crime is for nice places and nice people and if I believe that then this shame falls on me too.

But you're no killer.

I'm no killer. I'm no killer. Who else? If not me?

If I could make Saskia believe he'd turned on our own, she'd think he was a traitor; she'd kill him for sure.

There I am, telling her, even convincing her. And she's taking his side, telling me it was necessary; the men were losing heart and talk talk talk. She's telling me I'm the traitor. Would the blackbirds have taken the town if—was Makemin right?

Would the blackbirds have killed everyone in the town, or anyone in the town, if they'd taken it? They wouldn't. Why would they?

Who cares who owns what? What possession is like life? What possession is like life? I'm surrounded by idiots! All these crazy whores have sold their bodies and souls to the war.

I'm looking out at the fire.

The scene flashes in my mind again. I hear the man below call "help!"

I contract, and clutch my hands to my chest in terror. I hear that shattering cry for help and see Makemin's cruel answer; that man cries out for my help now. What is humanity if isn't help? It's simple.

My mind clears and my body relaxes. When Makemin killed men who had called on him for help, he stopped being human. The back of his tent. His shadow. It's all a fantasy. The back of his head is good enough for me if it was good enough for him I'm not interested in proving anything.

I don't move. I don't budge. I hear that cry for help fall away from me and the night swallows it.

*

Jil Punkinflake drinks his whiskey and sneezes.

Thrushchurl kneels, bends his cheek nearly to the floor, and rattles his long index finger in the mouse hole.

We are in the crypts whose backs line the cisterns. The two funeral men were drawn here reflexively and, as long as I stay underground, I find relief from the feeling of being watched. The light of our lamps, though dim, is warmer and more enlivening to colors than the washed out grey light of the day—I'm greedily looking around at the richly yellow fringes of the woven mats, and the paprika red poms that adorn the picture frames.

Night returns outside. I feel thunder through the stones. Jil Punkinflake slumps against oozing slate, a greedy, vicious light in his look.

I also have drunk, and I'm stupid, like a ghost, but disembodied simply as an accident of perspective since I do not bother to sway my eyes to see the rest of him, Thrushchurl's hand deposits a candle on a packing case. I look at the flame boring into space; it's like a hot coal burning a path through a snowdrift. The base is a misty blue cup, and I see a mote, like a grain of pollen, trickle up its curve toward the hollow mane. The tapering upper part of the fire kernel is the color of buttermilk. The flame plummets into a dark opening at its center, hovers over it, and is held to the wick by its suction. I imagine standing at the base of the flame as it ignites, seeing it column up and close around me like a multicolored alembic.

Thrushchurl is gone again, and I don't want to be alone with Jil Punkinflake now. I hear the clink of liquor in the glass as he raises and lowers the bottle with mechanical regularity, and in between these sucking pauses a soft, mirthless chuckle takes his place.

I get up, thinking that, should he ask me where I am going, I will say either that I need to piss or I am trying to get back to the tent before the rain no that would only encourage him to join me and what I most want is to get quit of his company. He does not address a word to me, but, as I climb the narrow passage to the surface, stagnant chill air daubing my face, the noise of his step slides in behind me and a stripe of repulsion sinks into my backbone. I go toward the bushes working my fly open and he drops his bottom onto a porch stoop. I will have to pass him to escape.

A honey-colored young woman is sulkily pacing up and down. A man, who might be her young father or her older fellow, comes and goes, bringing parcels out of the house and loading them into a wheelbarrow. Getting out, or something. She is impatient and urges him on with grim looks. Jil Punkinflake is eyeing her with a look at once intense and glazed. His face is five other faces at once. She's noticed his look and is adding extra movements to her pacing, turning away and folding her arms, her gaze scampering nervously from one object to another. Every time her man comes back she throws him a demanding look. Finally she says something and points to Jil Punkinflake, who is reclining limp against the stoop, bottle in his hand. The man stumps over to him.

"You want something?" he barks in accented Alak. All the work, and her fuming, has made him short-tempered.

"I want to make off with her," Jil Punkinflake says softly and fondly with a dreamy smile. Almost bonelessly he slithers upright before the man, driving the smile of his dreamy teeth into the man's vision. The man swats at him like a bear, and Jil Punkinflake is knocked down. He smiles and picks himself up, eyes glittering weirdly.

It's not until he's on his feet, though smeared with dust, he says, "I answered you."

But the man is already lumbering off. I don't believe he cared much one way or another, but felt he had to make a gesture.

"That was unkind, friend," Jil Punkinflake says into his teeth.

I take him by the arm and guide him away. We're barely out of sight of them when I feel his face mash into my shoulder and he slumps limp against me. The next moment he pushes me roughly away with a sob he can't hold in, and leaves me.

*

Another storm hurtles down the mountains at us, a cloud black as smoke. I take refuge in a small house, raised as most of them are here above the ground on short stilts.

It sounds as though every joint in the place adjusts to my every step. Empty except for a few cushions on the mats, a table, a lamp. I get the lamp going nicely—it has an adjustable wick that can be dimmed out to nothing at all but turned up again to full brilliance without relighting—and lie down to listen to the roar of water. It's hard to stop my mind, or to rest, because I am not certain someone with a better claim to the place might not appear at any time. I keep hearing the fumbling of what is trying to become a knock at the door, the sound of footsteps—a visit just barely trying, and failing to take shape, failing to compose these intractable elements into an event.

I decide I want to sleep. I turn down the light and the room shakes with deafening laughter. I turn the light up at once. The room reappears as it was, silent, unshaken. I listen to nothing but pounding rain.

Presently, I extinguish the light again. The laugh explodes in the room and when I turn the light on it illuminates only a face inches from mine from which is pouring that shattering, mind-annihilating laughter.

I rush outside and the ground is dry—there is no rain. I walk in haste. The city is deserted. Ruined buildings, litter, bones in the street.

The sudden appearance of a red lantern draws my eye to the brothel whose window I am passing, and through the window I see the Lieutenant lunging back and forth in uniform on top of a cooing woman whose dress is gathered high above her waist like froth and whose hands are widely splayed on his back; he is facing in my direction the circular eyes rolled up in blemished rings as she kisses his exposed upper teeth with dreamy abandon. His dangling lower jaw leaves viscous dabs the size of thumbprints where it flaps against her chin and throat.

I recoil from the sight into the blackness of a side street. It takes me past many brighter streets that I feel I must avoid, and I continue to follow this dark side street until it gives way, expels me into the utter darkness beyond the city altogether. I stop and start, go forward and stop again.

I look out over the battlefield again with a feeling of terror brimming in me at the idea of the bodies lying there in total darkness.

In the darkness I dimly spy a form dashing purposively here and there, gathering the bodies of the enemy in its arms and tumbling them with a kind of hasty decorousness into several heaps. This figure works tirelessly, moving with almost fantastic speed in its work. Then it alters its activity. It goes from one heap to the next, with long intervals at each. Then it retires I don't know where. I get up higher to search it out but my eyes are baffled by so much dark.

A pale and glowing tendril slithers up from within one of the heaps, fluttering its wormlike end against the sky. More rise around it, and from the other heaps. The fires are seeping up around the sodden clothes and catching the short hair. I watch every blaze expand and do its work.

*

Always the sickening feeling, like a lid dropping down on me, to shut me forever in the dark.

I was just asking someone for something—paper, I think—and someone said—

"Was that yesterday?"

I am looked at incredulously. I realize they mean the battle I witnessed—but that was days ago, weeks, wasn't it?

How many nights?

I climb to the spot again. I can see the marks I made in the earth, my knee and foot prints. Still there even after the rainstorm. I wander here and there, looking away from the stinking ravines ahead, streaked with blood and swimming with flies whose drone rumbles like far away thunder. The charred heaps of bodies still smoulder there, and from time to time a whiff comes this way.

What's that? I have been staggering a bit—it makes sense, I haven't eaten. I am on my knees, looking straight ahead no doubt stupidly and there before me I see a heap of those ferrous rocks and a crevasse there, the size of my hand, made by a jumble of smaller stones in among the larger ones. This crevasse has bewitched my attention so that I can't look away from it. I draw closer and peer in—there's something tickling in my head. I push the stones apart and peer more intently into the little crevasse, and a blue light begins to sift down among the veering edges of the stones ... only a bluish dust, but it catches the light strangely, because that light doesn't illuminate anything else. My own breath becomes audible to me and switches on its own to my open mouth as I look, because the arrangement of these edges, the pebbles, the fine-grained light, the chalk white, is what I want but can't deny precisely corresponding to the arrangement I would see every time I returned to my home from the town as I would look down from the pass—I don't know what to do—

I see my home again, the serene-looking College. I feel my breath stop and start, and hot lines down my face, but what do I do—it is too painful to go on seeing but it's too beautiful to push away—I can only fall into my seeing it until I am exhausted?

Then noises well out of me and I paw at the little stones as though I could reach out and stroke the vision, ruining it. I expect I'm making a disgusting racket.

*

I can't do it. Let's say I come away, back to the city, and I eat, eating badly. I push food into my mouth chew and swallow it as though it were all still new to me. The mechanical action of eating as I am eating now has no relation at all to whatever it is I feel the irritable, kinked feeling in my middle. Walking away from the table, whosoever it was, I can feel the jagged food lodged in my stomach; the effort I had put into gagging it down has drained me of my strength. I sag into a cellar doorway and lie down at the base of the stairs.

Now I am sleeping again.

Our characters are all crudely stamped on us along with our silly names and our tics, and now that I'm forever brushing first my left and then my right cheeks I have mine as well. Try explaining, rather than being understood, I think profoundly. How do you feed stone fishes?

Now it's a story—around the little farm house the young man calls on the eldest daughter, and they refer to him by a name that's never quite the same way twice; first, Taddy. Then Keddy. Then Kedded. He's talking with the girl as he stands in the tall grass by the window; they all love him there and the family is gazing fondly at him through the window. Deep blackness swollen up in the treeline beyond the high grass, shaggy branches make a line like the side of a half-melted candle. He's still chatting happily with them, and blackness stands now only a few feet behind him like a night wall. A cloud dims the sun, and when the light returns the two of them are gone from the tall grass and the family calls from the windowsill "Kaddy! Where are you?" He's gone forever.

"Thrushchurl? I thought he deserted."

"He's around here somewhere." Setting fires. Placing fires. Putting fires. I gesture halfheartedly; I'm being asked to shake off powerful fatigue in order to explain something with many parts. I see the beating lights before I find the flames. Everyone has come unmoored from the ground and hurtles around me in the air, like Wacagan, but without the stopping and starting, back and forth.

Rumor has it Makemin is unhappy. Well fancy that. He wants to pursue the enemy into the interior but the Predicanten are holding him here until reinforcements from the mainland arrive. So we are waiting and he is fuming. Let him. I stay in the cellar until a few other soldiers blunder in bickering. I go looking for another hiding place like an elderly dog looking for a moment's peace.

The wind blows the battlefield stink into town. People

light torches day and night and march brandishing them in the street, trying to thin out with fire the plague of flies. The fog returns from the sea, and in it the flies look like black leaves swirling in milky tea.

I've been sent to bring a message to Saskia. Everyone who has seen her can tell me immediately which way she went— they're that careful of her. I find her where she does her target shooting, on one of the slopes where the gorse trembles close to the ground. Sitting on a stone with her right arm resting palm up along her thigh, opening and closing her fist with mechanical regularity, she doesn't see me coming. Her eyes never leave her hand. Getting her attention is like being suddenly illuminated by a permeating, judging light.

She looks up as I approach. I fix my eyes on the air over her head, stop within arm's reach and hold out the note. It is snatched from my hand. I wait, trying to go to sleep or to find some soft way to resist the spell of her dominating, pitiless stillness.

"No reply," she says, and again I'm disarmed and shaken at the deep, incongruous voice. Despite myself, I bang my heels together in a gesture of efficiency I've always hated, and turn to go. To make up for it, I take my time; veering from the threadbare path I amble instead over the shrubby ground. After a few minutes, a movement catches the corner of my eye, and I turn to see Jil Punkinflake approaching Saskia. She is on her feet, her pistol in her hand. I imagine she's been loading it. Now she holsters it and watches him.

He is pale and puffy, with rings beneath his eyes. He also holds an envelope gingerly in his hand, and offers it to Saskia, the whites of his eyes very bright. Makemin must have guessed that he would be the one to find Saskia, wherever she might be. She takes the note, and he stands with his hands at his sides, a little more on one foot than another, breathing through his mouth, fear and yearning gushing from his stricken eyes.

Saskia has read and replaced the envelope's contents and shoves it slowly into her pocket, looking at him. Her back is to me. She slaps him. It's a glancing blow, her fingertips knocking against his chin's edge. His head jars, more with nerves than with the weak force of her hand, his eyes widen.

She slaps him again. I hear the sound. This time his head swings to the side and back at once; he stares and pants, white as milk. She slaps him and advances a step, slaps again and steps again, and he recedes before her, with an astonished, joyless excitement in his face. Suddenly she pulls her arm well back and strikes him to the ground. He does not cry out, but falls on his side and elbow. He raises his head and looks up at her with such a bleak longing in his rapt eyes that I turn away. I leave them there, Saskia towering over him.

*

The wind grows stronger. A cave breaks open in the fog, sweeping into the ferns, and in a moment I see a form through grey transparence and then that fog is swept away and I see her plainly. She is clearly there.

At the same moment you stride into an illuminated archway in my heart's spot like a little goddess. You had had another name before, and I learned it from your lips. Your fine lips pressed each letter carefully into my ear. Later you ordered me to forget it, not to say it, think it, or remember it. I don't, but I feel it stir anyway in the air in my open mouth, because your face glows through mine. I see your two eyes glisten through your veil—the intensity they stir in me stops and starts with my breath and grows like the intensification of light at dawn.

I take a step toward you. As always, a great spiral foam of dreams spins out of you like a galaxy but what do I know about galaxies? Your arms hang nervelessly at your sides and you hold your head up and back straight. You seem to want to draw me in under your chin, raising it at me. I see again the swell of your dress at your waist, where it is broken up by so many creases, all bowed to you—near your throat there is always a warm lineny smell a little like lemon rind. I close my eyes, still seeing you, and the gauzy dreaminess of your house and body close over me like a cold spring, offering me a whole life in sleep. You would be a monumental hourglass towering over the landscape, sifting out my time without seeming to. I'll resolutely stand here with my eyes shut dreaming myself out from under the hood of this nightmare with all my will until I find myself back in Tref, and Makemin dead and stinking in a ditch on the island, and you before me.

Fog creeps up toward the peak, and mires itself in the trees.

I have to escape.

*

I am beguiling my time sitting under a tree with a little blue guide to the city. A hermit lived here ages ago in a hovel built into the side of the mountain. Shepherds led their flocks into the vicinity and disturbed his meditations with their songs and their pipes and their bells and baas, and, in frustration, he picked up a piece of ice and flung it against a stone. The stone disappeared and water sluiced out of a "porcelain hole." The noise of the water drowned out the sound of the shepherds and the hermit was satisfied. Unfortunately, the entire fabric of the slope was gradually undermined and soon water began gushing out everywhere, forming the many waterfalls that still provide the city with its water. The destiny of the hermit is not described. "In the beginning was the end," someone's written here.

All around me are deep prayer platforms and mills, droning chants. They are eliciting the help of the spirits. I don't really understand.

I watch a Predicate form over the roof of the shrine. A lopsided gobbet, grey and lavender in color, spins there like clay on a potter's wheel, and long carrot-like stalks begin to droop out of it. It flails, convulsing away into the air like a bundle of dirty laundry infused with an antic simulation of life. Glancing down, my thumbnail has inadvertently indented a line beneath the sentence "although some say this spirit worship grew out of a primitive monotheism, and did not merely supplant it" end of page.

Flip the book aside and walk. Deep within the hood of this shrine is an enormous stone idol I've seen many times: a stone book. It is swarming with tiny, shivering leathery forms. Bats. Clappers and Spirit Eaters stand in rank and file before it, bolt upright with their feet together, chanting stanzas. Edeks tilt in and out of the slender wooden pillars, Predicanten perch in the dim rafters. One of them points to something with its lean bent arm, the wing hanging down like a voluminous sleeve, and it rasps a few observations to its glassy-eyed, ring-mouthed neighbor. A Clapper comes in from the right carrying blood in a paper basket, red soaking steadily into the white, and it is set down on a table beside the idol. With one continuous motion the bats begin to slither down the book, smelling their way toward the blood.

Shadows crumbled into the branches of the majestically calm trees like galleries of dreaming statesmen see how the foliage breaks up the light; I could use its example to illustrate the action of scintillation to anyone who was not familiar with the meaning of the word. There goes a woman by me; her body stiffly shudders with each step as she carries heavy bags in either hand. I see a boy of about four years go by with an older boy who lets him push their modest cart along. With great profundity I note the pleasure one gets or takes in pushing wheeled objects, as opposed to the depression involved in pulling them. Everyone here wears a scarf over the nose and mouth—I ask a man going by, carrying a bag of tobacco, why this is, and he explains that today is a holiday and points toward a narrow, crooked alley not far from me. There is an algae bloom in the sea, and this puts something into the air—I have noticed it, a bloody note under the smoke and trash smells of the city. The air is slightly caustic.

The alley is long and so irregular I can't see more than fifteen feet or so at a time. The chanting dies away to a faint grumble, and through it I hear a cricket … It's nearby … two thoughtful chirps and the beginning of a third, at even, medium-length intervals. Here and there I see silent people going to and fro in the alley, slipping into it from side passages that are even darker and narrower, while others just stand where they are, preoccupied, or lean against a wall. I have to wait for a while as others file past going the opposite direction. The cricket gets louder.

Here's a mass of people jamming the alley. I don't want to start ramming my way in among them but others are bustling me from behind and I move in anyway. High over us, in a window under a pointed roof, there is a lofty cage. The cricket, it seems, is in it, although I can't make out the contents of the cage from here. Everyone is silently listening to the cricket, and a drowsiness is settled in among them so that even I, who just awoke after such a long sleep, begin to nod again. I look from one person to the next—almost all but I have kerchiefs over their mouths and noses.

One fellow in particular catches my eye—a man right up against the wall. There's something complicated about his kerchief. I'm behind him, and it takes me a while to figure it out: he's wearing a wig. I wouldn't have known, since he's also wearing a shapeless cloth cap, but his wig has slipped a bit, and I can see he has a second kerchief or bandage under it. The bandage goes up around his head under his wig, which, along with the hat and kerchief, hides the bandage that binds his jaw like a corpse's. I look again up to the cricket.

When I try to find the pale man who hid his bandaged jaw so well, I have to force my way through the congregants. There is a door near the spot he's just vacated, and hidden inside it there is a hall lit with gas lamps. The vast chamber or cavern that blooms out at its end is partitioned into many smaller rooms without ceilings, elevated on planks. All manner of activities, crafts, mostly, take place here. In time I fall in with a group of three men, who sit on benches leaning their elbows over watches on a gleaming glass table. One is bald, all of them are scruffed and unshaven, but their hands are clean, their shining nails are immaculately trimmed and dressed. They wear rough clothes of fine materials.

In another room a ghostly-looking man sits reading; his cat, or a cat, is slenderly nosing along the edge of the floor, dabbing at the wood with its nose. The man looks up and gives me my first beckoning look from among them. I go through the doorway to him.

"Are you lost or something?" he asks. His snowy smile is beautiful but it brings me no closer to him nor him to me.

"No, I'm looking." There are books here in low towers, piled on the floor. One stack stands in reach of his hand from the high-backed chair.

In answer to his querying look I say, "I've been hearing much talk about the interior, but I don't understand what I hear."

"I'm not surprised," he answers at once. "There are ruins in the island's interior whose foundations were laid before the Limiters; not at all a city in any way any one of us would recognize, but what would have been the past's idea of a city. It's all full of spirits now."

"From the ruins?"

"In the ruins, and in the land."

"Ghosts?"

"Yes." This did not sound final.

"Other things than ghosts?"

"Yes—any thing. *Their* Predicanten. *Their* Edeks."

He speaks to me for a while, without any special eagerness or any sign of boredom. He makes constant reference to a cemetery, deep in the interior, where the spirits gather together in great abundance and may be safely contacted by a medium. Some other people are called in, until the enclosure is packed with people talking to me, and I hear several versions of a story about a Pepecaui named Jidjikuk, an intrepid youth in some versions and, in others, a resigned old man, who leaves home to find the burial ground and petition the spirits there for assistance against the pirates that used to harass the islands before they confederated.

One after another they tell me their versions, and when the last one has finished, they stand where they are in distracted silence. I've just had a thought—and I go, breathing excitedly, through their mass, and through the mass of congregants in the alley.

I remember Wormpig's neighborhood and I go back to look for him; I stand speculatively in front of a row of three houses there, trying to catch the eye of the few people milling, but they avoid my uniform. A woman emerges from one of these narrow houses and stands on the porch, her hands on her thighs, regarding me with neutral attention. She has dark pulled-back hair with silver needles shot through it, a square face with soft features; she looks practical and self-possessed.

"You're Low the interpreter, aren't you?" she asks in a slightly lofty, airy way.

"Low Loom Column," I say.

"I'm White Dead Nettle," she says, lowering her eyelids a bit and speaking as if she were enjoying a private joke. In the same manner, she adds, "Wormpig is my husband, if it's an audience with Pepedora you want."

"Pepedora is Pepecaui, isn't that right?" I feel as though I'm speaking too loudly.

"Yes," she says, lifts her eyes to me with a small toss of

her head and resets her mouth. "Won't you come in?"

A plume of steam runs from kettle spout to the rafters directly before me. After she has seated me on a padded wicker chair and put a mug in my hand, she resumes her place at the table by the window, sorting brass fittings with soft tinkles.

Wormpig comes in without a sound, and she greets him in a flat, easy way. He noticed me as he came up to the open door, and strides over to me at once. I set down the mug saying, "I want to see Pepedora."

Wormpig smiles and swivels once back and forth from his hips. "I am glad to assist the foreign officer," he pipes.

So I am conducted into Pepedora's presence a second time.

Once he was a dandy. Now he sits where the shade covers him. Only his legs, one bent flat on the floor, the other leg doubled up in front of him, emerge from the bisecting diagonal of the shade. As I approach, he adjusts a white stocking with a piebald hand. A froth of dangling lace brushes back into the gloom as he withdraws it. Wormpig tilts his head and rolls his eyes toward the farmhouse where we waited once before, indicating that's where I will find him when I'm done, and leaves us.

I turn to the breathing, half-silhouette in the mill. He grinds his teeth. It's a steady, automatic sound.

"I want to leave the island," I say. "Will you give me safe passage?"

I watch the slow descent of Pepedora's head; my eyes pick out the severely-tapering jaw, blurred spots on skin mottled as lichenous rocks, but smooth and shiny and firm as hard rubber.

"You have no ship," he says. The booming voice he'd used with Makemin is gone.

"I can take one."

Pepedora says nothing. I wait.

"If I give you safe passage, will it be for your use alone?" he asks eventually.

"Mine, and anyone who wishes to accompany me."

"Who will defend my city if you take the soldiers away?"

"Surely most will stay. And Wacagan are routed—they won't come back."

"They will if they find help in the interior."

That stops me.

"What do you mean?"

I already have an idea. I know he's not talking about soldiers, more of their soldiers, landing on the island's far side.

Only now Pepedora's voice changes, dropping to a deep, purring baritone.

"Anyone can win the favor of the spirits, if he petitions them in the right way."

"Is that what they're trying to do?"

"It's what I would do," he murmurs. He strokes the backs of his upper front teeth with the fronts of his lower front teeth. I can see his jaw slide up and down, and I can hear the teeth scraping together softly, like glass against glass.

"Your commander knows. It's what he would do, too. If he could. If they'd let him."

I feel a sharp thrill of fright at the idea.

"He and the lady are determined to set out after the blackbirds, but the Predicanten, and the Edeks, won't allow it."

He chuckles, nothing more than a gush of breath through dry nostrils.

"Someone has to make a *decision*."

I'm thinking about the ocean, about being alone in a boat. I see myself discovering I hadn't brought on as much food or water as I needed, unwittingly making one navigational blunder after another until I'm lost beyond hope of discovery. My hope, my plans, are withering away in me. They collapse from me like burning clothes. And the Edeks would know. They might even catch up to me on the open water.

Pepedora leans forward, so that his face is veiled only by the thinnest membrane of darkness. I know he's narrowed his eyes, his upper lip risen toward his dagger-like nose.

"Shall I give you my disease?" he says, deeply and softly.

I take a step back, shaking my head. He said it as though he meant something other than leprosy, and I wonder if *his* disease, as he calls it, isn't something else. He speaks as though he were offering to show me a secret, treasured property.

Now he is reclining back a jerking piece at a time, each muscle flexes along his lip as he tips back. When he speaks again, he speaks officiously.

"The harbor is closed. We'll need all of those ships if Wacagan return with help."

"Can you hide me?"

"From the Edeks?" The answer is in the tone of the question.

After a moment, I lower my head and mash my fist against the rough ends of the floorboards, pushing down on my fist with my elbow in the air, breathing through my mouth.

I can't get away. *There isn't any way.*

Flat and neutral, Pepedora's voice breaks in on me suddenly.

"I have something I can give you, but you must agree to teach me ... me, and Wormpig ... some of your Alak language, and characters. I want to know what is being said in my presence, and what is being planned. You will have to be resourceful, to teach us quickly. And I want my own alphabet."

"I've never made one before. I'm not certain I could."

"Try. You have time. ... Some time."

"In exchange for what?"

He sets a pearly blue vase on the floor in front of himself, removes the lid with a little porcelain rasp, and plunges his arm in to the elbow. Out he pulls a squat, faceted bottle a bit smaller than a fist. A bubble like silver lozenge at the top tells me it is completely filled with some thick, clear liquid. The stopper is neatly covered over with thick seal of black wax.

"This is a charm. It came from the interior. Give me what I ask, and I will give you this, and show you how to use it. The principle is the same as the compass—it will lead you safely *through* and out again."

"I'm not going into the interior!"

"Yes you are. They will *make* you go, because you're the only one who can read Lashlache, and Wiczu, and they already know they will have to read the inscriptions there to get what they want—the help of the spirits."

"For themselves?"

The smile on his face creaks.

"Of course."

"I don't want to help them!"

"They'll probably kill you if you don't cooperate."

Everything he says is true.

"The interior is a labyrinth that devours people. Almost

nobody who has gone in has ever come back out again. A reliable guide is the greatest treasure a visitor to the interior can possess."

He seems to tilt his head back in the gloom, as if he were daydreaming.

"Conceal the charm from them. Don't mention its existence to anyone. Let it guide you. When they see that you know where to go and where not to go, they will wonder why. They will want to know how you know. Let them reach the conclusion that you are gifted with an intuition about the interior, that the spirits of the interior favor you for mysterious reasons of their own. Tell the others nothing—don't make any claims for yourself—just show them, and lead them to believe they have discerned this supposed faculty of yours by themselves. They'll like to believe in their own acuity. When they are convinced you possess an uncanny knack for guiding them safely through the perils of the interior, they will preserve your life at any cost."

Confusion creeps palpably across my face.

"You can protect your friends, and yourself as well. It's the best chance for you all."

I feel my mouth bunching, breath tight in my chest and harsh in my nose.

"And perhaps, when you arrive at the cemetery, you will petition the spirits for *yourself*. They might then help you, instead. *Just* you."

"Could they end the war?"

He leans forward.

"War is the spirit that seeks your life. War is a spirit, and you need the help of spirits against it."

"It's Makemin will get me killed."

"Why? Does he hate you? What reason does he have to kill you?"

"He has only to see I'm not with him. Or he'll drag me into death somewhere ... I can't ... He'll know, or he'll guess ... "

"He's possessed. They all are. You've *seen* that."

He's talking about the insanity I saw bellowing from every face. He's right.

"Will the spirits really help him, if he asks them?"

"They might very well."

Makemin must die, not get what he wants, whatever that is.

"Have you gone in there?" I sound desolate.

He opens his arms.

"As you see."

"The spirits made you sick?"

A motion that looks like a nod.

"But, with that—" I point to the charm in his fingers.

"I was already afflicted when I discovered it. I found it as I fled. Fled from what killed all the others."

"Couldn't you use it to go back?"

This seems to strike him as a completely novel idea.

"Why would I go back? ... Why would I go back?"

"You might find a way to be released from your sickness, with that." I point again.

"I don't want to be released yet."

"But," I falter, "surely you must be suffering!"

"Yes," he says, thoughtfully. "Suffering, yes."

Pepedora seems to drift off.

"But it's all so interesting," he says finally. "And it can't last forever."

He smiles.

*

I don't have to think twice about what to do. I set out for the woods and the graves again. Not far outside town, I run into Thrushchurl, high-stepping toe first on his coffin-shaped shoes and swinging his arms jauntily.

"You don't look like yourself," he cocks his head. "Are you going hunting? You haven't got a rifle."

"I'm not on a proper sort of errand. Do you have gloves on you?"

Without a word he pulls a pair of elbow-length, shiny rubber gloves from his coat pocket and hands them to me.

"And your scalpel?"

"Always," he replies, and hands it to me, the blade thrust into a long bit of cork.

"Spit on them all before you use them," he says. "I don't want anything being traced back to me, you know."

"I will."

We part, he heading to the city. After a few dozen steps he turns and calls to me, not too loudly.

"You might keep an eye out for a pile of rocks, or a quarry."

"A quarry? What for?"

"That's right," he says, as though I'd expressed perfect understanding, one palm held up at me as he walks off against flat light.

Now the woods press on both sides of the road, which begins to wind. With each bend, the way narrows. I turn a bend and the road is now only a yard or so wide, and a man is creeping toward me on its opposite side. He is all in dark, loose homespun and a sweeping garment over that; his white head droops down and he scours the bare ground with his eyes. I want to avoid him, but I fear the results of trying. He has a weirdly smooth way of walking, and he holds his arms straight at his sides, all the fingers of both hands splayed out to their fullest extent as though he were trying to stretch his cuffs. He looks up at me with a gasp. His milky face has a sharp little nose, a white moustache with braided ends dangling past his lips, and a long beard hangs straight from his cheeks. Thick white hair is pulled straight back from his square forehead. He stands bolt upright now and steps over to me, so that I haven't time to see his eyes.

"Have you seen my dog" he asks, and adds another word at the end I can't make out. It might have been "miss." There was no question in his tone. Now that he stands in the gloom of the trees and the dusk I can't see for myself, but he speaks like a man without a tooth in his head. His jaw works obscurely in the shade, behind his beard, and I hear the loose cheeks and lips slop and flap a bit.

Not knowing what else to do, I actually try to recall noticing any solitary dogs, but after only a moment, during which he lists a bit back and forth, he says "I have many fine dogs," in the same abrupt way, and the impression that I'm talking to a fool or a madman solidifies. He is fingering the fabric of my tunic in the front. My eyes rest on a patch of bald shabbiness along the shoulder seam of his cape or robe, whatever it is. He gives off a strong, ammonia-like smell, but there's no human gaminess in it.

"Yes," I say simply, moving off.

When I turn a few paces later, I see him standing straight where he was, still looking at the spot I'd just vacated. I round the next bend and stop, return stealthily to spy on him. He creeps along as before, out of sight.

I leave the path at once and strike out into the woods. Staying within view of the path, I find the spot where we had left it before, the rocks and trees are familiar. Following them in, I know I can follow them out again. I spit on Thrushchurl's gloves and the uncorked blade of his scalpel, then I go in.

A colossal Predicate's head, hairless, half shapeless, boneless, and partially transparent with a grey hue, hangs in the sky, wreathed in clouds. The bulging eyes are dark balls visible through the tissue, crossed by the slender edge of closed eyelids. The mouth is a lipless arch. It is a dreaming head, sinking toward the forest.

As I stand, still as I can, where I am, I can hear noises begin to fill the woods. I hear flapping wings and vocal noises, soft cries, a rustling and mutter, first here, now there, all around me and gathering, but no sound is distinct enough to name. They are only noises, some punctual and some continuous, and they seem to call to one another. I imagine a ring of those sounds forming around me, and then closing, but I don't budge from my spot—only crouch down on my haunches to help myself keep still.

I hear the regular beating of feet on the leaves—it rushes up swiftly, and passes me. I never saw anything.

More feet, slapping now. For a moment I see, flickering into the cover of the trees from the bank of a paltry stream, a vast sea lung, clear as glass, borne along on many naked human legs. Its sides are trickling, and white foam oozes down the legs—are they attached to the thing, or are there many men carrying its mass?

Rapid, singular steps, distinct from the sound of bare feet on clay and purposefully marching through the leaves toward me. I pick my way as quickly and silently as I can toward a defile of stones that tumbles from a low rise down to the stream. Hiding among the rocks, I try to pick out the source of the steps, but I can't see anything and the steps have stopped.

Faint groan of metal. Two shapes travel up the bank of the stream, on my side. They come near enough for me to recognize the man from the road, sitting in a two-wheeled cart, snowy head softly glowing against the mounded wrap he's bundled in. A pair of huge cats draws the cart; one is grey and haggard, with a pelt like unshorn wool, and the other is a buttery golden-ash color with dark rings around its eyes, a swaying, bloated gut, and scrawny legs. Both are slobbering with effort, lashed between two poles. They stop, and the man alights, raising his arms to the huge sea lung, fingers still rigidly outstretched. The lung flutters like billowing glass, all but invisible on the opposite bank, hidden among the trees.

I'm certain he's a Predicate. I leave my hiding place and stalk up to him. Never in my life have I missed my footing on rocks, so I dare to stay on the defile until I'm within a few paces of him.

I step softly up to the Predicate. His trembling hands are still out in the air before him, and his cats are laboriously backing up and lurching forward again, trying to angle the cart toward the stream. I suppose they are thirsty.

Slowly I lift my hand. His long hair hangs in a braid to the small of his back, flanked on either side by long unbraided locks swept from above his ears. I pinch a bit of the left lock away and double it in my fist. I put Thrushchurl's scalpel through the loop and, in one motion, sever it. I pocket the hair and slip back to the rocks, from there up the defile toward the low rise.

His toothless mouth gurgles and clicks—he has turned and seen me—he leaps up onto the stones with an acrobat's speed. Now the cold fear has me and I straighten up and sprint, picking my steps, up the stones moving in a straight line and looking for a place to hide—I am already within its confines when I realize I've found the rock pile Thrushchurl meant. While the old man is still out of sight, I dart in among the big stones and conceal myself there.

The ammonia smell, and then that clicking gurgle in the mouth. A dark shape flashes by the gap in the stones before me. He's missed me, and is searching. Then, near me, another thing moves—dry steps on the stones. I can hardly stifle a shout when something hairy bounds past me in the dark. Silence. Slowly I lift my head.

Now I can see out among the rocks. In the open space, the old man stands motionless, staring. Opposite him, a huge black hare sits, returning his gaze from eyes that are just two starlike glints in liquid black. This hare is strange—its face doesn't twitch. It stares at the old man, who begins to back away, hands held out in front of him. He turns and moves off over the stones, picking up his robe, looking back again and again with sweeps of his white locks.

I don't like that hare either, and I climb out of my hiding place. The moon makes a faint radiant patch on the fog, and I follow it back to the path.

*

The hairs have turned brittle and hard as glass in my pocket. I instruct White Dead Nettle to boil a pint of the cleanest water available in a clean pot, and wait for a bit to boil away before I throw in the lock. The steam turns bitter at once, with a musty, vervain smell of dank stockings.

"Give me my dose now. Pepedora must know it works."

"I put myself at great risk to get it."

"Don't worry. Pepedora will keep his word."

"How do I know his charm will work?"

"How do we know yours will work?" Wormpig replies affably. He takes up the glass and looks at the contents in the light. "Is there any risk?"

"Nothing serious. But it will be a bit of a shock, I imagine."

"Feh," Wormpig flips his hand at me and downs the glass in a gulp, pinching up his face. I cry out at the same time—

"You drink it so fast! You'll regret that!"

I can see he already does—his eyes are starting from their sockets and the muscles of his face are pulling his features flat out to the sides. He sinks rigidly to the ground one hand flat by the base of his throat and wheezing like an asthmatic, reels backward eyes spreading apart.

"Oh, you fool!" White Dead Nettle is at his side, holding his arm and trying to force water down his throat. She has the right idea, but the water rills back out of his mouth and down his chin.

"Is he choking?" she asks me, more irritated than alarmed.

"He won't choke if we can get the new words to start coming out."

She thumps him flathanded on the back repeatedly

and I start barking questions at him in Alak. His red face darkens swells and creases, his voice begins to thread into his wheezing. From his stricken face his eyes fix on my face in desperation. I bellow—

"What time is it!? Lovely day don't you think!? Which way to the station!? Is that the post office!? When does the train leave!? What time is it!? Would you like to play cards!? Do you know any songs!?"

He is mewling, tears stream from his face, but now and then a more or less appropriate sounding vowel emerges from his mouth.

"Isn't the weather lovely this time of year!?" I scream.

"YES AUTUMN IS MY FAVORITE SEASON THE DEAD LEAVES SEEM SO DELICATE!" he roars in Alak, the words audibly scouring his throat.

And soon the Alak language gushes from his lips. His relief is obvious.

*

Speaking Alak together, Wormpig and I determine that a number of small doses, taken within the space of a single day, wouldn't put Pepedora's delicate health in danger.

I go to the shrine with the statue of the giant book and steal a flask full of the mare's blood offering, laced with the poisonous saliva of the shrine bats. Three times the following day, I set a bowl of it in the vicinity of a big wasps' nest Wormpig showed me; its paper mass bursts from the infested wall of an abandoned house. The wasps consume the blood, and on my two subsequent visits I collect those less hardy specimens whose bodies litter the ground below the nest. These I take to White Dead Nettle, who crushes them with indigo powder and adds them to the ink we brew together in the meantime. When a good quantity of this ink is ready and bottled, it joins my writing tools and a roll of special wasp paper I've secreted in a cave.

Now, as night is falling, I take several cups of a strong herb mixed with vinegar and return a fourth time to the nest. I peel back my sleeves, take up a stick, and give the exposed nest a strong blow. The groan of the nest swells, the air burrs with their heavy bodies, I feel the flutter of their legs on my skin and immediately pain like a dull knife heated up in a fire lances into my arm—these are the heartier wasps who drank the poisoned blood and survived. That poison is now mixed with their venom.

Crying out with pain I run for the moat, trying to sweep the wasps from my arms and neck—one tumbles down into my tunic and the next moment I feel a pain in my solar plexus that punches my breath out of me—it's like a stone the size of an apple were rammed into and lodged in me. I've traced this route before but I am reeling and flailing with less and less control over myself, and I fight every moment the instinct to shut my eyes altogether made worse by the wasps flitting on and off my face.

Nearly unable to breathe, I throw myself into the water face first, lifting my head out of the water and plunging it back in again over and over, trying to move away from the heavy black darts. Finally I take hold of the far edge. A wasp lands at once and languidly thrusts its sting into my hand. I wail in despair and put my hand back into the water. Bursting with pain it swells and I believe it will drag me to the bottom like an anchor. I can feel the poison like mint in my blood—I have to get out of the water at once. My arms are pin-and-needle numb, stiff. I set them on the bank and drag myself out of the water with them as though they were wooden fakes. The wasps have gone.

My veins and arteries are turning to glass bundles and my muscles are cold as ice, the bones under them ache as though they've been hammered out on an anvil. My shivering is painful, and for a moment I wonder if there are wasps inside. Every few moments an unbearable feeling, like a cold tissue crumpling, flares across me. Just ahead of me, a spot of no particular importance lights up brilliantly, as though a gigantic bull's eye lantern had illuminated it from directly above.

One by one, spots in the landscape light up, and now I'm looking at an irregular streak of clear, colorless light in circles, some overlapping, looking like the sun shining through a leaf that's been bored by caterpillars. There's a smell in my nostrils like jasmine, if it came from an animal and not a plant, from a fragrance gland. Like the glandy saliva of a flower-eating animal. And a deep, delicious warmth cracks in a little seam across my chest, starting just above my breast bone on the right side and tearing down toward my abdomen. My arms and legs tingle and the bursting feeling fades. I raise my hands and flip the fingers, relishing the fine control I have of these many joints. I bend my knees easily, and become ecstatic. I get to my feet, and the blood pounds hot in my temples, my whole head goes hot and I stagger. The rest of me feels light and insubstantial.

Like a ghost, I turn and enter the cave where my lamp and supplies are. Lighting the lamp, its glow falls across an oozing paper face, a figure hunched against the far wall opposite the cave mouth. It has come to help me, at my summons. It speaks viscously through its clogged mouth and its words sound in my mouth; I speak, the words flying from my mouth at the top of my lungs. Though they are loud, I don't hear them, but only feel bright flashes against my ears. In my hand I take the stylus and I write the letters of Pepedora's alphabet.

*

I put the roll in the tray.

"That's my end."

He pulls it toward him on a cord, so that the tray rolls on the loose kernels without disrupting their perfect distribution. His hand shakes in the light.

"Don't look at it all at once. That's advice I would give anyone." I add in Alak, "Did you take the treatment?"

"Yes," he says, in Alak, reaching for the roll.

"Then don't look at more than the first character. I set it on a line by itself. You can't be all that strong yet."

I hear the roll open. Then silence, for a long time.

At last, I hear a long, irregular exhalation. I don't ask whether or not the work is satisfactory.

Pepedora sets the charm bottle on the tray, and now it's my turn to pull it across the floor. The glass is warm in my hand. I can see the tiny, carved figurine of a capering man floating in the viscous stuff that fills it. I turn the bottle this way and that, but the figurine always turns away from me. I can't get to see its face.

"How do I use it?"

Pepedora seems to have slumped back against a timber,

the roll in one hand, the other hand empty on the floor. I repeat my question. His voice, when it comes, seems to emanate from a far away place.

"The outstretched arm will point the right direction. Hold it up, thumb on bottom ... index on top ... right-handed. Hide it away carefully. Tell no one about it. Never turn it upside down. Never tamper."

Now the voice grows stronger again.

"Never disobey."

Sixth Chapter

I don't want to think of anything that might soften me.

*

Makemin, Nikhinoch, the Captain, Saskia, Silichieh, and I go together. The path here is all a dead grey dust, with a wall of black rocks on our right. We pass a black granite stele marked over with characters all blurred by weathering, turning round the stele. A platform house of unpainted grey wood, with a nearly flat slate roof, appears before us, some chickens pecking in front of it in silence. There's a little smoke coming from behind the house and it sags in the air blowing back the way we came. A huge, malodorous puddle reflects it. Flies tumble in the air over the water and sometimes land on it, dimpling its scum with their claws. I'm breathing hard, feeling stifled again; my face seems to burn against the chilly air.

The front wall of the house, inside the veranda, is rolled aside on rails, and there are a number of old men sitting on the benches that line its walls. Their chins are bare. They wear colorless wool jackets and vests. A murmur comes from them, punctuated by coughing and throat clearing. We are not, it seems, meant to go in, but to stand out here and wait to be addressed. The musty atmosphere in there is not inviting. But, gradually I become aware that the one furthest from us, sitting in the middle of the bench against the wall opposite the opening through which we look in at them, is addressing us, and has been ever since we arrived.

He sits in the obscurity, leaning a little forward, his eyes closed, head a little back, speaking without pausing. It's a series of admonitions about the interior. I begin to translate: don't drink any water that isn't clear and that means perfectly clear, don't cut or burn green wood, don't trust anything seen from a distance, only fruit from plants with white blossoms is safe to eat, don't catch or eat game, don't in any way molest any hares we might see, no fires bigger than a few feet across and never set one before dusk ... a bewildering stream of mumbled advice coming out too fast for me to catch it all. The recitation is relentless, the speaker and the others, who continue to mutter amongst themselves, seem bored. Perhaps they don't believe we'll venture to go after all. Or they might set so little store on our chances that they don't think there's much point in concerning themselves with our safety. The effort of hearing and translating drains me quickly, and I begin to feel so tired I want to plop forward onto the steps. I can't possibly catch everything I hear.

Saskia shakes my shoulder nearly knocking me down.

"You're babbling!" she says with a jab of her head.

... Further down the road, the column has gathered. Another group of Clappers appears as we rejoin the other soldiers. They have a cart filled with long rolls, one for each of us. They're thick leather bags, big enough to hold a man.

"What are these?" Makemin asks incredulously.

One of the locals seems appointed to speak to us, introduces himself to me and gives Mushwit as his name. I translate.

"You will need them. We have that on the word of the last one to come back."

"Someone came back?" Makemin's eyes harden, looking first to me and then to the other. "Who? Where is he?"

Mushwit's face alters in slight surprise as I relay the question. "I heard he strangled himself—didn't he?" He turns to his companions. They nod slowly.

"Did he say anything else?"

"No, not that I remember." Again Mushwit looks to the others, who remain long-facedly silent. "He didn't speak much to anyone when he got back."

Makemin seems uncertain, looks at me. He gathers his mouth up.

"They're not heavy. All right. Silichieh, see to it everyone gets one."

I take mine, watch Silichieh dole out the others. These preparations for what we're about to do only make it more unreal. The early morning light, my lack of sleep, my hatred for Makemin, seem to flay me. Last night I dreamt of her round arms again—a woman I never knew. I am gazing into soft eyes through a veil.

Now we're marching again, and the grey men by the house are watching us go with blank baffled faces. I think of the story I was told, and I don't believe they get it right when they say the Pepecaui left war behind to go into the interior. Perhaps it was different then.

I feel as though I'm going toward war, that towers vastly above around and behind its pawns, the enemy soldiers, and us. War fashioned the interior. The war story is waiting to be lived again and to make all of us into its own characters. We will step into our places while the overture plays a medley of themes that will play out in full and in order later on. It's magic, because I *do* what I don't *want* to do, and there's no power that I can feel being brought to bear on me. If a hand had me by the collar, and I were being dragged away, I could struggle. If Makemin or Saskia would only point at me, order the others to catch or kill me, or even only threaten me, I could run. But there is no power here to resist. I simply go along. Hating, and rebelling at heart. Something like the sweeping power of the tides sets everything all too smoothly in motion. I feel war's unreal presence, like blank mindless insanity shining happily from these rocks, watching us bring ourselves to it, for its delectation. We're going to kill and die at war's fiat in this beautiful place, nothing more.

My eyes cling to what they see around me. Everything says to me, "you will never see us again."

I am trying not to clutch at the charm, seeming to want to squeeze it into the flesh of my hand and absorb its powers, if it really has any. In a flash I see Pepedora scheming with Wacagan to get rid of us, set me up with this charm of his. But how does that make sense? Leave his town open to invasion? I shake my head—this is foolish thinking. Makemin is the one dragging us into the interior, against the orders of the Predicanten; Pepedora had nothing to do with that.

Our standard is wobbling in the air. Jil Punkinflake struggles forward, and his dog is there at his heels, tripping him up. It takes the tails of his tunic in its jaws, braces its legs, and pulls him back. He curses and kicks at the dog. We are stealing in between the slopes. The land is still—you can hear the air move through it. Silichieh marching with his head flung back, a look of exaltation on his face. He and Thrushchurl are walking together for the first time, and I can see wild expectancy flicker across Thrushchurl's features. They both want to see the magic for themselves, no matter what. Thrushchurl in particular seems completely at home, even a little oblivious, as though it were already entirely familiar to him.

White vapor sifts in the air on the trail ahead. The ground is spotted with mirror puddles that reflect the sky. There's the white passage up there. The wind goes through me as though I'm not there. Thrushchurl gazes at the passage and says "Death." I hear a shot and the entire column jerks—Jil Punkinflake stands over the body of his dog with the standard in one hand, pennant shaft end braced against his hip, then holsters his pistol.

Cinnamon ground, the powdery earth here is saturated with rust. The passage takes us high into the mountains, the time goes with the passage and we are threading along a rocky course. Glance back and I can make out the remote, crumpled form of the dog where he died on the path behind us. The sounds we make, our voices, are muffled. Makemin stops us and sends a man up a shingled incline toward a house standing alone there against the rock. It seems to suck the breath out of my lungs; the house seems to stand outside time. It is plainly as it always was, an octagonal brick house with small-paned windows. The man comes loping back down to the column breathing hard. He explains that the house is on the far side of a chasm that runs down out of sight, hidden behind this mound of shingle. He saw signs there was a stone span there once, but the house is now completely inaccessible. He called to it, but there was no answer. A light burned in the window. Makemin strides up the slope to see for himself, and returns quickly, his face pale. With a terse order we are set in motion again.

As the sun sets, we come to a rise and get our first clear look at the interior. The land below us is flooded with dark purple dusk, while the pink and orange light of the setting sun still shines around us up here. Above the duskline the sun shines between me and the ground, sheeting it, so that the light hides the ground on its far side. Makemin's face is coated with a shock of sunset light, like a transparent, hot mask of glowing red gelatin. The sun is setting closer than the horizon, looks like a dome protruding from the clouds; the cloudline to the north is a long grey sabre blade with its keen side to the indigo of the upper sky.

We camp along the path, before dimming blue dome and a cloud floor. No moon rises. We crouch in the fluttering air, wind thrashing soundlessly in our clothes, and eat sullenly. The stars come out. The clouds below erupt in a distant flash that brings Makemin to his feet not far from me. There is no noise of thunder and so it takes a while to realize we are seeing lightning below the stars. Makemin stalks back to his letters, weighted down by rocks on his portable writing desk. His little fume light burns behind me, projecting his shadow past me and out into the air over the valley below. I fall asleep with white violet and blue spots flickering in the grey in front of me.

*

Our descent, the next day, is steady and swift. We make our way down the slope toward a foaming ocean of clouds. By midday we are already on gently declining land, the foothills, and the tepid, seeping fog has covered us over. The ground is littered with lumps of broken mortar, evenly laced with fine slivers of rusted metal like long grains of red rice. We pass something like a massive stump, but, examining it, I find it's the severed end of a cable, ten feet across, protruding from the ground. Hairlike wires festoon the disrupted earth at its base, as if they had sprouted and grown down into the soil like vines.

A wind blows back the fog. While it hangs in a sheer wall ahead of us, the sky over and behind us is clear, silky blue. Again I see the rare sun, slipping along the edge of that cloud wall, wisps passing invisibly between us causing its light all but imperceptibly to vary. The ground is levelling out more and more, and we are approaching a low flat space that is weirdly colored, all pale green with a little blue, and glinting sharply. It's like a field of translucent, thin-hued gems. We will have to cross it.

Now it's only a few hundred yards away and the words of

the man in the house begin spelling out in my head just what there is to be frightened of as I get a smell of something rancid. The charm seems a very distinct shape in my pocket. For a moment I clutch it surreptitiously, and then nearly drop it, afraid to crush it, afraid to drop it. I peek at it hastily, a feeling of unaccountable terror welling up in me because I can sense yawning beside me the empty forsakenness I will feel if it's a cheat—but the small man inside turns and points away, very deliberately, back toward the road. As if it understood my confusion and wanted to explain, the figure turns and points to the east. I follow its pointer, and for an instant I see a remote cloud of churning, shimmering motes, which fades at once. The air formed a lens there for a moment. Now the pointer again turns to point away up the road where we came. Shaking, breathing with gratitude, I hide the charm and run up to Makemin. I repeat what I was told, as though I were the man who spoke.

"After the mountains you will come to the Lake of Broken Glass. There's only one path through, and its location changes with each storm—without warning, terrible winds gush down from the mountains and stir up a blizzard of glass shards that can mince a man bones and all in the blink of an eye."

Then I revert to my own voice again.

"Sir, there's a storm coming," I point to the east. "We must pull back until it passes."

Makemin peers at me as if I'd run up to wish him a happy birthday. He glances at the glittering field.

"There's no wind. Return to your place."

"I'm not guessing and I'm not being nervous," I say levelly. "I know the signs. The wind is already on its way down the mountains."

"I see no storm."

"No one *sees* them!" I say sternly.

The loonies' eyes are trained on me. Their heads rise like a field of heavy blossoms in a breeze. They're listen to me.

Makemin pulls down his goggles and turns.

"Show me, then!"

I point to the spot where the motes had been.

"I see nothing."

"Look!"

"I see nothing." He pulls down on the lensed visor and releases it—it chunks back up into his helmet. "We advance."

"I won't go."

"Then we'll drag you," he sneers, turns to two of the men standing near. "If he won't walk, carry him—and keep his mouth shut!"

I am starting to shout, dropping onto the ground, trying to warn the others, when a blast of wind thuds against the column and a scintillating cloud shoots up into the sky like a snapped sheet. It tinkles and crashes with a demon noise. Makemin is stock still between me and a hurtling wave of glass.

"Get into the bags—the leather bags!" he screams.

I am released—already I can feel stings, hear cries—I pull my bag from my pack unroll it and scramble in headfirst, trying to gather it around my boots, the way they showed us. I turn my back to the wind, pulling up my legs and lying on my side. The bag is pitch black, hot and stinking—I feel the wind battering me, stings on my uppermost arm and leg, I can feel the leather flap, catch, pluck loose, but it's very thick. There was a welter of voices, screams and shouting, as I climbed into the bag—but now I hear nothing but the roar of the wind, the tinging and crashing of glass ...

Gradually the wind dies. The bag is stifling, but I don't want to leave it. I am rebreathing my own breath, sweltering in my own heat, but I can't move.

A hand shakes my shoulder loosely through the stiff leather. I am the medic.

I crawl backwards out of the bag, pushing the soil back with my boots so as not to crawl too much on glass. I don't look up. The soil before my face has no glass at all in it. I turn my head warily to one side and the other without raising it too much, and see no glass on the ground anywhere. Now I am hearing groans. Despite myself I look up, see a soldier a few feet away sobbing, bent over a livid, tranquil-faced head. The body attached to the head dribbles away along the ground, churned to a red morass. I blink at the soldier.

"I told you so," I say, "I told you so."

*

"There was nothing to see. How did you see?" Makemin staring me in the eye.

I stare back at him. My hatred for him, my contempt of his opinion, are giving me strength, weight, steadiness. "I don't know," I say.

Makemin and Saskia glare at me almost with outrage.

"How could you have known?" Makemin asks.

"I saw it," I say bluntly.

Makemin grimaces and, with a glance up at the descending sun, turns abruptly. "Up! We march!"

Saskia shambles out among them, where they crouch or

stand shivering in groups. She lumbers, bellows like a bear, gesturing to them to stand. Jil Punkinflake walks behind her, accentuating her gestures with his own, face like a ghost's. He's perpetually at her side now, and she seems to tolerate him. His eyes are like smouldered out holes in his head; they gleam like the glint of fish scales deep in a well. The soldiers are rising to their feet now.

Silichieh passes me on some errand, with no expression.

"This wind blew all bits of glass away again. There must be something that keeps it from dispersing in all these windstorms."

That's the kind of thinking he relies on.

The land on the far side of the Lake of Broken Glass is split by a ragged, turf-lipped crag. The exposed chalk wall bends acutely down to barren white ground dotted with small clumps of brush. The fog is denser before us, and nothing of the land beyond can be seen. It seals us in behind as well. Not far from the point at which we approach the brink, one of the scouts finds a subsidence, where the ground seems simply to have lost cohesion and melted apart. A cleft in the crag opens like a harelip, its mineral filling lies in an oddly neat, conical heap, the tip trailing from the cleft's base. We can employ this as a ramp.

Even without the assistance of the scouts, Makemin picks out the confused footprints of booted feet in the cindery dust around the top of the cleft. Here, perhaps shielded from the wind by the irregularity of the surface, we can still make out footprints the blackbirds left behind them.

The taling heap is loose as gravel; the men come down slowly, waving their arms, half-crouched to keep their balance. The pack animals have to be led down, and this takes time; then the carts are unloaded, their contents portaged down; finally the carts themselves are lowered, restrained by ropes the men above let out hand over hand. By the time we are assembled on the ground at the base of the crag, the dim sky darkens to black within a few minutes. It feels less like the onset of night than being suddenly engulfed in smoke.

There's a small building made of metal plates down by the base of the crag, mostly buried in the talings. I wander in as the carts are being let down. A steel implement a little like a can opener hangs from a peg on the wall trembling in the wind without stopping, still glinting. A skeleton lies on the floor. I brush dust from a long bone uncertainly. Do I cover it up, or uncover it? The metal implement taps irregularly on the wall as I think ...

Makemin has already ordered camp to be set, but he paces up and down, hands behind his back, at the far edge of the circle of light thrown up by our fires, barely able to contain his impatience to go on. The night is completely silent, but there's no peace in it.

I see Pepedora preparing the charm, filling the bottle with lymph from his sores—but that's all right, the charm works.

The next day I am jangled awake by Silichieh's hand on my shoulder. My head feels lead heavy. I can barely drag myself upright, blinking in pain at the insipid, fog-watered light. Silichieh tells me we are two hours past dawn. And here the light is no more intense than in the wan blush before sunrise. Everyone is oversleeping. I can hear Makemin snapping at someone somewhere.

*

We move along a stretch of bare white land, and there in front of us is a wall of trees, a little arched with the rise of the land. The treeline stalks out of the fog, which is thin lower to the ground but smotheringly heavy overhead. The column slows, cowed by the sight. The trees are uniformly huge, thrown up in a black wall across our path, but there is a break ahead and to the right like a colossal, shallow furrow gouged across the woods, its mouth angled away from us. The trees resume on the far side, across the oblique opening. I know what's coming, so I head off to mime urination in a knot of bracken a few dozen yards from the column, take the opportunity to consult Pepedora's charm. It points toward the gap.

As we close on the furrow, a long white regularity becomes visible inside it, raising at an angle into the air. It's something like a huge stone rail, flat and broad, maybe fifty feet across. To our right, it vanishes into the mound displaced by the furrow dug for it; to our left, it vanishes in the distance, driving a straight line through the trees like a wide avenue. While its course is straight, the rail isn't level—it looks as though a great hand had pushed the far side down deeper into the ground, tilting the near side up. It is however not so slanted we couldn't use it as a road. Makemin peers out at the black woods. Then, with a sharp draw of breath he turns and gives the order, walking away calling out instructions.

We make our way up the mound, pushing the carts, and then down onto the very point at which the white abutment is first exposed to the air. Setting foot on it I feel a flutter in my chest that makes me sigh, like a heart palpitation. There's a crisp, snapping feeling this substance imparts to me when I step—I crouch to run my fingers across it. A fine-grained smooth material, like ceramic or unpolished marble, without veins or glints, opaque and a little dingy, like dusty snow. Everything tells me it is older than the Limiters, but no one seems inclined to ask about that. I notice Silichieh rubbing it, too. He sees me, and points to the upraised edge.

"Still perfect," he says wonderingly, and I feel his curiosity is noble and saving.

The column slows, quietens, and we listen ... a sound like the clap of a horseshoed hoof on a cobblestone street, but without that rhythm. It comes from no fixed location, knocking here and there at random. We consult together—I have no opportunity to check my charm, but I feel we are still safe, and that the noise is natural and not threatening. Makemin sends the scouts ahead, and we continue. The woods seem to envelop us swiftly, in one gulp.

I feel vertigo, looking out into the trees, trees endlessly succeeding each other. The soil is white. Completely bare of brush, only the inky trunks of the trees emerge from soil like fine ash, and only the blue shadows of the trees darken the white ground.

The trees are huge, funereal, with heavy branches and peaked crowns. I can see the metal-colored bark is scored in a regular way, almost a grid, and glistens as though it were oozing grease. Each trunk is sheathed in amber, of a dim, barely-discernable blue color.

The hoof sound comes from all around us—it is the noise of these heavy, mineral branches knocking together, and now and then there is a chiming of glass in among the leaves, tingling. It sounds like a headache.

*

It's the middle of a silent, suffocating afternoon. I follow pointing fingers—off to our right, something massive droops above the tops of the trees. It looks a little like a wheat sheaf made out of badly rusted iron rods, melted together at the top into an uncouthly shapeless globule. Slowly its scale becomes clear to me as shreds of mist drift in front of it; I have to raise my head a little to see the top, and it must be at least a mile away.

Late afternoon. A droning knell, like the muffled reverberation of a bell, pitched almost too low to hear. The sound is continuous, but with the pulse of a slightly higher tone going through it.

I recognize it; I've certainly heard it before. Where, I don't know.

The drone comes from a towering structure that rises to the left of the path. The structure is round, drawing in as it sweeps upward, flaring at the top to make a platform. Below this platform, a sort of mast protrudes out over the treetops, and attached to it is a cubical object. This object is ochre colored and streaked with what looks like verdigris, studded with frozen bubbles and big granules. These streaks form stalagtites that hang down like frost from the cube, which has a few square openings in its sides, and seems very solidly mounted.

I find it hard to understand what I see at the top of the tower, something like a flat wedge. A slot opens along this wedge, and one side erupts in an irregular fan, smooth like the inside of an oyster shell, and stained a dull green. This fan must be thirty or forty feet high, and it looks strange coming out of the top of this structure, like an ear growing out of a pyramid. The tower looks like a bottle that has been attacked with a hot torch, and partially melted.

As we draw nearer, I begin to see a lead-colored urn or something inside the slot. Some of the soldiers around me are walking faster, craning their necks. One of them suddenly gives a long moan and drops straight to the ground. I have his slack face in my hands and my thumbs on his eyelids—his glistening eyes roll and focus on my face, and he mumbles in confusion. Bad breath, a shrivelled-looking beard around the lips. I help him to his feet again.

Now I turn and look. My eyes make out the urn, the rolled-up thing—a weak sizzling feeling around my eyes, my head swims. The back of my head hurts, and now, unaccountably, I am lying on my back, and faces are peering down at me. I rub my temples. There's a garbage taste in my mouth.

"Don't look at the tower!" I groan. "Don't look at the top of the tower."

Some men have fainted. Others mill around, unsure what to do. Suddenly afraid, I check the charm, keeping it hidden inside my tunic. Not broken. I let my breath out. It still points down the abutment.

Makemin is giving orders. "We need to get a look over these trees. I want someone to climb up there," he says, pointing to the cube. "You should be all right if you don't look at the top."

The Captain asks reasonably, "Are you sure? It could get worse the closer you get to it."

"I tell you we need to know if the enemy is near and where he is."

"Still, in that case, we wouldn't want to lose a man."

Makemin's mouth tightens. In a voice straining to retain its even tone he says "We will put a rope around him, put it over the top of the box, and he will not fall if he faints. Who will go?"

He turns suddenly to the rest of us. At once, Thrushchurl raises his hand.

"I'll climb it," he says, grins and nods,. "Only let the rope be tightly cinched and I'll gladly climb, and look for you."

We stand strung out on the abutment, watching Thrushchurl climb the secure rope. The sides of the tower are decorated with a mosaic of diamond- and disc-shaped tiles, all grey in heavy dark borders, all a little dissolved, and blackened strands with fossilized bubbles frothed into them run down from the tiles in long blisters. Silichieh stands at the base, keeping the ropes taut, and staring in a kind of rapt amazement at the tower. There's no telling how long ago it was built.

Thrushchurl dextrously climbs the sides; he clambers up onto the top in a few lunges and vanishes from sight. That ditty of his still drips from his lips. Cats have got their lice. With a moan of complaining iron, three ribbons of reddish-brown liquid spew down from the side of the box opposite the road, but the box and its arm have not altered position or relation. The fluid stinks—it's as if the box had been precariously balanced and filled to slopping with a broth of fluid corruption, steeped decomposing bodies, and Thrushchurl's weight has tipped some of it out.

The stuff runs out and the ribbons turn to rags. A

rumbling exhalation breathes from the top of the tower, a new, even drone that rises and falls, filling space above the trees, wafting up between us and the sky.

Now Thrushchurl lowers himself hand over hand, still smiling, down to us.

"There are ruins just up ahead there," he says, pointing off to the left, "and a clearing further up, within a mile or so. I could see persons milling there, and rows of white bumps on the ground, all in a peculiar, lovely sort of dim light from the ruins."

Saskia suddenly looks very animated.

"No, no, no," Thrushchurl says quickly, "they're not blackbirds, I'm sure of that."

"Sure of it? How can you be sure of it?" Makemin snaps.

"They—they ..." Makemin is making Thrushchurl nervous, his grin pulls up in the center and down at the edges in a volatile grimace, "They're all quite naked, sir, and appear to be starving."

"Does this—" Makemin waves at the abutment, "continue much further?"

"As far as I could see, sir," Thrushchurl says. "Dense as the fog is, I would say it goes on for two or three miles yet from here."

"How far away are these people you saw?"

"Less than a mile, sir."

Makemin glances up at the sky, lifting his chin. The tower chants its great note above us.

We march, putting the sound slowly behind us. After twenty minutes, Makemin orders us to halt again. We are to divide into groups, some to go along the abutment, others to go into the woods to the left and make our way toward the clearing, so as to have two sides open just in case. I don't want us to leave the abutment and say so, but I still haven't been forgiven my true warning about the storm.

Angrily I follow my patrol into the woods, jumping down with them from the high edge of the abutment and landing in the gravel, which bounces away from our feet as spongily as bits of dough. Keeping the weird ivory flank of the abutment in view, we slip in through the trees that seem to pour heavy, aching silence down on top of us. The tower drone is gone. Where have I heard it? I am off to one end of the line.

Then with a start I realize I'm hearing a new sound. A hum. The noise draws me. I see ahead of me some one crawling along the ground, draped in a churning mantle of flies. A livid patch of skin is exposed for a brief instant as the flies swarm and cloud the air, making a spinning column above the crawling figure, and alighting again. It's their hum I heard, like but not quite the same as the drone from the tower. Pictures flash in my head of those fly-infested lips coning out to articulate speech; I rush forward but the hum is growing farther away. The crawling figure is disappeareing. I want to hear the words she breathes in exhalations of flies. I see her again, crawling painfully, one arm stretching out every few heartbeats toward some absent object.

Now she's gone. I'm alone—no one followed me. I call out and rush back in what I think is the road's direction. I don't find it.

I stop calling. The woods seem to grow even more silent, so that I yearn after that irritating clopping noise. Figures are crossing between the trunks; the trees are thinner, the light brighter, in the direction they're taking. They are so lean they look elongated, and walk barely moving their bodies, shuffling, heads thrown back, swaying, shadowy stiff and lean they look like wooden figures broken loose from the trees. As I begin to move in the direction they're taking, parallel to them, they disappear in the confusion of thin dark trunks slipping by me. I wonder if these trees were once people like them, who simply stood still too long in one spot.

A clearing, like a scar in the forest. I stop at the tree line. Completely bare ground, with a ravine running through it. Here and there, emaciated people, naked or with a handful of rags at most, stumble from the forest near me, hair dishevilled, bodies withered, charred-looking but bloodlessly pale, faces and chests streaked with fluid. Near me, a woman stalks in a circle on sticklike legs, her arms wrapped around her stark ribs. Her buttocks are two knobs at the base of her pelvis. A wizened child sits by the edge of a brackish puddle, angrily striking the mud with his fists. Now and then I hear a growl or some other sound of anger and irritation, or a sob of pain, or the gagging noise as another one vomits. The ground is spattered everywhere with thin streaks of vomit; every one of them is vomiting intermittently. The stale air is permeated with a thin, acidic reek of vomit.

Some lie in exhaustion, chins and chests spattered. Others sit among the rocks, many convulsively kneading at their heads from time to time. The noise of the trees is back, and it seems to grating on their nerves. It takes me a long time to realize that an arresting object—it looks like a brown leather sack, glossy and hard as lacquer, with many odd ridges and an angularly kinked set of straps—is the shrivelled corpse of a woman lying on her stomach not ten feet from where I stand.

Moving quietly, I make my way around inside the tree line to a higher piece of ground, where there's a confined space bordered by stones and bracken I can use as a blind. A harsh rasp of breath from my right makes me lunge to the left, turning my face toward the sound. A tattered man in a black uniform is staring at me from the other side.

Simultaneously our eyes fly to each other's holsters. His is empty. I hear his frightened breathing. Reflexively I put out my hand and address him in Laschlache. His eyes open wider and he leans toward me. I see the insignia on his armband. It's the same. A narrator, like me.

*

He was cut off from his unit a few days ago. He says he hasn't kept the time attentively, and he seems wilder and farther gone than he should be after only a few days. The qualifiers he uses are strange, and make me second guess my grasp of the grammar. The details of his account seem to flash up at me randomly; he describes closely things that seem incidental to me, and omits what I would have assumed were crucially important points, but I can't strictly make out what his criteria of importance is.

There was a fight further in, past the end of the abutment; howling men flew at them out of the trees.

"Do you know who attacked first?" I ask.

He shakes his head, clutching at the front of his uniform where the buttons have all been ripped away, leaving ragged, angular holes. I can't understand the expression on his face, but it suggests he thinks this is not an important question.

"There all of a sudden was just corrupt noise, and then they were on all sides of us ... My friend right next to me was killed; we all started, only just started, running doggedly back toward the marble-semiprecious abutment. I was the only one who was reaching it. They purposefully didn't follow me."

I pat my pockets, looking for something to give him, but I have no food on me. I offer him water from my canteen. He eyes it glassily, but won't drink. With blue fingers dry as twigs he pinches at the rock in front of him.

"I didn't go immediately back. Not being sure I could find them again was the cause of that, if I left. I had only the marble-semiprecious abutment to guide me, but I didn't dare to try to walk even with caution because we knew on it that after us would come you. So I took to the stone woods, and stopped here myself.

"That we came here at all," and here his voice grows bitter. "Without the moment of uncertainty, but flew here by the straightest of ways, shows that we also are as insane."

"Were you trying to reach the cemetery, too? The spirits?"

Now he stares pale blue eyes at me, light lashes in blanched face.

"They're utterly insane," he says quietly. "They think the disembodied spirits will give them an invincibility."

The expression on his face seeps around and alongside his features like a vibration, blurring them.

"Your bloodthirsty men have had that very dream themselves." His voice seems to come from deep underground, humming up a long dulling tube.

Something subsides, caves in, inside me. "How do they know where to—"

The narrator's face coils in a brief, mirthless smile. Bending toward me, his hand unerringly seeks out and thumps the charm through my tunic.

"Pepedora?" I ask. "He gave you one?"

He moves his head, and his face droops again. He sighs, so that his head drops and stays lower than it has been.

"They set great store by it," he says.

"Do you have it?"

"I never was entrusted with that."

Getting a new idea, he points his finger shakily at the opposite side of the clearing.

"Just in the trees there, wholesome mushrooms can be found, and a pit of nonvenomous serpents. These people resignedly dig out and eat them every now and then."

"Aren't those the same wild men that attacked you though?" I ask.

He shakes his head looking older and older. "I call them vomiters. They constantly, they vomit. They are as notably thin as they are for that reason. Their jaws and chins get warts over them, and their teeth are nothing to see, meltings."

I look out at the people, sitting on the ground, and plants thrashing in the wind beyond them. One, sitting with his legs outstretched, puts his hands to his head and drops onto his back, rolling to and fro on his shoulders in intense pain.

"What's wrong with them?"

The narrator's mouth is slack. He's looking out at them with an alarming dullness in his eyes. Then he seems to recover.

"The grey light from the ruins does that to them," he says

without looking at me. "It appallingly fouls their insides and they never can be well again. Why they don't leave it, I don't know. There is water here, maybe that's their better reason for staying."

"Are the ruins far?"

He shakes his head, looks at me the whites of his eyes showing all around the iris. "Not far, but you will be killed if you draw too near to the gloomy light and the bad air off-given-off by them."

"Do you know what those rows of white bumps are out there?"

"... Those are elderly. There they drag themselves into the glow out of fear of the others, choosing instead to grow sick and die in mounds of clay, with only their heads sticking out.

"Food and water is brought to them by the stronger ones. I don't know the reason why they do it. It would be so much obviously better if they let them die. One might be inclined to suppose they need of others to feel sorry for."

He shivers, and rubs his teeth with a knuckle.

"I think we will have to go by them," I say. "Will they attack us?"

"They may." He throws a look around himself that is nervous but not exactly frightened. He is excited and terrified.

"Sometimes they attack on sight. Other times, they watch and do nothing, or take no notice at all. But might they. But these are so weak, not really dangerous. The stronger ones are further inside, to cope."

"They aren't affected by the ruins?"

"No, just the noise. The ruins they stay away from. I

think they dig up or dowse for or perhaps they even drill for their water."

"Do you mean the noise of the trees?"

"They are compelled to fight irritably," he says. "That noise, their condition, all this—" he gestures around himself vaguely, "—sibilantly grates on their nerves until they can't help themselves.—Your men are near? ... These people I've seen fall on each other for no cause at all. Once, I saw a group of no more than six of them sitting together in a rough circle. One of them began to sway and squeeze his head in his hands. The sound was driving him mad. Not another instant could he stand it. He began to cry out—"

And here the enemy narrator actually imitates him, a series of forced howls ringing at the back of the throat, each one a single breath.

"Then he vomited naturally, and, still vomiting, he turned on the one closest him. It was all he could do, he had no choice."

The narrator's voice seems to be choking him.

"They flew at him, just to have the relief."

His breathing becomes labored with emotion.

A voice calls my name, not too far away. The patrol is looking for me. The narrator can't have failed to hear them, but he keeps talking.

"They beat him to death. Then they went back and resumed their places conscientiously."

He turns his eyes to me, something wrong in them.

"There's a noise within the noise, like glass rubbing that nobody can take that forever and ever, without a moment's suspension."

He looks at me, and his breath is ragged, something

horrible coming into his face.

Voices call to me again.

He stares at me, horror in his look. A thin, wheezing cry comes from his convulsing mouth.

"It's the war," I try to tell him. "You've got the war!"

He gulps, his brow crushed in anguish. As if moving on its own, his right foot swings forward and plants itself in a step toward me. His face implores me, tears jostle loose from his eyes.

"War is the spirit that seeks your life," I say, not knowing what I'm saying. "Don't—... Don't let—"

With a sob, he reaches out and shoves my chest with both his palms, driving me a step back. Strangled sounds jerk out of his mouth. He advances again and shoves me harder, head flung back, eyes shut, desperate bleat in his throat.

I turn and run from him. Not wanting to lead him toward the patrol I bear to my left, and eventually duck down out of sight behind seething black shrubs. He dashes past me, arms flung back his whole body rocking from side to side as he runs. His head twists on his neck and as it twists in my direction he sees me and stops. Legs apart, he stands with arms held out like a man who's just been dowsed with cold water, and his face congeals in a mask of horror. Helplessly he stretches open his mouth, screams with unreasoning rage and despair, and runs at me.

Sharp voices to one side—I see my patrol, drawn by his cries. Their guns sputter and not seven feet from me, two or three shots pluck at him, and he falls. But he lunges to his feet again and runs from side to side before their guns, half bent and bloody, crying out for someone to turn to. Shots thump into him as he runs, head thrown back his mouth bawling, a shot hits him and he crumples to his knees, droops forward. A bullet tears across the curve of his back. I hear his faint, mournful "uh," when that groove appears as if by magic there.

"It's me!" I shriek, my voice breaking. "Stop shooting!"

For a moment he is still. The fading sound of the shots echo into the mineral forest. Then the war inside him forces him back up onto his broken legs, and with a scream he blunders forward. Half a dozen gunshots hit him, and he collapses onto his back.

I rush to his side, shouting, throwing up my hands at the others. The shooting stops; one bullet fired too late thumps into the ground a few feet from me. I kneel by his side. His fractured legs still struggle to set his heels against the ground. His upper body is rigid, his face shaking, every muscle contracted, horror, anguish in his eyes, terror in his throat coming out in a ragged, faltering cry, that momentarily sets his vocal chords ringing in the clear sweet tone of his usual, his real voice. As I peer into his eyes, the tension begins to dwindle from his features. They slacken with his feeble scream, and release his face as the sound stops with his breath. Something jealous is finally relinquishing its grip on him. He dies, and leaves the war.

Shots are resounding from the abutment, and all along the treeline around me.

*

The ground is littered with bodies. The vomiters stood or sat impassively watching the others die. With an impatient upward snap of his hand, Makemin orders me to rise and join him, then stops when he sees the dead narrator at my feet.

"Who shot this man?"

Some of my patrol stand together, nearby, eyes on the ground. He struts up to them and begins staring in their faces, one at a time. They shrink under his look. Abruptly he turns back to me.

"I will find the culprit later—or," he momentarily twists back from the waist looking at them while walking toward me, "perhaps you will all be responsible?"

Now he marches up to me.

"And *you*—" he says almost with disgust, "I suppose you were too busy embracing your comrade to interrogate him?"

Keeping my face expressionless, I tersely repeat the narrator's story. Why not? Makemin's face remains tensed but he is soaking it up, every word. When I'm done, he is silent and staring for a moment, but I have told my story in such a way as to answer any questions he might have before he asks them.

"Good," he says finally, and it isn't a compliment. He likely mistrusts me. If he doesn't, so much the worse for him. He should mistrust me. I intend to kill him. It feels false when I write the words. Marching back toward the abutment, he cries out to my patrol.

"Strip the body and return to the road! Get any papers and bring them to the interpreter! Interpreter is with me!" He makes a backhanded gesture over his left shoulder to show I should follow him.

We return to the abutment, where the other soldiers mill. Those nearest us snap to when Makemin bursts out of the woods. He picks out four men with his finger, saying "you" each time. Then he turns and surveys the clearing.

"Bring him here."

He points to a man sitting on a stone a few dozen yards away. The soldiers rattle over to him at once, take him by the arms, and bring him.

The man is naked, scrawny but not as wasted as some of the others. Tufts of black curly hair still grow from the sides of his head, and his discolored lips and chin are partially concealed by a threadbare beard. The front of his body is marked by an inky vomit stain from chin to groin. He walks between the soldiers, who are meaty, enormous in contrast, without resisting, head cocked a bit to one side. They bring him to a stop a few feet from us. He swallows loudly, and a brown streak escapes one corner of his mouth, stops in his beard.

Makemin begins relaying questions through me. The man returns my look expressionlessly. After three or four repetitions, I see his mouth beginning to work. He stretches out his lower lip, the upper one is gone exposing crooked teeth, and a hawking, shapeless rasping noise comes retching out. A few minutes of this, and then his rasps end in a short gout of bile that splatters noisily on the ground at our feet. The soldiers step back, releasing his arms, and he totters a little where he is.

Makemin selects a few more, all with comparable results.

"Leave them," he says finally, gazing around at them with disgust. "Get back onto the road!"

*

Dusk makes everything fluoresce blue around us. I have

watched as one head after another swivelled to the right, fixing on the vast shapes that flicker there deep in the trees. The line falters to a stop.

"You mean to say you're not going to investigate any ruins?" Silichieh asks Makemin incredulously, with no interrogative inflection in his voice.

"We will explore ruins only if that helps us find the enemy."

Silichieh looks peevishly down, brow crumpled. Makemin, still facing down the white abutment, adds, "There will be all the time in the world once we have beat them."

He is thinking.

He turns to us and raises his hands in a peremptory gesture of attention.

"Comrades! Don't let yourself be cowed by what you see and hear! Remember," his flinted voice clatters against the trees, turns into a knife cutting their noise, "you are soldiers of the greatest empire in the world!"

Each tree whispers secretively to each of us—"... you are soldiers of the greatest empire in the world ..."

"We march now in pursuit of our fleeing enemy, but also with the prospect of a great prize!"

He points down the white abutment.

"That way, there is a place of powerful and ancient enchantment. Spirits wait there to receive us, and offer us their aid in our glorious cause, if only we may overcome the obstacles that separate us! That is what we are struggling for now—a miraculous power, that we will bring to bear on the blackbirds to destroy them here, to destroy them on this island, and finally, to blot them out everywhere, once, and for ever!"

Nikhinoch, at a signal not meant to be seen by many, steps forward and strikes up the Red Earth Chant; the asylum soldiers take it cacophonously up at once, but the din emanates a familiarness that draws the regular soldiers in.

We are marching again. The trees salute us as we go by, whispering "you are soldiers of the greatest empire in the world ..." and showing us glimpses of the ruins far away, buried in the wood. I see blue-white sky through a lacy, rent wire spiderweb; stone tracery, the acute curve of a tower or silo, a bellied-out white expanse looking like bone. The walls groan with exhaustion, longing to split apart, to collapse with a sigh, and rot.

The noise of the forest is almost the sound of chewing teeth in a closed mouth. I imagine disembodied voices speaking flat, factual words in Lashlache. The idea is so vivid, I seem to hear them, saying nothing, speaking at random, in fragments of ancient conversations still hanging in the air like unmelting breaths. My balance sways a little in me, and I veer a step or two; I imagine the influence of the ruins had something to do with this.

I am inspired. I exaggerate. I let myself stumble, and pretend that I've suddenly gone woozy. Silichieh steps up to me and I feel his arm clamped across my back, his flat hand gripping my upper arm. Rolling my head forward I sag and stagger, mumble a little. I don't want to overdo it.

"What is it?" Silichieh asks in a bewildered voice. He's been watching me ever since I first warned of the glass storm. I hate to play with him, but that hate ranks low on the list of things I hate just now.

I pretend a little recovery. I want them to believe I have a special sensitivity to this place, that spirits are meddling with my finely-tuned nerves, so they will listen when I tell them which way to go, and not ask too many questions how I know. It's not so hard. I've always been the sort of person who would sink under the weight of an ordinary day.

"I'm all right," I insist again and again. I must act irritated, and give the impression that I want to avoid attention rather than attract it.

Silichieh looks hastily in the direction of the ruins. A few others saw me falter as well. Did I imagine I was pretending? Did something *make* me pretend?

I breathe out through my mouth, feeling less and less a master of myself. This pretending has brought up such a heavy sadness in my chest, and sudden misery. Death ... death, waste ... violation of every single precious, horrifyingly vulnerable, precious thing. All at once, it seems to me there is nothing in the world but terrifying frailty and the nothingness that waits for it, that will always inevitably overwhelm and violate it. The whole world is untasted ripeness rotting.

My breath keeps catching on my throat on its way out my mouth, I feel as though boiling water were streaking down my face in searing lines, and I taste salt.

In my mind, she sits in the brilliant day, in the regal gloom of her veiled trees, only a memory and that not even so clear a memory. Can I remember what she looked like? Looks like? I'm exhausted, and I'm going soft—my own young hands, the trees, this soft eerie air and light, Silichieh's worried eyes, Thrushchurl looking at me too with a weird knowing concern because he's seen through me but won't betray me, the kindness of my friends, all too beautiful.

Aren't I a man? Why am I still playing idiotic games like

this? I can't do it—I should reveal the secret of the charm, give it away and disappear into the woods, melt into their emptiness. I'll never write anything—what could I possibly say when I haven't understood anything? What one word could I possibly write about war, as though I could pick it up and handle it like it were a sane thing? It's more than I can handle—I can feel the war close like black water over me—it has me—I'm in its stomach. All my strength is pouring out of me.

*

Sticky air, trees, that irritating noise.

That noise is making us all angry and hasty—it's bad. It bodes badly.

Grey sky. Now there are trees ahead of us as well. Looking up, I catch sight of flying wings, the first birds I've seen in the interior. They soar above us, just in the fringes of the fog, fuzzed shapes. Their dull bodies look like iron. Those are *their* Predicanten, the most ancient ones. They feed in the ruins, I think, maybe they feed on that poisonous light. A few shots split the quiet and we all fling ourselves flat—the loonies are trying to bring them down. Makemin grabs the nearest of them, shakes her violently and slaps her face.

"You shoot at the enemy and only at the enemy! Ignore them!"

How—how—how—?

The white abutment ends and we climb laboriously down to the curdled white ground. The trees here are less crowded together. It looks like there's open country not far ahead. The trees, air, rocks, soil, the movement of the wind, even the noises we make ourselves, are all hiding places for spies.

I have a suffocating sensation of being watched, peered at in silence, and with it I experience oppressive, hot closeness. It's like I've been stuffed into someone's pants pocket.

Now that we're out in the open, the space itself stares at us. The trees give way to a wide rocky place in the fog. The ground here is sandy and trackless. The land ahead is curtained in mist. The perennial noise of the trees falls away, but I experience no relief. Feeling a million eyes on me, I put on a dreamy face and point wanly into the distance, the direction the charm pointed last time I checked.

"There ..." I murmur, trying not to overdo it. I step forward as if a mysterious force were pulling at me, and raise my hand—I don't thrust it out, nothing too emphatic—just point loosely.

Silichieh is watching me.

"What is it, Low?"

Thrushchurl says very loudly "He's in a *trance!*"—angling his head so Makemin will hear.

"That's the way," I say softly.

Other voices—"He was right about the storm ..."

Silichieh turns to Nikhinoch, but speaks loudly enough for Makemin to hear.

"Well, our scouts haven't turned up anything—I mean, if there were enough of us to fan out, maybe, but ... but as it is ..."

Makemin consults with Nikhinoch.

We move out in the direction I indicated, moving quickly to get out of the open.

The air all round us is thick with that feeling of watchfulness; a baleful sniper stare I can feel drop down on me like a lead mantle.

A wave from one of the scouts—they've found some empty ration boxes hastily buried in the loose earth. Makemin inspects them personally, then throws a sharp look at me.

We go on, following the course the charm indicated. Makemin calls me to the front, takes me familiarly by the shoulder—he keeps me close—sends me out to scout ahead telling me to report back directly to him. I can run out ahead and check my charm easily.

The day passes without seeming to. Nothing changes, not even the light. The land ahead is blackened, sprinkled with flat shapes, dark against the pale ground; they are slashed and bullet-riddled bodies of wild men, their upturned faces powdered with blue mold. Saskia strides indignantly among the bodies.

"Those monsters!" she snarls, drawing a Yashnik sabre out of a dead body she holds down with her foot. No dead blackbirds, but here's one of their caps.

I orient us again and we move out, trying to put the site of the massacre behind us before the sun is gone. Makemin walks with me. I feel his probing eyes every moment, with hate. Finally, he orders us to set up camp on a low rise and the men collapse in silence. Makemin takes me aside and we stand looking out into the mist.

"If you try to undermine my authority with the men, I'll shoot you. If you try to leave us, I'll shoot you. You will always be watched, and if you are shamming, if you are leading us into their hands, I will shoot you in the head. Understand—you are *my man*. You are not inexpendable."

He looks at me, preparing some further words he plainly does not want to say.

"One more thing. If you guide us correctly, I will see to it that you receive whatever you want."

*

Empty, colorless expanse.

Sandy gravel under our feet. Damp, stale air in our mouths, that leaves a drably insipid film on the tongue, like rebreathing your own breath. The iron birds appear to make wide circles at the extremity of our field of vision, keeping us in a vast, invisible ring. They are not watching us themselves—they may not have eyes—but their circling seems to attract a monstrous gaze to us. As the interminable day wanes, trees break through the mist before us like ocean cliffs. We pass through them almost obliviously ... there's that old clacking sound again, that until this moment I had thought I missed, and no reduction of the feeling of malevolent watching.

The trees give way in a few hundred yards to an oblong, clear spot, like a barren meadow, open at one narrow end, trees thick all round. Despite the exposure of the spot, the sun is going down and Makemin feels we risk being divided if we camp in the trees.

Camp again.

*

Shouts—

—and something beating me—

—rain is falling hard—men are veering this way and that in it.

I lurch up and a hand yanks at me.

Shots—a man slops up near me aims and fires—turn and see another firing in the other direction. Jil Punkinflake sprints by, face and eyes white, his black mouth open, groaning with a kind of rage again and again, like a stricken horse. Dark shapes run and shots snap all around—the night explodes in shooting.

A despairing voice wails somewhere near me. "Where did they get guns?"

I run, I get down, I want to ask somebody something—man splashes to within a few feet of me raises his gun aiming and it bursts in his hands swatting him to the ground and he's clawing his face and kicking on his back. I get to him and start trying to stop the bleeding, sew his face shut. He screams at me the bone of his jaws bare on one side his eye is red black jelly his nose is a rag. He punches and rips at me gulping and crying a flurry of explosions comes down like an avalanche on top of me and I can't think, I'm staring weirdly at my own sopping hands streaked with rain-thinned blood fingers pale thick and nerveless like sausages fumbling stupidly with the suture—a yakking face shoves into mine—

"He's dead! He's dead! He's dead!"

Figures dropping down onto their knees around me with heavy thuds thrusting out their rifle barrels like lances firing jubilantly and I swim past them in the other direction. I hear them sing out all around me like men at a wedding party. What are they shooting at in this pitch dark? Shapes in the rain. Saskia yelling "Press forward!" Which way is forward? All of them? The mud by my left calf shudders flying up into the air—dressed only in a long shirt, one of the women from the asylum staggers toward me making a convulsive animal sound in her throat, six or seven carbines hanging on straps from her shoulders and arms. She empties the smouldering one she has in her hands— and just shot at me with—firing now over my head into the mayhem behind me. She drops the empty carbine and unslings another still making that noise, a depraved giggle, firing into the movement, shooting anything that moves, and I know there's no one back that way but our own. I throw my hand out toward her.

Someone comes up from behind and to the side of her, opposite me; Nikhinoch, even in the mud he is neat and orderly his step still springs light as a jackknife. With one smooth continuous motion he pulls a compact gun from his vest pocket and fires a bullet into her head. She collapses in a heap of rattling carbines. Nikhinoch steps over to her body and checks the guns. He takes a loaded one and continues looking, his pursed blue face unhurried, lit sideways by muzzle flashes from the soldiers at the tree line. He takes another loaded gun and tosses it sideways to me, economically indicates I should follow him and walks toward the shooting with the same heron step he always uses.

We stop by a clump of trees. Nikhinoch fires into the dark, I can't see at what, but he aims with precision and fires swiftly and surely. Empties the gun, turns to me and for a moment his rain-streaked glasses, which must be impossible to see anything through, glint into me. His hand snatches the carbine I uselessly carry. He coolly aims and fires again, then walks back in toward the worst of it, flicking open his vest pocket pistol, pinching out the spent shell, and sliding another one in, snap it shut and pocket it again, all while

picking his way unerringly through the puddles and stones.
Not a glance for me.

I spot a man cowering by a stone—he's only nicked, but
he lies trembling, staring. There's a group of soldiers not
far from him, gathered in a knot, guns pointing out in all
directions, aiming and firing at who knows what. Silichieh is
there among those men; I can see him searching desperately
for the enemy. I can't get near them for the shooting, pull
away toward a rockier place. I cross toward the far tree line.
To my left I see Thrushchurl hunching along the ground—
he gives a sickening jolt and spin his hat flies off and he is
on the ground with a cry—I rush toward him but the air is
alive with bullets and the rain is blinding me. I search in the
mud calling his name—I can't find him. Searching toward
the tree line—

I can't mistake Makemin even in shadow nor can I
mistake his voice—"Spread your fire! Bring them down!"
Shadows fan out from him and aim toward the group I've
just left, blasts rip up and down their line. My pistol is there
by my side, heavy, fully loaded. I want to see him cut down.
I want it so much it shocks me.

"Those are ours! They're ours!" That's the Captain's voice,
from somewhere nearby. "They're ou—!"

Cut off, as though he'd been struck in the stomach—I
go toward the sound, but legs drive hard through the mud,
racing men ram me back; I lose the direction.

I run back toward Silichieh shots flying by me—screams
in the dark—a figure silhouetted against a clot of firing
men and their muzzle flashes, this one with something
flapping from his shortened face—I follow the screams to
the soldiers Makemin had shot at and find them rolling in

the mud bellowing in pain pushed out from the bottom of the heap. They flail and claw at me, drag me down as I try to help. Hands shove my face down into muck and I taste the blood that soaks it, I twist and push my brow down to tilt my chin back and keep my mouth free, rainwater sluicing down into it and my nose. I kick wildly hitting out with the back of my heel and though I barely feel what I'm doing the weight is suddenly removed from my head and I haul myself forward with both hands.

I'm in a broad, flat hole—I get to the brink and look back at bodies. A man falls spilling with a scream not six feet from me—I scramble over to him—he lunges at me trying to grab the front of my tunic drawing back his knife—tiny droplets of blood tremble on his eyes—"I'll kill you!" he croaks, "I'll kill you!" flopping toward me on his side, dragging himself over his own spilling bowels, knife shaking in his upraised grey hand ... then his eyes go out, and he slips forward, slowly, onto his face as the war leaves him. His bent arm stiff at his side. The knife presses into the mud by his limp features. The knife is driving its own blade into the mud under the weight of his hand, the night is exploding in the roar of guns all around me.

We're slaughtering each other—I catch sight of Makemin pointing, crying out his orders—I slap my hand to my side but my pistol is gone—Will I find a gun? I pull one up from a dead man's hand—grip it—point it at Makemin and jerk back in anticipation of a shot but the gun thuds inert in my hands. I throw it down with a grunt of frustration and search the dim ground for another going from one corpse to the next—a rifle lies there across some stones—I seize it and turn. In the sluicing darkness I've lost Makemin. I rush off into the deeper part of the rain and dark hunting him, shouting his name ...

*

This is a dream of mine war took from me. It owns it now, and owns me. I am and have been leaning up against a tree, my shoulder at the trunk, with the carbine I shouldn't have and that isn't mine in my hands. The branches keep some of the rain off, but I'm drenched through, numb and heavy. Frail daylight is gathering in dense ropes of rain. I watch it, drone of rain alone in my head. I'm alone. I'm not alone. The rain watches.

A sound of wet bracken breaking nearby. I turn abruptly toward it raising my gun—all my frozen joints squeal and I can't stop myself pitching over onto the ground. I've stood there too long and my body has seized up. My mouth stinks. Gibbering in panic I thump the mud with dead fingers trying to find my dropped carbine with deadened fingers when the weight of a hand drops on my shoulder and flail weakly away from it. I look up at Thrushchurl's head, rain ribboning from his viny locks, silver on broadcloth shoulders. He strides forward and shows me his upper teeth.

"I'm not a ghost," he says seriously. "You had better get back up again."

I find a carbine and climb it, regain my feet. I have many lives—the lonely one, that was just here, is melting, and the other, that I've lived so far, is returning, unwelcome.

Thrushchurl has already begun moving off out of the trees toward the clearing, and I want to ask him something. Back in the open the weight of the rain pushes down on me.

Gun in both hands, barrel lowered, I rush to catch him up. I raise my head, and beyond him see the struggling party. With desperation I feel it begin all over again—nothing's changed.

There is Silichieh, and I am happy to see his bearlike figure there swinging his arms in his sopping sweater. But there is Makemin, an inflexible blue shadow in the streams, pointing, shouting orders. There is Saskia—her arm launches out to catch a slipping soldier before he can fall, thrusting him roughly forward onto his feet. Jil Punkinflake's face is swollen and rigid with freezing rain, drops fall from his dangling lower lip. Everything will go on and on the same—I've stopped in place—Thrushchurl brings himself up short a few feet away and looks back at me with an expression the rain smears out. Guns have been lifted. One of them cracks. I just stand and stare wanting them to kill me while I'm still numb with cold. Makemin's arm flies up into the air and I hear his order to hold fire. His cruelly keen eyes have determined that I am one of *his men*.

Thrushchurl takes my shoulder again with a glistening hand, and I go dumbly with him. The carbine I carry suddenly seems disgusting to me, like a runny rotten leg, and I throw it down. Out of the rain glare Makemin steps toward us, solid, compact, strong high steps, and I watch him come into my heart like a worm flopping over. His face is hard and severe as a block of wood. I am turning into nothing, just water. I know I will have to cling to him just like all the rest of them do, and even clinging to him will take all the strength I have.

"Good, you still live," he says flatly. "You will march with me. Your guidance is essential in this rain."

We go on. Behind us, there is a field littered with our own soldiers.

*

The carts bog down and force us to stop again and again. As we scrape through the mud, we come quickly to the flat, uniform surface beneath that it covers. I peer ahead, where another line of trees has gathered like a barrier, and above them a vast looming presence of something I can't quite make out, like the shadow of a mountain. Looking back down the column from the front, I see the same behind us.

Regular shouts through hard sound of the rain. One of the carts lurches forward as its wheels come free. An object jostles out from the back and drops at the feet of the Captain, who twists like a top, mud belches up in a cloud around him with a muffled splat.

Muck plops back down to earth.

I rush to him, my heart pounding. The grenade blew the Captain wide open.

*

When I was young I read a story about a madman who drowned two people, crept up behind one while he was at his shaving basin and thrust his head down into the water—for months I felt him behind me, I hated to get near to water. Now I feel him again. It feels as though it had already happened.

I'm walking with Silichieh.

"What do you think?" he asks me abruptly, tossing his

head in Makemin's direction. As usual his voice doesn't go up at the end of his question.

"He's insane."

Walking.

"I think you are right."

Walking.

"I know it ..." he says gravely, his eyes downcast. "Because I catch it too, every time they shoot. It's kept me alive I guess so far ... I'm maybe afraid to think how much farther though."

"Who's alive? I don't feel alive."

"Don't be silly. You're more alive than they are," he says evenly.

*

The trees come up around us again. The rain stops quickly, like a faucet shut it off, and the white ground dries, the pale grey mud that clings to us dries. Marching, the air space and silence staring at us as we grind ourselves down past nothing. We camp in three tight groups in line of sight around the base of some bigger trees, with more open space under their branches. I almost falling on my face, roll over and sleep, the last respite. It isn't rest. Makemin and Saskia seem to have endless endurance—I can hear them still, from time to time, behind me. I've never known fatigue like this before, and I'm far hardier than the others. I gaze indifferently at the trees and their wonders ... and then I sleep, despite the rapping of the boughs.

I awake in darkness with a heavy weight on my chest. I can't see what it is—I take it in my hands, a weird, irregular, cold, thing, gritty, too—it moves, loathsome to feel under my hands like a slug. As I struggle, and breathe out, its weight keeps my chest from expanding. It's crushing the breath out of me—I struggle—I foam, snarl madly and push off the ground with my feet and as I turn myself sideways I feel it topple from me at last.

I pitch back gasping for breath, and two black pinions spread in the air with a glassy scream. The wings whip through the air and clash together—a blast of oily-smelling wind and I get a brief glimpse of flapping against the light between the trees.

It's gone. I sink down against the roots, shaking.

*

Crusts of blue mortar thrown up in waves show where outskirts of the city once were. The unnatural white soil is part of the ruins. We are already within the city limits, although the trees are just as thick. Between them, I see the shape of a black hare, ears up, motionless as a statue. From far off in the distance a ripple comes waving through the trees, though there is no wind.

The branches clatter together. The black hare is gone.

Men in Wacagan uniform hang from the trees here. We've wandered right in among them. They dangle in space, chins on their breasts. I see some tangled in the boughs high overhead, as though they had dropped into them from a great height. Far ahead, I see a shape perched on one's shoulder, picking fiercely at its head. The bird stops and stares at us. From its head rise two long leaf-shaped ears, and it flies straight up through the canopy of dead branches, disappearing into iridescent sky.

Thrushchurl half-climbs a trunk to look at a hanging man. The body is covered with a thin integument of clear, shiny material, like clear amber, that seems to have dripped from the branch, down the rope. The swollen, discolored face shimmers like a bright mask. They'll be preserved here forever.

Makemin's voice splinters the quiet, again and again. His barked orders press down on our exhausted heads and we blunder further, blunder further again. We are becoming stupid and forgetful. We are losing ourselves. Soldiers drawn away by the beckoning sunlight of golden afternoon that seemed to melt the trunks of the trees from behind, melt them into softness like candles. The soldiers melt into empty space that sucks up cries of "Come back, will you— come back!" One woman who fell ill said she saw a little wild pig, all naked, snuffling at the roots of the trees. Its brief grunts were loud there, as if she and the pig were alone together in a small room. She shot the pig in the head, and it flopped over on its side instantly limp; slaughtered the pig and tried to eat it, but the meat was bad. The flesh was layered with flakes of rust. Her skin turned a dingy yellow and she weakened, but she survived and marches on with us now, though all her hair has fallen out.

Saskia stares out into the trees, by the carts—turns to me abruptly as I come up.

"What do you want?" she snaps. I came to serve myself and wanted nothing from her. Jil Punkinflake stands, I notice, nearby, eyes on the ground; shot his dog and then became her's. I choose to point to one of the bundles of rifles. She stares at me, then turns, removes one, inspects it with a glance, and holds it out to me. Her eyes probe me with a look so knowing or expectant I almost don't take it from her. There's the butt of the gun, steady in the air; my hand floats up and closes on it. The weight is transferred to my hand and arm, so that the top of my forearm goes taut. The trace of satisfaction in her eyes puts me off.

She is the least changed of us all—or is she? I can't tell. But her face is, it now strikes me, white, and drawn; the doughty oratorial spirit of her is frayed to threads.

Something unnameable, with many layers or many heads, suddenly returns my gaze from her eyes; her brow contracts a little as she turns to go.

Jil Punkinflake's face is blank, like a corpse's, eyes glazed. He snaps his arm out and punches me. His fist drives into my chest making a disc of pain there, and I go down, off balance.

"Stay away from her," he says hoarsely, his eyes barely focussing on me before he walks away. At first the sounds make no sense. I have to think about them for a while before I understand them. I'm not hurt. The cold and the rain have cured me, made a numb rind of my outside.

*

Thrushchurl and I are chosen to scout together. No one leaves the group alone. We leave stakes to mark our path back, while the others regroup in one place. Thrushchurl turns his face like a dog catching a scent—he rushes forward, leaving me to hurry after planting stakes. I call to him, but he is preoccupied. I rush up to him, and as I catch him I see a shape loom ahead of us; the shape draws Thrushchurl to it. He is panting for it.

The trees have not encroached on the structure, which is a many-angled squat shape buttressed with tapering, inverted cones whose regularly-spaced flat round tops form a crown. The roof is irregular, with many gable-like shapes. The white enamel skin is like a tea kettle's, cracked and flaking to reveal a drab black subsurface. The whole thing sits on a raised, smooth stone foundation that runs on into the wood shadows showing where the much vaster original edifice had been.

Thrushchurl, open-mouthed, rushes forward and lays his splayed hands on the stone as if he were placing roots there. He caresses the surfaces in rapture. I follow him, now oblivious to my presence, around to the opposite side. Here the building has been ripped open, and the rest of it is gone without a trace; not even a single loose stone or bit of broken glass, nothing but the unscarred, unmarked foundation to show it was ever there. The exposed edges of the small remnant's walls and ceiling are shockingly jagged where the building was ripped away, with long triangular edges projecting out into space and many fine needle-like teeth in between.

We face a rounded inner wall that folds back on itself to make an aperture. Passing through it I feel a sudden oppressive vibration, like an organ droning at its lowest registers. We enter a hall-like space tall for its width, its floor strewn with cinders, tools lying in discs of dried grease, broken glass vessels and shards shoved rudely aside to form a rough path lined with curled bundles of green wire.

Now into the colossal main room. Thrushchurl dashes forward arms flung open. Everything is slightly phosphorescent. The floor is springy metal with a rectangular central panel of a glossy hard black substance like glass. Set into this panel are thick, transparent hexagonal tiles a little more than two feet across, and a corpse floats upright, head up, beneath each one, in honeycomb-like cells filled with a grainy scarlet fluid. Thrushchurl kneels crooning and running his hands over the tiles, his palm sweeping a dim shadow over dark heads.

Tables are bolted to floor around the walls. There's a dark booth projecting from an upper story with a spiral staircase drooping from its underside. The dim glow of the chamber illuminates a few dials on the back wall of the booth—I see their needles flicker convulsively every time Thrushchurl touches the cells. I point this out to him, and his reverie breaks. He crosses to one of the tables and picks up a pink-red vessel of glass or ceramic; the vessel is heart-shaped and pearly, like a red conch turned inside-out. There is no lid, and Thrushchurl sniffs at the contents, then pours out some of the thick scarlet fluid onto the table. Setting the vessel aside, he crouches down and peers at the stuff, sniffing and prodding it with a piece of metal that might once have been something. I detect a thin sour odor, like the smell of rotting brawn that came from the square structure on the tower.

Thrushchurl withdraws from his pocket a pinch of mercury—where did he find that? has he always had it?—and drops it into the center of the dish-like pool of scarlet fluid. The shapeless mercury gathers itself in the center, its blue-white radiance brilliant against the red. I'd barely noticed how his hands shake now. The grooves in his fingers seem all filled with dark mercury.

I notice that the scarlet fluid on the table has coagulated

into a single layer, with the mercury resting like a wafer on top of it, without mixing. I feel the steady earthquake of the building and dizzily suggest we get outside.

Thrushchurl breathes, "For a moment ..."

Our going is interrupted by a machine sound, and sharp knocks.

The black panel in the floor sinks a foot or so and slides out of sight moving in our direction evidently under the floor. A few of the cells on the edge opposite us emerge a bit from the floor, their lids tossed back. A body drops from an enormous ragged hole in the ceiling and, flashing down, lands in the capsule with a thud. The capsule slides into the floor closing itself, and, I can see, filling from below with red fluid. This happens until there are no more empty capsules.

Another sound of distant machines. The bodies drop down out of sight as though each had been tugged down by a single hand, and withered black hares rise through the fluid, are squashed against the transparent upper panels.

From the hole overhead comes a familiar sound with no perceptible beginning. I recognize the drone of the tower Thrushchurl climbed, but the timbre of this sound is clearer, with many transparent layers like sheets of breath. The tone is deep at its heart, and wind stirs through it. It's as if the sensation of being watched, like barely palpable wisps of air slithering on the skin of my back, or creeping just below the skin, were given a counterpart in sound. It billows over us like a sail. It's the drone I heard the tower make, but I'd recognized that too—now I remember Keen howling on the floor of the house we'd visited outside Tref, and the inhuman drone, like the deep groaning buzz of a resonating box, inside his howls.

The laughter suddenly erupts from him again.

"The war!" he raves, "The warrr! We won!"

His head snaps up on his neck and he stares into my eyes, hissing "*We* won!"

Keen subsides into idiot chuckling, his face folded down against his throat. He's laughed himself out. His laughter trickles around the room, his voice comes from the walls, the furniture, the fireplace. It jumps from the window, runs cackling into the distance. We can hear it go, we can hear it for a long time.

From outside, through the wall, I can hear an even, answering note, like the whisper of air escaping from a reedless organ pipe. Let me be there, let all of this have been a long vision and I am back in Tref.

"That's the trees ..." Thrushchurl says.

I almost believe I see something like an envelope of light in the open space between the floor and the ceiling. The note from overhead elongates me, as though I were being pulled off the earth.

It's music—that comes in a flash to me. The idea makes me smile. Who would have guessed, who else would have guessed, that they made this to make music—and the tower as well? Dead body, music, and Predicanten, always associated. The dead hares against the floor haven't changed at all, but they seem to peek out at me with an expressive look of mutual understanding. Thrushchurl stands abstracted, listening; I can't tell what he's thinking, but a secret has been entrusted to me and I intend to keep it. Let him find out on his own.

*

"What do you see?" Makemin is barking.

"I don't know yet—" I bark back.

"Well use those slanty eyes of yours damn you," strangely tired there. Weary of me, not too tired to go on with his war.

"It's a clearing like any clearing."

Brightening up for a change, icy light although the day is ending, brilliance soft on the eye, not dazzling.

We camp again. My legs don't want to bend as I lay myself on the ground, observe the droll spectacle around me. Dry voiceless laughs are shoved out of my trap with each contraction of my diaphragm; it's an interesting feeling.

They're all paralyzed. I see, on every face, blankness, just blankness. That blankness is on every face now.

"Little mice, little mice,
Even cats have got their lice,
Run-run, run get away—"

"Dead as cinders, grey as ashes,
Cold as ice, now its eye flashes,
Too too late to get away—"

That's not Thrushchurl but one of the privates, drooping on a flat rock right by me. His face, a moment ago inert, cracks open with a fierce, berserk energy. He leaps up again, slapping his canteen, rapping it smartly each blow quick on the last, and he gives a short laugh with a schoolboyish gaiety his eyes seem only barely able to contain, and I know he's gone crazy.

Now Thrushchurl is beside me after all, perhaps he sang or perhaps his appearance behind me ...

He sits, light streaming past his face turns it half to ether. Puddles everywhere. Aren't I good at describing things? Thrushchurl stares at them, like the mercury he enjoys playing with, and they are bright and shiny enough to be mercury. It doesn't take long to see reflected in them things that aren't occurring outside of them. In them I see four or five identical objects fixed in a motionless row high in the sky above us. They're like the white squares of a box kite.

The crazed soldier comes back and sits again. He's making note of something on an official form like an old rag. I can tell he's not writing the sort of thing they're intended for; he finishes his statement, and, trying to insert the nib of this pen into the cap, his eyes gleam, and he deliberately jabs the nib into his left hand, in the flesh between the index and thumb below the joint, his teeth set in a grinding smile like a slot. Blood spurts across his right hand as he pulls out the nib and drives it deeper into the wound, pulls it out and dumbly thrusts it in again, then watches the blood, turning his dripping hand this way and that, smiling fiercely.

It's dusk, when lights and darkness seem to form small scurrying shapes ... lie down certain a sticklike dwarf with a long thin knife will bound up, perch on my back and stab and stab. At the edge of the clearing beyond my bleeding friend, I see a black hare observing us, half in shadow—the shadow darkens, and it disappears. No one else saw it.

*

Silent shapes wheel around us with long nasal shrills

splitting the air like bugles—figures detach from the trees ahead swinging crazily back and forth in the air. Shots patter all around us and our guns return fire—Makemin leads the snipers and Saskia is whipping through the air already flashes over my head firing, her voice cuts under the screamed alarms. Soldiers and trees flash by my sights but I can't line up my shots, fire always too late. They stay in the same area directly ahead of us, dim flashes in the trees, pale moonlight on their shoulders and helmets, caps. Suddenly the flying shapes break and fly toward the enemy still wailing, and Wacagan retreat.

Makemin snaps to his feet and we are charging headlong through the dark and dark trees against the white ground—still firing at the retreating figures I see Makemin run his rifle level and the enemy are being cut down, punched in half, wrenched round and torn apart. The carbine butts and jolts in my hand like a bucking snake but I'm not shooting at anything, I can't manage it somehow. I glance around—the enemy shoots back at us but not one of us has fallen, a mob erupting with flashing guns like a churning thundercloud ...

... ahead and to my left the Captain stands in a plume of brass fire with his arms flung out, warding me off with his hands in a flash that leaves a shadowy scar in my vision, blotting him out. Did I see him? What did I just see? The blackbirds ahead scatter and bound off to the left—a few of them stand out distinctly in the moonlight—they are not swinging back and forth as they usually do: they are *leaping with both legs, like hares.*

Around Makemin, Saskia and the others, I see the wan dream tremble in the air like diamond haze, the chance at last to crush the enemy, hammer their bodies and break them open, dash them to smithereens—the same dream drove me forward against my exhaustion and flooded my arms and legs with miraculous, fresh strength, but now it recedes from me, though it wheels all around in them. No one is really dying.

Those aren't people. Their guns aren't guns. None of our number has fallen—what kind of ambush works like that? Following their charge a body of our soldiers on the left plunges after them and I don't see them any more. From out of invisibility ahead I hear them scream. The screams are cut short, each one.

Makemin suddenly drops to a walk and calls "Halt! Halt!" Saskia barrels up to him in a flash demanding to know why we've stopped—he wants us to advance slowly, expecting a trap.

"They may have found help. Those birds warned them we were coming."

In the dark and the cold the bitter grin on my face goes unremarked—they aren't *they*.

We close on them carefully.

"They've carried their bodies off with them," Saskia says hoarsely.

There are no bodies, no arms to carry bodies.

I hop up on a stone and see it, wave Makemin up to this higher vantage and show him the chasm standing there hidden by bracken and heaped scurf. Chasing "them," we'd have plunged right into it.

Three of the "enemy soldiers" stand there between us and the gap, all their impersonated Wacagan lightness gone, staring coldly back at us their eyes like stars shine with piercing light.

"*Those* aren't people," I say. I sound like a boy.

Silichieh half raises his rifle jerkily—

"Don't shoot them," Thrushchurl says without taking his eyes away, and Silichieh looks, and seems to understand, lowering his gun again.

The figures turn together and calmly walk over the chasm's brink, dropping out of sight.

*

I listen carefully to the slightest motions of the air in the branches, the sifting noise it makes as it slithers along the ground. My every spare moment is spent like this, in a painful effort to hear the music. Saskia tramps by making an enormous racket; drawn as she is, she never seems to get tired. I wish she'd tire right out into thin air, and wishing tires me. They created those vast buildings, that are musical instruments, to sing a neverending spell over all the land here. The soldiers we found hanging from the trees in mineral varnish were the "rests," I suppose. The song is performed by all those dead musicians, and its notes are also moments in our story, like that bit of improvisation with the counterfeit soldiers. The hares and the birds, their Predicanten, are conducting. It's so tidy I can't quite believe it. But it couldn't possibly be as quiet as this if there weren't some great booming sound shoving the quiet down into our ears. The music shakes its vast body of wind over me, and the quiet between us only intensifies until my breathing interferes with my hearing. The musicians must be dead, with no breathing or pulse, to be able to hear what they play. The soldiers hanging in the trees, or lying smashed at the bottom of that chasm, so far down we couldn't see them, are all listening to the music now.

Sometimes I think Thrushchurl hears it. He loves it here.

Dusk coming on. A Yeseg corporal near me gives a sudden yelp and snatches his gun from his back—I follow his eyes to iron wings high in a tree. The wings gape apart and the shape leaps aloft. The corporal starts blasting at it wildly, gibbering curses. I only watch him do it with cold curiosity. Silichieh rushes up, slows as he approaches the corporal from behind.

"What is it?" he yells. "Stop shooting!"

The corporal empties his gun, oblivious.

Thrushchurl is leaning against a tree. He catches Silichieh's eye without unleaning his head from the trunk.

"Oh, let him shoot, if it makes him feel better," Thrushchurl lowers his eyes. "It won't do any harm."

The corporal stands panting and glaring in the silence his shots made. Nothing has changed, except that some bullets are gone.

"You can shoot birds but not soldiers?" Silichieh asks suddenly. The smile that scales my cheekbones has to strain against my creaking muscles.

Thrushchurl answers him calmly, "It's not the same thing a bit. You don't shoot where your form and the Predicate's form correspond. It doesn't go through."

And I add, "If they model themselves on you then— injure the image, injure the original."

Silichieh looks from me to Thrushchurl and back again. I see plainly he has his own struggling understanding, and for some reason I feel abashed as though I'd just pulled a trick on him.

Seeing his confusion, suddenly I stop trusting this knowing, collected feeling; I stop forgetting the danger we're in.

Seventh Chapter

Through sparser tree tops towering, irregular spars, impossibly high mounds, crossways are dim blue grey against slate sky. We've stopped, and a cart wheel is being repaired; I lie down on my side facing away from everyone and gingerly draw the charm from my pocket. This fragile thing is my life. I don't dare even hold it, and my hands shake. So I slide it along the ground up to my face. The figure inside points unerringly in a single direction, toward the high silhouettes. Tatters of sky are reflected in its glass, grow blurry, now I see a sort of a gateway, a rubble road by a titanic pinwheel-shaped building sprouting hoses, and the cemetery beyond. Has this thing all along been thinking pictures silently to itself in my pocket?

Soon I am pointing the way again, Jil Punkinflake

glowering at me over Saskia's shoulder. He should thank me for the opportunity to feel something different.

*

Solitary buildings among the trees; no matter what the light, their insides are always completely dark, and the flaking rust walls are radiant with dark. Enormous trees erupt out of a few of them, transforming them into shapeless skirts for tree trunks.

Vast shapes of light shine at us, through the trees ahead. Our emergence from the woods is sudden; there before us is a smooth wall, bellied out like a sail, that looms and spans. The surface is chipped enamel, buff streaked with rust. There's a regular series of tapering, protruding openings, like the wide ends of funnels, high above.

The gate isn't far. It comes in view after a half hour's walk along the base of the wall, which vanishes directly down into the soil. The wall turns away from us at a place where the land breaks, and we look out now from a crag, not too high or steep. Just below it is a tangle of collapsed derricks scabbed with rust, some of them curled up on themselves like dried worms. Bolt-shaped metal pillars that rust has roughened and bulbed over like coral are thrust up among the derricks, which crushed the building they belonged to when they fell. The ground before us carpets itself with enormous shards of glass, warped metal beams orange with rust and tossed together like twigs, and what look like great blankets flung haphazardly down, all of rust metal mesh. There are some deliberate-looking streaks on the earth to show where buildings once stood.

The crag slumps off to our left, with an easy way toward the gate, which is now only visible sidelong as a complicated bus on the shield-like wall. It turns into direct view as we go—the oblate mouth of the gate is pitch black, set into a wide winged structure emerging from the wall. The sunken ground immediately before the gate has filled with water, and the mouth is reflected in it. From the near side of the pond emerges a brown-orange streak of what had been a paved road, its surface now gathered into tiny pellets that stir a little in the wind.

The wall simply stops a hundred yards beyond the gate, the edges of the outer skin stick out in angular segments, and mammoth rusted rods, each one a man's height or more in diameter, droop from within the epidermis like brown intestines. Blown out, somehow.

Predicanten explode from their red rookeries high over the gate and circle as we come—their beaks are closed, the shrieking is the noise their wings make against the air, and the groaning of their own rusted joints as they flap. We stand at the brink of the pool, and only now is a white coin visible deep in the gate, like the full moon reflected down a well. Without hesitation nor too long a look at the Predicanten, whose shrill noise chitters against itself in my ears, Makemin wrecks the wind-riffled surface of the pond with his boot, and we wade through to the ramped opening of the gate.

Its black arc hoods us. We are in the even darkness of the gate, in cool, dry, iron-smelling air. Sharp squeals and the sound of our feet and wheels rustling the water, hum and blend dully in the tunnel. The city's ruins draw near, in the egg-shaped opening ahead.

There's a small open space on the other side, gigantic wreckage all around it hampering our view of the rest of the city. Blankets of rusted mesh and elaborated metal beams with branches, mats of rusted wire, broken blue mortar, blue enamel shells like conches hundreds of feet high, crumbled metal plates beneath our feet. The shrieks of the Predicanten have died away; apart from the sounds we make ourselves, there is only the distributed creaking of a vast ruination to listen to.

There are ways through the ruins: I know which one. What we see is impossible, no sun's light *could* show it, but we see it through the dead white light of the fog that wreathes the spires and high ramparts. To the left, what looks like a metal honeycomb, all the steel frame's angles are wrenched and the building is leaning over and twisted on its foundation, with a long colorless cracked mantle of glass sweeping down one side like a cape, all flowed melted from the windows and made this mineral waterfall, and charred objects are frozen inside. On the right and all around are vast shapeless hives of coagulated rust. Rust like cinnamon powders the ground, which holds many white puddles. Silichieh points to slabs of the white substance the white abutment was made from, still impeccably white, studded with blackened wens of metal looking like warts, old black excrement on new-fallen snow. Shelves of blue cement between us and the foundation of the unbuilt wall, some stacked up with a few long branches of metal, like pillars or bridge pilings, that seem to have melted and slumped against the stacks, forming ribs or veins there.

As we walk, guns out, looking carefully this way and that, Thrushchurl nudges me and points to the buildings, where intermittent gestures are happening here and there, parts of figures and parts of motions, like raising a glass, or handing someone a letter, flash there dimly and almost without light. There is nothing magical about them, they are banal shapes thrown around by the wind; I can see the wind has abstract faces in it, black eyes and black mouth in a round piece of wind going by.

Lights flit in the buildings ... a human skull protruding from a mound of rust as big as a house ...

Some blackbird droppings, too. Charred remains of stamped-out campfires, and a few tin cans, still wet inside.

Thrushchurl is turning round and round, a weird, foolish sort of smile on his face. He stops, staring at something—rushes toward it. He so loves anything eerie, and he never seems to get frightened. Dying doesn't scare him. He's like an animal that way, but I don't think it's because he doesn't think about it. His way of understanding doesn't involve fear.

We follow him, Makemin snapping at us to come back, but we haven't far to go. Thrushchurl has ascended a broad flight of shallow steps to a bare semicircular terrace of that white material, fronting a huge white building whose roof has collapsed and whose sides bulge and spill out. There is a crushed and blocked doorway there, but he is approaching the exposed wall beside it, which runs on for many feet, covered with the shadows of people who aren't there to cast them. Black streaks run from a spot by my two feet to climb the wall, join into a torso of a man with arms at his sides, facing, I think, toward the wall.

Thrushchurl caresses the shadows without touching them, a lingering sigh welling from his chest. Mutely imploring figures, knees buckling, arms flung up before the face, another kneeling hands outstretched in warding off. At one end, a figure caught turning to look. We look at them. Black and white. Snow spins around me so thick I can't see the horizon, the trees, I can't see what past I'm in, although I've remembered this moment so many times since out of black and white I swam together and became a "character"—

—now see the flash that scalds the eye, through the glare see the shining city's beautiful towers minarets domes and columns wilt sag and jet fire as the whole city seems to deflate, crazily lie down on its side on a bed of screams—I see people burning to cinders, and dying in the ruin of the buildings. I hear silence. The light destroys the air. Instantly the light turns to darkness, blindness, a sky without sun, moon, stars, clouds, as black and dead as charred wood. The land glows with transparent white flames that ooze along the ground, and everything they touch turns over and curls up, changes from one color to another to another, shrinks and then billows out flat.

Far off down the street I see someone, a woman, going to and fro, crossing and recrossing the busy street, approaching everyone, briefly stepping into every business on the busy street, avidly searching for someone. Her clothes are entirely unfamiliar to me. This concerns me, but I haven't got time to think about it. My time is not my own. Inside my head are many many long lists of things I have to do right away. I check my watch. I have to collect my rations before the office closes.

The train is idling on the platform; I sit across from the open door as we wait for the connecting train to arrive. I watch the passengers criss-cross the platform between the two trains.

The streets aren't too bad, people move swiftly in even files on the proper side of the pavement, slip across the street hastily when they think they're safe—not many dare. I want to save time by crossing the walled square diagonally but the prisoners are doing exercises there in the center and I have to go along the edges. The supervisor is a willowy older woman with a shaved head, who is surrounded by a few officers and a group of soldiers.

On her orders, a number of prisoners in white rags are compelled to lie on their stomachs. The soldiers stand over them and shoot them, through them into the ground; the noise is like a row of stitches popping. Now she directs another group of prisoners to take the bodies and pile them into a hopper set into a wall.

Out of my way a little more to avoid proximity of a loud homeless man, who harangues the crowd from this street corner. He is a local fixture, tolerated by the authorities because he exhorts passersby to remember the indignities and injustices perpetrated against us by our jealous enemies. His eyes rustle icily over me as I go by.

What I didn't get at the office I couldn't get, not anywhere. What I see is all a white that makes me feel a wave of illness, and I avoid the thought. A young man emerges from a knot of people drinking from steaming mugs, going round to greet another warmly, and a wearily smiling dog trails after him.

Gradually the crowd around me is stirring ... the bull-like bellow of the claxons, a pulsing, dead white howl.

Chaos, shouts and running; prisoners have escaped, armed themselves. I make my way to the side but the alleys are filling too—I shove through a doorway and race through empty halls, I come out in a darkened shop with cold steel hoppers, remnants of ice, odor of fish. Out the door—keep moving—I pass a mob that have set on a couple of prisoners—I can smell their blood. People are running by with hands that drip red. I want to join them, but the prisoners are dead. Police rush to the windows of their towers actually colliding with the ledges in their haste, their eyes staring they move frantically like electrocuted men yacking and fumbling with their rifles, so frenzied they can barely work them, fire them randomly in the direction of the fleeing prisoners, twitching hands jerk at the controls they fire faster than they can aim—the gun goes off before they've even got the site to their eyes—

Shots buzz past me and I throw myself onto the ground, collide with a woman who claws at my arm and back. The street is being cleared from the far end forward, everyone is rushing for doorways and side streets—I want to get low but I'd be trampled. I can only just get behind a bin by the lamppost—the police have run right into a group of prisoners with guns flaring on all sides—blasting, moving barrel first they move start stop shoot—the bullets go over me in both directions every instant—police prisoners and bystanders drop clawing their wounds or flop over like sacks of flour—the air is all made of gunshots and thuds of body hits cries howls of rage agony—no one is taking cover, no one is backing off—

I shake with seizure hysterics panic, I'm moving on all my limbs through bullets dying blood and pain they don't stop they run in among each other killing firing their rifles not a foot away from each other shooting as they are shot all eyes white, white, white.

I crawl away from the shots, booms that seem to drop

like walls from the buildings—if only *I* could find a gun—
how can I join in?

The lobby walls were all glass and broken out, no cover
for me, I run deeper and deeper into the building followed
by breaking glass, metal walls are pocked with bullet holes—

Metal walls are buckled over with rust ... a tree grows
here in the outer wall.

I am looking up at a boll of roots that coil down
corkscrewing in and out of the metal and down into the
floor, form basins of rainwater.

Everything is ruined—smashed, bizarrely old.

I am bizarrely old. Long dead. Low still lives, in the ruins
of the city, inside a vast ruined building by myself.

I look down to see my face undulating in the puddle
at my feet, step out of the water with an exclamation.
The sound rings down the length of a long, wide gallery,
its ceiling perforated by roots and trunks, hanging moss
of rust, icicles of melted glass, clumps of black wire hang
down like scalps. Through gaps in the wall I see high misty
air and building tops, I'm up high. The floor is wavy, rolling
like hills seen from high mountain tops.

There is a sort of apse protruding from the gallery. It
opens itself not far from where I stand.

How did I get here? Where are the others?

I walk down the gallery, lit by panels of thready sunlight
from the windy apertures in the walls. The apse is dark, and it
does not extend far. What grows at the far end is not exactly
a tree; a shapeless tree, with roots and branches intermingled
and a trunk like a bulging wall, like many trunks grafted
together. There's a charred cavity in the middle of the trunk,
a natural crêche, and something I can't make out rests in it.

The floor intervening is flat and clean, with puddles here and there standing upright inside silver wire frames. That stifling feeling comes back again, like troubled sleep with the heavy covers piled on top of me. The area above the cavity is glowing with luminous moss, a pale sulfur color. As I come near, an all but invisible halo appears in the crèche, a head conforming to it and causing me to recognize other objects there as the outspread arms and legs, the crumpled torso.

Over the breathing, the eyes, living, gaze steadily at me. Their color is obscured by a golden lustre that seems to be an effect of the halo, for beneath it I can see blackness. The face appears through a kind of glare, as though I saw it through a membrane. A pale, spear-shaped nose points down toward black whiskers as straight as straw on a thatched roof. Hollow breath crosses his hidden mouth. His cap and his tunic are black, the light paints two glistening streaks on his black boots.

I imagine he will impassively raise a gun and cut me down where I stand. Just an idle thought, because, though he lives, I see too where the light twinkles on his abdomen, on the blood that soaks the cloth of his uniform, and the ragged spot where the bullet entered. Arms and legs lie on the ground without the slightest visible tension—they are paralyzed, alive but inert. There is an armband on his right arm, with insignia identifying him as a Narrator.

His thought is the same, his eyes, which quiver with life although they barely move, seem to have fixed on my armband, which feels almost to burn or tingle with the intensity of his attention.

His halo shimmers from time to time, like a guttering

candle. There is an air of seniority about him, which convinces me the Narrator I met in the clearing must have not been a fully qualified Narrator, but a subordinate officer to this one, an assistant. At the same time, I notice his Narrator's bars are struck through with a black line, possibly only a loose thread, and I am not about to move it to find out, but perhaps he isn't yet a full Narrator either. We had no ranks ourselves.

The Narrator before me draws a long breath. A new vigor comes into his breathing, although it may be vigor borrowed against his life. His eyes, brimming with animation, have settled on my face with a heavy-lidded, dead fixity. Suddenly, I look to the side and step quickly to a puddle gathered there in the roots—my own eyes, I see reflected, have those same sooty waves in them, just faintly, there on the whites beneath the irises. His eyes are still on me, pupils halved by lowered lids. There is something so expressive in them, I forget my eyes and walk over to him, drop down on my knees beside him. The hand by my foot is white as snow; the white, powdery skin of his face is yellowed by the halo light.

His eyes seem to see all around me; he does not see me at all. At most, he sees my eyes, perhaps without seeing them either; he may be only staring into a space that seems, maybe, to be watching him from particular point. A faint movement of his chin ... he begins to speak a language I know in name only. His words are clear, but the tone is dull, as though the sound were being absorbed by the air.

Without any urgency I can detect, a distinct, earnest murmur escapes his lips. He may be speaking to me, but he seems instead to be speaking to space, or to an invisible presence. I've heard the language, and I recognize it, but something is wrong with my hearing, because it sounds like gibberish to me.

"A, ab ab ab ab a abab ab, ab aba ab abab ab ab ab ab ab ab aba ab ababab ab."

Some time passes, and I become aware again of his voice, which had not, I think, paused once.

Suddenly, I can't swallow. I work my muscles, feeling something like a clot in my throat, but my throat won't clear, and now I feel my lungs stiffening with the effort to breathe, all the while his calm, meaningless droning is in my hearing—there's something horrible, disgusting in the sound, in his calm, how wrong it is he should speak like that here, as he bleeds to death! I try pulling on the sides of my neck with my hands to open my throat, I swallow convulsively, feeling like I'm dying. I want to stifle his mouth—he's dying, let him die faster then—but it's just not in me, my hands just paw uselessly at my asthma. I stand up in desperation and get away from him.

At my back—"A, ab ab aba ab a, aba ab, a ab ab a ab a ab. Ab ab ab ab, a aba, aba ab a ab ababab."

Through one door after another, I put walls between myself and his voice, his calm, because even my body will not listen to him.

I find some water and try to drink. I get over to the blasted window and draw in long breaths against the belts cinched tight around my ribs. But I can't I won't listen I can't won't decide between can't and won't, thinking thoughts that are part of the suffocation.

When I'm myself again—I recovered quickly ... pretty quickly—his words reappear in my memory, but now I can understand them in snatches, or I seem to. The meaning is elusive, because I can only recall what familiar words his speech sounded like, I can't remember the words he spoke. I can only imagine what they meant.

I begin to think he did see me, and was asking me to do him some last kindness, like carrying him to a breach in the wall, to die in light and air, with arms, no matter whose, a fellow human being's, around him.

I go back. The hall looks unfamiliar. I return to the stairwell. These doors don't seem to be the ones I first came through in distress, but I see no others. I return again to the hall, go halfway or so down its length, and turn around, to see if it strikes me as more familiar looking in this direction. Nothing looks familiar.

Rust and a clear, hard elastic substance run down the walls in sheets and covers the doorways; passages are blocked by huge boluses of coagulated rust or massive worms of melted window glass. Fossilized stumps spill out the elevator doors and fill the end of the hall like a petrified wave, tufted with little spurts of roots.

I search for a long time, but I can't find my way back to the room and the Narrator.

*

I can't find my way out; I'm blundering around in another wing of the building. Something framed in a window stops me, and the charm strikes against my chest like a door knocker.

Off in the distance a magnetic building looms against a mercury sky; it is the only undamaged building I've seen in the city. A huge upright half-circle, its flat diameter turned toward me, stands between two bullet-shaped buttresses on one end of a sweeping, flat foundation structure with windows and vents. The thing reminds me strongly of the Bonant's sullen gigantism. The diameter of the half-circle is indented, and two deep, narrow grooves stand parallel to each other along its length; the grooves are angled inward, and might perhaps meet inside in a V. Squinting, I can barely make out what might be a pattern on the metal by the grooves; like a sawtooth, uniform row of black soot smudges or scorch marks.

The charm shudders in my pocket, the figure inside is rattling violently against the glass. I pull out the charm and look at it—

… The city is invaded—enemy soldiers in the streets, the buildings shine like new. The citizens have fled or taken refuge in shelters.

Enemy soldiers in the streets. They unwittingly trigger certain machineries.

A group of enemy soldiers, whoever they are, gather at the window of one of the taller buildings—this window— conduct a discussion over a map. One meanwhile surveys the town with field glasses. She sees a light appear in the window of the foundation building.

Moments later, a grating, howling alarm begins to sound from claxons on rooftops. A mottled whiteness spreads in seconds over the entire outer surface of the upright half circle as moisture in the air condenses and freezes on the metal. Flakes of frost break loose from the sides of the structure and fall crashing to the foundation below, where they hiss and bubble, mantling the hooded tower in steam.

The two long grooves in its face emit a weak, fitful radiance.

The soldier with the field glasses turns to point this out to the officers, who look up in alarm as the claxons begin rasping—consternation on their faces, they shrink from the soldier, who stares at them in confusion. Rings of blood run down from where she held the field glasses to her eyes. Blood streams from her gums. She takes a step toward them, wavers and falls to her knees, raising her hands to her head. She puts her hands to either side of her head to steady it against the dizziness, and with the lightest pressure of her palms on her scalp, the skin over her cheekbones tears like a wet leaf.

All the soldiers in the room are on the floor now, skin sloughing with the faintest motion, blood streaming from ears, eyes, nose, mouth, smoking pools spreading from their groins. Blood trickles on the floor and boils there.

In the streets, the enemy soldiers sway to the ground slobbering blood. They turn to flee and their skins flap off. They clamber over each other and pull themselves apart, the claxons blaring a long exasperated note again and again.

... I am shown the position of the detectors, most of which aren't working any more. Those that are, line the streets on the opposite side of the building to me. The traps they are set to trigger were built to last.

*

Glass lobby doors swing apart for me. I swim out into cool rainswept air, fresh smell of rainswept streets, wet pavement ... but there is no rain, only mist ... and that choking feeling still lingers anyway.

I sit on a rustbank. There is no aperture in the rubble, nothing I could have used as a doorway. How did I get in and out? Silence, air moving over fused wreckage. Corrosive, cold fear slides along inside it.

The street is still roughly there, a rust trough through the tossed city bones. I trot down its empty length, looking for the others. I don't have to look far. I see them walking in orderly files on either side of what once were streets, entering what doorways remain or crossing invisible thresholds pushing open unreal doors. Silichieh darts up a ramp with two-step-at-a-time strides, taking a hasty look at his bare wrist.

The private I once saw stabbing himself with his pen weaves drunkenly to and fro across a broad glass platform to one side of the street, scraping it with the end of his carbine, oblivious to the bloody wound disfiguring one side of his abdomen. He thinks he's sweeping. As I hurry over, he loses his balance, toppling down hard on the unyielding glass with the snap of a bone breaking somewhere. He's trying to get up when I reach him, his face bloodless, eyes glazed. His pupils are fixed. I talk to him, put my hands on him to calm him, and he is ice cold. Gradually his struggle to stand erect subsides. Examining his wound, I find it oozing, not bleeding, though it has not clotted. It's as though he has no blood left. His uniform is soaked with it. I put my ear to his breast, my eyes on his fingers still feebly curling and uncurling around the butt of his gun, but he has no pulse.

Silichieh is looking in my direction as I turn. He comes toward me, seeing me, looking past me to the dead private. Two feet away from me now he is staring into my eyes, and using them—I can tell—to swim back.

"He's dead," he says, now looking past me again. "Shot. How shot?" Gives his head a toss—"Who shot him?"

"I don't know. I heard shooting before, I think ... and I found a blackbird in one of the buildings. He had a bullet in him."

"They're here? ... What happened? Was I knocked out?"

"... Let's see about the others."

Saskia is in the square, foaming about the enemy to bypassers that aren't there. One of the asylum soldiers is listening to her intently. Her eyes flick from one spot in space to another, where the faces would be, as she shouts. The others seem to be coming out of it. Nikhinoch strides briskly up to me, but he's himself again, searching for Makemin.

Not far to look. We find him frenziedly barricading himself inside a sunken building like a roofed basement, all of thick rusted metal. The noise draws us, coming up from behind so that at first the protruding roof, round as a jar-lid, hides from us the bodies littering the ground in front. Most wear Wacagan uniforms, but many wear ours.

Nikhinoch goes cautiously up to the ground-level loophole and calls to Makemin in his high voice a little wavering. The whole structure booms with the report of a gun and I can hear the sharp crack as the shot strikes the inside of the roof. Nikhinoch lunges backward unhurt— Makemin fired right at him, as though the bullet could penetrate such thick metal. Out of the explosion comes a shower of curses.

Rapid footsteps, rattle of armor. Saskia pushes past us, draws Nikhinoch aside by the shoulder, and shouts back, her powerful voice battering through Makemin's fusillade.

"Wake up Makemin! Wacagan are here! They've put us all under their spell and we've been cut to ribbons, Makemin!"

She uses his name repeatedly—"Makemin!" she shouts into his silence. Then, as she pauses to listen ... uncoordinated speech, hard to hear, inside.

After a long while, there is a sudden burst of activity as the barricade is pulled apart from the inside. Makemin emerges, slowly and rigidly, his face livid, stony. An ugly wound scars the side of his head above the right ear, and the skin at his right temple, and around his right eye, is scorched red and black.

... Gathered all together, we are less than twenty. Everyone I know is alive. Thrushchurl crept up to join us from a stone-lined culvert. Jil Punkinflake we found sitting on the chest of a dead blackbird, doodling with a stick in the rust. When he saw us, he popped up smiling gaily as a child and scampered over to Saskia; she is the only one he saw. She glares at him, but puts her hand on his head, which he lowers the instant he sees her raise her arm. I'm close enough to see his nostrils tremble.

Makemin stands before our assembled number with his head down and his back to us, still silent as a stone. In our search, we found dead Wacagan everywhere. Many still bled from fresh wounds.

Everyone waking-dreamt himself valiant defender of the shining city, repulsing barbarians repulsing the invading kingdom. No one has set off the machine I saw yet, and I have given my warning about it.

Thrushchurl sits on a boulder of broken concrete not far from me, rocking slightly and humming his song. Makemin strides over and tears him from the stone, fistful of jacket in his hand.

"Revive them at once!" he bellows. Makemin is pointing to the bodies. A Yeseg militiaman lying there with his head flung back, his mouth a rigid, fibrous O. Makemin shakes Thrushchurl, who seems stiff and light as a scarecrow, eyeing Makemin back, with crazy fascination.

"You were at the mortuary school—you know how to do it! Bring them back!"

Thrushchurl's face writhes weirdly around his teeth in an expression of utter bewilderment. Makemin releases him and now he has me, shakes me, face in my face—

"You do it!" Pulls me closer with overpowering strength. "You were there, you saw them do it! You do it!"

I'm not saying anything—his eyes are like black pits and I can only stare at them. They don't budge even as he shakes me so hard my teeth rattle.

"Listen to me damn you—you do it! What did they teach you medics anyway!?"

What I'm looking into isn't even a face but a pitted crag the setting sun rusts over.

Silichieh's voice comes to me from somewhere—"Low, *can* you do it? Spirits here talk to you—can you talk back, and tell them to go back in?"

"Well can you?!" Makemin nails the words into my face.

"No! I don't know anything!" I hear my voice and try to put force into it and it only makes my throat knock shut. I strain out the words as though I were being choked—"I only patch wounds up! I don't know anything! I don't know why they talk to me it just happens!"

Makemin is gone. I can't take my eyes off of him. The bit of uniform he held me by is still bunched, slowly uncrumpling, and seems to retain his heat and venom, I want to pull off my tunic to keep it from seeping all over me like a pollution. It's like a fat spider fastened on me.

Makemin goes to Jil Punkinflake, who leans by a ruined wall, his head and shoulders lost in the deep shadow of the overhang.

"You!" Jil Punkinflake is now driven back against the wall. "You do it!"

I can't see his face. The voice comes out of the dark under the overhang, resonating in the stone.

"Do what?" It asks, bubbling with a wild derision.

"*Bring them back!*" Makemin roars, drawing forward and bashing Jil Punkinflake against the wall with one hand, pointing again at the Yeseg body stretched there on the rust.

Jil Punkinflake's shoulders are shaking. His flung-back head drops down and forward out of the shadows; his eyes shimmer like silver and his face is drawn up in a comedic mask, screaming with laughter. His brows furrowed and knotted, until tears trace arcs along the tops of his cheeks, the laughter the loudest the ugliest erupting out of him with so much force his face should break, as though he were being ripped apart from the inside out.

*

"We go on. Get in formation!"

The voice comes from a far-away projection, bounding back to us from the ruins. Makemin has turned toward the road. We stand there barely breathing; I look from one dirty face to another and every one of them says, "Let's go back"—but none of us dares to speak, none of us can speak. Makemin has no face.

Saskia shouts, "I suppose you think you can't be shot just as readily in the back?"

Her voice seems to snap around us like a low swirling wind. I feel a cold splash across the inside of my chest; the circle we had been drawing around us to shut them out, she sets on fire. Cold white flames are consuming it.

"They've suffered greater losses than we have—and we'll find all the help we need ahead!"

She turns to Makemin.

"*Won't* we?" she shouts to the back of his head.

Makemin is still waiting for us to obey his order. He doesn't answer.

Like sleepwalkers something tear loose rattling behind, left there as we leave like a shred of meat glued to a hot griddle we fan out onto the road like sleepwalkers like sleepwalkers. Blankness sleeps again on each staring, leaning face. We go on now like sleepwalkers following the darkness shed by Makemin's turned back.

A hollow howling noise, like wind sobbing at the mouth of a mine, rises behind us as we near the city's brink. There are the landmarks I'd seen in the charm, the road to the cemetery curves off to the right, through irregular, soft ridges, and trees bristle pitch black above them. The charm tugs at me and without even bothering to look at it I call to Makemin.

"We have to go into the trees."

Makemin stops. His head turns slightly, just enough so that I can see the darkness of his profile, his glittering eye.

"The road won't take us," I say. My voice is flat, lost. "We're not wanted here. If you want to get to the cemetery, you're going to have to detour through the woods."

With inaudible creak and groan, we leave the road. The trees dart in among us again. Saskia storms back and forth, keeping everyone in formation with rough words, shoves.

Roots flex and trip our feet, and the loose white soil drags our steps like a mire. The gaps in the trees and branches stare at us. Shallow pools of fog dot the ground, now mist floats down from the boughs. Almost immediately it is so thick we can barely see ten feet ahead, sluicing over us in a wet wind like snow flurries, dense in my lungs like water. No one wants to go on, but Makemin seems to draw us forward like an ox dragging many leads.

"Stop!" Silichieh cries, his voice nearly stifled. "We're crossing our own tracks here! We've gone in a circle!"

Now Makemin stops, and we all look at the ground, see footsteps ahead of us and doubled up behind us.

"Those are blackbird tracks," someone says.

I can't see Makemin clearly in the fog, but he has turned toward us again; his face sweeps to one side and then the other.

"How many of us?" his words are like trumpet notes, puncturing the air.

Count and count again—one less, one less ... the last of the Yeseg officers.

*

The charm is dragging me to one side. They are following me with their eyes, a dangerous, heavy, slow anger. If I tell them it would have been worse on the road, they won't believe me.

"There's a hill there," I say, pointing. "Let me go up and

have a look over this fog."

A muffled word I take for approval comes forward, and I go cautiously away, catch sight at once of a dark, irregular slope through the trees. They let me go alone.

The fog thins, as though it shrouded only us, and, stepping from the trees to the hillside I come back out into the white daylight of the sunless sky. Being alone doesn't frighten me; I believe the charm would warn me if there were any danger. I climb the hill covered with black flakes of stone, more like a great heap of rocks than a hill. From the top I see trees all around, and a fog bank smeared over the trees to my right.

There's the road, slicing toward the cemetery not two miles away—remote, dreamlike. There is something across the road near the forward edge of the fogbank, but I can't see what it is. There is no blockage on the road past that point.

I kneel down to consult the charm. It points to the path, then swings back toward me again, not quite pointing toward me, again and again. I'm putting the charm away when I feel something move over me and it's ripped from my grasp. Jil Punkinflake has it—the charm—in his fist; a look of demonic joy mutilates his face, and he laughs at me.

"This is how you knew!"

He brandishes it as I get to my feet.

"I knew you were lying!"

My mouth goes dry, his is gasping.

"What do you know *now?!*" he cries, and flings the charm down, shattering it against the stones.

His laughter breaks out again when he sees my face; it grows steadily louder and sharper. He steps forward fluting out his lips and punches, hitting my jaw so my neck twists and I drop, his laughter crashing over me like waves—my spine goes cold. I get up trembling, staring, nearly choking with rage, and take a swing at him.

"Jil!" a voice roars.

He scampers out of reach and from him comes the ugliest laughter in the world, a hagging insane laugh—I whip my arm at him but he evades me and capers down the slope, turning back still laughing at me. I lunge, stumble, and, on all fours, I see myself reflected against the sky in the fragments of the charm there in the rocks, my eyes blank.

"Jil! I'm coming!"

He turns when he hears me—steps, cackling, picks up a rock—he pitches it at me with all his might. I raise my arm and bat the rock aside. Now I'm after him. Spinning my way he kicks me high against the ribs, but I bash him across the face and he tumbles. I hit him square in the face as he gets up and send him teakettling down the slope onto his back; he twists as I come to kick him. Drawing back my leg, I lose balance and fall down. He runs.

"Jil!" roars after him. "*I'm coming for you Jil!*"

Having slip trouble with the rocks. Now I'm on foot and following him down into the trees. I can see his track in the loose soil. A dark shape dodges among the trees ahead, the lighter irregularity of the face appears every few seconds, still laughing.

So he does not see the soldiers up ahead of him rise from cover and begin to swirl in their weightless, swinging formation like a bank of leaves blown up in a wind flurry. He does not understand why I scream his name in a changed voice. Laughing he turns to look where he's going to. I hear cracks and snaps far off. Their roar races away, spreading rings in space, borne along by the endless trees. His left shoulder whips and he pinwheels forward. Punched against his right side he clops to a halt throwing up his right arm.

He takes two weak steps, his arm still high. The soldiers ahead vault away with great impossible leaps in among the trees, but two remaining swing there, aim and fire at leisure, before they go, in turn.

Jil Punkinflake crumples to the ground. Remote, smoke-hazed soldiers turn and skip away.

Low skids on his knees and pulls Jil Punkinflake's body off its face, putting his hands here and there, throat, wrist. Blood slimes his hands. The slack face is pink and purple … a blue-grey blush has already begun to spread across its cheeks.

Low jerks to his feet, the front of Jil Punkinflake's uniform knotted in his fists. Jil Punkinflake dangles lifeless from his two hands.

Low looks wildly all around. He rushes to one side of the small open space among the trees, dragging Jil Punkinflake with him. The limp legs draw grooves on the ground.

He rushes to the other side. First one way, then the other, where there's no way, as though he wants to catch the escaped life before it gets too far, throw the body down onto it and trap it there like throwing a blanket on a fire. Low's face has a searching, escaping look on it.

Now Low bends his neck slowly, and stares down at drooping Jil Punkinflake. His face bunches and swells. His chest heaves. Sighs burst from his wrenched mouth, and weak fluting from his throat. His eyes and cheeks drip down onto dead cheeks and eyes. The droplets trickle on a bent back neck.

With a loud sound, he swings the body of his friend onto his back and carries it in the direction of the hill, his reversed steps erasing Jil Punkinflake's last footprints. His sobs hasten to take their places, to stand forever among the trees.

*

"Doooon't!"

Talk, gestures, expressions.

"No!" A warning note.

The commotion settles. A deep voice sadness makes deeper speaks calmly, repeating a name, with variable combinations of "low." Lulom Lousce Lousche Lulom Low Loom, Low Loom Column, is me—meaning me is listening to a request of me to do something that needs to be done, that won't get done as long as I don't do it. Silichieh is the one who talks through to me.

They are gathered round me, or around the body of Jil Punkinflake that hangs from my shoulders. Appearing again in my mind, his name knocks the wind back out of me, weakness overtakes me, and I fall down with his weight on top of me.

I can only tell them he ran into a patrol. Why not tell the whole truth? Because I haven't the strength. Not to keep the secret nor to tell it. So I push my weeping face against the ground.

Thrushchurl and Silichieh have been gathering brush. I numbly rise and help him build the pile. If anyone else has anything to say to me, I don't hear it. I'm going to burn his body. We build the pile together, and burn Jil Punkinflake on it. I kiss him, right through the fire. There are shouts as they yank me back thumping my uniform where it smoulders.

Makemin's faceless face appears above me, black eyes through the smoke from Jil Punkinflake's burning body.

I tell him the road is clear ahead. We can make our way back to it now we're above the road block. The cemetery is two miles away. My voice is frail and orphaned and shaken. Stumbling blindly, weak in body my sinews are as limp as old rags, and every sensation jabs at my nerves. Makemin's fist jerks my uniform—

"Which way?" he barks.

I barely notice him.

I'm shaken nearly off my feet, only a doll on wire, "Which way damn you?! We've been going in circles again!"

They're counting.

Now there's one more, every time.

*

Did I point the way?

We are marching again.

I see feet matching pace with mine, just to my right.

Marching alongside me and in step, but his head is turned toward me, his eyes stare right into mine as the trees and white land flash by behind his head, his lower jaw swaying gently against the dangling tongue.

*

The cemetery appears like a buckle in a belt of trees, all buried hoops of walls with a staggered series of gaps leading through them into the place, big as a city. From it sprouts an hourglass-shaped tower all glistening with pearly mosaic walls, hanging a hundred feet over us, its head brushed by the clouds, its foundation still nowhere near us. Another tower stands further back on the other side, and another further back, still vague in the black mist.

Drawing closer to the outer wall, and this is where the road leads us, a sound rises out of the boom of the wind. The clattering of some cold fire like a halo around us, as if the flames were solid and hard, knocking together. Now it's also a trickling of dry gravel, each piece scraping another. The outermost ring wall is low and broad, made of what seems to be a single solid piece of pale grey metal, not much higher than a man, but yards thick. At the gap in the ring, the walls are sheared back at an angle, scored over with hairlike lines. The gap is not a complete break—the two ends are linked together with a single, slender, shining silver band that marks the line of the curved threshold of the cemetery. Makemin is the first to cross it.

It's only in looking back that I realize I stepped over the threshold as well. The rustling sound receded the moment I did it, but it's still there, more metallic, more focussed. The second wall is tall and lean, made of enamelled metal without a chip or crack. The third wall is like a hedge of woven brass. The spacious expanses between the walls are lined with evenly-spread white pebbles.

The fourth, innermost wall, is made of thin, dark grey metal with a low arch set into it. A boulevard runs into the cemetery, plumb to the mound at the center. We look ahead to the mound, which is topped by an isolated building, and on sight I know that is where we are going. The fire sound is joined by a regular choughing sound, like thick metal pier cables knocking together.

We're coming up the avenue now. It's lined with tombs the size of houses, made of metal time has turned to charcoal. They are solid, all cast in one piece without any seam. Filled domes stand on four legs with curved groins over stone platforms all carved with a regular serration pattern like choppy waves. Slots open into what must be shafts set down into the earth, the metal sarcophagi, featureless as eggs, are attached to spindles that rise from the slots, all in the shade of the filled domes. No decorations.

Streets open alternately to the right and left, breaking onto views of undulating ground stretching off into the distance, and narrowing streets of increasingly crowded, boxlike tombs. Very far away I dimly can see where they appear to be piled up on top of each other in heaps.

Thrushchurl walks beside me. While the others look warily for signs of the enemy, he is gazing about himself in awestruck abandon, almost sobbing with emotion. I wish I could feel it. Instead, a fear, like a robe of ice, is cinching and recinching itself around me, dragging the carbine in my hands.

Everywhere there are upright vanes and grills of black charcoal metal that don't look ornamental. Some are set into blind loops in the walls, others lie on their sides, jutting out like awnings, and others stand upright on rods, like flags. To our left, a low rim of rock slides up out of the earth to form a ramp-shaped caer with grassy sides, and what look like cenotaphs on top of it. A small, circular plaza is set in its lee. The tombs surround the clear space like quaint, well-maintained little houses. The plaza has a metal platter set in its center. There are no tombs set against the base of the caer, and in the corner formed by its straight side and one row of tombs, there stands planted in the grass a whip structure, like a parabolic sheaf of reeds designed to sway and clatter in the wind. They make the cable-knocking sounds. There must be many more of them. That sound comes from everywhere.

Now we are nearer the base of the mound, and the avenue rises very gradually to meet it. Alone at its summit stands a squat tower. The road is taking us directly to it. Looking ahead, I see iron birds perched like statues on the vanes, watching us come. They never seem to move, but their heads are always trained directly on us, motionlessly following us like a portrait's eyes. The sky is very dark, for daylight, and yet the shadows of the tombs are as deep and broad as if the sun were blazing across the sky at them.

Makemin takes two or three long steps ahead of us, turns stopping in place and raises his hands, calling "Halt!" He stands in one of the shadows of the tombs, and only his outline is visible.

"I will go on with the narrator, Thrushchurl, and Nikhinoch."

His voice is muffled as though he spoke through a scarf.

Makemin's silhouette lifts its arm and points off to the left, toward a jutting prominence of rock a few dozen yards away—the only high ground in the vicinity apart from the mound itself.

"Saskia. You take the rest up there and look for the enemy. If you see them near, signal us. If we receive no signal from you, we will go up to the mound."

"You don't think we should watch from the mound?" she asks.

"Don't argue with me!" he snaps. His arm lowered, his form does not move. "On the slopes of the mound you would be too exposed. We four may go up with a better chance of escaping notice if the mound is being watched, and we don't want to tell them how few we are. We've come too far to be sloppy now."

"Yes, sir," she says resolutely.

"If you see the enemy, fire on them only if you can get them by surprise. Otherwise, join us on the mound if possible. The wall surrounding the tower should be defensible. You will command these troops. When I return, I will bring back what we need with me."

Saskia's face almost glimmers. She salutes Makemin fiercely and turns on the spot.

"Come on—hurry," she calls, her voice not loud but intense, low and penetrating. We four stand where we are, watching her go. After a few minutes, I can see them appear on the top of the prominence, taking their positions with care. Minutes pass. No signal.

Makemin turns on his heel and strides up toward the mound, which is beginning to loom above us. Its slopes are bare packed earth, and tapering, slender flues of enamelled metal protrude from somewhere deep inside, crowning it about three-quarters of the way up like a ring of spears planted in the ground. Near to me I pass an iron pinecone of skull creches—the dry sockets of the builders don't stare down on us, the faceless faces of the skulls don't make expressions for us.

Just at the base of the mound, Makemin leaves the road and moves quickly up its margin, leaning a little forward. We follow him, passing monuments of black glass, formed into bulbs, flat flows and fat rings, looking like bizarre arms with useless articulations. Once inside the crown of flues, I can see the tower is not as large as I believed—what I took for its base is a free-standing round wall closely surrounding it.

The wall glows faintly against black clouds; it looks like polished brass. There is no gate, the wall is simply interrupted. The gap is high and lean. Perhaps a gate had stood here once, and rotted away, but the gleaming wall, the featureless ends, belie that idea.

We enter the enclosure. Though the high walls close out almost all light, there is lush grass growing in the interval of ground around the circular tower. It stirs faintly as we come, though I feel no breeze. The tower is made of something the color of brass and the consistency of marble. It is not quite a cylinder, the circumference at the top, modestly adorned with egg-shaped knobs, seems slightly smaller than it is at the base. There are two narrow windows high above, one facing the gap in the wall, the other looking off toward the city. Otherwise, the tower has no features at all, no joins, only the door, which opens right at ground level. The road's end is its threshold. There is a lintel of black stone with two thick golden lines across it, and thin raised pilasters, the diameter of a forearm, descending from it down the length of the tall doors. There are two doors, narrow and massive, shining mustard-gold, with heavy diamond-shaped and circular bosses in their panels and upright rail handles.

Makemin seizes the handles and flings the doors back. They swing out toward us in complete silence, onto darkness inside. A billow of tepid air drifts over me, the smell of dust and varnish, and a barely-perceptible sour odor underneath.

We step into palpable silence, dense shadow, and stop. The light from the door barely reaches past our shoulders.

We peer together into the dark. After a moment or two, I begin to make out faint reflections high in the air, from some high, curving surfaces. They shine gold. My vision is growing rapidly accustomed to the dark. I begin to see tall, gigantic shapes standing in rows to either side, and a wide openness ahead of us. My vision is not growing rapidly accustomed to the dark—light is very gradually collecting high ahead of us, a shimmer, like a haze of light thrown off by gold coins.

We're gazing into a chamber of some depth, not especially large, with pillars running along either side of the open space before us, facing a sort of altar or screen opposite us.

A phantom luminosity gathers along the tops of the pillars. Delicate, long-petalled lily-like flowers of milky glass descend in corsage rows and all evenly grow radiant as they come down, filling the upper air with frosty light. The pillars are mineral trees, their branches lunging up into an abyss of darkness overhead, and grey globes dimly floured with pale blue-white light are visible there. A vaster tree stands facing the door, its base surrounded by a low brass wall with panels of white stone. There is a raised apse behind the tree, its rounded surface lined with a rich scarlet tapestry covered with small golden spots. As the light continues to grow, I see the flowers are strung together on weblike golden vines. Thrushchurl gasps and sighs in transports of astonishment moving out into the room, head thrown back. Then he notices something, and I see him tentatively approach an object between the pillars. Between each of the pillars, coffins of gleaming rosewood are standing on simply-carved wooden trestles. The coffins have no lids, and it is plain even from here that human bodies lie naked in them.

The glow intensifies by gentle degrees. Beyond the far end of each coffin there is a rounded opening in the walls, lined from top to bottom with tiny haloed figures, made of some shiny material like colored glass. Each figure is distinct and seems to hover just in front of the wall. The light shines up behind them, and their haloes are angled to catch it and shine gold.

Now the light has reached the floor, and, glancing down, I start and cry out softly, without meaning to. The floor is paved with transparent, tea-yellow hexagonal panels; each panel seals a chamber, like a honeycomb, and in each of them naked corpse lies curled. Thrushchurl immediately drops to his knees and peers down at first one, then another. They are well preserved, only slightly withered, slightly leathery. They have their hair, their nails, noses and ears. The eyes are only slightly sunken, dark eyes like blueberries, visible through the lids. All ages and sexes, all curled naked in their honeycombs.

Makemin suddenly stamps up to Thrushchurl, points in the direction of the large tree, the low brass wall, the white tablets.

"Go, invoke them!"

Thrushchurl looks up at him—I can see his frantic eyes running all over Makemin's face.

"Hurry!" Makemin orders, his voice sharp.

Thrushchurl goes over to the tree. We all follow, gather near him. I can see him looking at the tree, the white tablets. He has no idea what to do—none of us do. He puts out shaking hands.

"Oh spirits ..." he calls in a trembling voice, the air guttering out of his mouth. I can feel something congealing around Makemin and again the robe of fear that wonder had displaced cinches around me. All the same, I want to laugh. What are we doing here? What are we doing here? My eyes fly here and there looking for any hint or clue I could use, if this place is even the right place, if this is even the right or possible thing to do here, and I see the white panels in the brass wall around the base of the huge tree are covered in Lashlache written in Wiczu characters—immediately I see this I begin to intone them aloud. I have to shove my frail voice out of my mouth through a throat almost sealed with fear and I take Thrushchurl's shoulders in my hands as I begin—he is half-stooped over—and push him to the side, feeling him go as if I were lightly pushing his floating body across the surface of a pond.

The inscription is a strangely-worded general memorial whose meaning I find difficult to pin down, although it is plainly an official statement of recognition and remembrance. Boilerplate. What do I care what it says? Makemin doesn't know and Makemin must be made to *believe*. Made to believe—that we tried—but every moment he can be forestalled must be used—just to hold Makemin's hand, to hold Makemin.

With a crack as abrupt as a pistol shot, a light appears high in the branches of the huge tree above my head. I'm so desperate I hardly notice it, keep reading, and more lights crack on, little starlike lights at the points of gemlike leaves and the tips of green stalks, old boughs. Soon the tree above is sending out arrowlike shafts of piercing but somehow not blinding light in all directions, making a thicket of light over me. There are dark, open doorways flanking the apse the tree stands in, and from these now bursts the groaning of many deep voices, resonating as if they emerged from a huge iron vessel.

I raise my own voice to compete with theirs, groaning long syllables in Lashlache, and the words fill the chamber with a smell like heated metal. I have reached the end of the first tablet and switch to the second. The words are flying from my lips without my understanding any of them; they are being dragged out of me like links in a chain that those other voices are pulling. Something really is happening—I reach the end of the inscription and suddenly I drop on my knees as if my legs had been hooked and dragged down, I feel my eyes jerk up into my head—I put my hands to my face, feel it stretch and work forming long low syllables in Laschlache, feel it hum with those words, and my throat swollen with the veins tendons standing out from it nearly tearing with the bell-like words I shout.

Off to my right and high up I hear two sharp raps, and a series of rapid taps in three different pitches, several playing simultaneously, like a mechanical operation there in the corner, but I can't pull my eyes down out of my head to see it. The taps seem to follow the droning voices from the doors, from whatever it is that stands behind the apse. The taps stop. A moment later, I hear two knocks off to my left, high up and behind me, and the same series of taps. Before it ends another two knocks far behind me high and to the right, and halfway through what I think is the same sequence another breaks in from my left and another again near the end of that from the right. As the last tap comes, I feel as if a great hand that had been squeezing me suddenly lets me go. I spring forward on my legs, my eyes drop down and I can see again, my voice has stopped my throat raw, everything has stopped. Before me, I see a great white arch—the tree is far away, deep beyond in the space through the arch where I feel a powerful yearning to go, there is darkness, silence. The lights are all out, the sounds have stopped.

I wait. Time passes.

I turn, afraid. Makemin is between me and the faint light of the door.

"Nothing!" he says. The word fills the dark.

"Go see if anything has changed outside."

Nikhinoch's shadow goes to the door, vanishes for a moment. The sight of him outside the doors, in daylight, is strange beyond my power to express, as though I saw a living man from the point of view of a dead one.

We wait in silence.

He returns quickly. He stands near Makemin, invisible in the dark, and quietly tells him,

"I see no change."

Silence. Growing out of the silence ... I hear Makemin's breathing rasp in his nostrils faster and faster. He is fumbling with something.

Fire erupts in the dark, shining on his face, features as unyielding and hard edged as a stone face; he is setting light to a torch. Match in his right hand, torch in his left, eyes staring blank and white as fog.

"What are you going to do?" Thrushchurl asks. I can see his long face there in the chaotic light of the torch.

Makemin fixes him with that blank look, then points to the nearest coffin, standing between the trees.

"They're made of wood," he says hoarsely.

"Oh, but ..." Thrushchurl's brows contract, he looks stricken. I feel my insides turn to ice and my hands grow numb, my voice bolt up and gag itself in my throat.

"We'll *make* them listen!" Makemin shouts.

"Oh, but you mustn't *burn* them!" Thrushchurl explains, afraid, taking Makemin gently by the left arm.

Makemin tears his arm from Thrushchurl's fingers, draws his pistol aims and shoots Thrushchurl in the chest.

My cry seems to draw the sound of the shot down into my own bosom, and it shrivels in me as I watch Thrushchurl drop to the floor. He lies face down in spreading black.

I take three steps dropping to my knees beside my friend. I touch him blindly and clutch at him.

"Traitor!" Makemin's voice breaks near me I look up just as he fires.

Nikhinoch's wan blue face twists in a streak against the dark, and shock, outrage, incomprehension flash out. With a faint noise, like someone tossing a pair of shoes into a corner, he falls forward onto Makemin, who staggers back. Silichieh is rushing in the door and Makemin, still staggering with Nikhinoch sliding down his standing length on the way to the floor, shoots Silichieh.

Silichieh cries out in pain. He rolls to the side as he goes down, diving into the impenetrable shadows around the bases of the pillars. Makemin rushes toward him, lunging around the column gun ready. I see a motion in the dark. Makemin veers back to the near side of the column. Silichieh jerks his rifle one handed from the floor and shoots Makemin in the stomach. The crash of the rifle makes my ears ring, and for a moment it's as though nothing happens.

Makemin falls. Makemin's all but unrecognizeable voice groans from the floor. Silichieh, gasping, lies on his stomach, I see now, rifle still extended in one hand, the other, streaked with blood, clasping his injured leg. Makemin is between us, in the streak of light from the open doors, on his right side. Slowly, he tilts over onto his chest and begins to push his upper body off the hexagonal tiles dripping blood. His bare head inches into the air.

Silichieh shoots it. I cry out and throw myself backward—I feel warm droplets on my face and upraised hands.

Makemin's headless body lies there. Long black tree roots sprout from his neck flat across the floor, dotted here and there with lumps.

Silichieh rolls on his back, arm flung out, rifle resting on the ground. I can see the outline of his chest rise and fall, hear his breathing. I look down, and see faint light glint on Thrushchurl's upper teeth. I lower my head to his face, I feel for life in his throat. I lay him down again. I go to Silichieh, keeping close to the dark wall behind the pillars, calling his name softly. I come round to him and crouch by his head.

Silichieh's upside-down eyes flicker up to me.

"What happened?" he asks.

Makemin's bullet perforated his thigh through the muscle on the outside. I work smoothly for a while, feeling weightless.

"Listen," he says. "Saskia sent me ..."

Only now do I begin to notice the sound of shooting.

"They're here," I say.

He nods.

"Do we have a chance?"

"Maybe. They are nearly as few as we ... and they haven't got Saskia. I think they could be low on ammunition. They shoot sparingly."

"Do you think they have any help?"

Silichieh just breathes, looking up.

"I don't think so ... Did you ...?"

"No."

"What happened?"

"Nothing. It didn't work."

From far off come shots, cries.

"He didn't get you, right?"

Thrushchurl, he killed.

"I'm not shot," I say. "Any better?"

"Yes, thank you," he says.

I sit by him.

"We should get back," he says.

"You wouldn't get there," I say. "I'm not going to just leave you here."

I put his pistol in my empty holster. I look up at the open doors, thinking I should shut them.

"We never should have come," Silichieh says to himself.

Nikhinoch lies on his face across from me. Silichieh is resting.

I go over to Nikhinoch and turn him over onto his back. The look of suprise is still there. I try to lay him out with some dignity. It reminds me of the mortuary college, my friends. I start gasping, and I stagger away from Nikhinoch. My eye falls on Makemin's body. I go over to it and stand, looking down.

I can't hold my body steady—my hands shake, my legs sway, my head swivels on my neck, my breathing catches. I swallow thick saliva with effort.

"You idiot ..." I say.

I shout at abuse at him, and I kick his corpse, hearing only echoes of my own disjointed words as I jump on him with both my heels, stumble off balance from his body then jump again. I pick him up and throw him, his body collapsing a foot or so from me where I seize him up again and throw him down, take him and run with him, fling him up against a pillar. His body tumbles back to the ground hands slapping the floor.

Thrushchurl lies where left him, on his back, his spine curving off to one side. I go round to where I can face the door and straighten him out. I fold his hands on his chest, but then I take back the right one, and hold it.

Rattling—Saskia stops short in the doorway, bending over Silichieh.

"Where's Makemin?" she asks, her voice ragged.

I haven't heard any shooting for a while, it seems.

"He's there," I say, indicating with my head.

Saskia jerks at the sound of my voice, peers and sees me—"Who's that? Low?"

I come forward.

"He's there," I repeat my words and gesture.

She straightens and takes two steps. Silence. Saskia whips off her helmet and dashes it to the ground. I can see half her shadow there in the strip of light from the door, see the helmet roll.

"Thrushchurl gone, too?" she asks.

I can't see where she looks. It wasn't a question. I hear the scrape of her boots as she turns in place—"His secretary?"

Silichieh's voice is weak, "Makemin killed them both, for no reason. I came with your message, and he shoots me too. If Nikhinoch hadn't been falling all over him just then, I'd be dead ... and Low as well."

Although I can't see her, I know Saskia is looking at me. "You shot him?"

Silichieh answers—"He was coming to kill me. What else could I do?"

I hear her head swing to listen to him, then, again she addresses me.

"Why—did he shoot ...?"

"There's no help here," I say.

"That's impossible. We're in the right."

"What does this look like to you?" I ask, spreading my hands, still clasping Thrushchurl's in my left.

"They wouldn't help?"

"I don't know. I don't know anything, even if they heard us or noticed us. What about the others?"

"We've lost. We must retreat."

Saskia crosses slowly to retrieve her helmet. I see her put it back on.

"Let's get him out of here. Hurry."

She points to the bodies with a sweep of her finger.

"Take their rations."

We lift Silichieh between us and carry him outside, hastening down to lower ground almost headlong. Saskia tosses her head to the left and we begin to make our way through the side streets. A plume of smoke comes from the direction of the prominence.

"The others?" I ask jerkily, Silichieh's arm around my neck, looking across his shoulders to Saskia. She does not take her eyes from the path.

"... There are no others."

We go as fast as we can. Over us, the sky is growing darker.

"We were overrun. The survivors fell back. I made a sortie alone and lived. The traitors sent a group in behind me I couldn't stop. I couldn't stop them. I got back, and a few were still living. They drove off the enemy, made them regroup. Everyone was wounded, then they all died. The enemy is still regrouping on the other side."

"How many? How many?"

"Fifty. I'd say. At most. No more than that. No more."

The clouds are denser still. I see the outer wall coming near. We draw close. I hear sounds off in the distance, a few shots, raised voices.

"They're at the prominence."

"I thought you said everyone was dead ..."

"They are—I don't know why they shoot."

We're through the first gate.

"Can they see the gate from there?"

"Yes. If they look."

Second gate goes by, and the third. I startle to one side wildly as a bullet clangs off the brass wall a dozen yards away. We break in to a run, Silichieh hopping on his free leg in wild discoordination, another bullet bangs into the brass closer to us and we veer to one side passing through the last gap into the open, putting the wall between us and the enemy. Breathing hard, we run for the trees.

*

Deeper into the woods now, out of sight of the walls. Silichieh drops swooning to the ground as we let up—his face is grey. I check his bandage—soaked through with blood—his wound torn open by our flight. His breathing is weak.

"Will he be all right?" Saskia asks.

"No."

I am redressing his wound as fast as I can.

"We can't move him any more."

"If they come for us, we'll have to leave him."

"You'll have to leave him," I say without a thought in my head.

I can tell he's conscious, but he doesn't speak. His face goes whiter and whiter, rigid with fear. The light in his eyes turns fixed, glassy. He's watching something coming for him that he knows won't stop. I call his name. His hand is clutching my arm, squeezing it with all his strength. His hand rests on my arm. His white face is turned up, in terror forever.

"He's gone," I explain.

*

She wanted to return through the city and start the machine I'd seen from the window.

"The machine is set off by light tripwires that are too close to it for you to be able to get away before being affected, or even killed," someone is saying. "They might already be in the city themselves anyway, waiting for you."

*

Trees, walk, dark, sleep, wake, walk, trees. Come out into colorless clay heath covered with puddles, some mountains bathed in fog in the distance. Muffled, close, hot my face against the cold air. We are heading toward the mountains.

"We can get out through the mountains," she says, more to herself. "The reinforcements should be there by now. And we'll come back. And this time we'll win."

"We should never have come," I say.

"It was supposed to be."

Suddenly I want to argue—it's the first feeling I've had for so long—I almost feel nostalgic as the words burst from my mouth—

"What kind of nonsense is that?!"

"The spirits or gods whatever they are—"

"Gods?"

"... I don't know anything about religion, but they must have brought us here to test us."

"They *must* have?"

"Don't parrot me!" she snaps, her chinstrap banging against her neck as she turns to me.

"Tested us why?"

"We have to prove our worth to them before they will help us."

"What worth?"

"The worth of our side, you idiot! Our worth!"

"Worthy to do what? Make the whole world like this?!" I stop, wave my arm around, at the land, and the ruins in the distance.

She stops too. "Worthy because we are willing to die for what's right, that's what nobility is! When they see we are noble, I'm telling you, they will send us the victory we've earned."

"What victory?"

"What victory?! Are you out of your mind? Who are *you* to say 'what victory'—you want them to win?" She jabs the air with her finger in the direction of the cemetery.

"What you're calling victory is just *death*—can't you get that through your thick head? It's all just death—that's the only enemy I know or care about and who wins against death? What kind of victory is that? Who ever won a fight against death?"

"—And so Makemin and the rest, your friends, they all die for nothing?"

"Makemin was a murderer! He deserved to die! He deserved to die a thousand times! And just what price are *you* going to get us for their deaths? You think the enemy won't try to make us pay for all the ones of theirs we've killed? Show me where you *go* to make these final payments you're always talking about!"

"It's not something you see happen—history in the future will show we were right, and say everything I've been saying to you. Now will you belt up and move?"

"Right about what? If you're right you're right whether you win or not!"

"Who's going to tell the truth if we lose? If we lose, there won't be any one to tell our story at all!"

"To hell with the story! It's a stupid story! It's a worthless story! It's a shameful story! What do I care about stories when I'm dead!? Which of these dead people is going to tell the story?"

"*You.*"

"I won't tell! I won't tell a word of it!"

"You will," she says. Panting and hot eyed she grabs me by the front of my uniform and shakes me. "You *will* do it. You are the narrator."

"I'll say they were all insane, I'll call them murderers, and you too!" I shout it into her face, waving my head back and forth.

"You! You're nothing!" Shaking me, "You tell lies and

nothing is all you are—even a traitor tells lies for a reason! You'll tell the truth!"

"I won't do it! I won't say anything! If I get back, I'll say I never went anywhere! I was never *in* the army!"

I tear open my tunic, the buttons fly in all directions.

"I won't say a word about this obscenity! I'll say it never happened!"

She pushes me away from her.

"You think history can't do without *you?* I can talk too you know—I can tell the truth better than you ever could! I'll see to it every name is memorialized in a list of heroes, except yours! I'll leave you out altogether, like you never lived at all! Or no, that's not what I'll do, I'll tell everyone you were a hero just like the rest of them, then no one will believe your lies anyway. You'll do your part whether you like it or not!"

I fly at her, she throws me to the ground so hard my breath is knocked out.

"If I didn't need you—! " she snarls.

"You don't need me!" I shout back from the ground when I can. My voice is squashed flat.

"I could have been in those mountains by now, if I hadn't held back to keep up with you! I'll never understand why the spirits talk to you—that's one thing I can't understand."

I get my breath back.

"The spirits never said anything to me you cretin! Pepedora gave both sides special compasses that showed the way in. I was following it until your boy broke it for me in service to your great cause, so don't stick to me on your own account! I never knew any more about this place than you or the rest of them did—I knew less!" I'm getting onto my hands and knees, trying to rise.

"You're not a traitor," I hear her say, livid in her voice.

"You're the one who's thinking like war, not me," I say gingerly, pausing until a twinge of pain in my gut fades.

"You're not a soldier—you aren't anything at all!"

I look up as she turns and begins to leap, each step growing longer and longer—now she is bounding away from me, toward the mountains, streaking just above the ground like an ice skater. She disappears into the trees.

The damp air is chilling me. I regret tearing open my tunic. I start rooting the buttons out of the mud, and sewing them back on as best I can. I work for a long time, and the air grows darker between my eyes and the buttons.

Dusk comes down.

I look to see just what a bad job I'm doing, thread jabbed in and out of the cloth everywhere. Buttons and tunic slip from my nerveless fingers and my hands fly up to my face.

"Saskia!" I scream through my hands.

Weak I droop over onto my side—I imagine the victorious stories rolling out like crawling smoke from the cemetery, the city, the capitals of both sides, and rolling us, the ones who lived and died the story right off the page like we never existed for ourselves, we were just characters. I look up and see nothing around me, no people anywhere—not even me.

"Saskia!"

Does my voice even make a sound?

I'm calling her name to the distant woods, the gathering dark, the empty fog—

"Come back! You were right!"

*

The cemetery is nearby, but the landscape is monotonous trees and clay land, trees again and clay land again. I never see my footprints ahead of me so I can't be going in circles. Even in the open spaces I can't see above the trees, or through the mist. I can sense the mountains without seeing them, and I keep them in to my left.

I'm not alone—the woods and open places are filled with people, going up and down on all sides. Nardac is here, the Captain, Silichieh, Jil Punkinflake, Thrushchurl, the Lieutenant, Makemin. They're all too preoccupied with what they're doing, with their own thoughts, to talk to me, but they look happy and well, only very busy. I can't get close to them—whenever I draw near, they have somewhere else to go, and withdraw faster than I can follow, always with the air of people who have some private matter to attend to; but they always show me, never with words, but by means of very slight gestures that a less astute observer might not notice, that they are aware of me and entreat my indulgence a little while longer.

Soon they will have time for me, I'm sure.

*

"Cemetery can't be far a happy thought."

Happy thought. Happy thought.

No thinking, no thought at all.

"I will go on long enough find my way there."

The cemetery? Or the coast, what name is used to mean what isn't the interior? Another clearing.

"I'll get *out*."

—"Then?

"Happy then?

"Then what?

"Happy?

"How?"

—"Then I'll be out of this."

—"War is everywhere.

"Out there too."

—"I'll be out of *this*."

—"This won't get out of you.

"Happy?"

—"Better."

—"Happy? Or just not afraid, not tired?"

—"That's a cynical definition of happiness."

—"Who are you calling cynic?"

—"You talk like one."

Who am I talking to?

The air is settling like a pond after someone threw in a rock. Who was talking?

It might be the cemetery up there. Now I'm alone I can feel it pull me in. The others were the only ones keeping me from being pulled in. I don't want to go. Where's out?

I'm struggling, moving this way and that like a dog straining on his leash. I know where the mountains are—thinking all mountains are the same chains you enter here you can come out anywhere in the world there are mountains ... mountains are mountains. All I need is snow to feel at home, but here there's only this white ashy ground that's a pretty poor counterfeit.

I'm alone, but someone in an identical clearing only a

few yards from mine is imitating my movements as precisely as a mirror would, although his jaw whips and snaps in the air with his more abrupt movements in a way mine never could.

*

A place like the cemetery—the light here seems to ebb and flow with the air, and my breath, which at times is so thin I feel my lungs grow heavy through their emptiness and drag me toward the ground and at other times is so full I feel buoyed up with its glassiness and freshness. I came in, in a dream of mine, shared at the same time with some others, but now the dream has sprung free from all of us. It's rioting now all on its own. It has turned into a disembodied insanity, that can touch down in souls like lightning. The flash already passed off, stand and look at the devastation on all sides, and then a deafening crash breaks on the air, spreads unhurriedly in all directions, resounds with morbid deliberation back from the landscape.

I'm not nothing. Approaching the white being, I hear Thrushchurl's song, maybe I sing it, although there are many voices I hear. As long as I can go on speaking like that, I'm not nothing. I'm sure this is some other part of the vast cemetery but there is a persistent feeling that this is some other cemetery in the vicinity but separate. It's too dark to see the monuments around me clearly enough, and the light there is so intense—I turn my head to see what it illuminates but the brilliant streaks it sheds around me block my view, and I can't stop or turn all the way around it I am certain will get darker everywhere else if I do, and that thought is like death, dying to be alone here when everything goes completely dark. A bowl of light in the earth, a shallow bowl, with a white figure or some figure in there, lying there in such brightness that I can only see some of its outlines, a pink glow through the fingers ears and toes, the thin tissues, and the shadows where its legs are pressed together. It looks naked and is lying down. It lives because I see some regular palpitation and it rolls, now on its back, onto its side, back onto its back. It's having a nightmare. Out of the egg of its sway I see the paper thing shake its body of wind on the far side of the bowl, a dream I can see but only from the vantage point of another dream that I'm in at the moment. I'm still alone. The dream is real in the world—I see the person having the nightmare is the paper thing at the same time—he lies like a corpse there in the light, then shakes roll onto its side, then onto its back again the head turning back and forth, dimly dark opening of the mouth, like its decomposed belly is swollen with the gases of its decay and now it belches them in a long harsh voluminous emission that seems it should splinter the throat, as full of pain as a scream, and the dream-rotten thing is still twisting at my feet, now so small I could squash it with the toe of my boot. The serial nightmares all together say I am the war: and now the war is over.

Alone, I am lost in the nightmare now. We won. We won. I'm turning into a tower. I am growing vaster than the mountains, my head rising far above the world, staring down at the bare ground by my feet miles across miles away, I am becoming transparent to the darkness of the surrounding space, everything around me is intense light, and I am rolling over retching transfixed and suffering, I am darkness and empty space.

*

A musical voice from the doorway suffused with diaphanous white sunlight. "Sosska! Is that you?"

Orvar stands in the next room, smiling politely at her. The woman enters from outside, light streaming around her veiled face.

"*Mother!*"

"Sosska, my darling! How changed you are." She lifts her veil and takes Saskia by the shoulders, lightly kisses her cheek. The firm grip of her fingers is palpable even through Saskia's stiff clothing.

"Are you well?"

Saskia only stares.

"You've been away so long! And never a word from you ..." she glances at Orvar, "We were worried, night and day."

Saskia stares.

"I won't press you. This campaign *has* changed you."

She stands back from her daughter.

"Is Low with you?"

"*Low?!*"

"Yes, that's what I said. Is he with you?"

Saskia stares.

"He didn't mention me, did he?" She glances again at Orvar, whose polite smile grows firmer. "I believe I said he could be discreet."

"What are you talking about?!"

"Please, Sosska, is he alive?"

"... He was when I last saw him."

She looks closely at her daughter, "Where? Where did you see him last?"

"I left him in the interior. He was useless—practically a traitor."

"What?! Low, a traitor? Nonsense. Was he hurt?"

"No."

"Why did you leave him? Why in the world would you leave him?"

Saskia is staring incredulously. "What—what is this?"

"Oh how *could* you do something like that?" Madame Mauvudza stamps her foot irritably.

"What is this? Why are you asking me about that Low?"

"Well, I'm sure he's alive. He's always been so clever."

"What do you know about him?"

"My dear, we're to be married. Try to understand ... Really, when you look at me like that ... I met him in Tref, when he came through to join his unit. The man at Yashnik had been stationed in Port Conget when you passed through, and I chartered the ship as soon as I could. We've only just arrived."

She sighs wearily.

"And we had thought you were still up north. Oh, my dear, how drawn you are. But, perhaps, in a few months, when I've recovered my strength, we can all go in together. Or, no, but you and Orvar can go, can't you? If he hasn't made his way back on his own by then?"

"Recovered—what's that you say, recovered your strength?"

Ohra Mauvudza's open lips bend upward in a meagre smile. "Oh—well, these are rather loose clothes, and the light in here is bad."

She holds her hands up in the air by her shoulders and turns her body a little sideways, glancing down at the slight, uncharacteristic convexity of her abdomen, and then back up at her daughter.

"You see?" she says, placing her hand on the spot. "I'm not in the slightest embarrassed, but I wanted him to know right away. Now the war is over, he'll be free to return with me, won't he? I don't imagine his commanding officer can keep him here that much longer—although, come to think of it, his commanding officer might perform the marriage himself? Don't they have that authority?"

"His commanding officer is dead! *Everyone in the unit is dead!*" Saskia shouts.

Her mother blanches.

"You said you saw him alive!"

"He's dead! He's *dead!*"

"*You said you saw him alive!*"

"... He must be dead by now. No one can live in there."

"Sosska, I've been told there *are* people living there."

No response.

"Isn't that true?" she presses.

"Yes, yes, but they're all insane. And so will he be, by now, if he still lives."

"*He* won't go mad," her mother says. "*You* didn't. You escaped. It can be done. Perhaps you and Orvar will go soon, and help him. You *must* help him if you can."

Saskia drops jerkily onto a bench by the window, her eyes averted.

"Sosska, you should rest. We all must rest, and be strong," she says, stepping outside. She doesn't look up at the mountains tufted with fog. Orvar strides past her, to fetch the carriage she insisted they bring with them on the ship. He brings it forward, harness jingling.

"Your sister is a good soldier. When the family is back together, she will teach you to be a good soldier, too. She and your father, both."

As the carriage pulls up to the porch, she is distracted, her hand on top of her abdomen, listening down into her stomach toward the baby.

About the Author

Michael Cisco is the author of novels *The Divinity Student* (Buzzcity Press, 1999, winner of the International Horror Writers Guild award for best first novel of 1999), *The Tyrant* (Prime, 2004), *The San Veneficio Canon* (Prime, 2005), *The Traitor* (Prime, 2007), *The Narrator* (Civil Coping Mechanisms, 2010), *The Great Lover* (Chomu Press, 2011), *Celebrant* (Chomu Press, 2012), and *MEMBER* (Chomu Press 2013). His short story collection, *Secret Hours*, was published by Mythos Press in 2007.

His fiction has appeared in *Leviathan III* (Wildside, 2004) and *Leviathan IV* (Night Shade, 2005), *The Thackery T. Lambshead Pocket Guide to Eccentric and Discredited Diseases* (Bantam, 2005), *Cinnabar's Gnosis: A Tribute to Gustav Meyrink* (Ex Occidente, 2009), *Last Drink Bird Head* (Ministry of Whimsy, 2009), *Lovecraft Unbound* (Dark Horse, 2009), *Phantom* (Prime, 2009), *Black Wings I* (PS Press, 2011), *Blood and Other Cravings* (Tor, 2011), *The Master in the Cafe Morphine: A Homage to Mikhail Bulgakov* (Ex Occidente Press, 2011), *The Thackery T. Lambshead Cabinet of Curiosities* (Harper Voyager, 2011), *The Weird* (Tor, 2012), and elsewhere. His scholarly work has appeared in *Lovecraft Studies*, *The Weird Fiction Review*, *Iranian Studies* and *Lovecraft and Influence*.

Michael Cisco lives and teaches in New York City.